Like One of the Family

Nesta Tuomey is married and lives in Dublin with her family; educated at the Sacred Heart Convent, Leeson Street and the National College of Art, she worked as an air hostess with Aer Lingus. She started writing for radio, and her plays and short stories have been broadcast by BBC and RTE. A winner of the John Power Short Story Award at Listowel and the *Image* Oil of Ulay Short Story Competition, her short stories have also been published widely in magazines. Nesta Tuomey's one-act play *Whose Baby* won the O. Z. Whitehead Play Competition in 1996, and her first novel *Up Up and Away*, depicting life in an Irish airline, was published in 1995.

Best wishes

Nesta

Also by Nesta Tuomey

Up Up and Away

LIKE ONE
OF
THE FAMILY

Nesta Tuomey

A Mount Eagle Original Paperback

Published in 1999 by
Mount Eagle Publications Ltd
Dingle, Co. Kerry, Ireland

ISBN 1 902011120
(original paperback)

10 9 8 7 6 5 4 3 2 1

*The characters in this book are entirely imaginary and bear no relation
to any real person alive or dead. Similarly, the incident involving the
crash of the Marchetti Aircraft is entirely fictitious and bears no relation
to any crash of that aircraft which actually occured.*

Published with the assistance of the
Arts Council/An Chomhairle Ealaíonn

Cover design: Public Communications Centre, Dublin
Typesetting: Red Barn Publishing, Skeagh, Skibbereen
Printed by The Guernsey Press Ltd, Guernsey, Channel Islands

"Love no flood can quench, no torrents drown."
Song of Songs.

For Larry and my children with love.

If anyone had said she was in love Claire would have pooh-poohed the idea. She might have felt love for her parents, but with the death of her baby sister they had been too occupied with their own grief to notice they were neglecting her. By the time they did, it was too late. By then Claire was helplessly, hopelessly enamoured with the McArdle family.

Claire was a solitary child given to reading a lot and playing imaginary games by herself in the wilderness that passed for a garden behind their house. Her mother had been a teacher and believed it was never too early to become acquainted with books. Claire's first memory was sitting in her bath turning the vinyl pages of *Puss in Boots*. She remembered the water slopping the shiny plastic cat and crooning sadly because he had gotten his fur 'all wet'.

Christopher, who was two years younger than Claire, never opened a book. He spent all his time hopping, throwing or kicking a ball, which pleased their father who was also sport crazy and spent his weekends glued to the television watching *Grandstand* and *Match of the Day*. Claire didn't feel much, if any, affinity with Christopher.

When Claire was ten, another baby had been born: a little girl with hair a shade blonder than Claire's and grey eyes fringed with sooty lashes. She and Christopher had doted on Bella, bonded together this one and only time out of mutual adoration. "Make an angel face," Claire would coax and the little darling would show her pearly teeth in a smile. "Now a devil face," and she would scowl and wrinkle her button nose obediently. Claire was besotted by this tiny sibling, willing the school bell to ring so that she could run home, eager for the reality of her.

The baby was her mother's joy and delight and her death from meningitis when she was two cast Annette into a deep depression. She lost her optimistic view of life, her sweetness of expression. At thirty-eight years of age she became weepy and withdrawn, lying in bed with her face to the wall, refusing to take an interest in anything. When she got up at last and resumed her normal routine she performed her tasks like an automaton, without flair, the spirit gone out of her. Claire's father, Jim, tried to cheer her but could not break through the barrier Annette had erected about her. There was a marked difference in their relationship. He became hesitant, almost apologetic, as if it was somehow his fault. Her mother no longer laughed at his clowning and he had lost his faith in his ability to make her laugh.

Claire's tummy began to hurt, a niggling discomfort at first, which deepened to a sort of sour ache. Somehow it was always night-time when the pains got bad and her moans woke her up. Her parents heard her but put it down to the trauma surrounding the baby's death. In the nights after the death, Claire had woken up sobbing, turning away from them, refusing to be comforted. They would have been slow to take action even in normal times, but now they were so locked in their own private misery that they hardly noticed her any more.

Eventually, they took her to a doctor who diagnosed colic and she was put on a gluten-free diet. Now her stomach pained from hunger and all that week she cried herself to sleep. When the pains persisted only a hot water bottle or her mother's hand moving in soothing, concentric circles brought relief. They took her back to the doctor, who put his hands on her stomach, poking and prodding and feeling her. He could find nothing.

The pain became a red-hot pincers which dragged her regularly from her dreams and demanded attention. She was frightened by the intensity of her tears. Other doctors were consulted, more examinations carried out. She would point to the middle of her stomach since, by then, the pain would have faded and she couldn't remember exactly where it had been. "Just somewhere around there." Back home again. For a while near starvation and then normal food until the next time. Claire missed school sixteen days that term, too tired in the mornings after a disturbed night to get up and dress herself in time for the bus.

Across the street a house was sold and two shiny brass plates went up on the fence.

"Two doctors, no less!" her father reported, coming in when the tea table was cleared and his liver and bacon lay crisping in the oven. He had a flush about his cheeks, an air of foolish bonhomie. These days he was never home on time, spending longer hours "at the office". "I suppose there's nothing like keeping it in the family."

"You mean they're married," her mother stated without interest. "I wonder have they children?"

Claire could have told her. She had sat at the window all afternoon watching the unloading of the removal van and spied a cot, a playpen and bunk beds. Later, the men had staggered in with a roll-top desk and a piano. Claire imagined herself in a long, silver evening gown, moving her hands fluidly over the keys as she was doing now on the arm of her chair. It distracted her from the dull pain in her stomach. If she pretended she was playing a Scott Joplin number she could almost ignore it. Her fingers bounced rhythmically up and down, her brow furrowed in concentration.

"Look at her," her father said with maudlin affection, "she'll be a concert pianist yet." He looked down at his own tobacco-stained fingers regretfully. Her mother turned the page of a magazine. She might have been stone deaf for all the notice she paid him.

That night Claire dreamed the walls of her bedroom were closing in on her like a tomb, crushing breath out of her, squeezing her forehead in a vice. Her screams wakened her.

"Hush, hush," her mother murmured, rocking her distractedly in her arms. She had got into bed beside Claire and was lying under the quilt. Claire felt raging hot. Bile rushed to her throat. She half sat up and then her throat spasmed and the stench and taste of vomit was in her nostrils, burning her tonsils. She began to cry with relief and fright.

Her mother got out of the bed. Claire heard her speaking to someone on the landing and then she was back, sponging her hands and face, towelling her down, putting her in a clean nightdress. "I'm going over now," Annette said. "I don't give a bloody damn if they have just moved in." Her laugh was mirthless. "Surely between the pair of them with all their qualifications they can find time to come. It's not ten o'clock."

Claire lay and drifted. It felt like the middle of the night. Every so often pain jerked her awake. There was the sound of feet on the stairs. The dividing wall between her room and the landing did not quite meet the ceiling and every sound was magnified, especially at night. A lamp was switched on in the room and she felt someone bending over her. She squinted upwards but whoever it was blocked the light. She felt gentle hands pressing her stomach.

Dr McArdle said kindly, "Does that hurt, Claire? Won't you tell me now if it does?"

She was surprised it was a woman and it was a minute before she could answer, "No." Strangely, it was true. Throwing up, or something, had eased the agony. She began to say so when something was put into her mouth and cool fingers held it there. She closed her eyes and she must have dropped off because when she opened them she was lying in a strange bed in a shadowy room full of sleeping figures. From a lighted corridor just beyond the shadows a voice said clearly, "It'll probably rupture before they get her on the table." Claire wondered what she was talking about.

She had her appendix taken out during the night. It didn't burst but it was a close thing. Nine inches long, her mother told her when she came out of the ether to find her sitting by the bed. Claire wondered why none of the other doctors had realised what was wrong with her. When she said so her mother explained that her appendix had not been in the usual spot but was tucked away behind some other organ, making it difficult to find. "Only for Jane McArdle you'd have been in a bad way." There was a note of respect in Annette's voice.

Jane? When had they become so friendly?

It turned out that her mother and Jane McArdle – or Jane Mannion as she was then – had been to college together. They had been great friends at one time and had even gone on holidays to Spain together.

"I couldn't get over it when she opened the door and I saw her standing there," Annette said with a reminiscent smile. "She knew what was wrong with you straight away, and to think none of those doctors I brought you to had any idea."

Claire wondered if her appendix had started growing when the baby died and if she too would have died only for Dr McArdle. She felt the beginnings of a sense of obligation to her unknown saviour, which was to increase upon acquaintance and to remain with her for the rest of her life.

Claire was in the children's hospital almost a week and ate her meals from pink plastic dishes which tasted of washing-up liquid. There were six other children in the ward, all younger than her, one a toddler with his torso encased in a plaster cast, who wept all day. Christopher only came to see her once. He was spending all his time playing with their new neighbours.

"There's a boy my age," he told her. "He's smaller than me." He went on to describe the dressing-up games they played in the McArdle's garage and the stage they had erected out of packing cases. Claire thought it sounded fun.

After five days they took her stitches out and she was allowed home. She was glad to go. The sound of the wailing babies through the wall kept her awake nights and reminded her of their own lost baby.

Her house seemed smaller on her return, darker too after the wide windows in the ward. Claire climbed the stairs gingerly, afraid of making her wound bleed. She lay weakly against the pillow and stared at her book through a blur of tears, suddenly lonely for the antiseptic efficiency of hospital routine.

As if sensing this, her mother filled a hot water bottle and slipped it comfortingly against her feet.

"There!" she said. "You could do with a bit of spoiling." At the unaccustomed kindness Claire's tears overflowed.

Next day Jane McArdle paid them a visit. She was a big boned woman, with auburn hair and an infectious giggle, which, oddly at variance with her bulk, conjured up a much younger woman.

"How's the patient?" she asked, coming into the front room where Claire was sitting with a rug tucked loosely about her, a book open on her lap. Claire felt suddenly shy.

"You needn't keep her wrapped up, you know." Dr McArdle twitched away the rug. "Not in this weather, Annette. The poor child is the colour of lobster."

Annette bristled. "There's been a cold snap these past few days," she pointed out.

They stared at each other.

"Why is it," Annette asked pleasantly, "that doctors seem to think they're qualified to give advice in all areas, even those that don't concern them?"

Jane laughed. "Touché! Part and parcel of the trade. We're a bossy lot, I'm afraid."

Annette looked mollified. "And mothers are inclined to be over-protective," she conceded.

"Don't I know it. You should see the bottles of vitamin C and cod-liver oil I dose my gang with."

At this Annette laughed. "How domesticated we sound, Jane. Imagine us having this dull kind of conversation way back when we went to college hops together."

"Booze, men and sex were about the height of it," Jane agreed.

"And in that order."

Claire sat forgotten between them as they chatted about people and places they had once known.

Her convalescence lasted two weeks. By that time the summer term was more than half over and there seemed little point in going back to school. Her father, however, pointed out she had missed enough already and would drop even further behind, so she returned for the last two weeks. There was a new girl in her class at St Catherine's. Although Claire had covertly observed her on a few occasions, this was her first meeting with Sheena McArdle, a slim, leggy girl with bold, merry eyes under straight black brows and, with her birthday just before Claire's in June, Claire's senior by nine days.

They hit it off at once. Sheena moved her desk beside Claire's and helped her copy out notes she had missed. They lent each other rulers and colouring markers, shared their fruit and sandwiches.

They were like twins, speaking at the same time and finishing each other's sentences. Claire forgot her appendix scar and ran all over the playground, whooping and shouting. Her pigtails slipped their ribbon and blonde hair haloed her perspiring forehead.

The nuns were amazed. Claire had always been so shy and restrained, but she was a different child in Sheena's company, excited and garrulous. Together they got up to all kinds of mischief. On painting days they tipped the contents of murky jam jars through a broken floorboard, drenching the unsuspecting heads of the class beneath. Once during morning break, they barricaded themselves into the kitchens and sprayed cartons of milk through the serving hatch at the children in the refectory. Sister Dunphy threw up her hands and exclaimed at their antics. Only that it was so near the end of term they would have been punished. As it was, she called them into her office, told them such giddy behaviour was unseemly in little girls in their first year in the senior school and she made them promise to reform. For Claire none of it was quite real; it was as if she had taken a step into another sphere. She had never even back-answered in her life and now she was making up in a fortnight for years of good behaviour. She bit her lip, struggling to keep from giggling outright. Sister Dunphy glanced at their bursting expressions and with a sigh brought the lecture to an end. Arm in arm, Claire and Sheena pranced unrepentantly down the corridor.

The summer holidays normally meant for Claire unlimited free time to read, sprawled on her bed with a quarter pound of scented pin cushions beside her, dipping two fingers into the bag as she turned the page. On daily trips to the local library, she'd made a friend of the librarian, who was young and sympathetic and more than ready to turn a blind eye to the number of books Claire borrowed. She had practically exhausted the children's library, although she wasn't actually old enough at thirteen to join the adult section. You had to be fifteen to get an adult ticket. Sometimes she had to go further afield to branches in outlying areas when the shelves of the 'local' turned up nothing new.

This was how Claire normally spent her summers. With the advent of the McArdles all this was changed. Now she spent her days playing with Sheena and the other McArdle children, enjoying the novelty of their big house and garden.

Unlike her own terraced house, the McArdle's house stood on its own ground, with a solid stone garage set some distance apart. This was the garage that Christopher had played in when Claire was in hospital, but since then he had fallen out with Hugh and now his allegiance was with another family, further down the road. Claire was just as glad. The McArdles were hers!

Claire had yet to meet Sheena's father, who was away all that month at a medical conference in Leipzig, but Sheena's mother made a great fuss of her, getting her to come in out of the sun when she was tired and spending time with her in the cool kitchen, where she snatched frequent coffee breaks between patients. Jane flattered Claire, gave her little jobs to do and rewarded her by treating her like a grown-up.

The garage was the centre of the children's play. In it they performed all kinds of dramas, ad libbing as they went along. A big part of their garage repertory consisted of hospital scenarios, in which Terry, Sheena's twin, insisted on playing his father most of the time, an old stethoscope dangling about his neck; and Sheena their father's receptionist or the bossy matron at his hospital, while protesting that she didn't get to be the doctor more often. Claire and Hugh uncomplainingly acted the young married couple about to have their first baby, who was of course Ruthie.

"Why can't Claire or I be matron sometimes?" Ruthie wailed, taking her cue from her sister. But Claire was quite happy to form part of a trio with the younger children. She was a little in awe of Terry, who succeeded in bossing everyone except Sheena, who was equally strong-minded. With his cleverness and agile tongue he could make Claire feel foolish, but she couldn't hate him, only dumbly suffer it, because he was too like Sheena.

The twins, though not identical, were very similar physically, with dark mops of hair curling untidily on their necks, and expressive dark eyes in smooth, round faces. Each exhibited an effortless, unstudied charm and consideration which at once confused and disarmed their adversaries. Together they were formidable. All of them, from Ruthie upwards, had inherited the McArdle charm. When they fought for her favours, Claire felt both privileged and embarrassed.

One thing wasn't the same any more. Claire was no longer Sheena's twin. Out of school, Terry was restored to his rightful place. Claire felt her separateness keenly and, although they included her in all their games, felt supernumerary most of the time. It helped that Jane singled her out as she did.

"Would you help me carry in the washing? It's lovely and dry and it may rain later."

Claire was down the garden with Jane, behind the apple trees. A line stretched across the patch of grass Terry had begun mowing earlier in the day. He had left the edges untrimmed, the mower abandoned across the path.

"I love my eldest son dearly but I have to admit he's a minimalist," Jane said, stepping over it. Claire took the basket from her and carried it towards the house. "Now Hugh is a perfectionist like his father," Jane chatted on. "As for Ruthie, that little madam, she's another Meryl Streep."

Claire said nothing. She was becoming used to Jane's way of talking about her husband and children as though writing their biographies.

As they passed the garage they could hear Terry and Sheena playing there. There was a steady drumming sound, punctuated by Sheena's high-pitched laugh.

"Come into the kitchen and we'll make ourselves coffee," Jane said, tiptoeing exaggeratedly past the opening. Claire smiled and followed her into the house.

"No need to disturb them." With a conspiratorial wink, Jane closed the kitchen door and locked it. "This way is more fun."

Claire seldom drank coffee but she liked the way Jane made it, sweet and milky. She sipped it slowly and munched shyly on a Kerry Cream.

"Have another," Jane urged. "Go on! Don't be polite."

Pleased, Claire obeyed, feeling flattered and a little overwhelmed. She glanced discreetly about her and wished that their kitchen at home was even half as roomy as this one so that they could have their meals in it like the McArdles did. The Shannon's kitchen was little more than a scullery so they ate in the dining-room, sitting about the round mahogany table which took up most of the space. It was very cramped, especially when they had company, with Claire and her mother squeezing awkwardly past, carrying plates and apologising all the time. Claire had thought everyone else lived like this until she saw how spacious the McArdle's house was.

Jane sat on a chair opposite Claire and cupped her hands around a china mug sprigged with flowers. She eased her feet out of sling-back sandals and leaned her elbows on the table. "Another five minutes," she told Claire, "then it's back to the grind." She pulled a comical face.

Jane's regular receptionist was on holidays and her seventeen-year-old daughter was standing in for her. After a minute, the girl stuck her head around the kitchen door to say that the next patient was in the waiting-room.

"Okay, Babs. I'll be right there." Jane yawned and sipped her coffee, looking as if nothing would ever move her.

There was a clattering sound outside the window and a face bobbed into view. It was Terry standing on an upturned bin. He sank out of sight until only his eyes were visible above the sill. "We want to come in, Mum," he shouted. "Open the door." He began lashing the bin under him with a stick.

"Stop that racket," Jane called, unperturbed. "Claire and I are having a chat. Off you go now. You'll get your turn later."

Having a chat. How grown-up it sounded. Claire was suffused with pleasure, which quickly turned to guilt when Terry fisted the window and roared a rude word. Jane just laughed. "Brat!" she said lazily, declining to go after him.

Released in the summer months from the discipline of school time-tables and evening surgery, Jane McArdle had become very relaxed. She let her children run wild, neglected to cut their hair and only remembered their toenails when jagged tears appeared in their canvas runners. Her own hair, which could have done with professional styling, she wore girlishly tied back from her face with one of Sheena's hair ribbons. During the rest of the year she had no time to go to hairdressers, she maintained, and in summer no inclination. To save herself the chore of cooking she sent Sheena out to the local delicatessen every morning to see what she could find, and their lunches consisted of ham and salami salads one day, pizzas or barbecued chicken the next, and half a dozen buttered baguettes to fill them up. She refused to exert herself more than necessary in the summer months and meals were as labour-saving as she could make them. At the same time, she encouraged Claire to eat with them, saying that it wasn't worth her while to run home and anyway she was a civilising influence on her own children.

17

"Look how Claire never grabs but waits for bread to be passed to her," Jane praised, horrified at the speed with which her own brood cleared the table.

"She'll be waiting," grinned Terry, swiping the last piece. He gave it a quick lick before his mother made him return it to the plate.

"Someone else might like it."

"They won't now," he said simply. "I've put my saliva on it."

Jane sighed. Sometimes she wondered why she was sending her children to good schools. They didn't have the first notion of table manners. Maybe they should all eat together more often. She met Claire's eye.

"See what I mean?"

Claire grinned sympathetically. Even if she got a bigger share at home, she considered the McArdle mealtimes were much more fun.

Sometimes Jane asked after Annette in an absent kind of way. Claire didn't say that her mother, after her initial pleasure in their reunion, was resentful of the fact that despite repeated invitations, Jane had so far failed to drop over for coffee and a natter. Just as she didn't tell Annette that she was no longer passing her invitations on.

Jane was inclined to fuss over Claire. How pale she was! Was she getting enough rest, eating the right food? She was a great believer in children drinking lots of milk and, when Claire admitted that she never drank a drop at home, slyly made her cups of milky coffee to get it into her that way. Pharmaceutical companies sent Jane packs of vitamin samples through the post and she often encouraged Claire to take some home with her. No one, not even her mother, had ever shown such interest in Claire's welfare. She felt warmed yet guilty to be the object of so much concern.

"Don't be!" Jane hugged her. "I can't help worrying about you, you little silly." Her manner was at once teasing and comradely.

One day, when they were on their own in the kitchen, she told Claire to pull up her dress and, when Claire shyly revealed her tummy, gave her scar a quick, professional glance.

"It's healing nicely," Jane pronounced. "Luckily, you'll be able to wear a bikini."

Claire hadn't thought that far ahead. The incision had been fairly neat and, over the weeks, it had lost its livid colour.

"By the time you're my age," Jane promised her, "it will be just a tiny mother-of-pearl seam." She made it sound quite attractive. In this, and in other small ways, she was extremely solicitous of Claire in the weeks after her operation.

Claire's parents paid her little attention. The truth was that while they were not unkind to her, they were going through a rough patch themselves and had little emotion left over for anything else. Her mother was silent and abstracted most of the time, deep in her own thoughts. Her father was less and less at home, and when he was there he devoted his time to Christopher, who had always been his favourite. Comfortably ensconced on the couch, the pair of them watched the Wimbledon finals and any other ball that hopped. Claire, passing through on her way to the kitchen, would hear their voices rising to varying pitches of excitement as they recorded the scores. She wondered what it would have been like if Christopher had been a girl instead of a boy. And went back across the road to play with the McArdles.

Sometimes Sheena dropped over to Claire's house but mostly left it to Claire to call on her. There was always some activity going on in the McArdle's garden and little or nothing happening in the Shannon's. Claire could see that two deckchairs plonked out in the wilderness wasn't all that inviting. Nor was the inside of the house any better. The kitchen was poky, with a damp, odorous dishcloth permanently draped on the sink, and there was never any iced lemonade like in Sheena's house. It might have been different if her mother had gone out of her way to make Sheena welcome but any exertion these days seemed beyond Annette. The odd time she remembered to buy biscuits Christopher made short work of them, snacking before the television.

At first Claire was disappointed by Sheena's failure to return her visits; it was all so lop-sided somehow. Then she was relieved. It kept her relationship with the McArdles separate, which was what she had really wanted all along. She held on to the hope that when she and Sheena returned to school and Terry was no longer about, it would be the same for them as before.

One consolation was her friendship with Hugh. Although he was two years younger he was surprisingly sensitive for his age. He owned a cocker spaniel called Hero and let Claire help feed and groom her. Hero had started out as Terry's dog – she was given to him for his tenth birthday – but became Hugh's when Terry got tired of taking her for walks. Or so Terry made out. But this wasn't the real reason. According to Hugh, Terry was secretly galled at having a dog that wouldn't answer his whistle or obey his commands to sit or beg, so he made a great show of giving her away. From what Claire already knew of Terry she could well believe this.

Towards the end of June, Hero gave birth to a sizeable litter, too many for her to be able to feed by herself. Hugh fixed up a bed in the tool-shed with plenty of fresh straw from a nearby riding stables and borrowed a doll's feeding bottle from Ruthie and filled it with warm milk. Claire was thrilled when he asked her if she would like to try her hand at feeding them.

It was evident that Hugh had his parents' dedication to preserving life and his father's skill with his hands. Watching him dose Hero with vitamins, Claire was amazed how smoothly he got her to accept the tablets. She was sorry when the pups got bigger and Hugh no longer needed her. She had never enjoyed anything so much in her life.

During their coffee sessions in the locked kitchen Jane McArdle sometimes chatted to Claire about the children's father and Claire couldn't help feeling curious about Dr

Eddie McArdle. She tried to conjure him up from his children's faces. Hugh and Ruthie were so like Jane it was a safe bet the twins resembled him. She wondered what he would think of her when he returned and found her in his house every day. Would he object to having an extra child about the place, an extra mouth to feed? She felt sensitive about such things, having once heard her mother speak crossly when a schoolfriend regularly lingered on past mealtimes. "Hasn't she a home to go to?" Annette had grumbled, annoyed at having to stretch the shepherd's pie to five portions when it was barely enough to feed four people to begin with. At the same time Claire recognised that the McArdles were different. They didn't calculate so finely – didn't have to! She had already seen evidence of this in the generous way Jane included her in all the picnics and treats she laid on for her own family.

Claire began to see Dr McArdle as a slightly romantic figure, physically a cross between Sheena and Terry, yet inexplicably grim and brooding, with granite-hewn features and jutting eyebrows. She was reading *Jane Eyre* at the time and had unconsciously cast him in the role of Mr Rochester.

It was a shock to find how closely he resembled a romantic hero.

Eddie McArdle was broad-shouldered and powerfully muscled, with curly grey-black hair and a beautiful sad smile, which seemed to suggest that no matter what dreadful secrets you told him he would not be surprised or shocked.

He arrived home from Germany one morning, not long after Jane had set off to collect him at the airport, having somehow got her lines of communication crossed. The children were playing in the garage when he suddenly appeared in their midst. Claire was lying on her back – they were enacting a childbirth scene – and Sheena was instructing her to 'breathe deeply' and 'bear down, my dear' while Terry pressed the stethoscope against the cushion Claire had shoved under her dress. The twins were noisily encouraging her to moan and scream and when they saw their father, they didn't stop but, pleased to have an audience, exaggerated their antics.

"Good God, is this what you get up to?" he asked, genuinely appalled.

Claire struggled up, feeling mortified. She saw herself as he must see her: an almost grown girl, legs sprawled, playing childish games. Her face reddened as she pulled the cushion from under her dress and quickly hid it behind her. She gave an involuntary cry and held her stomach.

"Labour pains reoccurring, no doubt." Dr McArdle sounded sarcastic.

Tears in her eyes, Claire stared down at the ground. Her tummy really hurt. She must have opened the wound.

"It's my tummy . . . I think I've pulled my appendix scar."

He stared at her for a moment. "Come into the house," he said, more gently.

Still clasping the cushion, Claire followed him into Jane's surgery, where he motioned for her to lie down on the couch. She put the cushion on the floor and eased herself up on to the couch. She felt a little shy, lying there, staring at the walls. There was the sound of water running as Dr McArdle washed his hands.

He came over and sat on the edge. "Let me see." His hands were gentle as he pulled up her dress and peeled back her pants. Claire stared fixedly at a spot on the wall behind his right ear. She wondered desperately which knickers she had put on that morning. Annette was very lax these days about taking her shopping or, indeed, doing anything that required effort. With school holidays she had practically abandoned all pretence at housekeeping.

"Nothing too catastrophic," he murmured, blotting a globule of fresh blood. "You'll survive."

She made to sit up but he gently pushed her back on the couch.

"Hold on. A swab of Betadene and you'll be right." He stood up and crossed the room.

She looked down at herself, her stomach bared, her faded

cotton pants pulled down, revealing pale skin. Oh no, there was a hole in them. She flushed, wishing she could cover herself. Sheena wore flowered sets of lingerie. She wished desperately to have had underwear like Sheena's. She looked away miserably. He was back.

"Be prepared," he warned, "it's cool."

She gasped as the solution drenched her warm skin. Quick, competent fingers swabbed the area and with a grunt he straightened up. She let her breath out slowly. He turned away to put the stained dressing in the pedal bin, giving her time to rearrange her clothing before turning back.

"How old are you, Claire?"

She was surprised he knew her name.

"Thirteen."

"I would have put you older. Got your periods yet?"

She stared at him. She felt hot, confused. No-one ever talked about such things, especially no man. She nodded dumbly. There had been brownish red staining a couple of times so far. Annette had discreetly left a packet of sanitary pads in her room some time before. She told him.

He nodded. "I have some booklets I can give you. Sheena found them helpful. She has hers almost a year."

Claire looked down at her hands. She and Sheena had not spoken yet of such things.

"You're both fairly young starting. Means you'll go on longer. Possibly have babies in your fifties . . . if you want that."

She shook her head. Was she really having this conversation? She tried to imagine sharing the same dialogue with her father and failed. But then her father wasn't a doctor.

"It seems rather old," she ventured.

"No accounting for tastes, is there?" He smiled at her. "Modern young women want to put it off as long as possible. Careers first, babies later. You won't be like that, will you, Claire?"

Careers! Babies! She didn't know how to answer him.

He laughed, reading her thoughts. "That's all a long way off . . . still, maybe not so far away." He looked at her consideringly. "You are mature for your age . . . your body strong, well developed. You are already taller than Sheena by an inch I should say."

Suddenly she became self-conscious. She glanced towards the door. As if recollecting the time he went at once to open it. "Off you go. You can take your cushion with you." He sounded amused.

She blushed and retrieved it. He waited until she was through the door then closed it gently after her. She walked back to the garage, her head in a spin. No-one had ever described her so intriguingly to herself before. She felt as if she were being created afresh and was drawn, almost against her will, to view herself as he did.

That night Claire stood on her bed, her feet sinking in the soft mattress, and looked in her dressing-table mirror. She badly wanted to see herself, all in one go. It was the first time such an idea had occurred to her.

By bending her neck and crouching she was rewarded by a foreshortened frontal: first midriff and thighs, and then lower and upper torso. Her hips and thighs had lost their childish thinness and looked nicely rounded. Her breasts were beginning to get fat. When she arched her body, they gently budded the bodice of her cotton dress. Was this what he had meant by well developed?

Next she angled the mirror so that she could see herself lying down on the bed. With her head resting on the pillow, she pulled up her dress and down her pants and looked critically across. In the months since the baby's death she had filled out and was no longer a little girl.

She dreamed that night, as she had in the period after her appendix operation, that she was in the operating theatre, except that this time he was the surgeon standing beside the table. She was aware that her hospital gown was ruched up leaving her naked below the waist, but each time she modestly tried to pull it back down he told the nurse to pull it up again. In the end she just lay there and let them. She remembered the dream long after she woke up.

In the days after, when Claire passed the surgery, she felt a faint excitement as though behind the panelled door Eddie was waiting to continue their conversation. Now during her coffee sessions with Jane she encouraged the older woman to talk about him, avidly absorbing every detail of his life.

Jane, who never needed any persuasion to talk about her family, was pleased at her interest and painted a generally accurate, if slightly biased, account of the doctor and the man.

Eddie was a brilliant surgeon and had been awarded several medical gongs for his research into ectopic pregnancy and the effects of certain drugs on bone formation in the developing foetus. He divided his time between his consulting rooms in Merrion Square and the city nursing homes. One day of the week he operated at the hospital. Jane said he was treated like a god by his woman patients and bullied and adored by his receptionist, who had been his faithful watchdog for thirteen years. This paragon managed to keep his appointment book filled without overcrowding it. New patients were encouraged to pay in advance of consultation and maternity cases prior to their six week check-up. No-one ever slipped past her and Eddie could not have functioned without her. Jane laughed and professed to be madly jealous of her. Claire asked Sheena later if this were true, but Sheena just laughed and said that the woman was almost sixty years old and the only threat she had ever posed was to her father's waistline.

"Somehow babies always seem to get themselves born around meal-times," Sheena explained. "She worries about Daddy and stuffs him with take-aways."

"Yeah," agreed Terry, who was listening. "He's getting to be a right fatso!"

Claire was struck by how casually the twins regarded their father. By comparison Hugh worshipped his father and was afraid of disappointing him. He thought of becoming a vet when he grew up but worried that it would disappoint his father if he didn't follow in his footsteps. Claire thought if only Terry had some interest in medicine it would have let Hugh off the hook, but Terry was not the academic type. His was a bold and adventurous spirit and when he grew up would more than likely become an explorer or a soldier. Terry climbed effortlessly to the top of the thirty-foot chestnut tree in the garden, swinging daringly on a branch and shouting boastfully down to them all, while poor Hugh got dizzy and sick if he so much as went on to the garage roof to recover a tennis ball. Claire understood and empathised with Hugh's fear of heights, but at the same time she couldn't help feeling a sneaking admiration for Terry's fearless show of courage.

Claire got in the habit of hanging about her own gate around the time Eddie came home in the evening. But as soon as she saw his car turning into the road she would go at once into the house. One evening she lingered on the pavement, throwing her ball at the wall. When he had stopped his car and got out she pretended suddenly to notice him.

"Hi, Blondie," he said with a smile and disappeared up the driveway before she could say hello back.

Blondie!

Another time she and Sheena were going upstairs as he was coming down. Claire had on a blue gingham skirt and a frilled top, her fair hair bound about her head in plaits. He murmured something in his daughter's ear and passed on with a chuckle.

"Don't you want to know what he said?"

Of course she did, but only if it was something nice.

Sheena giggled. "Daddy calls you the Dresden doll. I think you're more like Heidi." She linked her arm through Claire's affectionately. "Daddy thinks you're awfully pretty."

Claire hugged it to herself. The Dresden doll. It sounded delicate and exotic. Her heart went up and up.

After that she began imagining dramatic little scenes. Jane had been called away and Eddie had need of her help with a woman who had cut an artery and was rapidly losing blood. She stood beside him following his instructions to the letter and afterwards he admitted that the woman would have been dead only for her. Sometimes Jane had died (Claire felt a bit guilty even thinking such a thing) and he was lonely and seeking comfort. She sat with his head in her lap and tenderly stroked his forehead, ran her fingers through his grey-black curls. Beyond that her imagination did not go.

One evening, Claire saw Eddie and Jane, both smartly dressed, come out of the house on the way to some function.

"Don't forget to get out the hose and water the plants," Jane reminded Hugh. She had on a mustard and brown Thai silk dress, with a linen jacket draped over her shoulders, and very high heels. She was wearing lipstick and she had been to the hairdressers. Claire thought she looked almost pretty.

Eddie backed the Rover out of the garage. Terry had hosed it down and given it a polish, and now the chrome gleamed and the bodywork held a blue satin sheen. He put on the brake and got out. He had on a light grey mohair suit, red silk tie and a handkerchief peeped from his top pocket. Claire thought he looked very grand.

"And how are you, my dear?" he asked pleasantly. "No more bother afterwards I hope."

Claire shook her head. "Thank you," she said, remembering her manners.

"No trouble at all . . . only too happy." He made her an elegant little bow and smiled his beautiful, rather mournful smile.

"Eddie, shouldn't we be going?" Jane sat carefully into the car, arranging her skirts so as not to crush them. She had been telling Hugh which plants most needed water. She had recently acquired a camellia in a terracotta pot and wanted to be sure he would spray the leaves.

"Claire will help you," she called through the window, adding in a low flattering voice to Claire, "Keep an eye on him, there's a love."

27

When they were gone Claire and Hugh got out the hose. They attached it to a tap on the side of the house and took turns directing the jet of water across the flowerbeds. At first it was fun. They screamed and laughed, soaking plants and bushes, everything in sight. Then they turned the hose on the house and the water spurted up like they had struck oil, drenching windows and gutters. There was a muffled shout and Terry stuck his head out of the window.

"Hey, watch it down there, you eejits," he shouted. He leaned out, comic in hand, vigorously shaking drops from the pages. His irritated gaze took in the dripping figures below. "Aren't you getting a bit big for that sort of caper, Claire?" he asked scornfully. "Hugh will cop it when Mum comes home."

Claire flushed, reminded of Jane's parting words. She had betrayed a trust. "Sorry!" she whispered, washed now by guilt. But Terry had gone back inside. She looked uneasily at Hugh. His T-shirt was sticking to his ribcage, his hair falling in a wet lick across his forehead. Her own dress clung sharply to the lines of her body, emphasising the swell of her small breasts. She went hot with shame. What must Terry have thought! She turned away.

"What's the matter?" Hugh asked.

"Nothing," she mumbled.

He followed her across the damp grass, still holding the nozzle in his hand. "You're going home?" He sounded disappointed.

Claire wandered through the gate. She had made a fool of herself.

Claire hated it when the McArdles went off on holidays in August. They owned a holiday bungalow in County Waterford and went there every year. Jane took the whole month off and Eddie commuted for the second half, driving down from Dublin for the weekend.

Claire wandered about like a lost soul for the first week, just living for some word from them. Sheena had promised to send a postcard. Claire felt like someone on a life-support machine, merely existing until their return.

She haunted their garden in the evenings, slipping like a lonely ghost about the darkening perimeters. The trees were covered with slowly ripening fruit. At night they were a thick mass of sweet-smelling leaves in the gloom. She didn't like to pull an apple from the tree. It seemed ungrateful some-how, though why she couldn't say. Jane had always been more than generous to her. Claire rummaged on the ground for a windfall and bit into it. It was sharp and woody-tasting. She spat it out and reached almost defiantly to the tree. The apple that came away filled her palm and was sweet and moist on her tongue. She dropped it guiltily in the grass and went home.

By the time the McArdles had been away three weeks, Claire was counting the hours to their return. Sheena's card arrived at last, a few lines with the expected message: 'Hav-ing a great time, swimming and playing tennis. Disco danc-ing at night. If only you could be here!'

Dancing! Claire felt envious. Not so much for the boys Sheena was meeting – if anything she felt distinctly nervous at the prospect of them – but for the altered status it implied. Her friend had stepped into a different world while she played at home in short socks.

The same post brought a card from Hugh. He'd caught a whopper of a fish and only wished she'd seen it. But he'd got sorry for it and chucked it back in the sea. He signed his name and Hero's paw-mark. Claire laughed and felt a whole lot better.

That evening she wandered again in their garden. The tool shed was locked and she peeped in the cobwebby win-dow, hoping to see Hero's bed. The puppies were all long since disposed of and she felt wistful remembering their eager pink tongues, the warm solid feel of them. Hugh had wanted her to have the little black and white one she was so fond of and urged her to ask her mother, but Claire had known it was out of the question.

She could hear a radio playing in the bedroom in the house next door. She recognised the tune, "What's Another Year?" It had been very popular a few summers before.

The lights in the adjoining houses were being turned on. Claire stood listening under the trees by the side of the garage in the faint pink light, not knowing why she did so but reluctant to go home. The music stopped next door, and she heard footsteps approaching. She felt sudden panic at being found there and, opening the small door in the side wall of the garage, slipped inside. There was the smell of rotting potatoes. She stumbled on a coil of rope and shot out a hand to save herself from falling. She looked about in the gloom for somewhere to hide.

"I said one drink . . ." Eddie McArdle's voice sounded with startling clarity at the other side of the up-and-over door.

"You said!" The woman's voice sounded amused, incredulous. "What makes you think it's any easier for me."

Claire stood very still as their footsteps went on down the path. They must have been in the house all along. But where was his car? After a moment she heard the muffled slam of a car door and the engine starting up. He must have left it on the road. She waited an age, giving them time to get away, before she crept out, pulling the door gently after her. She ran full tilt into him coming round the side of the garage.

"What the hell?" He gripped hold of her, his breath coming short and quick. No less startled, she froze in his grasp as he dragged her forward into the light.

"It's me . . . Claire," she said timidly.

"Good God!" he exclaimed. "So it is. Where in the world did you spring from?"

"I was in the garage . . ." She blushed and hung her head. She began to shiver.

Eddie looked at her professionally. "Are you feeling all right?" He put the back of his hand against her forehead. "You feel a bit feverish." He reached for her hand to take her pulse.

"I'm fine," she said, teeth chattering slightly. "Just a bit cold."

"Mmm. Your hands are icy. Better come inside. I was just about to make coffee." He walked off towards the porch. She stood hesitantly until he called, "Come along," at which she followed him inside. The drawing-room door stood open, spilling soft lamplight into the hallway. She noticed two glasses on the low coffee table and a decanter, half filled with some golden liquid. She walked on past, down to the kitchen where he was bringing the kettle to the boil.

"Perhaps you would prefer cocoa?"

"No, coffee is grand." She didn't want to put him to any trouble. Besides, cocoa was for children. He took down two mugs from the dresser, scraped a spoonful of instant into each, and filled them up with boiling water.

Claire thought of the way Jane made coffee, almost entirely on milk, and wrapped her cold fingers about the mug. "How are they all?" she asked shyly.

He looked up and smiled. "Enjoying themselves."

"And Hero?"

"Off on endless forays, following scents. She's a country dog at heart. Wouldn't be surprised if she decides not to come back at all."

She stared at him. What would Hugh say?

He laughed at her concerned face. "Only funning," he said. "Hero's no fool. She knows when she's well-off."

She nodded, relieved.

He took her mug away from her. "It's cold in here. Let's go into the drawing-room. It will be pleasanter there."

He put his arm around her, ushered her down the hall and into the drawing-room. He set down the mugs on the coffee table.

"Sit down, Claire."

She sat in the armchair closest to her. He lowered himself into another and took up the whisky decanter. With a pleased grunt he poured himself a drink. She realised he was a little drunk.

She sipped the coffee, wondering when she should go.

"How have you been enjoying the summer?" Eddie took a swig from his glass and waited, head on one side. When she was silent he prompted, "Go on . . . tell me what you've been doing? I'd really like to know."

She said she went to the library every day, took out a lot of books.

"You've spent all your time reading!" He laughed. "In this hot weather?"

She coloured, stung by his air of amusement.

"I like to read."

"Absolutely nothing wrong about that," he conceded. "I only wish the same could be said of the twins. Those two never open a book."

"Christopher . . . my brother . . . is a bit like that," she admitted.

"Younger than you, isn't he?"

"Yes . . . two years . . . but he acts a lot younger."

He smiled and nodded. "Boys mature more slowly than girls. I'm not surprised an astute young lady like yourself has already noticed this."

She felt inordinately pleased by his approval.

"Tell me your favourite authors."

She did. This was the real world, more real to Claire than her own. She became animated. She was aware of his eyes upon her and felt excited and a little carried away by his attention. "I mean, in *Jane Eyre* she's merely a governess and Rochester is the master of the house, but when he challenges her opinions she has the courage to stick to them and even when he's terribly fierce and rude to her she doesn't allow him to intimidate her. You see, although Jane cares for him passionately she preserves her detachment from him," she concluded earnestly, trying to remember in which textbook she had come across this observation.

He looked at her thoughtfully. "You're really quite smart, aren't you, Claire? And romantic too."

Yes, she supposed, she was. Certainly she loved reading

about people in unequal circumstances falling helplessly, hopelessly in love and cleaving together, despite dreadful opposition.

"Apart from reading how else do you enjoy yourself?"

She searched about but could find no answer. With Sheena away, reading and visiting the library were her only pastimes.

"I expect you play tennis?"

"Now and then." Why on earth had she said that when it wasn't true except for knocking a tennis ball against the back wall?

He nodded. "I like a game myself. We have plans to build a hard court at the back. Not this year. Maybe next. You must use it, of course." He got up suddenly and leaned over her head to switch off the lamp.

"That's better, isn't it?" He sat down again. "More restful." He began talking about Sheena, the fun she was having flirting with the boys in the neighbouring cottages on their holiday site.

"She's becoming very mature, filling out. Her breasts are as developed as a sixteen-year-old." Eddie laughed. "Driving the young lads mad. Sheena will give them a run for their money."

Had he said breasts? She felt a sudden shock and went hot all over.

"Had your first date yet?" he asked her.

She shook her head.

"It won't be long." He smiled across at her. "You are very mature for your age, Claire. Anyone would take you for older. Did I tell you that before?"

She was silent.

"And extremely pretty. But that's not the only thing . . . you have an air of fragility that is very appealing. You don't mind me saying so?"

Her head swam, her mouth felt dry. She had a sense of unreality again. The room was bathed in the reflected glow from the lantern in the driveway. Meeting his intent gaze in the pearly half-light she became shy. A little scared. She sat rooted, unable to move as he leaned over and stroked her bare knee, pushing her skirt right up till his fingers brushed against the vee of her pants. He talked dreamily about Sheena's exploits with the Waterford boys and stroked her as if he weren't aware of what he was doing. Her head felt thick, confused; her blood was drumming in her ears.

"Do you like that, Claire . . . it's nice, isn't it?"

His whispering voice seemed to come from a long way off. She licked dry lips and lay back helplessly as a warm glow spread up her thighs while from on high, another self looked down, noting what he was doing and registering a feeble protest. His fingers slipped inside her pants and the sensation between her legs became so intensely pleasurable that she was terrified she was going to lose all control and wet her pants. She closed her knees convulsively on his hand. He gave a long sigh and sat back in his seat.

She got up. "I must go home." She looked uncertainly at him. He sat slumped in the chair, a hand covering his eyes.

"Yes, do that," he said, without looking around.

She let herself out of the house and ran across the street. The *News at Ten* was on the television as she passed the sitting-room door and went on up the stairs. In the bathroom she took off her pants and looked at them. They were in a damp string. She scrubbed them under the tap and hid them at the back of the hot press.

The next evening she wandered in his garden again. She saw the light in the kitchen and knocked on the window. He came to the door and looked at her almost angrily.

"Yes, Claire . . . what do you want?"

She was taken aback. She thought he would be glad to see her. She looked at him tearfully. She didn't quite know what she wanted except to be with him.

"I saw the light."

He stared at her, obviously uneasy. His unease communicated to her and she glanced behind at the darkening landscape as if fearful of someone or something watching them.

34

"You'd better come in."

She stepped inside and he closed over the door. He went at once to the window and jerked across the curtain although the garden was not overlooked.

"So why have you come?"

She was silent. She stood before him, eyes cast down. She was trembling. He gripped her by both arms and shook her. "Oh, what have I started," he said, so softly it was almost a whisper. He stroked her hair back from her averted face and, with closed fist, gently bopped her chin. She was trembling in the agony of expectation.

"If you had any sense," he said, "you would run now and not stop running until you were far away from here."

Sense didn't come into it.

He took her up to Ruthie's bedroom. There were posters of tigers and lions on one wall, giant Pandas on another. She looked at them as he sat her down on the edge of the bed and stroked her small breasts through her T-shirt. The tiger's eyes seemed to follow the movement of his fingers, bare his fangs at her. She closed her eyes. He bent his head and pulled gently at her nipples, worrying them through the cloth, leaving damp patches where his mouth had been.

When he lifted her skirt and began the slow pressure, she involuntarily arched against it.

"You are a very quick learner. Do you know what part of you this is?" he asked, stroking his finger up and down between her legs.

She shook her head.

"A very important part. Without your clitoris you couldn't achieve orgasm."

The telephone rang in an adjoining bedroom and he went to answer it. Claire fiddled with her socks, stretching and neatly turning down the tops.

"No, I can't . . . not tonight."

It was just possible to hear what he was saying.

"Look, another time. Yes . . . yes. Soon. I'll let you know."

Pause. "Oh, for Christ's sake! Don't be like that. Tonight's just a bad night for me. Okay. I'll call you."

When he came back he was smiling.

He switched off the light and left the door open so there was enough illumination from the landing to see by. He lay down beside her, on his side, stroking her hair.

"We shouldn't be doing this, should we?" he murmured.

What did he want her to say?

"Is it so wrong?"

He laughed. "Only if you believe it is. Some people are of the school of thought that all pleasure is sinful but then again there are those that believe a little masturbation is a healthy thing."

She lay still as he placed his hand on her stomach and gently traced her appendix scar, slipped lower to massage her belly and crotch. She was reminded of her mother's hand soothing her in the night. It wasn't so very different.

The next time she was with him he asked her if she realised that the family would be home at the end of the week. She said that she did. He sighed and caressed her.

"You're a lovely girl. I'm going to miss our evenings together."

She had vaguely hoped they would continue.

"Will you tell anyone about us?"

She shook her head.

"Good girl. We have something precious. We don't want to spoil it." He rocked her in his arms. "Claire . . . pretty little Claire. Strange to think that in years you aren't much older than Ruth. Yet she's still a babe with her animal pictures and toys. My men-aja-wee," he mimicked his daughter, not unkindly.

Claire felt sudden hatred for him and, at the same time, anguish and shame that no matter how hard she tried, she wouldn't be able to keep away from him.

On Thursday, the day before he went down the country to collect Jane and the children, he handed her a little package.

In the package was a delicate gold cross and chain. He made a big thing of putting it on her and fastening it about her neck.

She felt both disappointed and uncomfortable with the gift. How nice if instead of a crucifix, she thought wistfully, he had given her gold stud earrings like Sheena had, or maybe a Claddagh brooch. She would have loved that. She had absolutely no jewellery of her own.

She brought it home and hid it at the back of her cupboard (she didn't know how she would explain it to her parents), thinking she would leave it there for ever.

In County Waterford the weather held as fine as at home. For Jane McArdle the holiday had gone very much like any other except that she was conscious, at the start of this one, of feeling more carefree than other years. Thankfully the three older children were well and truly past the clingy, dependent stage and Ruthie, just turned four, was prepared most of the time to trek off in their care. It left Jane free for what she desperately needed: time to herself.

Sheena was always complaining that her little sister cramped her style with boys, but Jane was just as pleased with anything that put a halt to Sheena's gallop. Girls grew up far too fast these days. Teenage years should be as they were intended, happy and carefree and unclouded, in so far as possible, by money considerations or sexual pressures. There would be enough of these in the years ahead.

Even with Ruthie determinedly tagging along, Sheena was still the most popular girl on the holiday site.

"Quite the belle of the ball," Eddie remarked to Jane with a pleased grin. Jane had grinned herself, amused to see that her husband took his daughter's success with the opposite sex as a personal compliment to himself.

Now they were into the last hours of the holiday. In a little while Jane knew she would have to begin the chore of packing up. "But not yet," she told herself, clinging to these last precious moments by the sea. She dug her hips more comfortably into the sand and draped her cardigan about her shoulders. The day was becoming decidedly cooler. Pity, but it would be less of a wrench heading off next day.

Jane did not really mind going home. These few weeks had been pleasant enough, but she was a city girl at heart and became restless when too long away from the bustle of town. She only regretted not bringing Claire on holidays with them. The sea air would have done the child good, Jane thought, and she in turn would have been good for all of them. It was an undeniable fact that the children behaved far better when Claire was around. She would, besides, have been a help with Ruthie.

Not that Jane was looking for a mother's help, but she was aware how popular Claire was with her youngest child and, indeed, all her children. Even with Terry, for all his pretence to the contrary. Jane had seen the way her older son showed off in front of Claire, airing his knowledge and making witty remarks at her expense. Typically male, Jane thought with a sigh, and so like his father.

She reluctantly reached for her book and marked her place. Better get moving. She gathered everything up and, shading her eyes, spotted her children dashing in and out of the waves and called strongly, "Time to be going."

As they came running back Jane was reminded again of Claire. Yes, she really regretted not asking her along.

Hugh had been sorry too when he learned how near his mother had come to inviting Claire. Oh, if only she had, he thought. He took from its hiding place the photograph Sheena had snapped of Claire holding the little black and white pup she loved best, and which he had wanted her to keep.

"She's so pretty," Hugh told himself, gazing at it. And she was really nice too, which was even more important. So many girls were full of themselves, he thought, but not Claire. She always had time for him, even though he was so much younger. Hugh rather thought he loved her.

In September Claire's mother declared her intention of going back to teaching. She had applied for a vacancy in a privately-run Montessori school teaching six-year-olds. It was time to take it up again, Annette said, before she became too rusty.

"It will be nice," Annette said, "although I expect it will take some getting used to." She shrugged and sighed. "You get out of the way of small children."

Claire wondered if she was thinking of the baby. She would have been three that year, just starting play-school.

"I'm getting to be a right old lazybones," Annette said. "Should have gone out and looked for a job months ago. So it's back to school for both of us," she smiled. "In a way I'm quite looking forward to it."

So was Claire. August without Sheena had been lonely, and with all the rush of buying their uniforms and books for the new term they had met only twice since she returned from holidays. School started in less than a week and there were too many things to be done.

Claire had grown three inches since June and the hem of her gymslip, which had already been let down twice, was way above her knees. Her mother had considered adding on a false hem but, to Claire's relief, decided against it.

"Just as well I'm going back to work," Annette said. "We never needed money more." Claire nodded, knowing how much her mother dreaded September with all the extra expenses to be met. At least Chris still had another year to go at the National School. Annette had applied to several secondary schools for him and he would be required to sit the entrance exams in the spring. With a bit of luck, he would be admitted to one of them. Christopher didn't care which one, so long as they had a good football team.

Hugh McArdle did not have this dilemma. He had been in the prep school at St Gabriel's, Terry's school, since he was eight and when the time came would automatically pass into the senior school. Like herself, Hugh had shot up a few inches over the summer and he had acquired spectacles. Claire thought they looked out of place on his chubby face and gave him an elderly, slightly scholarly air. Christopher expressed relief that he didn't have to wear glasses. They would have interfered with football. Once the term started he was never home before six o'clock in the evenings, either training or playing matches with other schools.

Claire did not care much for sport, preferring to go straight home after school and get her homework done so that she could tuck up early with a book. Normally she dreaded the winter term because of having to play hockey. All those fierce Amazons hacking at her shins as they flew down the field unnerved her, but this year she viewed it less fearfully because Sheena would be playing alongside her.

The day of their first inter-school match Claire was surprised to see Eddie watching from the sidelines in the second half. It never occurred to her parents to come to watch her matches, though her father sometimes went along to see Christopher play soccer on Saturdays. She had seen Eddie only once since the night he'd given her the cross and chain, driving through his gates one evening as she was returning from the corner shop with the evening paper for her father. He had waved casually to her and gone inside.

She peeped at him out of the corner of her eye as she hovered, stick in hands, waiting for a piece of the action. When the ball came her way she surprised herself by the fearless way she tackled the full-back, slipping past her guard and neatly tapping the ball to the waiting centre-forward. She felt like cheering as the other girl sped it past the goalkeeper, scoring a goal and bringing the score up to two all. Claire was normally a timid player but now, conscious of his eyes upon her, she felt supercharged, darting from the wings again and again to tackle and harass her opponent.

The days grew colder as September gave way to October. Claire had got in the habit of calling over to Sheena's after school and doing her homework with her. The heat in her own house was never switched on until Annette came in and it was nice and cosy in the McArdle's front room, she and Sheena sitting at opposite sides of the big mahogany table, their heads bent over their work. Sometimes Teresa Murray,

Jane's receptionist, brought them in steaming mugs of cocoa which made it all the more cosy and companionable. Claire was not so happy, though, about the way Sheena unashamedly copied her maths homework.

"You don't mind, do you?" Sheena asked the first time she did it, already drawing the copy to her side of the table.

Claire shook her head, but she did. Claire had a natural aptitude and loved spending time working out problems and neatly setting down the answers. By contrast, Sheena's work was hasty and erratic, pages of her copybook disfigured by numerous crossouts.

Claire tried hard not to let it affect their friendship and even went to the bother one day of explaining to Sheena how to work out a ratio problem, jotting down an example on a sheet torn out of her notebook.

"Thanks, but it's a waste of time," Sheena brushed it aside. "Fling us over your copy." When Claire hesitated she held out her hand, impatiently wiggling her fingers. Suddenly, Claire wanted to slap her for being so careless and ungrateful and selfish. "No!" she wanted to shout. "Go and work it out for yourself." Maybe I should tell her out straight, she thought. She stood up and gathered her books into her satchel. Sheena did not even notice her going.

For the next few days Claire kept away from Sheena's house, doing her homework at her dressing-table, but it was chilly in her bedroom and lonely. By the end of the week she was back across the street again.

A few days before Halloween, Eddie came in unexpectedly one afternoon and said he needed Claire's help. He didn't say what it was about, but he laughed and winked at Sheena as if he had already discussed it with her. He was dressed in sweater and pants, not the dark suit he wore to the hospital, and Claire thought he was very jolly and relaxed.

"Just you, Claire," he said. "I won't keep you long."

Sheena went back to her books, a little smile playing about her mouth.

41

Claire got obediently to her feet. She wondered what he was doing home so early.

Eddie went out the door, leaving it ajar. He seemed in high good humour. She followed more slowly, uncertain as to where they were going.

In the hall he reached for her school gabardine and handed it to her.

"Better put it on," he said. "It's cold out.' He opened the front door and stepped aside to let her go before him. His car was in the driveway. He motioned for her to get in.

Eddie drove out the gate and turned on to the road. Claire fastened her seat-belt and leaned back. She watched absently as the roads became narrower and darker. They passed Daly's farm, where Hugh had got straw for the pups, and went on up the mountainside.

"Where are we going?" Claire asked.

"You'll see in a minute." He kept the nose of the car steeply climbing. Every so often he glanced at her and chuckled. Once he put his hand lingeringly on her knee and squeezed it. She shivered at his touch.

Eddie turned down a dirt lane and brought the car to a halt outside an old farmhouse. He got out and crossed the yard to knock on the door. A man came out and led the way to one of the out-houses.

Claire waited, wondering what it was all about. When they reappeared, Eddie was carrying a box which he placed on the back seat. She twisted around to see half a dozen globular orange-coloured fruits.

"What are they?" she asked, curious.

"Don't you recognise pumpkins when you see them?" His tone was light, almost gay. He got into the driver's seat and drove back along the lane. Then, instead of returning the way they had come, he drove on up the mountain for about half a mile. He turned off the road and parked amongst the trees.

It was very dark. Claire could just distinguish his features in the gloom. He moved her closer to him so that his arm was cradling her. She grew rigid.

"I'm not going to touch you," he whispered, "unless you want me to."

She wasn't sure what she wanted. She was excited and afraid as he aroused her with the deft touch of his fingers. That part of her yearned to be stroked and, almost of their own volition, her hips lifted towards him. When he slipped his hand between her thighs and gently caressed her she involuntarily arched towards him, sickened by her own shame and desire. He angled her on the seat and continued to stroke her. She moaned with pleasure, feeling dizzy, light-headed almost. She heard herself as if from a very long way off.

"How is that . . . good, is it?" He sounded pleased.

She struggled up but he firmly held her and pushed himself against her, hurting her, but not unbearably, until a hot drenching pleasure juddered her lower limbs. He sighed, "Claire . . . little Claire," and it was over, and he was driving down the mountain again, moving quickly through the darkness to come out into the lighted suburbs. Rain bespattered the car windows, making it difficult to see.

The house was ablaze with light. Jane was home. They carried the pumpkins into the house, Eddie taking most of the weight, Claire shyly supporting one side of the box, for the look of things.

Hugh and Ruthie ran out to meet them, having been alerted earlier by Sheena as to where they had gone. Ruthie was wearing the bottom half of a furry brown monkey suit Jane had made for her out of old car seat covers. She carried her tail in her hand to prevent it getting wet.

"Can I have one?" Hugh cried, reaching into the box for a pumpkin.

"All in good time." Eddie playfully swung the box out of reach of his son's clutching fingers and carried it, on high, into the kitchen where Jane, helped by Sheena, was preparing the tea. Jane swung around from turning sausages in the pan, her face flushed from her exertions and the heat of the stove.

"Goodness!" she said, staring in surprise at all the pumpkins. "Where did they come from?" Terry, hearing the commotion, strolled in to find out the cause. The children clustered round the box, excitedly laughing and chattering. Unobserved, Claire retreated to the hall and slipped quietly out of the front door. The sound of their merriment faded behind her. As she ran home, she felt sudden aching loneliness.

Six pumpkin faces, with hollowed-out eyes and jagged teeth, lit by guttering candle stubs, lined the ledge over the McArdle's garage. Claire could just see them from her bedroom window. Earlier, Sheena had run over to invite her to the Halloween party but she had not wanted to be in the house when Eddie was there and pleaded a headache.

Now darting eerily about the garden were three sheeted figures, carrying torches, and one small capering monkey. The children's excited shouts carried faintly on the night air, tantalising Claire. She thought she recognised the in-between figure of Hugh but couldn't be sure.

Clouds scudded past the moon. Two taller sheeted figures came out of the house to join the others. They all joined hands and danced on the grass in a collapsing circle. After a while they disappeared round the side of the house and, a little later, there was a high-pitched whine, followed by the sharp crack of fireworks. It went on all evening.

When Claire fell asleep she dreamed she was in the kitchen when a huge serpent reared against the window, battering the glass with its head, seeking a way in. She rushed to close the windows but she wasn't quick enough. Then they were all about her, in a seething mass on the floor and the only way she could get out of the kitchen was to kneel on one chair and, with another in front of her, push-drag herself down the hall. The snakes entwined themselves about the chair legs but she managed to escape. When that dream ended another began. She was running upstairs pursued by a rampaging black bull and only just managed to gain the safety of her bedroom. When he charged the door with his horns she ran to the window and climbed breathlessly on to the sill, jumping the moment he came crashing in.

She awoke feeling tired, played out. For a long time afterwards she could vividly remember every detail of her dreams.

Annette talked all the time about the children she was teaching, recounted the clever things they said, and was happier than she had been for a long time. She finished work at two o'clock but usually bussed it into town to 'unwind' as she called it, before returning to cook the evening meal. She might have been taking a Leaving Certificate class, Claire often thought, and not a bunch of infants.

These days there was a more cheerful atmosphere in the house. It was not enough to encourage their father to spend more time there but Claire found her mother more approachable and less inclined to irrational outbursts. It was possible to mention that she needed a textbook for school without encountering either a stony stare or lists of domestic articles claiming priority. Claire was even able to ask for, and be given, a new fountain pen, something impossible before. Sheena, who had two of everything, had loaned her one for the first few weeks of the term.

There was less tension in the atmosphere but she and Christopher suffered more in other ways. These days they lived on hamburgers and chips, Annette having invested her first week's wages in a new deep-fat fryer. Sometimes she substituted fish for meat but the end product was much the same – a plate heaped high with fried food. Christopher loved it but Claire's stomach had begun vaguely to trouble her again. She put it down to too many greasy, indigestible fries. As Annette's interest in housekeeping further declined, the airing cupboard was in a worse state than ever before. It took half a day to find anything and continually provoked their father to violent language.

In an attempt to combat chaos Annette wrapped bundles of drying clothes in damp towels, to make ironing easier (whenever she got round to it, only she never did) and left household detergents and disinfectants strategically dotted about the house, as aids to on-the-spot cleaning.

Claire was the only one who took the hint and adapted to this new do-it-yourself regime. She rinsed her school blouses and hung them over the bath to drip-dry. Her father's socks and hankies were always a crackling bone of contention between her parents: "For God's sake, Annette! Just a few clean hankies and socks. Surely, it's not too much to expect."

It didn't take Claire all that much longer to wash them with her own. It was a small price to pay for harmony.

One evening, her father came home while they were still having their tea. Claire could not remember the last time it had happened. Jim was very flushed. He sat at the table with a glass of gin in his hand, and watched them eat, cracking jokes, making them laugh.

Annette got up and went out to the kitchen. She came back with a slice of cheese and tomato pizza on a plate and pushed it briskly across the table. "You should eat something," she said. "It's not good to drink so much on an empty stomach."

Claire looked at her father. He was watching the television flickering in the corner, the sound turned down. But it's only one drink! But perhaps he's already had a few, she thought, and stayed in the pub till now and wishes he hadn't come home.

Annette sighed extravagantly. "That's right, ignore me. Don't pay any attention to what I say. Get an ulcer, if that's what you want."

Claire, too, looked at the television. Christopher knocked over his glass. It hit the table with a thud. He walked his fingers uneasily through the spilt orange.

Jim said, "Don't exaggerate, Annette. I'm just not hungry, that's all."

"You mean you're not hungry for pizza."

"No, since you ask."

"Well, what do you expect?" Annette said bitterly. "You

46

come home when it suits you. Walk in without letting me know. You're lucky to get anything."

"I don't want anything," Jim said. "I told you I'm not hungry." He was frowning. "Stop making a big production out of this, Annette. Let the children finish their tea."

"I'm not preventing them." She stood up, her eyes angry and tear-bright.

"Please stop it," Claire whispered to them.

Jim set down his empty glass and pushed back his chair. He went across to the drinks cabinet. Annette watched him intently. He lifted the gin bottle and set it down with a bang. "Nothing," he said in disgust. "Not even a drop."

"I suppose that's my fault too," Annette said, beginning to cry. He left the room.

"The one evening he comes home," Annette said, through her tears. "The one evening!" She struggled to control herself, succeeded, and began clearing the table.

The next morning Claire woke up at five o'clock, having dreamed that she was in a pet shop choosing a puppy from a tea-chest full of squirming animals. She wanted a black and white one and looked and looked but couldn't see one anywhere. One puppy, jumping up, seemed to be saying 'Take me, take me,' but for some reason she felt this particular one would mean trouble, so she burrowed down deeper and lifted out another pup with silky blue fur. She was cuddling it in her arms when all at once it became the curly-headed baby sister who had died, looking up at her with brimming eyes.

She lay awake, watching the sky growing pale beyond the curtains.

For weeks Claire kept away from the McArdle's house, opting to do her homework in her own house. She had not been back across the street since Halloween. She was afraid of her feelings when she was with Eddie. She told herself it wouldn't happen if she never allowed herself to be alone with him again, both sorry and relieved at the prospect.

One evening Claire was doing her homework in the sitting-room when there was a ring at the door. She went out, thinking it was the milkman collecting the milk money on Friday night, but when she opened the door Jane was on the step.

"Claire, dear," she said, "Can I come in a moment? You haven't been over in a long time. Is there anything wrong that you have abandoned us?" Jane spoke in her usual light, affectionate way but her eyes were concerned.

"N . . . no . . . n . . . nothing," Claire stammered, taken aback.

"Ruthie is always asking for you."

"I'm sorry."

Jane put out an arm to hug her. "Claire . . . Claire . . . you don't have to apologise. It's just that we're fond of you and miss you, that's all."

Claire said nothing.

"But that's not why I came," Jane said. "I wanted to see your mother."

"I'll call her," Claire said, but at that moment Annette came into the hall. She stopped short at the sight of Jane.

"Well, look who's here!" she said. "What a nice surprise." But there was an edge to her voice. "Why don't you come into the heat."

Claire stepped back to allow Jane precede her into the living-room.

"I've been meaning to drop over for ages," Jane said as she sat down. "You know how it is . . . you work yourself, Annette. Weekends are the only time to get anything done."

"Oh yes," Annette said vaguely.

Jane smiled. "Oh well, I never was a very organised person, was I? Look, Eddie and I are having a few friends to supper next Saturday night and we're hoping you and Jim will come."

Annette brightened. "That sounds nice," she said. "Can I let you know?"

"Of course," Jane said expansively. "No rush. I'm doing a

fork, plate, rice and something or other, so a few more or less won't make any difference. And that's another thing." She looked at Claire. "Would you be a love and give Sheena a hand with the serving, Claire? I'd be eternally grateful."

Annette said, "Of course, she'll be glad to. Won't you, Claire?"

Claire could hardly say no.

On the evening of the supper party Claire went across to the McArdle's house early. They had strung fairy lights in the macrocarpa tree. Claire thought they were very pretty.

She met Hugh in the hall. Of all the McArdles she had missed him the most. She smiled at him shyly.

"Hero's in trouble," Hugh said glumly.

"But why?"

"She tried to bite the postman."

"But she's so gentle," Claire protested. "She wouldn't hurt anyone."

"It isn't her fault," Hugh said. "The bastard is always hitting her with his bag. It's making her vicious." He looked like he was going to cry and Claire ached for him. She went on into the kitchen where Sheena was.

"Why didn't you change?" her friend wrinkled her nose at Claire's school uniform.

"Didn't have anything decent to wear."

"You should have told me," Sheena said. "I've loads of things would fit you. Let's go up quick and have a look."

"No really, it's all right," Claire said embarrassed, wanting to get off the subject. "Honestly. Anyway I'll be in the kitchen most of the time."

Sheena looked as though she were going to protest then shrugged. "Okay, have it your way. Give us a hand with these." She indicated a bowl of grapes she was stuffing with cream cheese. Claire stood beside her, slitting grapes with a sharp knife. There was a big pot simmering on the stove.

"Beef stroganoff," said Sheena, lifting the lid and releasing an appetising aroma. "Hope there's some left over for us."

Claire eyed the pavlova and the tempting array of mousses laid out on a sidetable. She could have given the stroganoff a miss, desserts she adored.

The first couples began arriving soon after eight-thirty. Claire peeped into the cosy drawing-room. Flames licked about a freshly placed log and lamps glowed at opposite ends of the room. Centre ceiling, the unlit Waterford Glass chandelier shimmered palely. Beneath it, the guests stood about, glasses in hand, their laughter as tinkling as the translucent lobes overhead. Jane had deliberately left the velvet curtains open so that the fairy lights were visible through the patio window. In front of it stood a huge vase of chrysanthemums, perfuming the air.

Claire and Sheena went about offering little bowls of crisps and peanuts. Claire shyly and Sheena with gay impudence. No-one seemed to take offence at her bluntness and only laughed when she said, "Go on, make yourself fatter." One or two of them admired her dress and the velvet bow in her hair as they scooped up fingersful. "Quite the young lady," a man said to the woman beside him.

Claire might have been invisible in her school uniform. She looked about for her mother and father but, despite having such a short distance to come, they had not yet arrived. She wondered if, after all, they might not come.

Then she saw Eddie standing by the mantelpiece, head bent, talking to a woman in a black dress. He looked very tall and handsome. The woman laughed up at him, a jewel glinting at her throat. Claire swallowed hard, her own throat dry and constricted.

Her parents were still absent. She and Sheena took it in turns, between trips with fresh drinks or canapés, to stir the beef stroganoff. Every so often one of the younger McArdles, usually Ruthie, would run into the kitchen. She helped herself to so many cheesy grapes that Claire was afraid she would be sick.

Ruthie loved the house filled with people. She clung to Claire's skirt, anxious to be in on the excitement as more and more guests arrived. There must have been fifty. A few people to supper!

Claire peeped into the oven. Any minute the garlic bread would be ready to take out of the tinfoil and placed in the baskets Jane had left ready. She turned and caught Ruthie with her hand in the pavlova, her lips rimmed with cream.

"Oh, Ruthie," Claire sighed fondly. She picked up the little girl and Ruthie squirmed in her arms as she ran the tap and washed away the evidence.

"But it'll all be gone when I get up," Ruthie wailed.

When Jane came in to put her to bed Ruthie was reluctant to go, then with a tired little sigh she suddenly capitulated, holding up her arms for Claire to carry her. She placed one small hand in a proprietary fashion on her mother's silk-clad arm, and the three of them went upstairs to her room.

The tigers and lions, the giant pandas on the wall were the same, yet somehow the room looked different. Claire told herself what happened that night had been a dream, another of her fantasies, that she had never actually lain there with him, done what they did on the bed. She was only a schoolgirl. How could she have?

"Can Claire-bear tell me a story," Ruthie pleaded. It was her pet name for Claire.

"Would you be an angel?" Jane was anxious to return to her guests. When Claire nodded, she kissed Ruthie and slipped away, turning off the light as she went.

Claire sat reluctantly on the bed. Party sounds filtered through the ceiling: laughter, the hum of voices, doors opening and closing. She heard Jane welcoming the last of the guests, heard her mother's nervous laugh, her father's deep voice. The drawing-room door closed over.

Claire decided to tell Ruthie one of her favourite Rufty-Tufty tales that she had read many times to the little girl, the one where the golliwog floated high in the sky holding on to a balloon and came to rest in a faraway garden. Ruthie listened, thumb sleepily plugging her mouth. Claire heard the light footfall outside the door and looked up. Sleep banished, Ruthie bolted up in the bed.

"Daddy, come in and sit down," she cried, patting the coverlet imperiously.

"What! Are you still awake?" He pretended to be cross but his manner was playful. "This won't do at all, young lady." He came in and sat on the end of the bed. "Go on," he gently prompted Claire, "Don't let me spoil your story."

Haltingly, she continued, aware of his quiet breathing beside her. Quickly she brought the story to an end.

"Quite a guy that Rufty-Tufty," Eddie approved. He got to his feet and bent to tuck Ruthie in. "Go to sleep now, poppet." He disengaged her clinging arms. "Claire must go down and you must get your beauty sleep."

He stood aside politely for Claire to precede him on to the landing.

Claire was happiest in the classroom. There, somehow, her other life did not impinge upon her at all and she could lose herself in her schoolwork. In fact, she came out near the top of the class in the mid-term exams.

She was not unfriendly with the rest of her class but kept remote from them. She shuddered when they giggled about dirty old men.

June Kelly's next-door neighbour was always trying to feel her up, she said. Some of the other girls had similar experiences. They shrieked and made faces. Sheena laughed along with them.

"There was this man on holidays," she began, choking so much with laughter that she could not go on. "If you'd only seen him!"

"Go on . . . go on," they urged her.

"Pulled down his pants and showed his thing!" gasped Sheena. More delighted shrieks. Sickened, Claire turned away. Was that what Eddie was?

Eddie didn't seem old to her, not like her own father, or some of the other girls' fathers. If he hadn't been Sheena's father she might even have told Sheena about him. It would have been a relief to have told someone. Her own mother perhaps, if she had been at all like Jane, or Jane herself if she weren't his wife. It seemed unfair that the only people she might have talked to were out of the question.

Hero was in trouble again. She attacked the postman again and although the bite was not severe, the man's trousers were torn and he had gotten a bad fright. He complained to the Gardaí and Eddie received a summons to appear in court. When he did the judge ruled that Hero be put down.

"She's not really vicious," Hugh told Claire earnestly. "I've a good mind to find out where that judge lives and bring Hero along to his house. Then he'll see how gentle she is." He was almost in tears.

Claire listened to Hugh's anguished plans and wished there were something she could do to comfort him. She felt as miserable as he did.

As the date of execution drew near Hugh insisted that he would do the job himself and in his own way. Jane and Eddie tried to dissuade him, thinking it was too fraught a situation for an eleven-year-old boy to handle, but after they saw how determined he was, they withdrew their objections.

Hugh decided he would get chloroform from the vet and choose his own time. Mr Halligan gave it to him, telling him, "If you feel you can't handle it, bring her to me." Hugh still kept putting the moment off. He just couldn't bring himself to do it.

Eddie secretly tried for a repeal of the sentence. He offered to muzzle the dog and keep him chained, anything to save him for Hugh. But it was no good. The judge refused to reconsider.

"I'm sorry, son," Eddie said. "I did my best."

Hugh nodded. It meant a lot to him that his father had tried again. "Thanks, Dad."

"There are only another few days left," Eddie said. "Best get it over with quickly."

"Your father is right, Hugh," Jane said gently. "You're only prolonging the agony and causing yourself unnecessary pain."

"Okay, okay," said Hugh. "I'm going to do it. Don't go on about it."

"Right." Eddie brought the discussion to an end. "No more delay. You've got until tomorrow or I'll bring him to the vet myself."

Hugh listened in silence. He couldn't bear for Hero to be put in a cage and given an injection by a stranger. Next morning when his father drove away he got the chloroform and steeled himself for the grim task ahead. He had to be the one to do it, he thought, as he went to release Hero. He owed her that much.

Hero was delighted to see him. She frisked about, glad to be free after weeks of being chained up. When she came back to him he patted her and clipped the leash on to her collar. Hugh went up the back road, past the stables where he had got the straw for Hero's puppies, and kept walking until he reached a rutted track, high above his home.

He took his dog into a field and let her off the leash. Hero tore about, enjoying her freedom. When she calmed down, Hugh threw sticks for her and watched her race and fetch, her paws skidding in the mud. Together they rolled and romped on the damp grass.

After a time, Hugh took the bottle from his pocket. Hero watched her young master, her eyes bright and intelligent, ready to spring forward whenever he threw what he was holding. While Hugh hesitated she whined with excitement and jumped up against him, muddy paws scrabbling at his gabardine.

Hugh ran his hand caressingly over Hero's head and down her flanks. "Good girl," he whispered. He gritted his teeth and grabbed her in a fierce necklock. Hero looked trustingly up at him and whined, believing this was some new form of play.

Hugh grimly reminded himself that the vet had assured

him this method was quick and painless, no matter how terrible it seemed. He prised open her jaws and prepared to pour the chloroform down her throat, as Mr Halligan had instructed, but she moaned and struggled so frantically in her efforts to get free that the bottle was knocked from his trembling fingers and fell into the long grass. Although badly shaken, Hugh still kept a tight grip on the moaning, struggling animal, feeling her paws scrabbling at his bare legs and drawing blood, but counting the pain as nothing compared to what he was suffering in his heart. He knew then that he couldn't do it, and let her go.

Hero tore off down the field and vanished through a hole in the hedge. In a state of near collapse Hugh blindly felt about in the grass for the half-empty bottle and, hardly aware of what he was doing, screwed the cap back on and stuck it in his pocket. His breath rasped painfully in his chest and the muscles in his arms and shoulders trembled with the shock and effort of the ordeal. He hadn't enough breath in him to emit more than a feeble whistle as he went in search of Hero. When he found her eventually on the roadway, she wouldn't come near him but slunk along at the far side of the road. He went slightly ahead of her down the mountainside, calling repeatedly. He should have listened to his mother, he thought in anguish. There was no use in hoping for a miracle or messing about any longer. He had only succeeded in putting Hero through further distress. He was stricken when he remembered the stark look of terror and dismay in the dog's eyes.

Now he whistled sharply, and Hero came reluctantly towards him, her tail between her legs. He clipped the leash on her collar and, going down on his hunkers, made a great fuss of her, stroking her and praising her, and feeding her the lumps of sugar he always kept for her in his pocket, until gradually she perked up a bit.

At the end of the road, Hugh resignedly turned in the direction of the vet's house. He paused outside the gate bearing the familiar wooden sign, then he braced his shoulders and with an encouraging word to his dog went on up the path and rang the bell.

The vet greeted him warmly, taking in his pinched white face and dejected expression. He brought Hugh through the empty waiting-room to his surgery and, with a kindly pat on his shoulder, sat him down.

Ned Halligan chatted away easily, as he placed a bowl of water on the ground for Hero and ran a gentle hand over her silky coat. Then he turned away to fill a syringe with 10 ml of Euthatal.

When Hero had finished drinking she say back on the floor in her favourite position between her young master's knees, front paws splayed apart. Her tongue lolled out of the side of her mouth and she panted noisily, tired from her recent exertions. Hugh stroked her head, feeling choked and sad and desperately guilty. Halligan indicated that he should lift her up and hold her in his arms.

Hugh settled Hero as firmly as he could across his knees, petting her and whispering to her all the time. The dog whined a bit, as though sensing what was to come.

"Now, the thing to do is to hold her leg steady for me, there's a good lad," the vet advised as he approached with the syringe. With his free hand he fondled the dog's ears before moving lower and gently parting the animal's fur in his search for the vein in his leg. "Don't let her move on me now," he murmured. He withdrew the needle and straightened up with a relieved grunt. "That's it. Good dog now."

Hugh felt Hero jerk in his arms and saw her eyes rolling sightlessly in her head and her paws wildly paddling the air, before her head fell heavily against him. He cradled the shuddering animal fiercely against his chest, and his heart was unbearably stricken as he watched her in her death throes. After a few minutes Hero gave a last convulsive heave and lay still. Halligan went out quietly shutting the door after him.

Hugh buried his face in the dog's warm coat that he had always taken such a pride in and, as the familiar smell and feel of her filled his senses, the dam of feeling broke inside him and he sobbed into her fur.

In the period leading up to Christmas Claire did not see Eddie at all. She stopped back after school most days to rehearse a review her class were putting on in the New Year. Unexpectedly she found herself drawn into a group consisting of June, Imelda and Sheena, all of whom had aspirations to be actresses. They chose to do a skit on *Fawlty Towers*. Sheena, as Sybil Fawlty, wore an auburn wig and padded herself out in one of Jane's bras. Imelda, who was the tallest of them, was just right for Basil and blonde-haired June for Polly. Claire was blonde too but was unsurprised to find herself cast as Manuel. She discovered she had a natural ability to play comedy, which was strange because she was the shyest of the four.

Rehearsing for the review helped take her mind off the worsening situation at home. For a time after the McArdle's party her parents had seemed more in accord but during the Christmas holiday period, without the saving trips to work or school to distract them, there had been one acrimonious dispute after another.

One afternoon in January her mother called over to the McArdle's house for coffee and a chat. Claire was playing cards with Ruthie and heard Jane saying, "You could just leave, you know. Take the children and start again. You've got a job and he'd have to pay something towards their welfare."

"I can't see myself doing it," Annette said.

"Why not? You'd be better off." Jane sounded angry. "No one should have to put up with that kind of situation."

"I never thought it would turn out like this," Claire heard her mother say tiredly. "I expected better somehow. But there it is, the luck of the draw."

And now her parents were in the middle of another dispute. They had moved into the dining-room for privacy, but the door was not quite shut and Claire could overhear what they were saying. She sat with her head deep in her book, wishing she weren't there but unable to get up and leave.

"So I'm getting strident, am I?" Annette demanded. "Well if I am it's because I can't seem to get through to you any other way."

Claire felt a sense of inevitability sliding over her. The knot in her stomach tightened. Lately her father and mother acted as though they hated each other.

"I have tried," Annette went on. "It's not easy going back to work after so long. But there's not much use in me trying if you won't."

"We've been into all that," Jim said.

"I know, but I just can't believe you . . . you say one thing and then you go right on doing the other." Her mother sounded agitated, Claire thought.

"It means nothing," Jim said. "I've told you."

Annette banged the table with her fist. "You keep on saying that. But I can't accept it. I mean, it must mean something or you'd give her up."

This is awful, Claire thought. She turned the pages of her book but she hadn't read a line. If only she had somewhere to go. She glanced towards the door leading to the hall, but she didn't want to go up and sit in her cold bedroom. She could go over to Sheena but *he* would be there, so she stayed with her head bent over her book.

Their review went down very well on the night. After they had finished their act Claire and Sheena changed out of their costumes and slipped down to the back of the hall to sit with Hugh and Terry. The four of them sucked lemon drops and watched the rest of the programme. In the front row Jane sat with Annette as Eddie had a medical dinner which prevented him coming. Her own father had promised to be there. "You can book me a seat in the parterre," Jim had joked, but although, at the start of the night, she had peeped through the curtain and anxiously eyed the darkening rows, there had been no sign of him. Claire was not really surprised.

Hugh thoroughly enjoyed the review. He thought that Claire was the best and funniest actress, but then he was prejudiced. Inspired by the stage show, he made a whole series of sketches, colouring the costumes in pastels and mounting the lot on cardboard. He hung them on the walls of his bedroom and when his father remarked on them, he flushed with pleasure. After that he began to take his drawing more seriously and spend more time at it.

Hugh propped his one and only photograph of Claire against his transistor radio and made several pen and ink drawings of her holding the pup, but he wasn't really satisfied with any of them. She was far nicer, he knew.

Hugh was too shy to show the drawings to Claire. He kept them hidden in a box under his bed, knowing that if Terry ever found them he would never stop ragging him.

Towards the end of January Eddie and Terry began planning a duck shoot, as they did every year at this time. For days their conversation was totally centred on the most ideal locations and conditions, the best rifles and cartridges. Terry, like his father, was a natural with firearms, as he was with anything needing co-ordination and skill. Hugh had no interest in blood sports and invariably found his attention wandering at the first mention of guns, until one evening, when sprawled behind the couch reading a comic, he heard them mention his name and sat up and took notice. Eddie was saying: "How about taking Hugh along with us on the shoot this year?"

"Oh Dad! Do we have to?" Up to this their sporting confraternity had been exclusively limited to his father and himself, and that was how Terry liked it.

Eddie laughed. "We don't have to bring him but he's old enough I think." Eddie had noticed how low the boy's spirits were since Hero's death, and he was looking for some way of making it up to him.

"He'll probably cry when we kill anything," Terry said in disgust. "He's such a wimp."

Hugh reared up from behind the couch at that. "No, I'm not," he protested.

"Of course not. Our Hugh's no weakling," Eddie said staunchly, but with a sly grin at Terry, which seemed in Hugh's hyper-sensitive state to imply there might just be some truth in it.

The night before the shoot Eddie insisted on the boys' watching him as he cleaned and oiled the guns. Then he loaded up, slipping the cartridges into the breech and snapping the gun closed.

"Never point it at anyone," Eddie told them. "That's the first rule. And the second, always keep the safety-catch on until you're ready to take aim."

Terry looked bored. "I know all that, Dad," he said. "You've told me billions of times." He wanted to impress on Hugh just how often he'd been through it all before.

"It can never be repeated too often," Eddie said sternly. He emptied the shotgun and handed it to Hugh. "Now let me see you loading up."

Hugh took it from him gingerly.

"Treat it with respect but don't be afraid of it," his father advised.

Hugh fumbled for the cartridges and dropped some on the floor.

"Clot!" Terry said automatically.

Hugh bent to pick them up and hit the gun off the table. He flushed and looked at his father.

"Go on," Eddie encouraged him. "You'll soon get the hang of it."

When Hugh had the gun loaded his father made him empty it and do it all over again until he was able to do it without faltering. By this time Hugh felt more confident, although he knew that it was not the loading, but the shooting of the gun that troubled him. He only prayed he would not look a fool before his father.

Next morning they rose at 3.30 a.m. and drove to Wexford. The sky was still dark when they reached the sloblands and parked the car by the side of the road.

Three times that morning they heard honking and the

furious beating of wings overhead. Eddie and Terry brought down seven birds between them and all Hugh's shots went wide. His dejection increased with his brother's derision, his father's laughter. Hugh went out several more times with Eddie and Terry but though his aim improved and he even succeeded in hitting ducks once or twice, the whole business of killing sickened him. He was careful, however, not to allow Eddie see his revulsion and, whenever he could, made excuses to get out of going.

In February when Christopher had sat the entrance exam for his new school and been accepted for the following autumn, Claire's father told her that he and Annette were going to separate.

"Oh no!" Claire wailed, thinking with her mother more cheerful lately everything had seemed to be going better between them. When they had all gone out to New Year's day lunch in a restaurant, Annette and Jim had drunk a bottle of wine and been full of jokes and laughter in the car on the way home. And she had tried so hard herself. She had really thought she was succeeding. It was ages since he'd complained about having no hankies or socks. She stared miserably at her hands.

"Just for six months," her father said, "and then we'll see."

"But what about us?" She was nearly crying. "Chris and myself?"

"Your mother and I need time away from each other to think things out. Decide what's best for all of us."

"But what about the summer holidays?" They were to have gone camping in France this year. Oh how could they do it? Claire felt sick and trembling, her confidence all gone.

"It won't be so bad."

How could he say that? It would be terrible. Some of the girls in her class were from broken homes. They had the lowest marks in the class and were always in trouble. Claire hated to think that she now numbered in that unenviable statistic.

Christopher blamed Annette for everything. "She shouldn't have gone back to work," he told Claire shrilly. "That's what it's all about, you know. Dad hates her working. I've heard him say so. Mothers should stay at home or they shouldn't be mothers."

In the past their father had said something of the sort. While Claire honestly felt their home life would have been much easier if this were the case, she was struck by how unfair such a view was. After all, it wasn't Annette who stayed out late every night and only shared family mealtimes on Sunday. Her mother always encouraged them to study and, if needed, was there to hear their homework. If lately she had lapsed it was only because she was finding her return to work a strain. And why shouldn't her mother work? Claire thought. With the right kind of back-up support from their father and help in the house once or twice a week, she could have easily managed to keep the household running smoothly. At the same time, Claire loved her father. No one was entirely to blame for anything. She had learned this from the books she read. Her father and mother were made up of both good and bad. Young as she was Claire could make these distinctions. The pity of it was that they could not bury their differences and live in harmony. But she kept these thoughts to herself. Like Christopher, she felt despondent and rejected.

Claire's father moved out on a Sunday. Before he went away they all sat about the dining table and ate their last meal together.

Annette sat red-eyed and withdrawn at one end of the table, ladling soup into bowls. For the occasion she had cooked their favourite dinner of roast beef, parsley stuffing and roast potatoes. Claire toyed with her portion, too full of tears to eat. Her father looked at his loaded plate as though he didn't know where to begin.

"Will you say grace or shall I?" Annette asked.

He shrugged. "Whatever you like," and left it to her.

Grace? When did they ever say grace, Claire thought. But

Annette was determined to bless this last supper. "For what we are about to receive Oh Lord . . ." she began, the words fluid and familiar on her tongue. Suddenly her voice died in her throat. She bowed her head and a tear fell on her hand. Claire looked away uncomfortably. Please God don't let her cry, she silently begged. Her father cleared his throat.

"Now don't start that," he said.

"What?" Annette found her voice.

"This emotional blackmail."

"If you can think that there's no point in saying anything more." She spoke with painful dignity.

"Annette, just what are you trying to say?" He was frowning, but he strove to be patient. What he would really like to do, Claire thought, is slap her about.

"You must allow me some emotions after fifteen years of wedded bliss," Annette said ironically. "I'm not apologising for my feelings, nor am I using them as a means of getting back at you."

"Very well," he conceded. "I'm sorry. I spoke without thinking. I was afraid you were going to cling on to me. Make it all so much harder."

"I suppose I might if I thought it would make any difference," Annette said very quietly.

Christopher had been eating all this time but now he threw down his knife and fork with a clatter. He swallowed a sob and fisted his eyes like he used to do, Claire suddenly remembered with a pang, when he was a little boy. Centuries ago.

Claire laid down her fork, unable to swallow any more food. Christopher's sobs continued jerkily. The tears flowed in dirty rivulets down his cheeks. He had been playing ball in the garden before lunch and neglected to wash his hands. Jim moved his chair over beside him.

"We'll go to a football match very soon, Chris old man," he said, putting an arm about him. "I'll get tickets and call over for you one day. We'll have a great time."

Christopher tried to speak but only succeeded in making an unhappy sputtering sound.

"Stop now . . . for pity's sake, stop!" Jim shaded his eyes with his hand.

But Christopher could not stop shaking. He began to hiccup. Claire too found she was trembling and sick. When it was time for her father to go she threw her arms around his neck, and began to cry.

"There now," Jim soothed her, and tried to joke. "Isn't it a pity I have to be leaving home for my family to show any affection." Christopher moaned faintly.

Jim left the room. They heard his footsteps heavily climbing the stairs. Annette went to the window and fidgeted with the curtain. Claire and Christopher sat slumped at the table, not looking at each other.

Jim came downstairs again, carrying his case, and passed the diningroom. Annette turned impulsively from the window and took a few hurried steps forward as though to call him back. Then as the front door closed she sighed and stood still.

Christopher put his head down on the table and sobbed inconsolably. "He's gone . . . he's gone . . . and I really liked him." Claire sucked on her knuckles till they turned white. Annette stared at her children, then gave a despairing cry and rushed out of the room.

Later that evening as Claire passed along the landing she saw her mother in her room, just sitting on the bed. She went in.

"I've just been sitting here and thinking," Annette said.

"What about?" Claire asked cautiously. She didn't really want to know her mother's thoughts, but felt she must ask.

"About the last fifteen years." Annette smiled wanly at her, not really seeing her, still in the past. Claire noticed the small pile of snapshots on the bed.

"Pictures of you and Christopher when you were little . . . and Bella." It was the first time she had mentioned the baby in a long time. Bella was their pet name for her. Arabella Angela Shannon. After Annette's mother and an aunt of their father's.

"Can I see?" Claire felt a sudden desire to look at her sister once more. Annette fumbled amongst the photographs and extended one to her. Claire gazed at it for a long time.

"She was a dote, wasn't she?" Annette peered over Claire's shoulder. "When I was a couple of months pregnant I nearly lost her. I got a show and had to stay in bed. Do you remember?"

"No," Claire lied. She did not want to hear any gory details.

"She was such a little angel when she was born. I suppose I always knew she was too perfect to live." Annette began to weep slow, painful tears. "Maybe it would have been better for us all if I had lost her earlier. I wouldn't have known what I was losing."

Claire didn't answer. She wished her mother would stop. She turned away.

"Oh my baby, my baby," Annette sobbed, putting out her arms blindly to hold Claire. She sat quietly in her mother's embrace. Why can't I feel more than I do? she thought. She was not entirely unmoved by Annette's tears but felt disassociated from them, as though witnessing a stranger's grief. After a time Annette stopped crying.

"Sorry, sorry," she said. "I just felt so low. It seems I've made a complete mess of things."

"No, you haven't," Claire said staunchly. "You're not to blame."

Annette hugged her tearfully. "What a funny girl you are," she said, "and there I was thinking you had no feeling in you at all. But you do care, don't you?"

There was nothing to say. Claire stood up, suddenly longing to be in her own room, on her own. Her mother went sniffling to the dressing-table and scooped up tissues to mop her eyes. Claire hesitated.

"Are you all right?" she asked.

Annette turned around. "Do I look all right?" She attempted a laugh.

Claire regarded her gravely. "Yes, you look fine." Her

mother did look better as though the tears had released some of the awful strain of parting. She hung awkwardly in the doorway, waiting to be dismissed.

"Off you go," Annette said, patting her averted cheek. "Don't worry about me. I'll be all right now."

Claire nodded and turned away. She shut the door of her bedroom with an overwhelming sense of relief.

When Claire went across to Sheena's house after school the next afternoon, Jane looked at her and said, "Claire! Is something the matter?" Claire began to cry. Embarrassed, she put her hands up to her face and scrubbed her eyes.

"Claire, come into the kitchen." Jane pulled her gently across the threshold and put her sitting down. All control gone, Claire sobbed brokenly.

"I'm such a nuisance," she moaned through her tears.

"Nonsense," Jane said, "You're anything but."

That made her cry more.

"Don't bottle it up," Jane said. "Let it all out and then you can tell me what's wrong." She turned away to heat milk in the microwave for the milky coffee Claire loved. Claire dried her eyes. She felt very tired, as though she had been walking a long time.

"It's lovely," she said, taking a sip.

Jane smiled. "Good. You looked so cold and pinched when you came in. It's what you need."

Claire nodded.

"Okay," Jane said, after a moment. "Now tell me. Is it your father?"

At the mention of him the tears blinded Claire's eyes again. "Yes," she said, her voice hurting her throat. "He left yesterday . . . we were having lunch and he just got up and . . ." She couldn't go on.

Jane sighed. "It's hard, Claire. I know! But maybe it's for the best."

How could it be? She had lost her father as surely as if he were dead.

"What I mean to say is," Jane went on, correctly divining her expression, "your parents will now have a chance to assess and correct what's gone wrong between them. When you are too close to someone it's often hard to find the right solution. A bit of space can work wonders, you know."

Claire stared at her uncomprehendingly. What had all of that got to do with anything? Her father had walked out on them. He had left them, not for the best, but to go and live with some other woman. There! What she'd tried to keep from admitting was out. "I hate him and I'm glad he's gone," she said passionately.

"Try not to blame him too much," Jane said gently. "I'm sure he's as sad as any of you. Men find it much harder than women to analyse their feelings." She leaned across and squeezed Claire's hand. "You are such a lovely girl, Claire. It would be a tragedy if you became bitter and allowed this to ruin your life."

Claire allowed her hand to lie in Jane's trying not to weep again. Jane seemed to sense this.

"Don't be afraid of emotion, Claire," she said. "It can sweep us away, but isn't that better than being cold and unfeeling." After a moment she went on, "I would like to think if you ever had any little problem you felt you couldn't tell your mother that you would bring it to me."

Claire was startled. Had she found out, was that it? It was like someone hinting that they knew you'd stolen something and expecting you to give yourself up of your own accord. Only Jane couldn't know, or could she?

So successfully had Claire compartmentalised her feelings about Eddie that up to this she had experienced little or no guilt. It was all so fantastic, so out of the ordinary, so beyond her control. True, in fantasies she sometimes saw herself confessing and begging Jane's pardon. Then Jane was the one to take her in her arms and stroke and pleasure her. Claire sometimes saw herself like a small rubber ball bobbing about between the pair of them, veering rather more slightly towards the one than the other, depending on which way the current was pulling.

"Think over what I've said," Jane stood up. "Remember, love, I have your best interests at heart."

Jane was her friend, Claire told herself. She really was.

"I have to take the children to the dentist at five so I'd better round them up." Jane smiled at Claire, "Why don't you stay on a bit? Teresa went home early. You can pull the front door after you."

It was warm in the kitchen, a nice contrast to her own house. Claire felt drowsy and relaxed, like she felt in a warm bath, reluctant to move but knowing she should climb out and dry herself. She sat on, promising herself every minute to get up and go home. She always had a lot of homework on Monday nights.

She awoke to see him standing in the doorway.

"What! All on your own. Where is everybody?" Eddie advanced into the room, removing his topcoat and flinging it in a chair. He stripped off his gloves and laid them on the table. He gave her a little sidelong smiling glance, in high good humour.

"So we are alone at last, Claire-bear." He'd heard Ruthie calling her that. She didn't know whether she liked it or not. She felt muzzy from sleep. Her hair was dishevelled, her mouth dry. Her gymslip was crumpled, riding high on her bare thighs. She saw him glancing down at them.

He turned away. She thought he was going out again but it was merely to switch off the light. In the gloom she saw him coming towards her.

In late spring, just after Hugh made his Confirmation, the Irish government announced their proposal to add an amendment to the Constitution. By voting 'Yes' in the referendum Irish people would ensure that abortion would never be legalised in their country.

In their different medical camps Eddie and Jane McArdle were taken up with campaigning against the amendment on the grounds that it was unnecessary. Eddie maintained that the law, as it stood, provided for the physical and mental well-being of pregnant women who found themselves in a life-threatening situation. Doctors were making their own compassionate decisions and could be trusted not to allow a developing foetus to endanger the life of the mother. He claimed too that the wording of the amendment was faulty and, if passed, would leave the way open to all kinds of misinterpretation. He was ultimately proved to be right but none of all this was clear at the time of the referendum.

Jane was concerned that the amendment might even prevent pregnant women from leaving the country to seek abortions abroad. For some years she had been involved in counselling the victims of rape as well as giving her professional services to a birth control clinic two days a week. In no way involved in assisting in or procuring abortions, or even offering referral advice to patients, she supported women's right to freedom of choice and movement.

As polling day drew near everyone was becoming more and more confused, and debates waxed ever fiercer between the less restrained of the pro-lifers and the right-to-choose activists. There were some nasty scenes in the city following demonstrations and pregnant single women went in fear of insult and attack.

Because of the nature of her counselling work Jane was asked to go on television. She sat opposite the interviewer, smiling with an assurance she did not feel, and sincerely stated her views, saying she was against abortion and honestly believed all truly dedicated doctors were of the same opinion, but, at the same time, she believed in the constitutional rights of women and felt the amendment could jeopardise those rights.

"So in effect," the interviewer said, "you are saying that you support the right of women to seek abortion."

Jane shook her head. "I support their right to information regarding it and the freedom to make up their own minds."

"To have an abortion?"

"Or not to have one."

The interviewer folded his arms and tried another tack. "So if a very young girl came to your surgery and it transpired that she was pregnant as the result of incestual rape, you would have no qualms about turning her away?"

Jane had never been in such a position in all her years as a doctor but she had often wondered what she would do in such a situation. She tried to give an honest answer. "I cannot say for certain what I would do but my personal view on the matter is that in a very extreme case, for instance, where there might be a substantive risk not only to the life but the mental state of a women who was pregnant, say, as the result of rape or incestual abuse there might . . . just might . . . be an argument for abortion."

"Can you clarify this?"

"If, say, the trauma suffered by the victim at the prospect of carrying the child full term was so great that she became suicidal or showed indications of trying to harm herself."

Nine years later such a case would come before the Supreme Court and the judges would decide that a fourteen-year-old girl, reportedly pregnant due to rape and thought likely to commit suicide if she was prevented from having an abortion, could be considered to come within these terms. But at the time Jane was speaking no such case had ever come to the public's notice, although it was highly probable such cases existed.

The interviewer, delighted at having provoked her into what he regarded as a contradiction of her earlier statement, began to harass her and twist her words, querying whether it was possible for a doctor to hold a personal opinion as distinct from a medical one on such a serious matter as abortion.

Jane held her own as well as she could. She spoke movingly on the rights of the unfortunate victims of rape and sexual violence that she counselled in the clinic, but her compassion was the very weapon the interviewer used against her. By the time the interview was over the majority of viewers had gained the impression that she was actually in favour of abortion, irrespective of circumstance.

During and after the show there were the usual abusive calls from cranks and misogynists. In the Sunday papers there was a follow-up and Jane was denounced by a bishop who said it was a sad look-out for Irish motherhood when the likes of Jane McArdle were given peak viewing time in order to corrupt and seduce the youth of the country.

Jane tried not to be too cast down by the more vituperative of the letters that came pouring in. She felt she had been grossly misrepresented and contemplated writing a letter to the papers clarifying her views, but Eddie strongly advised her against it, believing that the less said the sooner the whole thing would be forgotten. Sheena enjoyed all the notoriety. She told Claire she was hoping her mother would go on the *Late Late Show* to vindicate herself. That would be really great.

Hugh may have fared rather worse as a result of all the publicity. He came home one day with his forehead badly gashed. Jane thought he must have been in a fight, although as a rule Hugh was peaceable enough. Terry was the one who regularly fell in the door with a cut and swollen lip. She was not unduly worried until one evening she noticed bruising on Hugh's back when he was undressing for bed. When questioned he mumbled something about slipping off the high bar at gym. He tried to make light of it but when she pressed him, reluctantly admitted there had been one or two bullying incidents on his way home from school.

"Don't fuss, Mum," Hugh said anxiously. "I can handle it."

But could he? Jane wasn't so sure.

It seemed that his spectacles had triggered off the first ill-natured remarks and after that the situation had escalated. Jane was incensed and rang St Gabriel's to make an appointment to see the headmaster.

He received her in his study with barely concealed dislike and, still seated, waved her to a chair. Jane, taken up with her grievance, hardly noticed his lack of courtesy. She told him why she had come.

He assured her that anything out of the ordinary, even something so commonplace as spectacles, could draw forth the venom of the bullies in a class. He shrugged and said that it was regrettable. He didn't seem to feel there was anything he or anyone else could do about it.

Jane proceeded to speak her mind with no uncertainty. It was disgraceful, she said, and not to be tolerated. The bullies should be singled out and suspended. The headmaster listened with a bland expression. When she ran out of words he spoke about the danger of jumping to conclusions. A tumble in the playground hardly constituted an attack. She fumed as she listened to this bland whitewashing of the incident. Tripped indeed! She came away in a fury of hurt and dissatisfaction.

Maybe the school authorities had seen the television interview. No one could say for sure, but her complaint received scant attention and the bullying continued. Hugh refused to discuss the matter, insisting he could defend himself. In desperation, Jane spoke to Terry.

"Leave it to me, Mum," he said. "I'll fix those bastards."

Terry and a few of his classmates concealed themselves in the bushes at the end of the avenue leading up to the school and lay in wait for the bullies. As they drew near Terry gave the signal and he and his chosen band rushed out. Terry caught hold of the ringleader, a boy called Mark, and slammed him into the ground. He sat astride him and pinioned his arms.

"If you ever lay a finger on my brother again," he told him, "I'll break your neck."

The boy struggled and squirmed under him but offered no further defiance. Terry had a reputation for being a formidable adversary, and after that they left Hugh alone.

The leaves on the silver birch in the McArdle's back garden hung like pods about to unfurl, and in the overgrown mass of vegetation behind Claire's house the broom fountained yellow-gold against red brickwork. There were only two weeks to go before the end of the spring term and she and Sheena were counting the days. The McArdles had decided to go away to their holiday bungalow for Easter and Jane had asked Claire to go with them.

"It will do you good," Jane said. "You've been looking very pale lately. Even Eddie has noticed. It's a beautiful spot and the sea air will be just the thing to put colour back in those cheeks."

Jane admitted she was feeling the effects of the past few months herself and looked forward to lazing about for two weeks. "Don't feel you have to be grateful or anything," she told Claire with a smile. "You'll be earning your keep looking after Ruthie as well as putting up with me when Eddie is playing golf. You may be sure Sheena won't be much in evidence. If I know that young lady she'll be off gallivanting with the boys."

Claire didn't really mind. She had no wish to meet boys. She really welcomed the break from her own house though, and especially her mother. Not that she didn't appreciate the efforts Annette was making since her father left home. Each week the two of them went to a film together and bought fish and chips on the way home. Some nights they got on really well, others they hardly spoke to each other. When this happened Annette would lose her temper and accuse Claire of being selfish and unsociable and then inevitably she would start cataloguing Jim's faults. Claire recognised that her father had faults, but he wasn't there to defend himself. When she said so Annette would cry in exasperation, "For God's sake, Claire, anyone would think from your attitude I drove him away. He was the one who strayed. It wasn't the first time either."

Claire considered that it would be a relief to be out of the line of fire for a whole fortnight. She deliberately kept herself from thinking of Eddie. There had been two further occasions of intimacy in the months since the February day in the kitchen, but even those she had put out of her mind and they had assumed a dream-like quality, as though they had happened to someone else. Actually, the intimate Eddie was becoming more and more distant from the father-figure Eddie, whom she met often in the presence of his family. This fatherly Eddie, unlike the other, presented no threat.

Annette did not raise any objection. She was feeling worn out herself after the spring term and looked forward to two weeks of freedom from early rising and Montessori teaching.

These days she felt all strung out by the time she reached home in the evenings. With the approach of the good weather the little boys and girls she taught were full of repressed energy, just bursting to get out of school and into the air. At home her own children were also taking their toll on her. Since Jim had moved out of the house the three of them had been thrown into the claustrophobic proximity of one parent families. Every little grievance was magnified and it took as little as the absence of a favourite breakfast cereal to spark off a family row. It seemed to Annette that in her children's eyes she was always at fault. Of the two, Christopher, although less analytical and probing than Claire, was inclined to be the most censorious and clearly still blamed her for the family split. So Annette readily agreed to her daughter going away with the McArdles for Easter, only too glad to have her burden halved for the next two weeks.

The McArdles travelled in convoy to Waterford and arrived in Dualeen in the late afternoon. It was a lovely day, like the middle of summer. Along the coast road the sea sparkled invitingly, the waves only lightly capped with lacy foam. Claire was sorry when they left it behind and turned inland.

The McArdle's holiday house was actually a dormer bungalow, and bigger than it looked from the outside. Claire found she was sharing an upper room with Sheena and Ruthie. The boys were across the landing. Downstairs, with a separate bathroom of their own, was Jane's and Eddie's room.

Wherever they went in Dualeen everyone seemed to know the McArdles and because she was with them Claire got friendly smiles and nods of the head. It was her first taste of life in a seaside town and she loved every minute.

On the beach, which was two hundred yards from the bungalow, the children played sand cricket and skimmed stones in the waves. Ruthie, helped by Hugh, made linked rows of turrets on the shore, endlessly filling, patting down and upending her bucket. The mild weather looked as if it would never end.

Jane sat on the rug, like a queen amidst her subjects, sunglasses shoved high on her forehead, a book dangling from one relaxed hand. "This is the life," she sighed every few moments, wanting to hold on to these first blissful moments of the holiday, not yet taking for granted the fact that she really was away, with no patients to see or urgent cases to consider for the next two weeks. And the weather! "Not like April at all," she gloated. "More like the middle of June."

Claire, like Jane, hugged to herself the thought of all those sunny days ahead of her. For the first time in her life she felt part of a family, a real family, with brothers and sisters to share her happiness. She wandered away from Sheena and Terry and lay down on a corner of the rug beside Jane. Contentedly she took up her book. *Villette.* Another great story and even better than *Shirley*, which she had just finished the week before coming away. When Claire liked a writer she read everything she could lay her hands on by that author, feeling it gave her a great sense of the person, almost as if she knew them. Sometimes she just let the book slide out of her hand and felt the sun an aching violet pressure on her lids. Lately she was feeling lethargic. She was just as pleased to laze about playing snap with Ruthie or noughts and crosses with Hugh. She thought she might be getting her period.

With her eyes shut, she heard the shouts and laughter as though from a great distance. She kept her eyes tight shut, afraid if she opened them she might find herself back home again. When at last she chanced breaking the spell and let them fly open, the sun nearly blinded her and she gazed in wonder at the sea and sand, the smiling faces turned towards her.

"C'mon, lazybones," Sheena cried, plumping down on the sand beside her, "we're going to play cricket and we need you."

Claire marked the page of her book and got up reluctantly. She could have lain there for ever. Jane watched her with a smile, glad to see her so relaxed.

Not far from the bungalow there was a hotel, a large white building at the top of a sandy sloping road. There was a pool table in an annex beside the bar and the hotel served delicious afternoon teas. Jane often took the children there and she would sit reading a magazine with a gin and tonic at her elbow while they sampled the cream cakes and petits fours.

"This is my Black Forest Gateau," she would joke, raising her glass. Eddie sometimes joined them and he and Jane would withdraw to the bar, leaving the children to their own devices. Claire always felt easier when he wasn't with them. It was a relief when he went away for two days to play golf in Rosslare.

There was a fun-fair set up in a field behind the hotel and the children went there as often as they got money from Jane. Hugh partnered Claire in the dodgem cars, and she hung in breathlessly beside him, her heart in her mouth. He knew she hated the jarring collisions and he did his best to ferry her safely out of danger, but every so often Terry and Sheena came at them out of the blue and the two cars would come crashing to a halt. Ruthie was not allowed to ride the cars and she would jump up and down, impatient for them to finish. Claire took her on the chair-o-planes and the two of them held hands and whirled screaming high above the crowd. Ruthie loved them but afterwards Claire felt so sick she thought she was going to throw up.

In the evenings they stayed home and Jane cooked up lots of chips and whiting in batter. Sheena and Claire took turns, lowering the fish basket into the hot fat. Sometimes they had party nights, when Eddie and Jane invited in couples from the other holiday bungalows and the adults either played cards or shuffled about the floor in lazy time to Elvis or the Beatles.

Sometimes the neighbouring couples brought their children with them and Claire and Sheena had to organise them in another room. Eventually the younger ones became cranky and would have to be carted home and put to bed, so the girls earned themselves quite a bit of money baby-sitting. By the time the partying parents came stealing shamefacedly in, Claire and Sheena would be fast asleep on the settee but, within minutes, they would be fully awake and hurrying out of their respective cottages, clutching fivers or even tenners. Stumbling back to their own bungalow, they would plan how they would spend it. Once it was so late that the first blush of dawn suffused the sky and they saw the men setting off in their fishing boats to bring in the catch.

Another morning, tiptoeing in the door, the girls found Eddie still sitting, glass in hand, by the fire. Although the weather was so mild as to be almost summery, the nights had a nip to them and the McArdles kept plenty of turf stacked beside the fireplace. Hugh was usually first up in the morning and, by the time the others struggled down, he would have the fire lit and be sitting by it, listening to his Walkman. Later in the morning it was let go out and only lit again when evening came.

Now the fresh sods Eddie had arranged on the previous night's dying embers had begun to catch, sending a flickering glow about the room. Jane had already gone yawning to bed and Sheena, perhaps fearing that her father would make her do the washing-up before retiring, fled upstairs crying, "Last one in bed's a rotten turnip," and abandoned Claire to him.

Claire hesitated, drawn by the heat of the fire, for she was chilled from hours of sitting in the unheated cottage. Eddie seemed half asleep, nodding over his whisky. She lingered, warming herself at the blaze.

Sheena's shout awakened Hugh out of his second sleep. He stirred and dozed until it became evident that he would have to get up and take a leak. He was reluctant to go down the steep wooden stairs to the toilet and contemplated peeing in the bowl on the washstand, but fear of Terry's wrath deflected him.

Hugh swung his feet on to the floor and shivered. Elsewhere in the bungalow the polished boards were warmer underfoot but in this room, which was really little more than a boxroom, lino had been put down. He looked longingly at the washbowl and then at the sleeping hump in the bed. Terry would almost certainly tell everyone if he used it. Hugh shuddered. He would be mortified if Claire found out. He opened the door and crept down the stairs.

The house was very quiet. At the turn in the staircase he looked through the banisters and noticed the fire still burning. Someone had piled on more sods and the flames were leaping high up the chimney with no guard in front of the fire. One stray spark and they could all burn in their beds. He was about to run on down when something in the corner moved, so slightly he might have imagined it, a sod of turf shifting in the creel or hot ash settling in the grate. Then he saw the bodies on the rug. For a moment he could not distinguish who they were. He peered closer and, in the shifting firelight, recognised Claire's long blonde hair fanned out on his father's bare stomach. He had always thought that hair so pretty. At that moment she lifted her head slightly and he saw what she was doing.

Hugh crouched down in the shadows and began to cry softly to himself. It was the first time he had cried since Hero died. He turned, almost in slow motion, and with great effort got his legs to carry him back upstairs. He crept into his room and quietly closed the door. Careless of Terry, or anyone or anything in the world, he peed in the bowl and got back shivering under the covers. When he closed his eyes he could not rid himself of the vision of Claire and his father.

Claire went through the morning feeling like she was going to get sick. Her throat kept gagging as though she had swallowed some of the stuff. She hadn't wanted to do it but Eddie had insisted, pressing her head down lower and lower until her face was pushed into his pubic hair. "Please . . ." she had said in a low voice. "Oh please!" But he had kept her at it. She was afraid if she refused or told him how much she hated it he would be angry with her and might even tell Jane to send her home. She hung over the toilet bowl dry-retching and would have stayed in there longer only Terry was banging on the door, wanting to get in.

Claire came out and went into the bathroom, which was separate from the toilet, to brush her teeth, taking a long time over it and repeatedly rinsing out her mouth. The memory came back to her, indelibly etched on her brain. She spat again and again, coughing until her throat hurt, remembering the force with which he had driven into her mouth. She felt violently ill again.

"Claire, my dear, are you all right?" Jane asked, coming in after her and gently closing over the door. When Claire looked up, white and exhausted, from the washbasin, Jane thought she had never seen such abject misery on a human face before.

Jane was too familiar with the early stages of pregnancy to be in much doubt about what was the matter with Claire, and was both shocked and saddened. How could it have happened to Claire? She was so young, not yet fourteen, still a child. Such a tragedy. Jane couldn't have felt more depressed if it had been Sheena or Ruthie.

She persuaded Claire to come into her bedroom and gently examined her. What she saw confirmed her suspicions. Claire's breasts were blue veined and rather fuller than normal, with a thickened, orange peel texture to the nipples.

"Good girl," she said, her heart aching for the shame she saw in the girl's eyes. "Now there's one more thing I'd like from you." She gave her a bowl and told her to go into the toilet. Later that morning Jane got a home pregnancy testing kit from the local chemist. As she had suspected, Claire was pregnant.

From the girl's bewildered attitude Jane surmised correctly that Claire was not fully aware what had happened to her. Like most youngsters of her age, her periods were scattered and light, and she wasn't even sure when she had had her last one. From what she could tell from her brief examination, Claire was at least ten weeks pregnant. Jane sighed and cursed nature's ill-conceived system, whereby girls hardly more than babies themselves were given fully effective reproductive equipment long before they were mature enough to cope with it.

Jane decided to take a trip back to town to consult a colleague who specialised in the area of rape crisis and she decided to take Claire with her. There was only a few more days of the holiday left and she was anxious to get the girl home before her condition became apparent to the others.

Jane decided she would say nothing to Eddie. In such a crisis, she considered, men were rarely much use. Eddie would more than likely tell her that it was Annette's business, not hers. Jane had no great confidence in Annette's ability to cope with this particular kind of situation, but while she was in town she would have a chat with her. Another suspicion was beginning to form in her teeming brain. She was visited by a memory of how upset Claire had been after her father had walked out on them and, putting this and a few other impressions together, believed she knew who the father of Claire's baby might be. And if her suspicions were correct . . . Jane shuddered at this new aspect of the situation and the effects of it upon the unborn child.

Claire packed her case with lowered spirits. She felt somehow as if she were in disgrace. It was nothing Jane had actually said but Claire sensed her reserve. She closed down the lid, thinking how happy she had been the day they arrived and what fun it had been taking out her belongings and laying them on the shelves along with Sheena's and Ruthie's things. How she wished she could reverse time and be starting all over again. She stood, eyes closed, swaying slightly until Sheena and Terry came running in to tell her that Jane was ready to go.

"I'm to bring your case down," said Terry importantly. He swung it off the bed and went rapidly out of the door. Claire and Sheena looked at each other.

"See you the very minute we get back," Sheena promised, almost recovered from her disappointment at being left behind. "Why can't I come too?" she had asked her mother indignantly. "I'd love to visit the book fair in the Mansion House," Jane's excuse for bringing Claire. Only her mother's promise to bring her back a treat had succeeded in soothing her feelings. Now she put her arms around Claire and gave her a hug.

"I'll miss you, Claire-bear," she said wistfully. "It'll be dull here with only the boys and Ruthie."

Claire hugged her back, feeling immeasurably cheered. She went to say goodbye to Ruthie and blinked back easy tears as the little girl clung fondly about her neck. Of Hugh there was no sign. When she went out to the car Jane was in the driver's seat and Eddie was lifting their cases into the boot.

Annette was taken by surprise when she opened the door to find Jane and Claire on the doorstep. She had not expected her daughter back until Saturday and now here she was on Tuesday afternoon. Annette could not help feeling cheated. She had counted on two whole weeks. Nothing ever worked out the way you expected.

While Claire went up to her room Jane sat down with Annette in the kitchen and proceeded to quiz her about Claire's health. Had Annette noticed anything amiss with the girl lately? Was she depressed or unusually nervous or unable to sleep? Was she as affectionate as she usually was?

Annette shook her head. She felt vaguely apprehensive and at the same time irritated by Jane's questions. They could have equally applied to any one of them, she thought. They were all of them going through a difficult time since Jim deserted them. Christopher had started smoking. She had smelled it the minute she came in the front door. When she went upstairs he had been sitting on the edge of the bath with the window open, puffing away. All his class were doing it, he'd said defiantly. Annette was shocked. He was only eleven, for God's sake! She herself wasn't sleeping well. And she often felt depressed these days. Why was Jane going on like this about Claire, who had just been away on holiday?

"Get to the point, Jane," Annette sighed.

"It's just that she seemed rather depressed away on the holiday," Jane said. "I was wondering if you had seen any signs of it yourself just before she went away. Whether you had noticed her any less affectionate or out-going? You know, not so inclined to give you a hug."

"Claire has never liked being hugged, not by me at any rate. Anyone would think I was her enemy. She has always been prone to nervous outbursts and nightmares, but if there is anything seriously wrong, please tell me."

Jane debated whether or not to give her the whole truth. It was a tricky situation. She could hardly say that she suspected Claire's father of abusing her. Jane had met Jim only once or twice and he had seemed nice enough. She could be making a terrible mistake. She decided the best thing might be to edit her declaration until she had discussed the situation with another doctor.

"I've noticed she's a bit run down, getting dizzy spells," Jane hedged. "She could be anaemic. I'm arranging for a colleague of mine to take a look at her."

"Is that all?" Annette was relieved. "Why didn't you say so? I was beginning to think she had leukaemia or something dreadful."

Jane got up. "Can I take it you're in agreement if I book her into hospital overnight?"

"Surely it's not that urgent?" Annette looked surprised.

"No point in putting it off," Jane told her. "Now is as good a time as any. Don't forget, she'll be back at school next week."

"Whatever you think, Jane. You're the doctor," Annette

said, half-joking, half-resigned, and secretly glad for anyone to take on the burden of looking after her children. She saw Jane out, then fortified herself with another cup of coffee before steeling herself to go up and hear all about the wonderful seaside holiday.

That afternoon Eddie took his sons to play at the local golf course. On the drive there he noticed that they seemed unusually subdued. Normally, Hugh noisily vied with Terry for his father's attention, but today he did not even seem to be listening to anything Eddie said. And Terry for once had little to say.

Glimpsing Hugh's pale, woebegone face in his rear-view mirror Eddie blamed his son's apathy on too many late nights.

"Bed early for everyone tonight," Eddie announced with a sardonic grin, and waited for an outcry. "And that includes you too, Terry my boy," he added, in case his eldest son believed his seniority would save him.

"Sure Dad," Terry said, gazing absently ahead. Eddie sighed and drove through the entrance to the club in silence.

That morning Terry had come upon evidence that Hugh had been too lazy during the night to visit the toilet, and vigorously tackled him.

"Smelly little wimp," Terry had jeered, disdainfully flicking drops from off the end of his fingers. Instead of humbly begging his pardon, Hugh had suddenly backed him on to the bed with such force that his head cracked against the brass bedstead. Next thing Terry felt an iron, unrelenting knee on his windpipe.

"Shut the fuck up!" Hugh said in a coldly menacing voice, "or I'll make you bloody well drink it."

"Oh yeah?" Terry croaked, but with a lot less force.

Who did Hugh think he was anyway, handing out threats like that? He had a bloody nerve!

Terry hoisted the bag containing the golf clubs on his shoulder and as they strolled on to the first tee, debated whether to raise the urinary incident. He cast a speculative glance at his brother's preoccupied expression and regretfully decided to hold his tongue. Terry frowned. For a while this morning he had felt – not scared exactly – but well, apprehensive. Definitely apprehensive. Despite himself, Terry felt the beginnings of a grudging respect for his younger brother.

Hugh played badly, every shot wide of the mark. By contrast Terry seemed inspired. On the second hole he placed the ball only an inch short of the green and with his second shot lobbed it into the hole. Terry was noisy with delight.

"Remind me some time to show you how to win, Hugh," he boasted.

"I thought you already had," Hugh said thoughtfully. Terry flushed and walked in sulky silence to the next tee.

Eddie played his shot. It landed on the green. Pleased he turned and ruffled Hugh's hair. The boy twisted away. When Eddie picked up his clubs again and moved on, Hugh was careful to avoid going close to his father.

Some hours after Jane had arrived back in town she sat in a small clinically furnished room with its surrounding walls covered by posters on every aspect of pregnancy and birth control and outlined her suspicions to the quietly listening woman who was her friend and colleague.

"Although I am not absolutely certain that it was the father, and short of asking the child outright I have no way of knowing for sure, yet somehow it all seems to fit. She was terribly upset when he left and yet relieved too in a way, saying she hated him and was glad he was gone. The mother also revealed one or two things which strengthened my conviction: namely the girl's inability to express physical affection, as well as her tendency to nightmares and nervy and irrational outbursts. Classic symptoms of this kind of tragic situation."

"It certainly bears all the hallmarks," Detta said thoughtfully. "How old is she?"

"Her birthday is around about the same date as my

daughter's and Sheena won't be fourteen until the middle of June."

"Only kids," Detta said soberly. "What I would be most concerned about is her mental state if she were forced to carry the baby to full term."

"My feelings exactly," Jane agreed. "Some years ago when her baby sister died Claire suffered severe trauma and is not entirely recovered from it yet. I honestly believe her present dilemma could be the unhinging factor."

"So Jane," Detta gave her an appraising look, "are you saying she should have a termination?"

Jane sat very still. Yes, she supposed she was. She had not thought she would be put to the test so soon. Jane shuddered and, realising Detta was still waiting for her answer, slowly nodded.

"Yes, having taken all things into consideration."

Detta reached for the telephone. "Okay, Jane," she said firmly. "I'm fully in agreement. In view of her shaky mental condition and the risks involved, the girl should not be put through the ordeal. The sooner she's seen to the better."

When Detta put the telephone down it was all arranged that Claire would be admitted to a privately run clinic next day, ostensibly to have a D and C carried out. She would be kept overnight and allowed home on Thursday.

As soon as she reached home Jane rang Annette and told her that Claire was booked in for her check-up next day.

"They may want to do certain tests so she must be fasting," Jane said. "If you like I can bring her there myself, but it will be early. Eddie is driving up from Waterford first thing to be at his consulting rooms before nine and I'm aiming to be back with the children by midday."

"I understand," Annette said bewildered, not understanding at all. At least, not about all the rush where Claire was concerned. "I'll have her ready. And thanks for everything."

Jane put down the phone and went to have her tea. She felt tired and was aware that she had just taken a huge decision on Claire's behalf. But now that it was done, she felt it had been the right one. It would have been too callous to allow her to continue with her pregnancy. As Detta so rightly said, girls at this age were still only children themselves and they must be protected.

Next day Claire followed Jane over the gleaming parquet floor, overnight bag in hand. She waited while Jane spoke to a woman at the reception desk and tried not to feel lonely when the woman beckoned her down a corridor and showed her into a room.

"Take off your things, love," she said, "and slip this on." Claire recognised the theatre gown from the time she had been in hospital having her appendix removed. She gazed at it uneasily.

Jane put her head round the door. "Don't worry," she said, seeing Claire's troubled expression. "There's absolutely nothing to be alarmed about." She came in, smiling encouragingly. "I'll wait with you until you've undressed."

Claire's back felt chilly. She slipped down deeper in the bed and gradually began to warm up. A dark-haired nurse came in with a hot water bottle and slipped it under the covers. That helped quite a bit. When Jane had kissed her and gone away, Claire lay looking at the light beyond the window. If felt strange to be in bed so early in the day. Various people, nurses and, she supposed, a doctor came in to sit on the bed and take blood from her arm and ask her to give them a specimen of urine. All of them seemed to think she was older than she was and that she was suffering from painful periods. Not that her periods were ever pleasant but Claire wouldn't exactly have described them as painful. She still wasn't quite sure what she was doing there.

"You won't know yourself afterwards," the nurse who took blood from her said. "You'll be glad to have it over with, pet." She stroked Claire's hair back from her forehead and said how pretty she was. "A right little blondie!" she smiled. Claire felt a sudden pang, remembering the first time Eddie had called her that. They were all so kind to her that she felt like crying. Lately she was becoming so weepy. She reached under the pillow for a tissue.

"Ah now," the dark-haired nurse said, coming in the door again. "You're a bit lonely I expect. I have something here that will relax you." She handed Claire a tablet and water to wash it down. In a few minutes Claire began to feel drowsy.

"What, still awake?" It was the same nurse bending over her. "You'll be going down to the theatre in a minute."

Theatre? Claire's head felt muzzy. She knew there was something she should remember but it eluded her.

She lay flat, gazing dopily at the moving ceiling. Then she realised that she was moving. She was rolling along, vaguely aware of a murmured conversation going on over her head. Someone was helping her off the trolley on to a high bed. She felt them doing something to her arm. More voices seemed to be telling her that she and Sheena had got first prize for best performance, script and theatrical production. So that's what she had been trying to remember! But as soon as she'd grasped it, there was a slight pricking sensation and the thought was blotted out.

"Wake up now, Claire . . ." She was at the bottom of a deep dark tunnel, and a voice far away at the top was calling down to her. "That's it, pet . . . open your eyes." She was back in her room, wearing her own nightie, and they had taken out her appendix. Again. Her hand moved sluggishly in search of the wadded bandage on her stomach, slid smoothly over the healed scar, and dropped lower to encounter the pads between her legs. So her period had come at last. She fell into a doze.

Next day Claire got dressed and sat on the bed expecting Annette to collect her. The door opened and the smiling dark-haired nurse popped in her head.

"Claire, dear," she said, "here's Dr McArdle come to bring you home." Claire was surprised. She had understood that Jane would not be returning until Saturday. Then Eddie stood in the doorway, smiling his beautiful sad smile.

"Well Claire, and how are you feeling?" He came and put his hands over hers. "I was sorry to hear you weren't well." He sounded infinitely kind. Concerned.

Claire struggled not to cry. She could feel it creeping up and taking over her. She felt her throat painfully constrict. Suddenly she could keep it back no longer. She began to sob.

"Oh now, now, pet . . ." the nurse came forward to put an arm about her. She rocked Claire comfortingly against her shoulder. "There now!" she said, delicately picking the strands of hair out of Claire's trembling mouth and looking apologetically over her head at Eddie.

Claire slept and woke and slept again, as though she were starved for sleep. Dehydrated too. Whenever Claire reached out for the glass of water Annette left beside the bed, it had miraculously filled up again.

Every few hours she struggled down to the bathroom. The tide between her legs flowed heavier than ever. She had never seen so much blood. She had cramping pains in her thighs and stomach and felt bewildered why this period should be so much heavier than any that had gone before. Maybe it was because it was so long since her last one. She wondered if it had any connection with what they had done to her when she was asleep. She felt frightened. If only she could talk to Jane, she thought, but Jane wasn't due back from Waterford for another two days. Weakly, Claire adjusted her clothing and slowly returned along the landing. Once she was back in bed she fell asleep at once.

She awoke a few hours later. It was growing dark outside, the light fading beyond the undrawn curtains. She drank and slept again. The next time she awoke the house was very quiet and the glass was empty. Claire lay there for a time, feeling it almost beyond her to get up until thirst forced her out of bed in search of water. She filled her glass at the cold tap in the bathroom and drank deeply. To her relief the bleeding had eased. She carried the brimming glass back to her room.

As she passed her mother's room she glanced in. The bedside lamp still burned. Annette must have fallen asleep with it on. Claire took a step into the room to turn off the lamp, moved as much by a desire to have contact with her mother as anything else.

The bed was empty.

She went to the top of the stairs and was about to go down when she heard voices and the clink of glasses, the drone of conversation. Every so often it was punctuated by her mother's high excitable laugh and Eddie's deep answering chuckle. Claire felt dizzy, unreal. Her knees began to shake and for a moment everything went black. When her head cleared she turned and stumbled back to bed.

Within a few days of her arrival home Claire felt well enough to get up and go about again, though she still felt tired and inclined to tears. The half-waking dream she'd had of Eddie's laughter mingling with her mother's she brushed aside, refusing to dwell on it.

Until it happened again, only this time the sounds she heard came from Annette's bedroom.

In Dualeen Jane took her children to the hotel for their tea and announced her intention of eating out for the rest of the week. She was feeling too worn out after the emotional events of the past few days to stay in and cook. The children were delighted at the prospect and noisily planned what they would eat.

"Daddy starved us when you were away," Sheena said. "I must have lost pounds."

"That's right," Terry agreed. "And he made us go to bed at seven. Seven!" he repeated in disgust. "Like Babe Ruthie here," he added mockingly, which brought forth a storm of protest from his little sister.

"I'm not a baby. Baby yourself, Terry." She pummelled him with her fists and he laughed and rolled playfully with her on the grass.

Hugh did not join in the bickering but Jane was too busy

with her own thoughts to notice how quiet and withdrawn he was. Before leaving town she had changed her mind and rung Eddie to tell him about Claire. If anything should go wrong in her absence, she wanted Eddie to be aware of the situation. He was an excellent doctor and she trusted in his judgement implicitly. She was relieved when he not only grasped the situation but even suggested picking up Claire himself from the clinic next day. Jane had put down the phone satisfied, but on the long drive to the country the enormity of what she had done began to break on her. Jane was no longer sure she should have acted so quickly. With time to reflect she was painfully coming to the realisation that she had acted on a wave of outraged feeling. Even if she had taken time to suss it all out, it still didn't alter the fact that the decision was not legally or morally hers to take. Ever since she had been engaged in a kind of mental dialogue as she attempted to justify her actions and make peace with her conscience. She was still uneasily tussling with the latter as she entered the hotel that evening.

Jane followed the waiter to the table he indicated and absently waved her children to their seats. But I only acted out of humanitarian feelings as a doctor and a friend, she took up her defence once more. Someone had to help Claire. "Yes," the relentless voice retorted in her head. "There's no argument about that but it wasn't only up to you." Jane sighed, weary of pursuing this avenue of thought, and picked up the menu.

"Mum, I'm starving," Terry complained. "Can I have steak?" It was the dearest item on the menu and he was delighted when she nodded, hardly aware of his request.

No, she couldn't regret that it was done, Jane's thoughts ran on. Only for originally keeping the whole thing from Eddie. And Annette, who had every right to be informed of the situation. Jane realised now that she had been afraid Annette might stop her and reasoned that for all she knew Annette might have been turning a blind eye. Statistics suggested that in many cases of child abuse the mother already knew the score. If this were the Shannon's case it would have been cruel to subject Claire to any more pain or mishandling. So Jane argued with herself as she toyed with her steak, feeling depressed, her appetite suddenly gone.

"Aren't you going to finish it?" Sheena asked, and was delighted when Jane allowed her remove it to her own plate. They were all acting as though they had not been fed in days. Ruthie was stealing chips from her plate.

Jane ordered a brandy and sat sipping it gloomily. Pull yourself together, she advised herself grimly. You only did what had to be done. Someone had to take responsibility and you were the one most qualified. Still, she couldn't help feeling guilty.

Sheena came over to see Claire the minute she got back from Waterford and Claire's heart rose at the sight of her, and stayed up. It was the beginning of feeling better.

"Daddy is buying another dog for Hugh," Sheena told her. They were in Claire's bedroom, sitting on the window seat. "The funny thing is, Hugh isn't a bit pleased and keeps saying he doesn't want it."

Claire was not surprised, knowing how much Hugh had loved Hero. "When is he getting it?" she asked.

"Don't know. Before he goes back to school, I suppose." Sheena lost interest in her brother and excitedly raised the bag she was carrying. "Claire! Shut your eyes and don't look till I tell you."

Claire obediently closed her eyes.

"Now!" Sheena sounded exultant. She was holding up a pair of shiny black patent-leather shoes, with tiny taffeta bows on the pointy toes. "Mummy bought them for me as a present for looking after Daddy and the others while she was away. Aren't they fab?"

Claire nodded. She loved them but was scared to death of them. Translated, they meant dancing and boys. Unknown territory. Sheena slipped them on and wavered up and down the room. "I can't wear them until my birthday, Mummy says, but that's light years away."

Another two months actually.

"I'll die if I can't show them off before then." Sheena sighed dramatically. Claire grimaced in sympathy. She was beginning to feel a dragging tiredness. She leaned against the wall.

"Oh, I nearly forgot," Sheena said, delving deep again, "I brought you a present." She pulled out a fluffy little pink bear with a striped bow and presented it to Claire with a flourish.

"Thanks!" Claire propped it in the window, feeling touched and pleased.

"It was Ruthie's idea actually," Sheena admitted. "She said 'Let's bring home a cuddly bear for Claire-bear'."

Claire laughed. Trust Ruthie not to forget her. When Sheena went home she sat him into the beer mug Christopher had brought her back from his school trip to the Rhineland. She got undressed and climbed into bed. It was a relief to be lying down again. She closed her eyes and thought about Hugh and his new dog.

Eddie had become concerned by Hugh's despondency and, thinking to cheer him up, bought him the puppy. It was another cocker spaniel but, unlike Hero, was male with white markings. When Hugh displayed no interest whatever in the new pet, Eddie was at first surprised, then angry.

"Very well," he said curtly. "Since you don't appreciate the gift it will be given to your brother." Hugh just shrugged and walked away. Eddie stared after him, baffled. No dog could ever replace Hero in Hugh's heart so there was no use even trying. It was like expecting Romeo to forget all about Juliet and console himself with another girl from the Capulet family. Besides, Hugh wanted nothing from his father. Once Eddie's most ardent supporter, he now repudiated his father utterly.

Jane was troubled. She could not exactly pinpoint the moment when she had first noticed Hugh's disenchantment with his father. She thought it might have been before the holiday but couldn't be sure. All she could remember was how excited Hugh had been about Claire coming away with them for Easter. He had talked of nothing else for days. Jane sighed. So much lately seemed to revolve around Claire.

Jane had called over to see Claire the day after she returned from Waterford, but beyond enquiring how the girl was feeling and if she was sleeping all right, thought it wiser to leave well alone. She had no way of gauging if Claire realised just what had occurred or even been aware that she was pregnant.

"You should be out in the sun in this good weather," she advised her. "Get some colour in your cheeks."

Claire said nothing.

"I'll put you on an iron tonic," Jane said, adding, "Don't worry. I have one that tastes really nice." She chatted on, unsurprised that the girl was listless and withdrawn. It was only to be expected, she thought. Nor was she surprised by her brief, almost monosyllabic replies. Claire had never been gregarious.

In one way it was a relief. What was the point in discussion at this stage? Jane asked herself, as she scribbled a prescription. Better to try and put the whole thing behind them. Jane shuddered at the thought of Annette finding out what had happened. She didn't know what she would say in expiation if Annette ever did.

She kissed Claire. "I'll come over soon again, love," she promised. "And don't be shy about dropping over to us. You know you're always welcome."

Claire gave a wan smile, her first lightening of expression since Jane had arrived in the door. Thank goodness for the resilience of youth, Jane thought. She gave Claire's arm a fond squeeze and went back across the street.

Taking everything into consideration Claire was doing very well, Jane told herself, as she went into her house. Not that she could hope to escape without some emotional scarring, Jane reckoned.

Jane made a deliberate effort to put the whole unhappy business out of her mind and almost, though not quite, succeeded. She had learned from her work as counsellor not to allow herself the luxury of wallowing in excessive pity or regret. To do so would render her emotionally unfit to help others with their troubles. In Claire's case, however, her affections were already so closely engaged that she had found it difficult to distance herself. Jane was also troubled by a vague feeling, almost a presentiment, that some day she would be required to pay dearly for her actions. She shrugged uneasily. Maybe she was being fanciful.

Strangely, she and Eddie had never discussed the matter. Although she kept expecting him to bring it up, he never did. She eventually put it down to reticence on his part. Claire was entitled to her privacy and, after all, it had really nothing to do with him. At the same time to have been able to discuss it with him would have afforded Jane great relief.

Which brought her back to her worries about Hugh. What was to be done about him? She only wished she knew.

That night Jane was awakened by sounds of something moving stealthily about the house and, thinking the puppy had been left in, threw on her housecoat over her pyjamas and went downstairs. In the dark she almost stumbled over Hugh, who was crouched at the foot of the stairs, seemingly in earnest conversation with himself.

"What are you doing up at this hour, Hugh?" she asked. He paid her no heed but just stared fixedly past her and it was only then that she realised he was asleep. She strained her ears to hear what he was muttering and thought she heard him saying Claire's name over and over. After a moment, she put her arm about him and gently guided him back to bed.

She stayed with him until his breathing became even and relaxed. Once or twice after Ruthie was born, when he was adjusting to the strain of the new baby and she herself had little time to spare for him, he had sleepwalked like this. She wondered if it had anything to do with the constraint between his father and himself.

When Jane was satisfied that Hugh was sleeping peacefully she returned to her own room, leaving the bedroom door ajar so that she would hear him if he got up again. As she eased herself under the quilt, Eddie opened his eyes and mumbled, "Where were you?"

"The loo," Jane told him, not wanting to go into the whole thing about Hugh, not just then.

"Cut down your fluids before bedtime," Eddie advised, and fell asleep again.

Jane lay awake for a while thinking about her son, slightly disturbed by the incident and wondering if the bullying at school might have started up again. He's at such a vulnerable age, she thought. Maybe the best thing would be to take time off to bring him to a film or the Zoo without any of the others, and he might be encouraged to confide in her. She would do that, Jane decided, and fell asleep herself.

Although she genuinely meant to carry out her resolution, Jane agreed soon afterwards to take on an extra couple of evenings at the clinic and became so burdened by pressure of work that beyond occasionally reminding herself to do something about Hugh, never got around to it.

Meanwhile the rift between Hugh and his father deepened. What he had seen that night in the holiday bungalow festered in Hugh's memory like an unpoulticed sore. As soon as he went to bed at night and turned out the light the whole scenario played again behind his closed lids, with the same shocking intensity: the flickering firelight, the two figures, Claire's softly pleading voice and the inexorable hand on her neck, forcing her to do that obscene thing. Hugh felt a chilling hatred for his father and thought that as long as he lived he would never forgive him. Never!

As love for Eddie withered in Hugh's heart, it flourished in Annette's. Her involvement with the father of Claire's schoolfriend gave her a flustered, clandestine feeling. She felt as though a nerve she had believed dead had suddenly

resurrected and come throbbing back to life. Her conscience, on the other hand became, as it were, comatose.

She took dangerous and exciting risks. Once when Eddie
called late at night she allowed him make love to her on the
living-room floor, where either of her children might have
chanced upon them at any moment. It was only later that
she realised the window blind was not fully down. Would it
have made any difference if she had known? Probably not,
Annette decided.

She was like ground that has not been tilled or watered
for a long time but, when the hard crust is turned over,
reveals rich arable soil. Under his practised touch she was
becoming the woman she had once long ago dreamed of
becoming.

Annette accepted that her behaviour was crazy, irresponsible. Honour, loyalty, commitment were only words and
meant nothing to her any more. In the end it came down to
her own desires versus that of her family's well-being, his
wife's and children's happiness.

"Why do I love him? Do I love him?" were questions
Annette asked herself constantly. There was no convincing
answer. She loved the feeling he inspired, if not the man.
That was the only sure thing.

Once again her household, which had already weathered
two domestic upheavals, suffered from her neglect. Her
children no longer expected things to be orderly as in other
people's homes and accepted that their mother was different. Annette did, indeed, feel different. She was overwhelmed by her awakening sexuality. She had never really
been loved before, she told herself. Well, not in the truly sexual sense, except perhaps for an unrequited love affair she
had experienced while at college.

So here she was again, Annette told herself, waiting in
another night for Eddie, on edge, smoking too much, with
Claire upstairs doing her homework and Christopher in bed
listening to his Walkman. Eddie was becoming like a drug,
she thought. The more she had of him, the more she had to

have. She wondered how she would endure the night if she did not see him.

It was after school on a Friday afternoon in May and Sheena loitered with Claire outside her house. "Want to come in and play with the new puppy for a bit?" Sheena asked.

Not that Sheena was all that keen on the pup – it left messes and chewed things – but she knew how fond Claire was of Hugh and thought she might be missing him.

Claire hesitated, then nodded. "All right."

With a pleased smile Sheena led the way into her house. "Look who's here," she called, going ahead of Claire into the kitchen.

Hugh looked up from the table where he was doing his homework. He stared at Claire in dumb embarrassment, a tide of red sweeping over his face.

Sheena noticed her brother's confusion and grinned. It was just as she had suspected. Hugh was soft on Claire. Sheena debated whether to rag him over it and then decided to keep her derision for another time. Not that she wasn't quite fond of her young brother but some of Terry's scornful attitude towards Hugh had rubbed off on her.

"Hello, Hugh," Claire said quietly. "Can I see your puppy?"

"He's not my pup," Hugh said abruptly, turning back to his books. Now it was Claire's turn to flush.

"Come on." Sheena pulled her towards the door. "I'll show you. He's out in the garden."

As soon as they were gone, Hugh regretted his rudeness. He got up and went to look out the window. The girls were at the end of the garden, standing under the apple blossoms. He thought they made a pretty picture, dark and blonde heads pressed close together. He wished now he had been nicer to Claire. He felt all mixed up, one part of him longing to run down the garden and share in the fun of the puppy, the other aloofly standing by, hating it and everything it stood for. He turned slowly away, holding in his mind the sight of Claire standing under the flowering apple tree, stroking the puppy on her shoulder. He went to the table and slumped down.

Hugh picked up his pen and sat turning it idly between his fingers and staring into space. But as soon as he heard the back door opening he grabbed up a book and stuck his face into it. He heard Claire's quiet voice uttering his name as she passed through on her way to the hall and in his mind he echoed her soft goodbye, but no words left his lips.

Jane's suspicion that the bullying had started up again was correct. Hugh had come to dread the moment each morning when he set off for school. Actually, the jeering and name-calling had never really ceased, only been suspended for a time. Now, added to the stigma of spectacles, was Hugh's weight. He was rounder, chubbier than his classmates, the perfect target for all those 'Hey Fatty' jokes.

Hugh detested his body and was convinced that, no matter what he wore, he looked fat and ungainly. At not quite twelve he was into men's sizes already. In another year or two he would be tall enough to carry it off and, with his fine eyes and good skin, he was already showing signs of the man he would become. But all Hugh could see when he looked in a mirror was his fat, rounded shoulders in the outsize school sweater and the size thirty-eight trousers, wider and baggier than anyone else's in the class. He could have got away with a size smaller but Jane was genuinely concerned about the harmful effect of tight, constricting pants on a growing boy. Hugh was mortified.

When Hugh returned to school after Easter, the going got rougher. Like blood on a wounded animal the bullies scented his misery and harried him unmercifully, vying with each other to see how far they could provoke him. They knew of his friendship with Claire, and Mark, the ringleader, who lived on their road, had somehow found out about Annette and Eddie.

"Your old man and her old woman are banging each

98

other," Mark told Hugh, making a lewd gesture with thumb and forefinger.

"You're a liar," Hugh said. "A bloody liar."

"Watch who you're calling names." Mark adopted a threatening stance.

"Liar!" Hugh repeated, his voice very high now and on the verge of tears. Apprehensive too, knowing what he already did about his father and Claire.

Mark, sensing some inner uncertainty, pressed his advantage. "Okay, don't believe me then. Go see for yourself. Look in the window late at night, the way I did, and see who's a liar."

Hugh swung a punch at him but Mark was very quick. They wrestled each other and then, conscious of his glasses, Hugh backed away and they stood facing each other, panting. "Specky-four-eyes!" Mark said scornfully. He gave Hugh a last disdainful push and walked away.

Hugh stared after him, choking back tears. Then, without really knowing why he did it, he took out Claire's picture from his inside pocket and tore it up. As the pieces fell from his hand, a wind sprang up and blew them about the gutter.

That night when Eddie went out for his bedtime stroll Hugh followed him. Eddie draped a scarf about his neck and shouted to Jane that he wouldn't be long. She had already gone up to bed. With her extra hours at the clinic she was perpetually tired these days and constantly popped vitamins for energy. Once she had cleared away the remains of the evening meal she couldn't wait to get her head down.

Hugh kept well behind his father and dodged into gardens to avoid being seen. At the top of the road Eddie did a quick turnabout, came briskly down the other side and went into Shannon's porch, where the door opened. Hugh had not seen him ring the bell. He hung about in the shadow of the hedge, then slipped up the path and round the side.

He crouched under the window and looked through the space beneath the blind. What was he doing here anyway? Hugh wondered, in self-revulsion. He was a bloody peeping-

Tom like that shithead Mark. He felt hot all over. What if anyone saw him? He'd really be in trouble. He was about to turn away when his father came into the room. Eddie crossed to the sideboard and poured himself a drink. He sat down on the couch.

Annette appeared in the doorway. She was wearing a silk, belted kimono. Hugh thought she looked very pretty. She walked across the room until she stood in front of Eddie. Smiling, she untied the belt and let the kimono slip off her shoulders. It fell in a crumpled heap on the floor. Hugh's heart did a double-take. She was naked.

Eddie said something to her. He leaned forward and pulled her on to his knee. Annette laughed and looked over his shoulder. It seemed to Hugh that she looked straight into his eyes. After a moment she stood up and with a slight swing of her hips, crossed to the lamp and switched it off. The room was dark now. Hugh could just make out their two figures coming together. He backed away so hard that he overbalanced and sat down in the wet grass. His heart thundered in his ears. It was useless, hopeless. His breath caught in a sighing sob. He had been sure that Mark was lying. It was excruciatingly painful for Hugh to find that his greatest tormentor, a foul-mouthed bully whom he feared and despised, could fling mud at his father and make it stick. As Hugh ran home, he could see nothing ahead but dishonour.

The summer term was half over when the pro-lifers came in a group to Claire's school and delivered their propaganda lecture on the sanctity of procreation and birth. There were four of them: three women and a man. Since the amendment had been successfully carried in the recent abortion referendum they were campaigning the schools with fresh zeal. The man, skeletal and morose, carried the grisly jar containing the pickled body of the three-month foetus. He placed it on the rostrum, where it remained throughout the lecture.

The women each took it in turn to speak, standing before

the rostrum and giving statistics and detailed descriptions of babies conceived and aborted. From womb to incinerator. One girl began to cry and another made retching sounds as though she was going to throw up. Sheena scornfully whispered to the girl on the other side of her.

Claire sat in the front row and looked at the jar. She felt there was something vaguely counterfeit about the contents. She stared at it, believing yet not believing. Had that thing really once been inside someone, brought into being by the fusion of two seeds? She saw them like tiny peppercorns. Claire felt sick in the pit of her stomach and she hadn't felt sick in weeks. Not since before her painful periods were treated.

No! She veered away in panic. She never allowed herself to think of that time any more. She stared hard at the pickled thing. It began moving tiny tentacle-like fingers and uttering piercing cries. It was alive. The jar swam before Claire's eyes. She heard someone moaning and it was a full minute before she realised it was herself.

Sheena was full of Claire's collapse when she got in from school. It was Jane's day for surgery and she was in the kitchen, taking a break between patients and, at the same time, hastily putting together a sandwich for Hugh, when her daughter came rushing in.

Sheena flung down her schoolbag and with her usual flair for drama, described the events of the morning, making it all sound more horrific than it actually was. She graphically described the ghoulish bottle on the rostrum and the effect it had on the class. "Three girls fainted," she exaggerated, enjoying the attention she was getting. "Imagine! A dead baby in a bottle."

Jane heard her in horror. She cast a quick glance at Hugh, not happy about his listening to any of this but trying to make sense of what Sheena was saying. "What baby . . . what bottle?" she asked.

"An aborted baby," said Sheena. "Yuck! It was awful. I think that's what sent poor old Claire off her rocker. She suddenly stood up and started screaming." Sheena's mouth trembled. "It was awful, really awful, Mummy. I just didn't know what to do."

Oh God! Jane thought. What terrible timing. Poor, poor Claire. She began trembling with anger. How dare they, how dare these people go about terrifying children.

Hugh listened gravely, his eyes huge in his face. He nibbled at the sandwich Jane absently thrust at him, then, his appetite suddenly gone, put it down and went to get his schoolbag and begin his homework. He found it difficult to concentrate, beset by images of dead babies floating like ships in bottles and of fair-haired Claire standing up at her desk, mouth open, screaming. Sometimes the image changed and became the one he saw every night when he put out the light and lay down to sleep. Normally it did not bother him during the day. This was something new. He was tortured by the memory of Claire's heart-broken sobbing, punctuated by helpless pleading. He felt like weeping himself. His head began to throb. He pushed away his books and laid his head down on the cool wood of the table.

Someone had left the door open. The puppy waddled in and whined about Hugh's ankles, gnawing fretfully at the toe of his slipper. The poor animal was starved for affection. It was not even an especially lovable dog. The runt of the litter, no-one had even bothered to give it a name.

The pup's whining increased the ache in Hugh's head. "Eddie's a proper bastard!" he said out loud, staring into the puppy's face. "And this bloody animal is his fault too." He pushed it away but it kept coming back, pathetically wagging its stumpy tail and trying to push its nose into Hugh's hand.

Hugh regarded it morosely. The poor beast would be better off dead, he thought. His eyes pricked with tears. Like poor bloody Hero, kicked and beaten by that shit of a postman. Well, now she was at peace. No-one should have to put up with this miserable, stinking existence, Hugh thought. A few drops of chloroform and it would be all over.

Looking at the pup Hugh saw Hero. And Hero was

doomed to die. The judge had said so. He found himself trembling at the thought of what he must do.

"Poor Hero," he said, stroking the pup's head, fondling its ears. "Poor old girl. Don't worry. I won't let anyone but me do it. I'll miss you but you'll be better off."

There was still enough chloroform in the bottle. Hugh stuck it in his pocket and went out to the back, whistling for the pup to follow. It waddled trustingly after him.

Hugh performed the deed quickly and humanely. He was surprised at how soon the puppy became lifeless, confused by some lingering memory of tussling with the full-grown animal. He looked at the bottle in his hand with an expression of distaste, then flung it from him and turned to go back inside.

The lights of his father's Rover lit the driveway. Hugh went in the back door. In the toilet he washed his hands, taking a long time and methodically scrubbing each finger, like he'd seen his father doing after stitching a patient. He dried his hands on the towel and went into the kitchen. Everyone except Sheena, who had gone to her piano lesson, sat about the table.

When Jane placed his dinner in front of him, Hugh took a potato and mashed it into the stew the way he liked it. He felt very hungry now and ate ravenously. Finishing before any of them, Hugh sat back and watched the others eating. His mind seemed to be floating in a different sphere. He heard their conversation as if from a distance, and although he listened with attention, even interest, none of it made much sense. The only thing he seemed able to latch on to was Claire's name.

"She's a bit disturbed," Jane said quietly to Eddie, with a warning frown around the table. Hugh wondered why his mother bothered to lower her voice. By now, all of them knew what had happened in Claire's school that day. And all the boys in his own school, thought Hugh, knew about his father and Claire's mother. He watched his parents almost dreamily. So far, he told himself, he was the only one to know the most terrible piece of scandal.

Jane was saying, "Might be a good idea if one of us was to pop over later and find out how she is."

Eddie nodded.

"Perhaps you'd go," Jane suggested. "By the time I've cleared up it'll be too late. You don't mind, do you?"

"Not at all." Eddie took some bread and neatly wiped gravy from his plate. He smiled pleasantly about the table, inclining his ear to something Terry was telling him. Hugh was no longer dreamy, his attention fully focused. His father was going over to see Claire.

He mustn't go, Hugh thought worriedly. He'll only hurt her again. All his calm deserted him. He felt hot and confused, churned up. The throbbing in his head, which had eased a little, began painfully pulsing again. Beside him Terry was noisily declaiming the need to study for the summer tests and Ruthie wailing that her tongue was burnt.

"Don't be impolite," Eddie told her as she spat hot stew onto her plate.

Hugh strove to collect his thoughts. He knew there was something he must do. Hero? No, he'd dealt with her and she was at peace. Something else. His father. Yes. That was it. He got up and left the room.

"Don't be long, Hugh," Jane called after him, thinking he was going to the toilet, "I'm just about to put out dessert. Your favourite. Apple crumble."

Apple crumble, Hugh thought absently. That's nice. He went into Eddie's study and crossed to the far wall. The guns gleamed dully in the glass case. He found the key on the ledge above the case and fitted it in the lock. It turned smoothly. Eddie always kept the locks well oiled, like his guns.

Hugh carefully lifted down his father's shotgun and sat it between his legs to load up. He knew exactly what to do. Hugh slid the cartridges into the breeches and snapped the gun closed. It was a heavy, solid weight on his arm. He went back to the kitchen, carrying it correctly, safety catch on, the way his father had shown him.

Jane was dishing up hot apple crumble and the air was spicy and clove-scented. She half-turned her head. "Come on, Hugh," she said encouragingly. "There'll be none left if you don't hurry."

Hugh sat down on a chair just inside the door. No-one was paying him any heed. He eased off the catch and took a firm grip on the gun. The kitchen sounds were a steady accompaniment to the throbbing in his head. He got his father carefully in his sights and, as Eddie had shown him, slowly squeezed the trigger.

Claire opened her eyes as the urgent wailing note of an ambulance siren sounded close to the house then faded in the distance. Annette came out of her doze and glancing at her daughter's face, was relieved to see that she was awake at last.

The girl had lain on her back in the same fixed position all afternoon, her blonde plaits, each one tidily resting on her collar-bone, framing her pale face. She was like an effigy of some martyred saint, Annette thought with a sigh.

Even as she watched, Claire closed her eyes and slept again.

At midday, Sister Whelan had rung Annette at work to tell her that her daughter had thrown some kind of fit in class and she was sending her home in the care of one of the teachers. When Annette reached home she found the pair of them already waiting for her in the front room. She had been shocked at the state of her daughter and noted, with concern, her trembling hands and nervous, wandering stare. The teacher gave her a somewhat garbled account of the pro-lifers' lecture and Claire's hysterical reaction.

Annette was incensed. "What in God's name are you trying to do?" she demanded. "Frightening the life out of fourteen-year-old girls with morbid stories of sex and abortion and putting entirely wrong notions into their heads. Is it any wonder Irish girls grow up deeply inhibited about sex?"

The young teacher, barely out of the teachers' training

college, stammered a reply. She hadn't much liked the idea herself, but the nuns thought the girls should be aware. Annette nodded grimly. Claire had been nervy and intense of late, prone to nightmares. On more than one occasion Annette had heard her daughter calling out in the night and had half gotten out of bed, prepared to go to her if she called again.

She realised her own nerves were strained, too.

Annette shifted tiredly on her chair and decided that it was time for Christopher to come up and take a turn at the bedside. She went to the door and called him.

"The match is on. Do I have to?" he asked, resentful at being dragged away from his beloved sport.

"Too bad," Annette said shortly, thinking there was always some match on. Normally she would have made an effort to jolly him out of his sulks but she thought that if she did not have a drink and a cigarette soon she would be a hospital case herself.

An ambulance went speeding along Nutley Lane, siren screaming, and came to a halt in the unloading bay outside the accident department.

When the driver jumped out and ran to open the rear doors, the paramedic kept the oxygen mask in place over the face of the unconscious boy and assisted the driver to lift the stretcher out of the ambulance and carry it through the swing doors of the emergency unit. When it was taken over by hospital staff, the ambulance men turned swiftly about and went back into the ambulance to bring out the second casualty, only to find that he had died on the way to the hospital.

Jane sat in a screened-off part of the emergency unit, her eyes, red and swollen from weeping, fixed on her son's face. Hugh still wore the bloodstained pants he had been wearing when admitted to the hospital. His upper torso was swathed in bandages and there were two drips set up by the bedside. Everything possible had been done to save him, but his injuries were so severe that there was little hope of his recovery.

Nearby, a nun sat praying with an audible click of her beads. Terry, who had accompanied his mother in the ambulance, stood just inside the screening curtain, his eyes also trained on Hugh.

Terry tried not to think of the scene in the kitchen but it kept coming back to him in vivid bursts, the colours and sounds magnified and distorted in his head like fireworks viewed up too close. Hugh, his father, Ruthie screaming. It had all been so incredible and shocking as to be unreal. Like some gunman had stepped out of the films he often watched in the cinema and entered their house to bring death to them all. Only it had been no outsider but his young brother who had shot their father and then turned the gun on himself. The sensation Terry had of being part of a gangster film was reinforced when the squad car had pulled up outside the house in response to the telephone call he had made to the police station immediately after summoning the ambulance. Two Gardaí had come into the house and assisted his mother, who was desperately trying to resuscitate Hugh and give aid to his father. Terry had stood by in a daze, gazing at the carnage all about him. Now he kept thinking how Hugh had always hated it when anything was killed, which made the whole thing impossible to understand. How had he brought himself to do such a thing? And why? None of it made any sense. Terry gulped and the wall he had erected around his emotions crumbled and disintegrated under the onslaught of feeling that suddenly engulfed him.

". . . pray for us sinners now and at the hour of our death, Amen . . ."

It is over now, Jane thought, and her tears began to flow again. She pressed her handkerchief over her eyes and doubled over in a wild paroxysm of grief, mourning for her husband whom she had deeply loved and would never get over, and her son whom she had also loved and been unable to help in his darkest hour

The old nun came forward and laid a gentle hand on her

shoulder. Her eyes were compassionate and she waited with patient detachment until Jane regained control of herself and got unsteadily to her feet.

Terry gravitated towards his mother and she allowed him to take her arm, then stooped over the bed and gazed sorrowfully down at Hugh. She smoothed back the heavy auburn hair, the same rich colour and texture as her own from his forehead, and bent and kissed the beloved, pale face. "My dearest, my son," Terry heard her whisper, and his own tears began to flow in nervous sympathy, not only for the lifeless body on the bed who had done such a shocking and incomprehensible thing, but for his father, lying equally lifeless and still, in another part of the emergency unit.

Sheena had stayed at home with Ruthie, both of them in the care of the woman police officer who had arrived at the house just minutes before the ambulance had left. Sheena had sat in the front room, holding her little sister close and trying to soothe the child in her first wild hysteria and fright. She had been barely conscious of the policewoman, who divided her time between speaking on the telephone and conferring with the two Gardaí in the kitchen while they were writing out their reports. Sheena was overwhelmed by her own desperate grief and incomprehension, and her mind ran in shocked circles, questioning and laying blame, so that she hardly noticed the little body relax at last in her arms as Ruthie slept. She had come home to find the house in an uproar. Just inside the kitchen door, she stumbled over her mother, down on her knees beside Hugh's fallen body, desperately attempting to staunch the blood flowing from the wound in his chest. Her father lay near by, his features twisted in agony.

"Daddy, my Daddy," Ruthie sobbed, trying to reach the prone figure, wriggling and struggling in Terry's grip. Sheena had wanted to go to him too, but when Jane looked up, her eyes wild and tragic as she worked over the unconscious body of her son, and told her to take the child at once from the room, she had obeyed. As she did, she heard Terry urgently telephoning for an ambulance.

Now Sheena sat on the couch, holding her sleeping sister in her arms and waiting out the long span until her mother and her twin returned from the hospital. The policewoman had made tea several times and kindly offered to take Ruthie from her to give her a chance to stretch her limbs, but Sheena had dumbly shaken her head, desperately needing the warm, live feel of the little body close to her own. At last she heard the key turning in the lock, and when she raised her frightened eyes to Jane's and Terry's faces she knew, from their stricken expressions, that her father and her brother were dead.

Jane went through the days of mourning and burial with her usual quiet competence, handling the funeral arrangements, legal formalities and social obligations which fell on the widow of an esteemed and highly qualified medical man. The hardship of her situation was not eased by the journalists who were lying in wait for her whenever she left the house. And when the excitement and speculation about the killings had begun to die down, there was the ordeal of the inquest to be got through, bringing in its wake the resurgence of unwelcome publicity. On this extremely distressing occasion Jane had cause to be grateful yet again for the reticent support of Teresa Murray, whose non-judgemental attitude impressed her more than any amount of syrupy sentiments.

Jane was outwardly composed but inwardly she bitterly railed against the loss of her husband and son and mourned the terrible waste of their lives. Even with the pills she prescribed for herself she could not sleep, and except for brief snatches of rest taken at odd moments during the day, remained awake for the three days and nights following the tragedy. Throughout the day she was possessed of an unnatural calm, but behind her closed bedroom door at night she lay suspended in a kind of limbo, alternating prayers with weeping, her love and misery rending her as she relived those last cataclysmic hours, over and over again.

The days and nights of grieving took their toll on them all. At the church and cemetery, and afterwards at the house, relatives and colleagues came to pay their last respects. Ruthie was querulous, only understanding in part what had happened, and Sheena was furious and frantic in her grief. She had relied upon her father, blossomed and basked in his approval. Although not seeing him as some deity, as her younger brother had, Sheena had nevertheless counted on him. He had called her the belle of the ball and she had hoped always to be that for him. She had been reft by the sight of his agony as he lay prostrate on the floor, shuddering in pain. For the rest of her life, she thought, that memory would remain with her. For her brother she could not yet feel anything but hatred for what he had done.

Terry had had, perhaps, the greatest affinity with his father. They had shared sporting interests and a fighting code. Eddie had been his mentor and guide and he an apt and willing pupil. He had loved and admired his father and dreamed one day of being his match. He felt bereft and cheated before his still irreconcilable loss. He saw his mother's great sorrow and pitied her, but felt heartened by it too, for her desolation was but an echo of his own. For those few days, he did his best to support her, comporting himself in a manner older than his fourteen years as he gave her his arm up the aisle of the church and afterwards at the graveside, while all the time, within himself, he held at bay the storms threatening to annihilate him. Later he was the one who attended the inquest with her – Ruthie was too young to be a witness and Sheena had not been present – and he gave his account of what had happened on that evening in the kitchen. He spoke with the awareness of his new responsibility as the only man in their sadly depleted household. Terry could tell by his mother's expression that she was proud of him, and after the verdict had been given – manslaughter followed by suicide when the balance of the mind was unsound – and they were travelling home in Teresa's car her whispered words of affection and her warm embrace compensated for the stress of standing in the witness box recounting the horrors they had lived through.

Some days after the burial as she was going down to the washing line Jane tripped on something lying in the grass and, bending down, discovered the puppy's limp body and the empty bottle. With a sigh, she went back inside filled with fresh horror and regret, and bitterly blamed herself for not realising there was something gravely amiss with her son. When Terry came in from school he got a shovel and buried the pup.

Jane stayed up, grieving and dry-eyed, until the small hours, and was still unable to comprehend what terrible trauma could have induced a gentle boy like Hugh to take his father's life and his own along with it.

Annette was in mourning too. On the night of the tragedy she had been expecting Eddie to drop over later in the evening. She had left Claire sleeping and was sitting before her dressing table, freshening her make-up, when Christopher, whom she had sent to the shop for the evening paper, came crashing up the stairs full of the McArdle slaying. Annette was totally unprepared. Dead. Both of them. She stared white-faced at her son, not sure that he hadn't somehow got it all terribly confused. But no, Christopher said, there was a Garda car right now parked across the road in the McArdle's driveway and there were neighbours standing all about saying that Hugh had blasted his father with a shotgun and then taken his own life. The ambulance had left for the hospital ages ago, Christopher said, and now the Garda cars were coming and going all the time. Claire, weakly eavesdropping from the landing, caught the tail end of her brother's disclosure and was unable to take any of it in. In her great confusion of mind, she assumed it was Hugh's new puppy that had been killed. It would be weeks before the full enormity of the tragedy would strike her.

With the exception of Terry, the McArdle family absorbed

the grief and shock. Jane seemed to accept her loss with an almost philosophical forbearance which at first puzzled Terry and then angered him.

In a way Terry was even more jealous now of his younger brother than when he was alive. Terry believed in retribution. Observing his mother gazing fondly and regretfully at Hugh's Confirmation photographs – the most recent pictures to be taken before his death – it seemed to him that Jane felt that it did not matter what terrible things people did to each other. If they died early enough they would be enshrined for ever in memory. With Jane apparently determined on sanctifying Hugh, and Sheena pretty much taken up with looking after Ruthie, Terry felt left out in the cold.

So Terry avoided his family and perhaps they, occupied with comforting each other, neglected him. He hardly ever mixed any more with his schoolmates, but found other friends. There was a reason for this.

At the time of the killings wild rumours circulated about the school that before his death Eddie McArdle had been having an affair with some woman in the locality. Terry spent half of his time in hot denial, the other half brawling with his persecutors. He was not, like Hugh, sensitive on the issues of integrity and honour. He held a very tolerant view on all things sexual and, if it hadn't been for the terrible manner of Eddie's death, he might have even been rather secretly proud of his father's sexual prowess.

Terry never told his mother the reason for his brawling. She had suffered enough already. He preferred to let her think it stemmed from his love of fighting, anything but the truth. Terry may not have been idealistic and introspective like Hugh but he had his own code of behaviour. So he dealt with his problems in the only way he knew how. Jane had got to the stage where she met Terry at the front door with the bottle of mercurochrome in her hand. These days his handsome brooding face, so like his father's, was constantly bruised and battered. She worried in case the damage might be permanent.

Terry often wondered about the identity of his father's amour. Stephen Rigney, a boy in his class, swore he knew her identity. Stephen was the elder brother of Mark, the ringleading bully in Hugh's year.

One afternoon Jane made herself go into Hugh's room and sort through his belongings. It was a task she had been dreading, but she steeled herself and set to work, methodically clearing drawer after drawer. She found poignant reminders everywhere of the child she had loved and lost. Hugh was a sentimental hoarder. All his summer and Christmas report cards since he began school were stacked in an Oxo tin. Jane, reading through them, saw that he had been consistently top of his class in everything but maths. She mourned the terrible waste of his young life and forced herself to continue.

He had kept his First Communion and Confirmation cards, and his red Confirmation ribbon, worn so proudly on the day, was carefully enshrined in its box. To celebrate they had all gone out to a restaurant for lunch, followed by a trip to town to see the latest Harrison Ford adventure film. Later Hugh had said in all seriousness, "Thanks for a wonderful day, Mum. I wouldn't mind dying now it was so great." Jane clamped down on her lower lip to keep from crying aloud the keening, despairing cry of all women down through the ages, when confronted by their dead. She doubled over, striving to regain control, knowing if she ever once allowed herself to let go she could never get going again. Gradually she calmed.

She opened the last drawer and lifted out the contents. These were mostly comic papers and drawings. The top sheets were sketches of Hero and her pups, some lightly pencilled, others shaded and completed down to the last detail. Jane was particularly struck by a sketch of a horse, head upflung, mane flying, perhaps glimpsed from a moving car, the pose beautifully caught in a few bold strokes. She had always been proud of Hugh's artistic gift, but she hadn't realised just how good he was. "Oh the waste," she sighed again, "the terrible waste."

No! she wouldn't let herself go down that road again. She lifted out the last bundle of sheets and idly glanced at them. They were drawings of persons unmistakably engaging in the act of fellatio.

Jane was horrified by the explicitness of the phallic drawings and the accompanying captions. They were not, as she'd first thought, erotic messages, but revengeful declarations.

Closer inspection revealed Claire's name scrawled everywhere with affection, Eddie's with loathing. Jane clutched at a memory. Claire sick and despondent in the holiday bungalow, eyes full of despair. "Oh dear God!" Jane moaned. Bile rushed to her throat. She felt trapped in some terrible nightmare.

It was Eddie's child. She rose from the bed and rushed into the bathroom to hang over the hand-basin, heaving and retching until all the sickness had drained from her body. Throat aching, she straightened up and pushed tendrils of hair from off her perspiring forehead. She felt shaky and ill. Slowly, she went back to Hugh's room and sat down on the bed, striving to make sense of her thoughts.

Oh God, what had she done? It occurred to Jane that in her rush to mend the wrong done Claire by, as Jane had thought, Claire's own father, she had killed her husband's child, the half-brother or sister of her own children. Tears spilled down her face as she thought of how much she had wanted another child after Ruthie was born. She had experienced an early and difficult menopause, suffering constant headaches and a loss of sexual desire, until gradually she had ceased all lovemaking. Was that what had driven Eddie to seek satisfaction elsewhere?

Jane still could hardly believe it. A mere child and her husband. And to think he hadn't even taken precautions to protect her from pregnancy. She felt shamed and distraught, heartbroken too in a way, for it effectively turned Eddie into a man she had never really known. A kind of monster.

She wiped her eyes and, carrying the sacks of rubbish to the garden, made a bright, burning bonfire of them. Oh, how differently everything might have turned out if only she had glimpsed the drawings in time, she thought in anguish. Truly, they bore all the signs of a deeply disturbed mind. Watching the leaping flames Jane felt infinitely older and sadder than she would have ever thought possible, even on the day of the funeral.

Jane found herself dwelling obsessively on all that had happened, continually retracing in her mind the lead-up to each incident and recalling words and gestures and accompanying glances. She knew this was not healthy, but she was past prescribing for herself. It was as if she were preparing to give evidence at a court of enquiry, at which she was the self-appointed judge, jury, prosecution and defence, all rolled into one. And the more Jane dwelled upon the past, the greater was her jealousy that Claire had had sex with Eddie and conceived his child. Erotic images of Claire and her husband, at various stages of arousal, with their limbs sensually entwined, tortured Jane, and she felt weak with hatred for the pair of them. Sometimes she tried telling herself that sexual abuse was not inspired by love, and tried to convince herself that she had no real reason to feel such jealousy of Claire. That Eddie hadn't really loved the girl, not in the way he loved her, but had merely indulged his lust. What a load of rubbish! she told herself the next minute. As if that lessened the offence. Anyway, what did she know about what Eddie thought or felt? The only thing she did know was that middle-aged Eddie hadn't shown much love for anyone but himself in seducing a teenage girl. Painfully conscious of her own aging body, Jane was filled with fresh envy. She felt a sudden rush of anger towards her dead husband.

And so it went on. When Jane was not castigating Eddie in her thoughts she was railing at Claire. Without being fully aware of it, her grief at her son's death was gradually being replaced by a baser emotion. No longer was Jane able to see Claire as she once had, as a victim, abused and taken advantage of. Instead she mentally derided her, calling her sly and sluttish, fanning the flame of her anger and resentment to the point of exhaustion.

It was only in calmer, more rational moments that Jane dimly perceived what was happening to her and felt horror at the awfulness of her own reactions. But most of the time she tended her bitter resentment like an ailing plant, discovering fresh excuses and justification for keeping it alive.

One day Ruthie confessed how much she was missing Claire and wished she would come and play with them all again. Jane's overwrought feelings burst out in a senseless tirade. She hardly knew what it was about, something to do with little girls learning to play with nice children of their own age and not depending on brattish teenagers for company.

"You don't like Claire-bear any more, do you?" the little girl said with pitiful perspicacity and, with a sorrowful glance, she left the room.

Jane felt a deep sense of shame. She covered her face with trembling hands, stricken at what she was becoming. How could she have reviled the girl, she asked herself, and before Ruthie who loved her so? Jane's eyes filled with tears; she felt worn out with the tussle going on in her soul. She was haunted by a vision of Claire as she had seen her last, nervous and wretched, and she began to cry in earnest. In that searing moment of clarity Jane recognised that she had nothing left in her to give but hate and began to feel truly frightened. Oh God, she prayed, let me have the peace of forgiveness, anything rather than go on like this.

It was Jane's first step towards recovery, in the slow process of healing. While more time would elapse before she was able to bring herself to visit Claire, and even longer again before her old affection for the girl returned, the unhappy vengeful spirit that had possessed her for weeks was banished at last.

For Claire the weeks had passed in a kind of dream sequence of waking and sleeping, not always able to differentiate between them. Whenever she opened her eyes, her mother was sitting on a chair near the bed. Annette held a book in front of her but seldom turned the page. Sometimes she was weeping but, on seeing that Claire was awake, she would make an effort to smile and enquire how she felt.

Claire's head felt swollen and heavy as though filled with hot pebbles. She wondered what she was doing in bed during the day and why her mother was sitting there. It would seem to suggest she had been ill, but from what and for how long? Once or twice the doctor came, the one they used to go to before the McArdles came to the road. He was an elderly man, kindly and loquacious. So she *was* sick, she thought, but when she asked him what was the matter with her he only patted her head and told her not to worry about a thing.

Claire tried hard to pierce the fog in her mind but the harder she strained the more confused her thinking became. Eventually she remembered being in the classroom listening to a lecture. Gradually, the strands of fog parted to reveal more details until she recalled the whole frightful day. What puzzled her now was why Annette was weeping. She tried to stay awake long enough to put the question but her lids grew heavy again and she slept.

Claire dreamed she was on her hands and knees in a dark underground tunnel, trying to crawl to a higher level, but the space got smaller and smaller until her head wouldn't go through the opening. She sensed something big was moving along fast behind her but there was no room to get out of its way. She was about to be crushed when she woke up.

She turned on the bedside light, then her eyes were hurt by the glare so she turned it off again. She called weakly to Annette, but it was Christopher sitting there, dozing in the chair.

Next time Claire awoke her father was sitting in the chair reading a newspaper. She tried to tell him something of her

117

confusion, but he just smiled at her and told her not to tire herself out with talk. As she lay there looking at him her lids grew heavy and to her dismay she couldn't keep awake long enough to ask him how he was or when he would come again. When she awoke and found him gone, hot tears of disappointment slid from under her lids. It was so long since she had seen him, and now who knew when he would come again.

And then she was dreaming that she was trying to get back to the holiday bungalow. She was pushing an enormous pram along the sea-front with all the McArdles in it. They were laughing and talking amongst themselves and didn't seem to notice her. She wondered why none of them got out to lessen the load or to lend her a hand. She pushed with all her strength but then she got very tired and let it roll away from her. She lay down on the road. A car came along and she tried to struggle out of its path but she was too weak and it went right over her. Strangely, she felt no pain, only a tremendous relief.

She was telling Jane all about her other dreams. She was lying on the couch in Jane's surgery and Jane was sitting beside her, jotting everything she said down in a notebook. And then Jane was gone and Eddie was bending over her, examining her. He wore a white coat over his shirt and tie but had no pants on and was trying to make her suck his cock.

She awakened sobbing and crying, struggling against the blankets which were tucked too tightly, not sure if she were still in the dream, trying to shake it off but remaining anguished and scared. It was dark outside the window. Slowly, she got out of bed, leaning against the wall until the blackness receded from her eyes. Holding the banister, she went down, carefully placing each foot on the stairs.

At first she thought the house was empty it was so quiet, then she heard her mother's voice in the kitchen. She pushed open the door. Annette and Jane were sitting opposite each other, sipping drinks. "Why, Claire," Jane said, half-rising, her expression concerned, "I was on my way up to see you."

Annette got up to bring Claire back to bed. Claire felt suddenly aware of her crumpled nightdress, the sour odour of her body. Shamed, she allowed herself to be led upstairs. She felt exhausted from the effort. A few minutes after her mother had gone out of the room Jane came in and sat on the chair.

"Claire, dear," she said, "how do you feel?"

"Sleepy," Claire answered truthfully. "Am I very ill?" she asked. "Is that why you're here?"

Jane looked pale and tired. She gave Claire a long, pitying look.

"No, love. I just wanted to see you. It's been a long time."

Claire felt uneasy. She didn't know what month it was, let alone what day of the week. There was something in Jane's subdued manner that frightened her. The light in her eyes seemed to have gone out, and her mouth was serious. Uncomfortable, Claire looked away.

"How is Sheena . . . Hugh?" she asked.

Jane's voice was steady as she said, "Sheena's very well . . . she and Terry are doing their summer exams . . ."

Were they into June already?

". . . and Ruthie, in her own way, struggling along."

"What about Hugh?" Claire asked again.

"You must hurry and get well," Jane said. "This year we'll be going to the cottage a little earlier and we hope you'll come with us."

Back to Waterford. How could she?

"There's plenty of time yet," Jane said, as if reading her thoughts. "You'll be fully recovered by the time we're heading off. Your mother has promised to come too, later on, so we'll have that to look forward to."

When she was gone Claire wondered again about Hugh. She suddenly thought of the day she called to see his puppy. He'd been abrupt, not exactly rude. Embarrassed. But why? He hadn't wanted the puppy. The thought was followed by a vague, terrifying memory about the puppy, and something about Eddie. She tried but the fog had come down again

119

and she couldn't remember.

Her father had to come and visit her before Claire found out that they were both dead. Why hadn't someone told her?

"You were ill, Claire," Jim said, sitting on the side of the bed, holding her hand. "It wasn't the time to trouble you with something so tragic."

No wonder Jane hadn't answered her when she asked about Hugh. Poor Hugh. Her head felt hot and heavy, as if the pebbles were overheating again.

"Why did he do it?" she asked, her voice breaking.

"No-one knows, Claire," Jim said. He stroked her hand, studying her face anxiously. "Try not to dwell on it, love. It seems the poor kid was bullied at school and just flipped under the strain."

Claire thought that her father was looking very well. He was wearing a blue, short-sleeved shirt. The colour suited him. His breath was free of alcohol. He had even cut down on cigarettes. She wondered who washed his hankies and socks now that he had left home. She felt a lump in her throat. She wanted to kiss him but didn't want to be the one to do it first.

"You get yourself better," he said when he was going. Everyone was telling her that. As if she didn't want to! She nodded. "You'll come and visit me soon," he said. "I've got this great thing for making lemonade. I'll stock up on flavours in the meantime. Chris can come too and we'll have a party."

Claire tried to smile but it went all wobbly. She wished he would stay and just go on talking. It seemed so long since they'd had a proper conversation. Years. And now he was going and he hadn't even kissed her.

"Hey," Jim said, coming back over. "Give me a glimpse of those pearlies." It was an old joke between them. She smiled in spite of herself. He bent down and kissed her forehead. Claire clung to her father, not wanting to let him go.

When he had gone she lay back with closed eyes, mourning for Hugh, remembering him that last day forlornly watching herself and Sheena through the kitchen window. And Eddie? His last words to her? She wished with all her heart she could remember.

In the middle of July Claire went with the McArdles on their summer vacation to the seaside. She sat in the back of the Rover with Ruthie and Sheena, quiet and withdrawn, dreading the moment of arrival at the bungalow.

The previous week her father had rung and asked her over to his flat. Annette was convinced that Jim was living with the woman who had ousted her and strongly condemned any association with the enemy. Longing to accept, Claire had hesitated, but in the end had braved her mother's displeasure and gone. It had been a pleasant visit. Her father had cooked up rashers and sausages and bought in a chocolate cake.

"I'm on flexitime this week," he told her. "I go to work at eight and finish at two."

Claire felt sudden jealousy for his new way of life. Why couldn't he have arranged his life this way for them? Paradoxically, he had abandoned his family in order to become like other fathers.

"This bothers you?" Jim asked.

She had not known what to say.

"You think I've selfishly gone off and left you?"

"I didn't say that," she managed at last to get out.

"You don't have to." He sighed. "In some ways I wish to God I hadn't left but there seemed no other way. Was no other way."

"You said it was only for six months," she reminded him, almost accusingly, although she had never really believed in it herself.

"I suppose it was wishful thinking," her father admitted.

Claire had suddenly hated the woman, whoever she was. It was all her fault, she thought miserably. She had come between her parents at a time when their marriage was too shaky to withstand her, when Annette was too sad and dispirited to fight back or even recognise the danger. If only the baby hadn't died, Claire thought.

"You have your life ahead of you to do with what you want, Claire," her father had said as he kissed her goodbye. "Don't forget that. You'll be cleverer than we were. Don't allow anything to spoil it."

Claire glanced out at the passing landscape and blinked away easy tears. It seemed to her that her life was already spoiled.

The holiday site was unchanged, the local people as friendly as ever, although now their warmth was tinged with pity. Nobody wanted to be the first to say anything, but they expressed their sympathy in gruff throat-clearings and lowered glances. Jane was aware of the warm tide of feeling but elected not to give them the opening they sought.

Claire found the hardest part was not, as she had expected, crossing the threshold, but the absence of Hugh. The bungalow struck her as cold and remote without him and, outside of it, she seemed to see him in every turn of the road.

When they were alone Sheena hugged and kissed her, swearing with tears in her eyes that she had never been lonelier in her life as in the weeks of Claire's illness. Like Jane, she looked grey and tired. It was as though the bloom had gone from her skin, the sparkle from her life. In the privacy of their room, lying together under the one quilt, Sheena told her that Ruthie had begun wetting her bed and for weeks now she had been getting up at night to change her.

Terry had got in with a gang of neighbouring boys, Sheena said, and was disappearing off all the time to drink beer with them in a waste lot behind the sports complex. Jane was worried out of her mind but was afraid to be too harsh in case she alienated him. Terry had always been stubborn and only had to be told not to do something to go out of his way to do it.

"I can't understand him," Sheena admitted, with a catch in her voice. "He is so moody and withdrawn that we're afraid to say anything to him."

Claire listened sympathetically in the darkness. From all Sheena said, she was really missing her twin. But most of all, from what Sheena did not say, it was clear she was missing her father.

Jane was missing Eddie too, even more than she had imagined she would on this first trip back to the cottage. Her worst time was when she closed the bedroom door each night. On previous holidays that had always been the moment when she and her husband would lie close together, their fingers linked, and mull sleepily over whatever antics the children had got up to during the day. Now taking up so little space on her own in the big bed that had been their soft haven, Jane felt beleaguered by the phantoms that returned with the fall of darkness to haunt her.

If Claire saw Hugh in every turn of the road, Jane was convinced that she saw her son in every corner of the cottage. In the mornings when she emerged from her bedroom she fully expected to find him crouched beside the freshly lit fire, his head to one side as he carefully placed each additional briquette on the flickering pile. With an almost unbearable pang she recalled how pleased he used be for any little word of praise she would give him.

Then there was Claire. At first, seeing her back in the setting where the seeds of the tragedy had been sown the previous Easter, Jane was affected so painfully that she was almost in danger of regressing where the girl was concerned. Soon, however, in the reality of Claire's gentle, self-effacing nature, all Jane's resentment faded entirely away. She now clearly saw how unbalanced her attitude had been when, half-crazed with sorrow, she had placed blame on a child for the misconduct of an adult. She felt such contrition that she longed to make it up to Claire and resolved never to give the poor girl any further cause than she already had to regret her links with their family.

That decided, Jane made a determined effort to put past sorrows behind her. She treated Claire with great gentleness and was eventually rewarded by seeing her become, if not light-hearted, at least not as troubled as before.

Annette joined them in Dualeen at the end of July, planning to stay a week, even two. With school closed for the summer she was not tied to any particular routine and was finding it lonely on her own with Christopher away in the Gaeltacht.

After a few days it was clear to everyone that Annette was drinking too much. Claire was ashamed of her mother's raucous laugh and unsteady gait in front of Sheena. There were times when she almost hated her. Jane was concerned but didn't like to say anything. After all, Annette was the guest.

One evening, having drunk more than usual, Annette became sad and vengeful. She began talking in a wild, provocative manner. She couldn't seem to keep off the subject of Eddie, probing ever deeper, trying to gauge the depth of Jane's sorrow and plainly irked by what she considered Jane's smug assumption that that Eddie had loved no other woman but herself.

If she only knew, Jane sighed, knowing only too well that she had no cause to be smug but, nevertheless, determined to keep up the illusion of her husband's fidelity.

"How can you take so much for granted, Jane?" Annette asked impatiently. "He was in a profession where he met lots of women. He wouldn't have been human if he hadn't taken advantage of it."

Strangely, this thought afforded Annette a certain satisfaction. If she had been just one of many in Eddie's life, so too had Jane. Annette was getting an almost sexual thrill out of the conversation.

"Please, let's change the subject," Jane begged at last, unable to hold back her tears any longer. She sat with a hand covering her eyes, at a loss to know why Annette was behaving in such an unpleasant way. Just what was Annette trying to do to her? Wasn't it enough to have suffered the loss of her husband and son without having to justify that loss? She looked at Annette's half-empty glass and decided not to give her any more whisky.

Terry came in and took an apple from the fruit bowl. Jane absently told him to wash it first. He went out munching.

Annette raised her glass to her lips, missed and slopped it over herself.

"Oh hell," she said, and began to cry.

"What is it?" Jane asked.

"I have to tell you," Annette sobbed, looking at Jane through a fog of tears. "I don't want to hurt you but I have to tell you." In her maudlin state she began to believe that her telling Jane was inspired by repentance, and not malice.

Jane listened without a word. Annette stopped crying. She looked frightened. "I know you must hate me," she gabbled. "It was like a kind of sickness. I know now that's what it was. When I let Eddie make love to me, I was trying to compensate for Jim's indifference. I told myself I didn't care but deep down I really did." She waited as if expecting Jane to contradict this. When she remained silent Annette hurried on, pouring out more and more of her passion for Eddie, how much she'd suffered when he had died. She began to cry noisy, harsh sobs, her face contorted and ugly.

Jane struggled to control her emotion. Forget she tried to steal your husband. Try to think of her as a patient. She leaned over and pressed Annette's shoulder.

"I never meant to tell you," Annette sobbed. "I never would have only I was so miserable."

She continued to cry noisily into her handkerchief.

"I think we could both do with some coffee," Jane said, getting up. She went down the passage to the kitchen. Terry was standing like a statue beside the laden hall-stand and she passed by without noticing him. She desperately needed to be by herself. Behind her calm facade Jane felt a kind of helpless rage that Annette should have the gall to tell her right to her face that she had been having an affair with her husband. She struggled to tell herself it wasn't malice prompting Annette but a kind of sorrowing bravado.

Like hell it was!

Jane took milk out of the fridge and closed the door. She pressed her hot forehead against the cool melamine and drew a shocked, sobbing breath. In God's name, what did Annette expect? Her blessing on her adulterous affair?

Jane made a pot of coffee and automatically put cups on a tray. Was there ever to be an end to these nasty surprises? Bitterly she thought of her dead husband and son. Was she to be left with nothing? Not even those tender memories of her early love for Eddie and their years of toil and laughter. It seemed to her that everything she had ever prized was being gradually taken from her, stripped away bit by bit. Jane's eyes darkened with pain. Surely to God she deserved better than this?

She thought of the almost triumphant manner in which Annette had revealed details of Eddie's infidelity. Jane realised what she had never realised before, that Annette was intensely jealous of her, only up to this she had managed to conceal it. With drink, however, it had all come spilling out like so much sewer water. Now she saw the reason behind it.

Claire, Annette, Eddie. A tragic, terrible triangle.

"Oh, Eddie," Jane moaned in wounded misery. "What deep, dark shade was in you that I never even suspected?"

Not now, she thought in panic. I can't possibly think of it now. Later, much later, when alone she would take it out and examine it. She heard Annette's sandals clipping unsteadily down the passage, coming to find out what was keeping her, and quickly straightened up. She took a firm grip of the tray and went to meet her.

Terry stole on up the stairs to bed. Annette Shannon and his father. He struggled to take it in. His father and Annette Shannon. Claire's mother.

He had a flash of memory. Stephen Rigney, in his class, boasting that he knew the name of the woman his father had been involved with. She had a teenage daughter who was a real looker, he'd said. Terry stood shock-still as he thought of Claire, asleep upstairs. Quiet, bookish Claire with a mother like that. He wondered if she knew.

Claire was awakened by Ruthie's cries. She got up and helped the little girl out of bed. Together they hurried to the bathroom. Sheena heard her sister's wails but soon went back to sleep, glad to be relieved of the burden for one night.

Ruthie sat on the toilet, her damp nightie ruched about her waist. "Finished," she said sleepily and eased herself off the seat.

Claire guided her carefully back to their room and wrapped her in a blanket while she remade the bed. The sheet was not very wet as Ruthie had fortunately woken at once. As Claire deftly turned the bottom sheet and tucked the damp patch under the mattress, she heard the door open. She looked around and saw Terry standing there. He stared at her, solemn-faced and silent.

He had hardly spoken a word to her since the holiday began. He was either rude and withdrawn, or else boisterously high and sitting on the wall talking to Susan Deveney, the over-developed teenager from the next cottage.

"Sheena is asleep," Claire told him, but Terry just nodded and continued to stare at her. She felt acutely conscious of him as she helped Ruthie back into bed and bent down to tuck the little girl in. Conscious too, of her own brief attire: because her only nightdress was in the wash, she had resorted to wearing an old school blouse which barely extended to her thighs; her cheeks grew hot. Ruthie yawned and fell asleep at once. When Claire slowly straightened up from the bed and shyly turned around, Terry was gone.

The excitement and speculation amongst the fifth years as to who would be selected to play the leads in the school opera was intense. Claire divorced herself from it and looked out at the garden to where the gardener's boy swept up the leaves in golden heaps. Like scattered doubloons on the mossy grass, she thought, taking pleasure in the sight and in the simile. In three years Claire had made very few adjustments in her life. Her friendship with the McArdles was, if anything, stronger. They were still her only friends and otherwise she continued with her solitary life, much as before. At first, the going had not been easy. Neither her mother nor her brother had any notion of what she had experienced or indeed been aware of the trauma she suffered and was still suffering, as a result of her early seduction and subsequent termination. She had tried to put it all behind her, but those events had left their mark. There were other hardships.

Since Claire had returned to school in September her mother had made no secret of the fact that she was finding it difficult to pay the household bills. She said she was sick, besides, of doing without the kind of necessities other families took for granted. What Annette really meant was she longed for the luxuries she had had to forfeit when the family was reduced to living on one salary. Annette had extravagant tastes, and in the days before Jim had walked out she had thought nothing of spending big sums on lace slips or silk blouses. Even now she occasionally indulged herself on a lingerie spending spree, but not as often as she would have liked. She was sick of having to make do; there had to be some legitimate way of improving her income. Claire echoed this sentiment. The years since her father had left them had been really lean. It did not help that her mother was such a poor housekeeper. She was a careless and impulsive buyer, and food either accumulated and turned bad in the fridge or was already past its sell-by date when purchased. At the same time, Claire recognised how difficult it was for her mother trying to manage on a Montessori teacher's modest salary and her separated wife's allowance. The only solution that occurred to Annette was to take in a lodger, and while Claire did not much care for the idea, she soon had to agree that the additional income made all the difference to their comfort.

Sheena weaved fantasies about Claire and the young teacher falling in love but Claire didn't think there was any danger of this. While she was willing to concede that

Austin was fairly good-looking, although still showing traces of teenage acne, most of the time he made her feel uncomfortable, wandering the house half-clad, showing bony knees and a thickly matted chest.

Now in the desk beside her Sheena was saying, "What's keeping Attila?" the fifth form's nickname for the mistress of studies. "I'll die if she doesn't come soon."

The school opera, held in conjunction with St Gabriel's each January, was the highlight of the year – and Sheena had set her heart on playing the role of Katya, the king's daughter, kidnapped by the dastardly bandit, Rodrigo. Although her own voice was sweet and true and she had performed well at the auditions, Claire wasn't even sure she wanted a part. But Sheena told her not to be mad; there would be parties every night and all the fun of rehearsals.

There was a muffled shout from the girl on look-out and, seconds later, Sister Whelan came smiling into the classroom and held up her hand for quiet. When Sheena drew attention to her own fingers crossed beneath the desk, Claire felt sudden excitement.

"I know you're all longing to hear the names of the successful actresses so I won't prolong the agony. I'm delighted to congratulate Sheena McArdle . . ." Sister Whelan paused for effect and, despite herself, Claire felt her stomach swoop, "and Claire Shannon!"

There was an enthusiastic burst of clapping and cries of congratulation. Sheena hugged Claire and confessed, "God! I thought I'd die of suspense," and Claire nodded shakily.

They rehearsed three afternoons a week during the term and every day during the Christmas holidays. *The Revenge of Rodrigo* was written and produced by one of the masters. Noel Ryan was tall and knife-thin with a beautiful speaking voice which he used with sarcastic effect, mainly on the boys. He was quite charming to the girls. Claire was a little shy of him. Sheena flirted with him shamelessly. She had got her wish and been cast as Katya, playing opposite tall fair-haired

Rory. Claire was Anya and her opposite number was dark and hirsute and renowned for his piano-playing.

Claire's assurance on stage surprised everyone, especially herself. She began to enjoy being caught up in the make-believe of *Rodrigo*, finding the melodramatic story-line innocuous when compared to the turbulent happenings in her own short life.

Her mind could never really let go of the past. Even after three years she was still full of regretful longings and remembered shame, and was constantly preparing herself for the moment when Jane would find out and cast her off without a chance to explain. The opera was a welcome distraction and left little time for brooding.

Then one afternoon, she arrived at St Gabriel's to find that her long-haired musician had got tonsillitis and been replaced by, of all people, Terry McArdle.

Claire did not know how she would ever get through the rehearsal. Sheena thought it very funny and kept giggling behind her hand. Terry scowled and folded his arms, darting glances at Claire from under beetling brows.

"We'll take the last scene next," Noel suggested. "It needs a good deal of polishing." His eyes wandered towards Terry. "In the final clinch your predecessor managed to look like he was about to be guillotined. Let's see if you can do better, McArdle. Remember, you may be a great man in the back of a car but on stage it's got to look real."

Claire blushed. Usually the kiss was taken as given and the four of them moved on to the next and final scene, holding hands and singing the quartet.

"Just bear in mind that you're kissing the object of your desire and, I might add, a very pretty young lady to boot."

Claire and Terry gravitated towards each other. Terry stood, hands awkwardly hanging at his sides. His face was flushed and he avoided looking at her. Claire tried to move gracefully but she felt all hands and feet. Sheena always managed it better, she thought, miserably conscious of the attention she was getting from the rest of the cast. The boys were growling appreciatively in their throats and giving the odd jeering hoot. Terry had a reputation for being a knock-out with the girls and this bashfulness on his part was highly amusing.

"Very well," Noel said. "Let's be having you."

Terry stepped forward and took firm hold of Claire. She settled back on his arm and gazed fondly up at him as she was meant to. His face was very close to hers, his eyes wide and alert, staring grimly into hers. She had never realised they were so light a brown, almost golden. Eddie's were a shade darker, she thought, just before Terry's lips came down, blotting out thought. Neither moved for several seconds. There was pandemonium.

"Cut!" Mr Ryan said, moving forward. Claire and Terry broke at last. Claire felt hot and confused, conscious that for a few dizzy seconds she had forgotten where she was. She had never been kissed by anyone but Eddie.

Noel lightly applauded and sighed, "Thank God for at least one scene bearing the mark of authenticity." Claire blushed for the implication and Terry shoved his hair off his forehead and slouched scowling to rejoin his cheering schoolfellows.

"Now let's take that scene of yours," Noel turned to Rory.

After rehearsal Claire ran off without waiting for the twins. If she had to face Terry he might say something to her and she would blush and say the wrong thing. She wondered how she could go through it all again. Two more rehearsals and then the night itself.

She was amazed at how well the whole thing passed off in the end. She was quite contained and even smiled at Terry before the curtain fell.

This year, the one before Claire sat for the Leaving Cert, was her best year, with more time reading for pleasure before the pressure of exams began. The other girls in her class went out with boys and talked about their dates. They were fairly explicit but so far none of them admitted to going any further than kissing and petting. There was a lot of joking done about close dancing and the rigidity of male partners. Claire refused to get into the discussion. When she told Sheena that she got more fun curled up with a good book, Sheena had laughed. But it was true.

Sheena was doing a hectic line with Rory since the opera and kept asking Claire to come out with them and one of Rory's friends, or even Terry, on a double date bowling or to the cinema, but Claire had no interest. It was true that for a while after the school opera, stimulated by Terry's closeness, she had begun coming regularly in her dreams. Otherwise, she had not experienced any sexual feeling in three years and definitely did not want to be turned on again. Although she was not happy, she did not expect to be happy, nor could she ever remember being really happy. Not, she supposed, since Bella. That was the nearest she had ever come to happiness.

By contrast, her mother was the most light-hearted Claire had seen her since her father had deserted them. Her brother seemed happier too. Christopher had missed another male in the house and Austin slipped easily into the absent parent's role of sports enthusiast and TV companion – only later did he take on an additional role of Annette's friend and comforter.

When the new contented Annette began urging her to go to discos and have fun (more, Claire felt, from a desire to get her out of the house than anything else) she gave her mother the same answer she had given Sheena. Anyway, there would be plenty of time for all of that in the summer months away with the McArdles.

By the end of the summer term, however, Claire finally gave in.

One Saturday afternoon Sheena arrived at Claire's door with Rory and a shy-looking boy called Alan. The four of them took a bus to Rathfarnham and walked up to the Pine Forest. There the boys produced a tonic bottle filled with whisky and passed it around. Claire drank her share and almost lost her footing coming back down the mountainside.

"Enjoy our double date?" Sheena asked when Claire called over for a chat on Sunday morning. "Great fun, wasn't it?" She grinned "Only don't let on to your mother about the whisky."

"No, of course not," Claire said. Whisky. Annette was getting through bottles of the stuff with the help of Austin, ever since the government launched its campaign to introduce divorce into Ireland. Although Claire's father hadn't actually spoken of marrying again her mother was convinced it was only a matter of time.

"But how can he?" Claire had asked shaken. "He's a Catholic."

Annette laughed grimly. "Once a Catholic always a Catholic, eh? That's what they used to say about priests, but it hasn't stopped them. No, depend upon it, if the bill is passed he'll make an honest woman of her and cast the rest of us off." Claire had shivered at the finality of it.

Now Sheena was asking, "Want to go out with the boys again?"

Claire nodded.

"Great! We'll call for you on Saturday," Sheena promised.

"I might go with you," Terry said, coming into the kitchen. He had been intrigued by Sheena's veiled hints and thought it might be a good idea to find out what she and Claire got up to when out with his classmates.

"Good idea, but bring some cans," Sheena told him, giving Claire an impish look which clearly read, this will give the fellows a bit of competition.

That Saturday afternoon when they got off at the bus terminal, the boys grouped naturally to kick a tin can further along the country road. They crested the hill. Ahead of them, up another sloping road, a stream wound its way down through rocky banks.

"Let's go for a paddle," Sheena said, tugging off her runners. She hopped across the pebbly grass and eased herself down into the water. "Come on," she called. "It's lovely."

Within minutes she and Rory were fisting water over each

133

other and Sheena was soaking wet. The other boy made quasi-helpful suggestions, like she should take off her wet shorts before she caught cold. Terry eyed his twin and said she'd never dare with them all watching her. At once Sheena stretched and did a sensual dance as she peeled off her shorts and T-shirt. Claire wandered away from the shouting group, bent to pull a blade of grass and place it dreamily between her teeth. She stood looking down the sloping road to where the foreshortened figures of three climbers could be seen moving ant-like, slowly upwards. Out of the corner of her eye she saw Sheena dash madly past pursued by the boys.

When they eventually rounded Sheena up and escorted her back to the rock, she was shivering and exaggeratedly chattering her teeth. Rory made a great ceremony of wringing out her shorts and T-shirt and handing them back to her. They were almost dry. Sheena picked up her bra and took her time putting that on. The boys watched her openly. They walked deeper into the forest. When they got to their usual place they sprawled on the ground and Rory produced the bottle. Claire soon began to get that, by now, familiar woozy feeling. Only this time the whisky taken in conjunction with beer made her feel not so much dreamy as out of control. How would she get herself down the mountain? She didn't think she could even stand up. The June sun shone hotly on the tender flesh of her exposed thighs, increasing her feeling of inertia. A hand ran lightly over her knees and coasted higher to settle on her breast. She felt a love-bite on the right side of her neck and turned in that direction. Her lips met other lips. She kissed them and was kissed back. Most of the time she was not quite aware who was doing what. For a time the kissing and stroking continued but none of them went any further than that, and after a while they all fell asleep.

Claire set off with the McArdles in July, her mother absently waving her off. Since the Divorce Bill had been defeated Annette had stopped anticipating the worst and was looking forward to a lazy summer, without the burden of her off-spring.

This summer, like the previous two, Jane commuted more frequently from their holiday cottage. Now that she was sole breadwinner, she felt she couldn't be away from her practice for more than a couple of weeks. Besides, work helped distract her from thoughts of past vacations when she'd had Eddie and all her family around her. She considered that Sheena and Claire were well able to run the household in her absence and, even more important, take care of Ruthie. In this regard Jane was more than ever glad of Claire's steadying presence. That Sheena was unreliable was regrettably true. Jane had long ago come to terms with her daughter's shortcomings.

Every so often, Jane took Terry back with her to town. Sometimes she regretted leaving them all so much on their own, and especially him. She secretly feared he would fall into bad ways, and might even display some of the darker aspects of his father's nature. These trips alone with Terry were an attempt to keep the lines of communication open with her teenage son.

In June, when he had turned seventeen, Jane had applied on his behalf for a provisional licence and Terry relieved her of some of the burden of driving, especially to and from the clinic at night.

Since Eddie's death, besides increasing her time at the clinic to include three evenings a week, Jane regularly took surgery each morning and afternoon, excluding Saturday. Summer made very little difference in the need for her services. There was, if anything, an increase in rape and violence at night on the summer streets. Jane's consciousness of the plight of women, which had always been acute, increased with the passing of the years. She was now committed to representing and improving the lot of her less fortunate sisters.

With Terry gone a lot of the time and Sheena opting out of her responsibilities, Claire was left looking after Ruthie most of this holiday. Not that she minded. Besides being a way to repay Jane's kindness to her, she loved the little girl as if she were her own sister and enjoyed the prospect of spoiling her. Sheena, who wanted to be off all the time flirting with boys, made no secret of the fact that she considered her small sister a drag on her, but Ruthie was never anything but a pleasure to Claire.

At eight years Ruthie was a biddable little girl, and although the tragic events three years earlier had left her shy and inclined to be clingy, most of the time she happily played her own made-up games. She had an insatiable appetite for books and the only demands she ever made on Claire were for more stories. Claire made some up out of her head but, by the second week of the holidays, was glad to resort to re-reading her own childhood favourites to keep Ruthie satisfied. It seemed to Claire that if she had been lucky enough at Ruthie's age to have had someone to befriend her, she would have grown up a happier, more integrated person, less likely to fall prey to the first sexual overture.

Claire wished that the whole episode with Eddie could be as cleanly wiped out as though it had never happened. That she could regain, not only her innocence but, with regard to Jane, her self-respect too. Claire would hold anguished monologues in her head, in which she tried to justify the whole sordid business. Failing, she would grow angry with herself, until she realised that Jane had never accused her of anything. It was her own conscience she had failed to convince.

Some nights Terry would stay in the cottage listening to the radio while Claire and Ruthie played Ludo or some other board game. When he did Claire never felt comfortable. She sometimes looked up to see him watching her with those tawny eyes, so like Eddie's, and then all the guilt would come flooding back. What if Terry was to know of her association with his father? She didn't think she could bear it if he did.

Claire got in the habit of settling down for the night at

the same time as Ruthie. She hated being downstairs on her own after dark and always imagined faces looking in at her through the uncurtained windows. It was much cosier up in bed, sipping cocoa and reading her book.

Terry never came into their bedroom. That was a blessing. Claire was loth to admit it but he stirred a feeling of excitement in her. She was coming in her dreams again and it had to do with that afternoon on the mountain. She realised that the lips she had kissed so dreamily and unknowingly had not been Alan's – how could they and he at the other side of Sheena? – but Terry's. Deep disturbing kisses that seemed to reach down into her soul and go on for ever. So it was a case of never allowing herself to be alone with him.

Before long there was another cause for guilt.

Terry and Sheena were taking money from the housekeeping to pay for their bottle parties and she, Claire, had never said anything for fear of being called a prig or a goody-good. Jane had treated her from the very beginning of their relationship like an adult, and now here she was betraying her trust yet again.

Jane had no idea of any of this.

Like Eddie, in the past, she worked hard all week, then drove back to the country at weekends, intent on making the most of these few days with her children. She was like a sailor home on leave, crowding the all too few hours with the kind of things she most liked. And once back in the bosom of her family, she loved and indulged them to an almost foolish degree.

Jane was not aware that she was doing it, but she deliberately blanked her mind to anything unpleasant that might mar these brief get-togethers with her children. There was enough grimness in the shape of illness and death awaiting her on her return. It was unlikely that she would ever probe deeply enough to discover that Sheena and Terry were getting high most nights on drink or that Claire was left minding Ruthie practically all the time, as well as shopping for

groceries and keeping the cottage tidy. On the surface everything was serene because Jane wanted it to be that way.

Terry understood his mother's attitude perhaps better
than any of them. He had that same ability to stick his head
in the sand in order to avoid tackling issues that were, for
one reason or another, distasteful to him.

Terry was a doer, not a dreamer and anything he was
unable to settle with his fists made him uneasy. He always
had to be in control and usually was. Since the previous
summer he had put on an extra four inches, which
brought him up to six foot in height, and although slim, he
was sturdy and strong. There was a fearless streak in Terry
which had the effect of disconcerting his fiercest opponent. The tougher and bloodier the fight, the better Terry
liked it. Once he had identified his enemy's Achilles' heel,
he coolly went for it, pounding away until he was victori-
ous. He was not a dirty fighter. He was even a chivalrous
opponent. But as he said himself, he just didn't take crap
from anyone.

For some time Terry had found himself strongly attracted
to Claire. The strength of his feelings puzzled him, for he
considered she was everything that he was not: intellectual,
refined, sensitive. Not his usual kind of girl. A real little Miss
Dainty-Dot.

He'd always had a curiosity about her from the days they
had played nurses and doctors in the stone garage. She was
so cool and fair, remote. The day up the mountains, seeing
her lying there in the sunshine, permitting liberties . . .
exchanging kisses like she was some high priestess conferring an honour, yet managing somehow to retain that
dreamy, untouched quality. She confused and excited him.
Ever since the school opera he had found himself thinking
of her, remembering the sensuous kiss she'd given him
before the whole cast. Terry hadn't encountered anything
like it, not even the night he had lost his virginity to an older
girl on the holiday site two years earlier. With that one kiss,
Madonna-faced Claire had relegated his earlier experience

138

to the inept fumble it had been. He thought of the other kisses stolen on the sunny mountainside and felt confirmed in his opinion that Claire Shannon, though she appeared so gentle and reserved, was breath-takingly sexy.

He wasn't the only one on the holiday site who was attracted to her. Denis and Barney, two local lads, were always angling for introductions. Down on the pier at night after the disco, the beer sizzling in their bloodstream, they leaned on the wall and spoke lewdly of what they'd like to do with her if they ever got the chance. Even Terry was a bit taken aback the first time he heard them.

The boys were older than him, which was part of their attraction for Terry. Denis was nineteen and Barney a retarded twenty-three, and they were hard drinkers, which also appealed to Terry. Most of the gang he and Sheena knocked about with were their own age or younger and were on their ear after one or two beers.

One night, after their usual drinking session on the pier, Terry and the two older boys walked back to the cottages. Well primed. Denis and Barney began jumping up and down scrunching the empty beer cans. Terry walked on ahead.

"Hey, McArdle," Denis called after him, tripping on his training laces and falling over. "Come back here, you effer!" Barney began shouting too. He did everything that Denis did. They were making an appalling racket.

Terry quickened his steps down by the side of the cottage, fully expecting Garda Deveney to open his window and bawl them out for disturbing the peace. Last time he'd threatened to take them down to the station. He was probably pulling on his pants right now, Terry thought, and would appear any minute like a maniac in the doorway. When it happened he, for one, intended to be safely tucked up in bed.

The kitchen light was on and he wondered if Sheena had brought her current boyfriend Killian in for a snog, but when he slipped inside he found Claire on her own, heating milk on the stove. Her skimpy nightgown barely covered her thighs. When she turned he noticed the childish transfer on the front. Sleepytime Bunny. At the same time his senses registered the swell of her breasts. He swallowed uncomfortably.

Claire angled the saucepan and poured milk into a mug. In her hurry to get away she spilt some on the counter. "Ruthie woke," she told him, mopping furiously. "I thought warm milk might get her back to sleep."

Terry nodded, for the first time struck by how little Sheena helped with Ruthie. He felt an irrational anger at his twin. Always out enjoying herself, he thought. It didn't occur to him that he was being equally selfish.

"You should come out with us more," he said lamely.

"I'd like that," Claire said. But who would stay with Ruthie? hung unspoken between them.

"There's another disco on Friday. Mum will be home then. You could come."

"Maybe. I'll see."

She turned off the stove. He stared at her indecisively. A picture flashed in his mind of Claire sprawled on the grassy knoll, eyes closed, knees apart. His desire flared. He wondered what she would do if he kissed her. Drink made him bold. He moved to bar her way.

She looked up at him, her face flushed, her grey eyes enigmatic. He bent his head and kissed her hotly on the mouth. She did not at once push him away.

To the boys outside the window, peering in, Claire seemed to be encouraging Terry. By the time she had freed herself from his embrace, they had ducked back around the side.

"Did you see that?" Denis rounded on Barney. "Standing there with her backside hanging out?" He pretended to stagger. "McArdle has it bloody made."

Barney chortled and went out of his way to kick a beer can. He would have begun stamping on it again only Denis shoved him on.

Terry roamed his room, all thought of sleep gone, his

pants uncomfortably tight. "Dynamite, she's dynamite," he kept telling himself. That one kiss had been even better than the ones he had stolen on the mountainside. Now he couldn't concentrate on anything, not even getting into bed. He thought he was in love. He was damned sure he was in love. He wanted to go and tell her, to kiss her again.

Terry went out on the landing, now thoroughly aroused and tapped gently on Claire's door. There was no answer. He went inside.

"Claire," he whispered urgently, overcome with a desire to kiss and hold her, find some release for this sweet aching tension. He stopped short at the sight of Claire and Ruthie lying side by side, with their eyes shut and their blonde heads nestling close together.

Claire opened her eyes and looked at him.

"What's wrong?" she whispered.

Terry felt as though he had been caught doing something criminal.

"I thought Sheena was back," he gulped. He turned and stumbled out of the room.

While Claire was away in Waterford, Annette took things easy. She spent a lot of time in the garden, sunning herself and reading blockbuster novels.

With the advent of the school holidays Annette had lost not only her children but her lover as well. Austin had returned to Cork, leaving a big gap in her life. She had outlined her summer to him, stressing how peaceful and private the house would be. Austin had talked vaguely of a walking holiday in Germany. Annette had still half-hoped that, missing sex if not herself, he would come up for a visit, but one postcard from Bad Godesberg in mid-July confirmed her suspicions that she was strictly term-time relaxation.

At the end of July Christopher returned home briefly before going on a camping holiday to France with his father. Annette suspected it was to be a threesome. She washed Christopher's grubby shorts and T-shirts and repacked them in the same fraying plastic bags he'd taken with him to the Gaeltacht.

Three days and he was off again. She missed him to about the same degree as before, which was a good deal less than she missed Austin, and settled back to her solitary routine in the garden.

A fortnight later they drove right to her front door: Jim, Christopher and the Other Woman. Annette invited them all in. As she made them tea – Marissa declined to have a drink and Jim shook his head in the slightly censorious fashion of one who has once spent his evenings drinking himself unconscious – Annette kept up a string of bright inanities. She was both fascinated and repelled by Marissa. So strikingly ugly. She searched her mind and came up with "belle laide". Annette thought Jim was out of his mind.

She wondered at his openly flaunting the relationship, until later when he phoned to tell her that Marissa was expecting a baby. He hadn't liked to mention it before her. Why not? Annette wondered. It was his, wasn't it? He said they wished to make the fruit of their love legitimate. His actual words. He was seeking a Church annulment. Annette put down the phone feeling that she had somehow been nullified herself, the past twenty years cleanly erased.

She reached for the whisky bottle and poured herself a stiff one, wishing there was someone with whom she could share this disturbing new development. What about Jane? She hadn't seen her in ages and maybe now was the right moment to bridge the gap. But when she went across the street and rang the bell, Jane's latest teenage assistant, yet another of Teresa Murray's many daughters, told Annette that Dr McArdle had just left for Waterford.

That same evening, in his mother's presence, Terry asked Claire to come with them to the disco. When she hesitated he appealed to Jane.

"Mum," Terry said. "See if you can get her to come."

Jane squeezed Claire's arm. "Off you go, love," she said

encouragingly. She was looking forward to an early night and had given in to Ruthie's plea to be allowed share her bed. They had taken the portable television into the downstairs bedroom and would watch for a while before falling asleep. "You'd like to go, Claire, wouldn't you?"

Claire nodded. She had been a little shy of Terry all week, remembering his kiss and the way he'd come into her room afterwards. Of course, he and Sheena often went searching for each other in the night, to share some plan or thought. Admittedly, not as much these days as when they were younger. Now she felt pleasure at the prospect of an evening out with other young people, dancing, having a good time. She wore a red skirt, over a lightly boned petticoat, and a white, sleeveless blouse. She left her hair loose on her shoulders.

The disco was held as usual in a hall near the quay. Claire danced with Terry a few times, and then other boys approached and took her on to the floor. Sheena, who was with Killian, looked plump and provocative on a diet of chips and alcohol. She was wearing her low-cut frock and a pair of red heels, which Jane hadn't yet seen.

Barney and Denis slouched about, feeling-up the girls. Every few dances the pair of them disappeared outside to tank up on beer. Claire could not understand how Terry was friendly with them. She shivered when Denis approached and put a hand like a brown glove on her bare arm.

Terry held Claire carefully, not with his usual careless swagger, shielding her from more boisterous dancers and, every so often, gazing wonderingly down as though to check it really was her in his arms. At the end of the evening, he hoped to kiss her again. Maybe even go a bit further and feel her breasts. Any more than that he did not envisage.

The disco over, Terry and Claire held hands and walked in step along the pier. They passed, without seeing, the usual intoxicated group under the quay wall, aware of nothing but each other. They spoke in short animated bursts, laughed self-consciously and then fell silent. An almost full moon shone luminously down upon a dark sea, quilted with waves.

At the end of the short pier, as if at some pre-arranged signal, they came into each other's arms and kissed. When the earth steadied they turned and went, hand-in-hand, back to the bungalow.

Claire felt she could never get enough of Terry's kisses. It was the afternoon on the school stage all over again, but with no witnesses. Not to begin with anyway.

They had come in to find the fire still smouldering where Jane had left it well banked.

In the beginning Claire had felt uneasy, though she didn't know why. She wanted to stop Terry when he began poking and easing the sods, making them burn brighter. The fire had not been lit regularly on this holiday, not indeed since the days when Hugh took it upon himself to light it each morning. Tonight it cast an eerie glow about the room, throwing light on a footstool and on the spines of books in the bookcase.

A tall figure was poised motionless to the side of the bookcase, but it was merely Jane's belted raincoat, hooked on the back of the door.

"Clairey," Terry sighed, holding her very close.

His passion thrilled her but, at the same time, made her self-conscious. As she returned his kiss, she wondered how much longer she could hold out. She was like a foundered fish, desperately gasping air through its fins.

When he unbuttoned her blouse she made no attempt to stop him. He undid her bra and consigned it to the darkness. Her breasts jutted rosy and startlingly plump in the firelight. Terry gently stroked them, his expression a mixture of lust and reverence. Claire watched him, her own expression shy and proud by turns. It was a long time since her body had been so openly offered to another. She felt confused and, at the same time, conscious of a sweet aching desire to surrender.

She grew even more lax and allowed him to remove her

skirt and petticoat. They were on the rug now. She had a sense of *déjà vu*. She shifted and made to sit up but he murmured pleadingly and she lay back again. He knelt between her legs, caressing the inside of her thighs with steepled hands, long sweeping strokes bringing her to a state of trembling arousal. Now he could have done anything with her, but Terry was holding back, unwilling in the throes of this new loving sensation to jeopardise their burgeoning relationship.

They were still in this position when Denis and Barney crept low under the window and reared up to look in through the uncurtained glass, blurry with condensation. In his eagerness to see better Barney shoved Denis and a stone from the rockery dislodged, and thudded softly on the grass.

The noise, thought slight, was enough to recall Claire to herself and she came out of her daze and looked down in horror at her exposed breasts and pearly parted limbs. She snatched for her blouse and, holding it against herself, scrambled up. What was she doing here? Oh God, was she out of her mind? On the very spot where with Eddie . . .

With a shamed, inarticulate cry Claire gathered up the rest of her fallen clothing and ran up the stairs. Terry watched her in surprise, his senses drugged by heat and the sweet uprising of flesh, not at once connecting her exit and the faint noise beyond the window. Then came the ribald shout.

Terry's mind cleared instantly. He hastily adjusted his clothing and went outside and stood on the moonlit roadway, his eyes raking the area. His earlier euphoria was replaced by a raging disappointment. Bloody morons! If he laid hands on them he'd leave them for dead.

The road was quite clear.

Terry went back inside and shot the bolt, then remembering that Sheena was still out drew it back again. He put the guard before the fire and went upstairs. Outside Claire's door he hesitated, full of regretful longing.

Jeeze! He'd really blown the whole thing. Really messed

it all up before it even got going. Remembering the sweet trustful way she had let him touch her naked body Terry felt like weeping. Oh Clairey. He turned away in despair and went into his room.

Terry threw off his clothes and went to the window. The sky had grown a shade lighter. Denis and Barney, he thought bitterly. Bloody bastards! As he reached his hand to jerk across the curtains he looked down and saw the pair of them, hunched like predators on the garden wall.

On Monday morning when his mother asked him, Terry was glad to drive her back to town. Claire avoided him, refusing to speak to him or let him explain. He didn't think he could have stuck it another day.

Left to themselves the girls passed the week much as usual. Sheena said that she was going to the disco with Killian, taking it for granted Claire would stay home and mind Ruthie.

Claire didn't much care if she never went to another disco. She was only sorry she had given in and gone to the last one. She would never forget Terry and herself hand-in-hand on the moonlit quay, talking, laughing, kissing. And then what had followed.

It wasn't fair.

Tears welled and fell on the toast she was burning. She threw it in the bin and cut more bread. She found it hard to concentrate on anything. All the time she kept seeing the firelight and her own naked body. She tried to put it out of her mind but it kept creeping back. She grew hot whenever she recalled the jeering shouts.

She piled scrambled egg on triangles of toast and carried the plates into the other room. Ruthie toyed with crumbling egg. It was not her favourite tea but sometimes it was hard to know what to give her.

"Eat it up," Claire told her. "It's good for you."

Ruthie pushed it away. She didn't care if it was good for her. Upstairs, Sheena was an inordinate length getting ready for the disco. She came down at last wearing one of her mother's silk blouses that was practically see-through.

Sheena winked and did a pirouette before going off to meet Killian. Claire raised her hand and let it fall. When was the last time she and Sheena had held a conversation? Sheena hadn't even asked her how she had got on with her twin. It hurt to think how little interest her friend showed in her life. Sheena seemed to see or hear nothing outside her own pampered existence. Claire sighed and went to get out the draught board. She sat opposite Ruthie, absently moving pieces from square to square.

"You're letting me win," Ruthie complained. She hated it when any of them played down to her.

"No, I'm not." Claire contradicted. She made a determined effort to concentrate. Even so, Ruthie won four games out of five.

"My game again," she said triumphantly, "and I wasn't even trying." She began straightaway laying out the pieces but Claire stopped her.

"Why don't we play beggar-my-neighbour," she suggested. Ruthie agreed enthusiastically. She loved cards even better than board games. Claire pushed all thoughts of Terry out of her mind and forced herself to pay attention but it was a relief when it was time to prepare the cocoa.

Claire tucked Ruthie into bed then went into her own room. She supposed it was better for the little girl to get used to sleeping by herself – Jane was trying to encourage her to become more independent – but she missed the warm feel of the little body curled beside her own. She took her time weaving the strands of her hair into one heavy, golden plait. She snapped on a rubber band and tossed it back, got into bed and picked up her book.

She was reading a writer new to her – F. Scott Fitzgerald. *The Great Gatsby* was like nothing she had ever read. So elegantly written. Claire loved a good story but liked good style even better.

She turned another page and lingered on a passage. This

wasn't a book to be read in a hurry.

Downstairs a door clicked open. Subconsciously, she noted it, her eyes still fixed on the page. It was early for Sheena and Killian. Sheena usually had to be dragged away from the disco while still calling for encores.

Claire read on absently, not really taking the story in, her ear idly tuned to the sound of the creaking stair. Seconds later her bedroom door opened abruptly.

She looked up, not yet alarmed, and saw Denis leering at her from the doorway. Claire sat bolt up in the bed.

"What are you doing here?" she asked, hearing the tremor in her voice.

"Looking for you. What else?"

She ignored what he'd said. This had nothing to do with her. If she admitted that it had she would start screaming. She got out of bed and stood facing him.

"If you're looking for Terry, he's not here," she strove to speak calmly, but sorry as soon as the words were out. Now he'd know she was on her own.

"But I'm not looking for Terry, am I?" Denis lowered himself on to the bed and bounced up and down, testing the springs. "Saw him going off in the car on Monday."

Claire put a hand covertly to her nose. Close-up, the stench of stale beer and cigarettes was overpowering. She heard the stair creaking again and grew dizzy with hope. Barney appeared in the doorway.

"What's keeping you, Denis?"

"Go downstairs," Denis ordered. "Go on. Look sharp."

"I want a beer."

"In the fridge. Take what you want."

With a pleased grunt Barney disappeared. Claire heard him lumbering down the stairs. She gasped as Denis pulled her back across his knees and forced his tongue between her teeth. She gagged. When he slackened pressure she pulled back, choking and coughing.

"I'll show you how good it can be," he promised thickly. "Not like that crud McArdle. You'll see."

"Oh God," Claire prayed, "Please help me."

She twisted away from him and tried to run to the door. He caught hold of her plait and yanked her back. The pain was excruciating. She staggered against him and almost fell.

"Let's see your tits."

He grabbed her pyjamas top. Only that he was so drunk he'd have had it off her back. She gasped as dirty sausage fingers squeezed her nipples. She shoved him away with all her strength but he easily overpowered her and knocked her back on the bed, then fell on top of her, holding her hands rigidly by her sides

Ruthie was calling her. Claire painfully turned her head and saw the little girl struggling in Barney's grip. He had his belt around her chest and he was laughing and letting her run a little distance from him, then jerking her smartly back to him, like a cat toying with a small, frisky mouse.

"Clairey," Ruthie sobbed. "Please help me, Clairey."

Claire made a determined effort to shake off Denis. She almost succeeded but he held on to her plait. Her mind was beginning to blank, but when she heard Ruthie screaming, her courage asserted. She kicked out and felt savagely glad when she heard his grunt of pain. Suddenly the pressure lifted and she gasped in relief.

Killian was in the room. Claire saw him striking Denis with a sweeping brush, great cracking blows across his head and face. Denis fell whimpering to his knees, blood streaming from his forehead. Sheena had her arms around Ruthie, unbuckling the belt, comforting her. Barney had run off. Claire sat up and drew in a sobbing breath. "Oh, thank God," she whispered brokenly.

That night they all slept together in the one room. Claire made Sheena promise not to say anything to Jane. Sheena protested, then seeing how upset her friend was, reluctantly agreed. Claire was afraid that Jane would think she had encouraged the boys to come into the house, afraid that Jane would think she wasn't a fit person to look after Ruthie.

149

It was almost dawn before they settled down to sleep. Ruthie did not hesitate between beds, just climbed in beside her sister. That she wasn't risking herself with Claire was obvious.

Claire felt a sense of isolation. She in her own bed and the sisters together. She did not sleep, just lay there, thinking that since she had come into their lives she had spelled nothing but trouble for the McArdles. Hugh, Jane and now Ruthie. She didn't at all see it the other way round. That would come later, but not for a very long time.

Jane arrived back on Friday evening and noticed at once how despondent the girls were. After one or two attempts to get them talking failed, she let it go and went tiredly to unpack her things.

Later, they sat about the kitchen table, saying little to each other as they listlessly ate the Friday night take-away. Terry hung about for a bit after the meal, hoping for a thaw in Claire's attitude, then took off moodily for his usual haunts.

Ruthie disappeared into the bathroom the minute he left. She was there so long that Jane sent Claire to see if she was all right. When Claire came back she said the door was locked and Ruthie wanted Jane.

Jane went out and spoke through the locked door. She asked if there was anything wrong.

"Come on out," Jane begged her. "We'll make cocoa and take it into bed with us. We'll be lovely and cosy and watch television together."

Ruthie didn't answer.

Jane's neck ached from the effort of bending and speaking through the keyhole. "You love it. You know you do."

There was no sound. Perhaps she wanted Claire. Jane felt a little jealous. She supposed it was only natural that Ruthie would want to be with the older girl, who spoiled her rotten all week. While she was away in Dublin working herself to the bone. Jane couldn't help a trace of self-pity.

"Very well," she said, trying to hide her hurt. "Sleep with Claire, if that's what you want. Only come out now."

The door remained closed.

In desperation Jane went up to Claire's room and was surprised to find the girl already in bed. Sheena had gone off earlier to the disco with Killian, admittedly with none of her usual bounce.

Claire laid down the book she was holding. Jane wondered why Claire hadn't offered to try and get Ruthie out of the bathroom.

"I can't understand what's the matter with Ruthie," Jane said, noticing that Claire looked unusually pale. She felt a sudden stab of conscience at leaving her so much with the little girl. Not that Ruthie was a difficult child but she was inclined to be demanding since her father died. Jane suddenly regretted not insisting that Claire go with the others to the disco.

"I think she's a bit upset," Claire said.

Jane stared at her, unable to understand her detachment. Something was definitely wrong.

Jane sat down on the bed. "What is it, Claire?" she asked gently. "Has something happened?"

Claire flushed and looked down at her book. Jane noticed the slim fingers gripping the cover, so tight the knuckles had changed colour.

"I'd like to go home," Claire said abruptly.

Jane was taken aback. This was the very last thing she had expected to hear. "But I thought you were happy here," she said, bewildered. "Besides, there's only another week before we all go home. Don't you want to stay until then?"

"I'm sorry," Claire faltered. "I didn't mean to sound ungrateful but I'd really like to go at once." She looked desperately at Jane.

Here she was thinking something had happened and it was only that Claire had tired of minding Ruthie and wanted to go home. Jane felt an enormous sense of let-down but strove to be fair. After all, it couldn't be much fun for a teenager left all day minding an eight-year-old She shrugged and stood up.

"Very well, Claire," she said, a little coldly. "If that's what

151

you want, I'll drive you to Waterford tomorrow. There's a train around midday."

"I'm sorry," Claire said abjectly.

"I'm sorry too." Jane was unable to conceal a note of disillusionment. "I had hoped you liked sharing these holidays with us. I know it's not very exciting left with Ruthie so much but you should have told me before if you weren't happy."

Claire winced. She looked as though she were going to cry.

"Well, it can't be helped." Jane tried to smile. She felt deathly tired. "We'll just have to get along without you somehow." A slight unintentional irony tinged her voice. "Goodnight, my dear." She went out without looking back or waiting for Claire's reply.

As soon as the door closed Claire burst into tears. She knew that she had mortally offended Jane. She pulled the pillow over her face to deaden the sound and sobbed as though her heart would break.

Ruthie finally came out of the bathroom of her own accord. She appeared suddenly in the kitchen as Jane was reading the paper and threw herself weeping into her mother's arms.

"There, there, everything's all right," Jane soothed her.

"Mummy, Mummy," Ruthie bawled. She was still dressed in her shirt and denims. Her tears soaked Jane's blouse. After a while Jane said, "Let's get you changed, love," and took her into the bedroom and undressed her. As she put her in a nightie she noticed the angry bruises on Ruthie's chest. She said nothing, but she felt a stirring of fear. Who or what could have caused such marks? She lifted the little girl into bed and pulled the duvet over her.

Ruthie sat up. "Don't go, Mummy," she cried. "You won't, will you?"

Jane shook her head. The child lay down again and watched her undress, her eyes enormous in her pale face. Now Jane was convinced there was really something terribly wrong. She put on her dressing gown and drew the cord firmly about her waist. When Ruthie was asleep she went to sit by the fire until Sheena got home.

Just before eleven o'clock she heard the key in the door and Sheena and her boyfriend came in. It needed only a gentle prompt to get Sheena going and she blurted out the whole scary story. Jane was horrified. No wonder Claire wanted to go home, she thought, and Ruthie spent half the night hiding in the bathroom, the only room in the house with a lock. The animals, Jane thought in a rush of anger.

"For God's sake, Sheena, why didn't you tell me all this earlier?" In her weariness, Jane's anxiety turned to exasperation. "I can't understand why you didn't." She looked severely at her daughter. "Most irresponsible."

Sheena burst into tears. Jane stared at her aghast. Sheena never cried.

"Oh darling, I'm sorry. Forgive me. I didn't mean it," Jane babbled remorsefully, shocked by all these disturbing revelations. "I don't know what I'm saying. You were marvellous, all of you. I was just so upset and worried. Please don't cry."

Sheena gulped and choked. She took the handkerchief Killian handed her and mopped her tears. When she could speak, she said, "But I wanted to ring you, Mummy. I really did, only Claire begged and begged me not to. She was afraid you'd blame her."

"Blame her . . . why should I do that?" Jane asked, genuinely puzzled.

Sheena shrugged. "Dunno. She gets funny notions, Claire. She even wanted to go home before you came but felt it wouldn't be right to leave Ruthie."

Jane sighed and stood up. Poor Claire. She might have been Ruthie's older sister the way everyone took it for granted she must accept responsibility for her. Jane felt ashamed at how casually they all used her. What an ordeal. She turned to Killian.

"I can't thank you enough for all you did," she told him. "I dread to think what would have happened if you hadn't been here."

"It was nothing at all, Dr McArdle," Killian said, looking pleased. He was really rather a dote. Jane hugged him and Sheena shyly squeezed his hand. Jane looked at her watch and smiled at them both.

"Off home with you now, Killian," she said gently. "It's time we were all in bed." She saw him out and shut the door behind him. Sheena went tiredly up the stairs.

Jane suddenly yawned. It seemed like an eternity since she had got into the car that afternoon to drive to the country. She would get the whole thing straightened out, she promised herself. First thing in the morning she would have a chat with Garda Deveney next door. But just now she couldn't wait to get into bed. Before falling asleep she reminded herself that this was a sensitive situation and she must warn Terry to be careful what he said to Claire.

There wasn't any need. Sheena already had.

For the next few days everything seemed back to normal. Ruthie appeared to be putting the ordeal behind her though she showed a tendency to wake up at night and cry for her mother. Claire too felt her spirits gradually lifting.

Jane had taken her aside the next morning and gently drawn the whole story from her. Claire cried as she told it, partly from distress and partly from relief that the air was cleared between them. Jane took her in her arms and comforted her. She told Claire she had decided to remain with them until it was time for them all to pack up and go.

"So I hope you'll think twice about going home. We really want you to stay."

Claire nodded, then blushed when Jane went on to say how proud she was of the way she had fought off her attackers and done her best to protect Ruthie.

"It's a debt I can never repay," Jane said and hugged Claire again, relieved to see the look of shamed desperation ease from her face. "I want you to know I trust you completely and there's no one I would rather have to mind Ruthie than you."

Claire looked embarrassed. "But Sheena is really good

with Ruthie," she protested loyally. "She's always getting up at night to bring her to the toilet. Honestly!"

"I'm glad to hear it," Jane said, unconvinced. She knew how little Sheena ever exerted herself. "So it's a bargain?" Jane squeezed Claire's hand affectionately. "You'll wait and come home with us at the end of the week?"

Claire nodded and shyly returned the squeeze. With Jane staying on in the cottage, she no longer felt such a desperate need to get away. One thing bothered her. Had Terry been told?

Jane nodded. "When he heard I'm afraid he got a bit carried away and took things into his own hands. You know Terry." She smiled ruefully. "I suspect he rather enjoyed himself."

Claire smiled, her heart lifting at the thought of him going to her defence.

By the middle of the week she felt so much better that she suggested to Ruthie that they get out the billy-cans and go into the field behind the bungalows to pick blackberries. They collected enough fruit to make a couple of pies and came giggling into the house, their lips and fingers stained purple. When Jane exclaimed over how much they had picked the two girls began talking at once.

"We would have had loads more," Claire said, with an impish glance at Ruthie, "only a certain young lady ate far more berries than she put in the can."

"Oh I like that!" Ruthie moaned. "Don't listen to her, Mummy. Claire ate twice as many as me."

"I don't think so!" Claire grinned at Jane. "I seem to remember someone saying, 'One for the billy-can, two for me.' Now I wonder who in the world that was?"

Jane laughed and hustled Ruthie before her into the kitchen. She pretended to be cross as she removed the evidence with a face-cloth and soap, but secretly Jane was delighted to see them so jolly. How could she ever have imagined that Claire resented minding Ruthie, when her affection was so apparent in every smile and caress she gave the little girl?

They were all very light-hearted that evening as they tucked into delicious slices of blackberry pie, topped with cream, that Sheena had generously offered to make. Besides, she was rather good at pastry and wanted to impress Killian, who had been invited to tea. Jane was just as glad to let her.

There were jokes made about Sheena's pastry but there wasn't a scrap left over. Terry sighed over his third helping and pretended to vomit. Sheena threatened to take it away from him and, while Killian held his arms, Ruthie ran giggling to get her brother's dish. They all insisted he take back his words or forfeit the pie and Terry, pretending to be scared, dutifully begged for mercy.

Claire loved it when the McArdles cod-acted like this.

Great to see them perking up again, Jane thought as she watched their antics with a smile.

It was the last night of the disco and the last night of the holidays. They were all a little sad that the summer holiday was ending but pleased to finish it off with a dance. Sheena and Killian were going. So were Terry and Claire. And Susan Deveney from next door.

Claire told herself she didn't mind. Terry hadn't even looked at Susan this holiday. All the same she intended painting her nails and begging a spray of perfume from Sheena.

Jane thought it might be nice to wind up the holiday by eating out, so she brought them to the hotel for a meal and ordered wine, pouring a little for each of them, even a drop for Ruthie. As the level of the bottle sank Jane became relaxed and giggly. The children watched her with tolerant smiles, liking this aspect of their mother they didn't often see these days. On nights out their parents had always taken wine with their meal and, afterwards, gone into the bar for brandies.

"Why don't you have brandy tonight, Mum?" Terry suggested, reminded of happier times.

"Okay, I will," Jane agreed. "Why not? It's back to the grind on Monday." When it came, she cupped her hands about the balloon glass and smiled around at them.

"Please let me hold it, Mummy," Ruthie begged, and when her mother passed it to her, sniffed with an ecstatic expression. "Mmmm. Nice."

"Our little connoisseur," Terry flicked her head affectionately with his fingernails. "Soon Coke won't be good enough for her. She'll insist on brandy."

"Yes," agreed Ruthie. "I can't wait." She reluctantly surrendered the glass as they laughed.

"To next year," Jane toasted, looking about with a warm expression in her blue eyes. "I suppose we should be more adventurous in our choice of holidays but I can't ever see us not wanting to come back here, can you?"

Claire was silent, thinking she had once felt this way but now wasn't so sure. Still, she told herself, she shouldn't let one isolated incident spoil years of enjoyment. "Experience in itself is not so important," she wisely reminded herself, "as the use you make of it."

They lingered, loth to break the happy mood, and when they eventually stirred themselves, they had to walk back fast to the cottage to get ready for the disco. Claire was about to run upstairs when Ruthie said she wanted to go to the shops for some fake sweet cigarettes she had developed a craze for.

"Oh Ruthie," Claire sighed. "Do you have to?" But she hadn't the heart to refuse her. "You go ahead," she said to Sheena resignedly. "We'll be back before you know it."

"Okay, but hurry," Sheena said. "I told Killian we'd meet him there and I don't want to be late." She ran off to get changed, as usual content to let Claire take care of things. Terry had already parted from them at the hotel, promising to meet up later.

Jane smiled her thanks at Claire. "Good girl," she praised, relieved after all that lovely food and drink not to have to go out again. She was looking forward to putting her feet up before tackling the packing. Anyway, it wasn't as if she could drive, she absolved herself.

Claire went round to the shed to get out the bikes. The light was beginning to fade. Let's hope we don't run into Sergeant Flynn, she thought. None of the bikes had lamps. She tucked her jeans into her socks and called out to Ruthie, "First one to the shops gets a surprise." It worked. Ruthie flung herself on her bike and pedalled strongly away. Claire grinned and followed her.

They flew down the road and turned right at the post box. Claire passed Ruthie, then slowed to allow her take the lead. The little girl shot past, her hair flying out behind her in a silky curtain. Her legs flashed, sturdy and tanned, in navy linen shorts. She was really becoming very pretty.

Taking after Eddie, Claire thought with a pang. Although she admired Jane, she would not describe her as beautiful. Eddie had undoubtedly possessed the best looks in the family. Terry and Sheena took strongly after him, and now Ruthie promised to be even more striking than her sister, which was saying a lot.

They covered the last half-mile in record time and with a crow of delight Ruthie leapt off her bike and waited for Claire to catch up.

"My surprise! my surprise!" she cried.

"Okay," Claire said, playing for time, "you wait here and I'll go into the shop. But you mustn't peek or the magic will vanish." Ruthie nodded eagerly and climbed back on her bike.

Claire went into the shop and picked out a packet of sweet cigarettes then, keeping a watchful eye through the window, reached across the counter for a Lucky Bag and a comic. She hid them under the evening paper and, as she glanced around again, glimpsed Ruthie cycling past. She waved but the little girl did not see her.

There was a queue at the counter. Claire glanced at her watch and prayed that Mrs Cummins would get to her soon. The woman loved a bit of gossip and was reluctant to allow any of them escape before she exacted her toll. Claire sighed and tried not to mind. It was just the country way of life.

Ruthie weaved her way happily about the perimeter of the shops. Head down, she pressed the pedals as hard and fast as they would go, speeding down the laneway leading to the sheds at the rear. This time, she told herself, she would go all the way to the far wall, touch it and come back. Empty cans and mineral bottles were strewn in her way and she deftly circled them until she reached her target then, extending her fingers, brushed the brickwork. Done! She was so intent on her game that she did not notice how dark it had become as she clocked up yet another trip.

Two figures materialised out of the dusk and stepped in front of the bike. Ruthie saw them too late and was brought down with jarring suddenness, collapsing in a tangle of spokes and rubber. As she tried to get up, the handlebars spitefully sprang back at her, jabbing her agonisingly under the chin. Tears stung her eyes and she cried out with the surprise and pain of it.

When she recovered from the shock, she pushed herself on to her hunkers and weakly pushed the hair out of her eyes. Across the waste ground from her, at the level of her own eyes, she saw a pair of scuffed canvas runners. Slowly, she lifted her eyes past the jagged holes in the tattered jeans to the face lit by the reflected glow from the neon light of the chip shop. She climbed stiffly back on her bike and tried to ride on past.

"What's your hurry?" Denis barred her way.

Ruthie opened her mouth and the words came tumbling out of her shaking lips. "Let me go," she begged.

"No-one stopping you." Denis moved closer and put his hand on her arm. His face still bore the marks of the punch-up between Terry and himself. "Where's that big tough brother of yours?" he asked.

"He's in the shop waiting for me." She twisted her head away as Barney put his grubby hand on her hair.

"Little Goldilocks," he said.

Again, Ruthie attempted to cycle past them and thought she had succeeded in getting clear at last, when she felt a heavy weight bearing down on her back carrier. As she was dragged to a stop, she turned with a frightened little cry to face her persecutors.

Claire came out of the shop with her purchases and looked about. There was no sign of Ruthie. She sighed and resigned herself to a brief wait, fully expecting Ruthie to round the corner or pop out from some hiding place with a triumphant shout. Nothing happened. It occurred to her that Ruthie might have cycled ahead.

She mounted her bicycle and headed back down the road. Even now Ruthie was probably with Jane having a giggle over giving her the slip. Little chancer, Claire thought with a grin, pedalling faster.

"No, she's not back," Jane said, looking up in surprise when Claire ran in. "I thought you were together."

"Oh, but we were," Claire said, upset. She had been so sure the little girl would be there before her. "I was in the shop getting her a surprise and she wasn't meant to know what it was – " she broke off.

"But surely you could see her from the shop?" Jane asked, her sleepy expression vanishing. She stood up.

"Yes . . . in the beginning, but then I thought she was playing a joke . . ." Claire's voice tailed away.

"Let's not panic," Jane said, a slight tremor in her voice. "We must go back to the shop at once," she decided.

Jane took the car keys from her bag and went outside. Garda Deveney was going in his door and she paused beside her car and called to him.

"No, I didn't see Ruthie," he said, then sensing Jane's agitation, "Do you want me to go down the road and look for her?"

"That's most kind of you, Bill. With two of us searching we'll find her in no time. We're heading back to Cummins' shop," she went on, as Claire slipped into the seat beside her. "That's where she was when Claire lost sight of her."

"I'll take the station road so," the Garda said, and seeing Jane's anxious expression added kindly, "Don't worry. She's probably just lost count of the time."

Jane nodded and drove off. She was down the road before she remembered to switch on her lights.

A new group had gathered in the thirty minutes or so since Claire was in the shop. Mrs Cummins sighed and shook her head at Jane's anxious questions. "Wisha, I know the young lassie well, so I do. And all of your children, Doctor. I'd surely remember if she was here. Indeed'n I would. She was in yesterday, right enough, but not today. Just that young miss there," she said, pointing at Claire.

"But hold on now," Mrs Cummins said, coming out from behind the counter. "Mick might have seen her, so he might. Nothing escapes that fellah's notice."

They all waited in silence while she went to the beaded curtain, dividing the front of the shop from the back premises, and called her husband.

But no, Mick hadn't seen Ruthie either. He came out, scratching his head and puzzling over when he'd last laid eyes on the little girl. Mrs Cummins appealed to those standing about the shop and they willingly entered into the discussion.

"Would she be about three or four?" one of them asked.

"Ah, not at all," said Mrs Cummins. "She's a big lassie, made her First Communion and all."

Jane tried to contain her impatience, on knife-edge with worry. They were well-meaning, but of no help. She felt hysteria slowly building up as in a leisurely manner they thrashed it out between them. She cut them short as politely as she could and, in the sudden silence, thanked them for their help. She was conscious of their voices starting up again behind her as she left the shop. Oh God, Jane thought. She had gained nothing, merely wasted precious minutes. It was now almost fifty minutes since Claire had last seen Ruthie passing the shop door.

Jane knew she was beginning to panic and took a tighter grip on herself. She bent over the wheel, agonising it out. Claire watched her, miserably aware she should never have left Ruthie on her own. It was all her fault.

Jane decided to go back to the cottage. Bill Deveney might have found Ruthie and brought her there. Or he might have heard something, anything which would give them direction. Quickly the Rover covered the mile and a half distance. When Jane swung into the driveway and saw two figures standing in the doorway, her heart leapt. But it was only Sheena and Killian, puzzled at finding no-one at home.

"No," Sheena replied in answer to her questions. "We haven't seen her. We just walked up from the quay to collect Claire and bring her back with us to the disco."

Jane got back in the car. At least that was another route they needn't take. She was badly frightened, hardly able to hide her fear.

"Will we come with you, Mummy?" Sheena called, but Jane shook her head. Someone should stay behind in case Ruthie returned. Or Garda Deveney.

With Claire beside her, Jane drove off again. She was now completely sober. It was pitch dark. She flicked on her full headlights. A car was coming towards them fast along the road. When it was almost up to them it slowed and stopped. Jane recognised Bill's car with – thank heavens – Ruthie's bike sticking out of the boot. Thank God, oh thank God. She braked and got out.

"I've got her," Bill said. "She's all right. Just shaken. You'd best go to her." She hurried around to the passenger side where Ruthie sat huddled on the seat.

Jane reached for her daughter and held her tight. It was a full minute before she realised that Ruthie's hair had been cut off.

"Here, Doctor," Bill appeared at her side. "Let me give you a hand with her."

With his help, Jane put Ruthie into her own car. Claire

climbed into the back and put her arms about the child.

In convoy, they drove back along the narrow roads to the cottage, Ruthie's bike bumping and clattering crazily behind. Bill carried Ruthie into the house and, in response to Sheena's gabble of questions, Jane tersely told her to make a cup of tea and sugar it well. Sheena rushed to obey.

Jane laid the shivering child on her bed and pulled the duvet warmly about her. Ruthie lay very still, her eyes closed, her butchered hair spiking unevenly about her head. Jane gave a choked cry and gathered her close. She sat like that for a long time.

When Sheena brought in the tea Jane gave Ruthie a sedative and fed her tiny sips of the hot sweet liquid. Then she left Sheena and Claire with her and went out to speak to Bill. He was sitting with Killian and stood up with a sympathetic cough when she appeared. The boy tactfully disappeared into the kitchen.

"Where was she, Bill?" Jane asked. She felt very old and tired.

"In the chip shop," Bill said. "They brought her in there after one of the lassies caught some boys tormenting her and chased them off."

Jane felt her knees give and sank down on the settee. The memory of Ruthie in her First Communion dress, her golden hair spread out on her shoulders beneath the snowy veil, came back to her. It was only last year. Another picture flashed into her head. Eddie's face the day he carried Ruthie home from the nursing home. Proud and doting, smiling down at the little silky head.

Her beautiful hair.

Oh God! Jane thought. What kind of brats would mutilate an eight-year-old?

Bill disappeared and came back carrying the whisky bottle. He poured a tot and handed it to her. "Take this, Doctor," he said. "You've had a bad shock."

Jane took a sip and thrust it from her. No. She wanted to keep a clear head. Enough had been drunk today. Oh, why couldn't she have stuck to the wine? she thought in anguish. She never regretted anything so much in her life as that indulgent glass of brandy. Without it, she would never have allowed Ruthie and Claire go off in the dusk on their own.

Jane took a deep breath and, turning to Bill, asked him who could have done such a thing. He said from what the girl had told him it appeared that it was two local lads. One was in his late teens, the other older and slow-witted.

Jane supposed she had known all along.

Which reminded her that Terry was still out. When Garda Deveney departed with a last sympathetic glance, she called Killian and asked him to go down to the disco and see if he could find Terry. They should all be home tonight, Jane said. He went off at once, glad to have something to do.

Jane went back into the bedroom where Claire was sitting with Ruthie and suggested to the older girl that she might like to go upstairs and begin her packing. Claire got up obediently.

"Thank you, Claire," said Jane, gently dismissing her and closing the bedroom door.

Ruthie was still awake despite the sedative, and she lay submissive and uncomplaining while Jane carried out her examination. She was as gentle as she could be, but it was important to know just what had occurred. The child's knees were grazed and there were ugly scorch marks like cigarette burns on her thighs but when she gently felt between her legs there was no evidence that she had been assaulted. Jane caught her breath on a sigh of gratitude and relief.

Ruthie lay with closed eyes all the while Jane tended her, saying never a word. It broke Jane's heart to see her so silent and withdrawn. She would rather have had her crying, screaming, abusive even. Anything rather than this terrible stillness.

When Terry came in shortly afterwards Jane left him in charge and went down to the police station. She told Sergeant Flynn what had happened and he listened with a

164

troubled expression. Dr McArdle was well liked in Dualeen. She had always been quick to respond to emergency calls, even though she was on holiday, and there was nothing but sympathy and respect for her amongst the townspeople. The sergeant remembered the tragic case of her husband and son and thought it was a terrible shame that such a decent woman should have so much hardship in her life.

"I'm really sorry for your trouble, ma'am," he said gently. "If there's anything at all in my power to do, believe me, I'll do it."

His sympathy snapped Jane's control. "Dear God, Sergeant," she said brokenly, "what kind are they to do such a thing?"

"It's a sign of the times," he said, with a troubled look at her. "Crazed by drugs and drink. They don't know what they're doing half the time."

"Oh no, Sergeant. I won't accept that one," Jane cried. "That's too easy. That lets them out of responsibility. Those same delinquents broke into my cottage last week while I was away and terrorised my family."

Sergeant Flynn looked alertly at her. "Did you report this?"

Jane shook her head. She didn't know why she hadn't. Perhaps she had been too anxious to believe it couldn't happen again. Or too willing just to try and put it behind them.

The sergeant briskly reached for pen and paper. "With this we'll be able to get them before the district court," he said. "Breaking and entering, assault and attempted rape. Then we'll take it from there."

Jane was relieved. The sergeant gave her forms, helped her to fill them out, then witnessed her signature. She thanked him and drove back to the cottage, feeling emotionally washed-out.

She found a subdued household on her return. Every last thing had been packed in readiness for the journey next day, the cottage swept and tidied and even the bikes lined up in the hall, to enable a quick departure. Jane was touched almost to the point of tears. How responsible they had become all of a sudden, she thought. There was nothing like trouble to hasten the maturing process. She only wished it could be some other way.

She went into the bedroom where Claire sat patiently at Ruthie's bedside and learned that the little girl had fallen asleep soon after she had left. She had been a bit restless at first, Claire told her.

Jane thanked her and went to make a pot of tea before bedtime. As she stood in the kitchen she glanced at her watch and could not believe that it wasn't yet eleven. The disco would still be going on, the music blaring away, young people dancing. Everything so normal and pleasant on the surface, she thought a little bitterly. How disappointed the children must be, missing the fun on their last night in Dualeen.

Sheena and Killian sat huddled together on the settee, sad at the thought of parting. They had vowed to write to each other every day and Killian was already planning a visit to Dublin at Halloween. Across the room Terry sat gazing into space, a grim cast to his features.

Terry had always been greatly attached to his little sister. After Eddie and Hugh died, he had in effect taken on the dual role of parent and brother. Terry had often keenly felt the loss of a father himself, but never so much as now. He felt out of his depth. He was only seventeen, after all.

He went into the bedroom at last. Claire sat beside the bed, a book on her knee, so quiet he was not at first aware of her. She met his eyes gravely and he was struck by her look of compassion.

Terry looked down at his sleeping sister. No one had prepared him for the butchered hair. He was horrified, remembering the feel of it, like silk to his touch. He felt a lump in his throat.

"Bloody shits," he railed in helpless rage. He should have killed Denis when he had the chance, he thought. Kicked the loathsome bag of tripe until he spilled his guts. One less load of garbage in the world.

Ruthie moaned piteously in her sleep. At the sound, Terry's mouth wobbled out of control. He turned his head sharply and felt his throat constrict again with tears.

The house was quiet. Jane had gone into her bedroom and quietly closed the door, careful not to waken Ruthie, and the older girls were upstairs preparing for bed. Terry sat in the living-room, too full of anguished reflections to be able to sleep. He threw another sod on the fire and sank back on the settee. He was so deep in thought he hardly heard the soft tapping on the outer door and it was a minute or two before he reacted.

When Terry drew back the bolts and opened the door he found Garda Deveney on the step outside.

"Goodnight, Terry. I hope I'm not calling too late." Bill stepped into the tiny hallway and when Terry turned back inside to call Jane, said at once, "No, don't disturb your mother. I've only dropped in for a moment."

He followed Terry into the living-room and kept his top-coat on while he explained his reason for calling at the advanced hour.

"I thought your mother would be anxious to know. You can tell her in the morning, but the young one in the chip shop is prepared to sign a statement as to the identity of the two lads who attacked your sister. We picked them up a short while ago and took them to the station for questioning. They'll be charged and will go before the district court in another week or two." Bill paused and cast a quick look towards the bedroom door then carefully drew something out of his pocket.

Terry shivered as recognised the shining hank of Ruthie's hair.

"Wait until you get home before telling your mother," Bill advised. "She's been through enough as it is and 'twill only upset her to hear about it tonight. Of course, we'll have to hold on to it as evidence in the event of a trial."

"But where was it?" Terry stammered. "I mean, how did

you get it?"

"We took it off the daft one." Disgust thickened the Garda's tone. "He was wearing it in his belt like some Apache trophy, the poor sick bastard."

Terry clenched his fists, swamped by feelings of rage and helplessness. He looked closely at the hair and burned afresh when he saw the piece of rusty wire binding it. His expression was grim as he searched about and found a bag. He placed his sister's hair in it and wordlessly handed it back to Deveney. Then Terry went to stare out of the window, struggling with his emotions.

Bill seemed to understand what he was going through and waited another moment before he said, "Those are the same young lads you used knock about with if I'm not mistaken?"

Terry nodded and his face reddened as he was reminded of the nightly racket that they used all of them make, returning from the disco.

"You seem a nice young chap," Bill went on. "Now what would you be mixing with the likes of them for?" When Terry remained silent he said, "Would you listen to a word of advice? Keep clear of the drink. It's all very well in its way, but too much of it leads to all kinds of excesses." His tone became gentler when he saw Terry's discomfited expression. "Good lad now, good lad. Sure, don't we all get led the wrong way at some time or other in our lives?"

He walked towards the door and Terry followed him, his thoughts painful. Bill stepped outside, then glanced back at Terry and said, "Don't think I don't know what you're feeling. It's only when it comes to our own doorstep that we recognise how primitive we are deep down. There's a lot of evil in the world and a lot of good too. Our job is to do what we can about combatting the one and keeping faith with the other." When Terry kept silent he said, "You're a fine strong young chap. Have you ever thought of joining the Force?"

"I've thought about applying to the army," Terry admitted, "but I'm not really sure what I want to do."

"Ah, there's plenty of time yet. You have more schooling

to get through?"

Terry nodded. "Another year."

"Well, have a think about the Force. There's a strong need for young men like yourself. But the army is a good life too. Plenty of discipline and plenty of action. You'll never be bored anyway." He chuckled quietly. "Ah, you mightn't believe it, but we see plenty of action ourselves, even down here in a quiet little spot like Dualeen."

Terry murmured in polite agreement.

"Well, I'll be off and let you to bed. I'm on the first shift in the morning."

"Sorry about all that noise," Terry said awkwardly, but Bill laughed and brushed aside his apology.

"There were times, I'll admit, when I could have clapped you in the cells, but sure wasn't I a rumbustious young divil meself once." Lifting his hand in a friendly salute he went back to his side of the fence.

Terry closed the door, feeling curiously comforted by the other man's warmth and understanding. Then he grinned ruefully as he was reminded how only a few short weeks earlier he had been comparing the man to a maniac.

Terry switched off the lights and placed the guard before the fire. Deveney wasn't a bad sort, he thought, feeling cheered. He might be right about the Force, but given a choice he thought he would prefer to become a pilot. As he went up to bed he was reminded of what Bill had said about the Gardaí charging Denis and Barney, and felt suddenly more hopeful than he had all evening.

The following evening Jane relaxed after the journey from the country, glad to have the long drive behind her and the week's shopping unpacked and put away in the fridge and freezer. She sipped her tea and turned the pages of *The Irish Times* and thought that in another few minutes she would go up and say goodnight to Ruthie.

She sighed. Ruthie was still deeply shocked from her ordeal but was thankfully beginning to come out of the daze

169

she had been in since Garda Deveney had found her the evening before. It was too early to say yet what the long term effect on her would be and Jane was uneasily prepared for the reaction, when it came, to be a violent one. She had decided it would be best not to leave the little girl for any length on her own. Sheena was with her now. Ruthie's sense of security had been badly shaken by this second fright in the space of a few days and it would take a long time to build up her confidence again. Jane reminded herself that it could have been a lot worse, and gave fervent thanks that the child had been rescued in time. Now she distracted herself by reading an account of the Ulster Unionists' protest against the Anglo-Irish Agreement and was moving on to another section of the paper as Terry came into the kitchen.

"Mum," he said gravely. "I've got something to tell you."

"What is it?" Jane looked up, surprised at his tone.

Terry sat down at the table across from her and solemnly related all that Garda Deveney had said the previous night, how Denis and Barney would be charged and go before the district court. Then Terry went on awkwardly, for fear of distressing her, to describe how Bill had taken Ruthie's hair from his pocket and shown it to him.

"God! Mum, it was held together with a piece of rusty wire," Terry exploded, unable to contain his anger. "Her lovely hair!"

Jane's face registered her shock. "But where did Bill get it?" Even as she spoke she knew. He got it from them.

"I got a bag and wrapped it up", Terry said, remembering his wish at the time that it had been tissue paper.

"For God's sake, why didn't you tell me before now?" Jane demanded.

"Bill told me not to," Terry said simply. "That it would only upset you."

Jane was silent, touched by Bill's consideration. He was a decent man. That decides it, she was thinking. Now she would do everything in her power to see that those barbarians were convicted.

Terry observed her for a moment, his own expression troubled, then he slipped from the room.

Much later that evening the telephone rang. Jane was preparing to go up to bed and when Terry called softly from the landing so as not to waken Ruthie, she went into her surgery to take it.

It was Bill Deveney and his voice sounded tired. "We've suffered a bit of a setback, Doctor," he said heavily. "I'm sorry to say, but the young one from the chip shop has withdrawn her statement."

Jane's spirits, already low, descended even further.

"'Tis obvious she's got the wind up," the Garda went on, "and as luck would have it she's our only witness. The two boyos are denying they had anything to do with the attack. They've concocted a story to explain how they came into possession of the little girl's hair. The daft one isn't reliable – he'll say anything the other one tells him – but he's the one that was holding the hair when we picked them up. The main thing is the other fellah has produced an alibi for himself that may just stand up under cross-examination."

"So can anything at all be done to them now?" Jane asked, her own tone as leaden as her thoughts.

"All is not lost yet, not by a long chalk," Bill assured her, "Ah, no, no. We still have the evidence and there's the child's own testimony."

Jane sighed, feeling she had come full circle. How could she put Ruthie through that ordeal?

"So what's the next step?" she asked in resignation.

"We'll submit the details to the Director for Public Prosecution and he'll have the final ruling on whether we'll proceed with the case or not."

Jane took a deep breath. "Tell me honestly, Bill. What are our chances of getting a conviction?"

Bill took his time replying. "With the young one's statement we'd have been home and dry. But as it is, we'd need to break the alibi and have your child go on the stand to give evidence of the assault. All other things being equal, we

171

might be able to make it stick."

Jane decided she could not let Ruthie be subjected to the stress of such an interrogation, not after all she had been through, but when she said so to Bill it seemed they no longer had that option.

"I'm afraid it will have to go now to the DPP whether we like it or not."

Jane felt as though the nightmare were going on and on. She listened to the rest of what Bill had to say in silence. He was obviously aware of her distress for he said gruffly that he would be in touch with her again when they received the DPP's findings. And with a last promise to do all in his power to hurry things along, he bid her goodnight and rang off.

Jane replaced the receiver and leant back in her chair. All her earlier desire for vengeance had quite left her. The price to Ruthie was too high. She felt all played out. They are best left to the Lord, she thought brokenly, and let us get on with our lives.

The weeks passed slowly and all the time Jane was conscious of the impending decision hovering over them like a storm cloud. How would it all turn out? Some times Jane felt it might be best if the case went to court. Horrendous though the experience might be, it would not last for ever, and once it was over they could, at least, start looking forward to better times. At other times, usually towards evening when she was tired and depressed or Ruthie had been more than usually difficult that day, she quaked at the very thought of all that was involved and desperately prayed it would not happen.

By the end of October Jane had got to the stage when she felt any decision would be a relief. The waiting and still not knowing was the worst part. Just when Jane was deciding she would go down to Waterford and find out for herself, Bill Deveney rang her at the clinic one morning with the long-awaited news. The DPP had declared that there was insufficient evidence to bring an action and recommended that they drop the case. Jane felt weak with relief. Thank God! It was better this way, she thought.

"I'm fierce sorry, Doctor," Bill said, sounding every bit of it. "'Tis terrible to think of that pair getting off scot-free. If it's any consolation to you, we'll be keeping a close watch on them from now on. Their sort always go on breaking laws until they get put away." Jane could not find it in herself to be really sorry. The memory of her own attendance in court for the inquest into Eddie's and Hugh's deaths and all the hassle involved made her want to steer clear now of any involvement in legal matters. But most important of all was Ruthie's well-being. Court proceedings would have been an intolerable burden to place on the child, not to mention the effect on the rest of the family. In the circumstances, the DPP's decision could only be regarded as fortuitous.

Several mornings later, not long after the children had left for school, the postman rang the doorbell and delivered a small package. Jane took it from him and glanced at the postmark. Yes, it was the one she had been expecting.

She got a scissors and snipped the string then carefully withdrew the contents. The soft mass of Ruthie's golden hair lay on the table before her and Jane caught her breath at the forgotten beauty of it. She sank down feeling suddenly weak, remembering how often in the past she had washed and dried it, given it the recommended one hundred strokes.

Safe from interruption with everyone out of the house, Jane shampooed the hair, handling it with great care. When it was dry she removed the barbarous piece of wire and tied the golden mane in a piece of white ribbon, one Ruthie had worn on her First Communion Day.

Jane's eyes were full of tears as she laid Ruthie's hair in tissue paper and locked it away in a drawer. Some day she would show it to her, she thought. Some day perhaps Ruthie might even wear it as a hairpiece. Jane wondered if that day would ever come.

As the months passed Claire was saddened to find on her visits to the McArdle's house that Ruthie was making so little progress after the trauma of the summer. The sunniness which had been the mark of the little girl's temperament had vanished since her return from the limbo she had occupied in the days after the attack, and now she was broody, inclined to sudden fits of temper, followed by weeping. She had never been a whingey child but this now became her normal conversational tone.

For a time Ruthie was hostile towards Claire and refused to listen to her stories or accept help with her homework. Sometimes she met her at the door with cries of, "Go away, Claire. This isn't your house. We don't want you here," and when Jane gently remonstrated with her, burst into noisy tears, crying, "You're all so mean to me. I wish I could die."

Claire was disconcerted by the change she saw in her and found it difficult to respond to this demanding, nervy little girl. It was as if Ruthie were saying, you let it happen to me, now see how you like what I've become. It was almost too much to bear Claire thought. She had been looking after Ruthie and she had let her down.

But after the initial defiant outbursts Ruthie clung to Claire more fiercely than she had ever done, as though afraid that Claire might reject her. Where before Ruthie naturally accepted affection as her due, now she grimly exacted it. Claire found this naked appeal as distressing as her short-lived animosity. Sometimes Claire surprised a wary, placating expression in Jane's eyes as she watched them together, as if she were afraid Claire's patience might snap and then there would only be herself to love and help the little girl.

One afternoon Jane broke down before Claire and confessed her earlier fear that if the case had gone to court the strain would have proved too much for Ruthie. From all Jane said it was clear that she had suffered intensely over the weeks of waiting for the DPP's decision. Claire realised that for Jane to confide in her like she was doing must mean that she was still very close to the edge. She realised too that, whatever about her own difficulties with Ruthie, it was much harder for Jane, forced to watch her youngest child change from an adorable innocent to this irritable, restless spirit. She resolved to visit oftener and try and help to lift some of the burden from her. When she did, more often than not Claire returned to her studies with an aching head and depressed spirits. It did not help that in her own house the atmosphere was equally fraught.

On the first day of the autumn term Claire had got a shock when she came into the classroom to find a new teacher on the rostrum. She had stared at her mother, unable to believe her eyes. Annette smiled coolly back. As she told Claire later, it was all part of work for her Masters, which she intended sitting the following year. Austin had been the one initially to encourage her, Annette said, but it was only that summer she had made up her mind about the course.

Claire did not quite believe her mother's excuse. She suspected her of not telling her in case she objected. Sheena was at first disbelieving and then amused. "I can't imagine Mum pulling a stunt like that," she exclaimed. "She discusses everything with us first."

Claire had seen the evidence of this for herself. Maybe it was because she had no husband to advise her. But then, strictly speaking, neither had Annette.

"Must be kind of nice having your mother teaching you," Terry said, overhearing. "She can't punish you if you don't do your homework."

"I always do my homework," Claire said seriously. Actually, Annette expected work to be handed up on time and marked it according to its merit. Out of school, she taught Claire how to analyse her own work and encouraged her to question herself.

"Always do my homework," Terry echoed in horror. "Oh my, what a pain!"

Claire blushed. "I must go," she said, picking up her schoolbag, aware that since the holidays he had adopted a rather mocking attitude towards her. She suspected it might be to cover his embarrassment but it made her feel uncomfortable and a little sad. "Bye, Sheena, see you tomorrow."

"That's right," Terry called after her in the teasing voice Claire hated. "Hurry on home like a good little girl and start your homework or Mama will smack you." She ignored him and went to have a word with Jane.

"Stay and have coffee," Jane said. She had bought an electric percolator and was loud in its praise. "How is school working out?"

"Fine. Mummy is really popular with the class," Claire said truthfully. Annette treated them all on a matey, woman-to-woman basis, and spoke quite openly to them about sex. Not like the other teachers who would have preferred the girls to believe the human race was spawned under a cabbage leaf. Her mother had already given the class her own reading list. Annette had advised them not to neglect D.H. Lawrence, insisting that he was essential reading for a deeper, truer understanding of erotic literature. She was erudite and articulate, even quite witty. Listening to her, Claire had been both proud and embarrassed, and got the feeling she didn't know her mother at all.

"I didn't know she was changing schools," Jane said.

"Neither did I," Claire admitted. "Not until she walked into the classroom."

"That must have been a bit of a bombshell."

"It certainly was!"

"She'll be able to give you individual coaching. That should be a big help with your exams coming up."

"She was always a great reader," Jane said thoughtfully. "When we were away together in Spain years ago she was never without a book. She sometimes read as she walked along the street. I was terrified she would be knocked down."

Claire was reminded of her thirteen-year-old self, walking up the long road from the library, with a pile of books gripped under her arm, another held open before her eyes. Funny, she hadn't thought she took after Annette in anything.

"I don't know how I would have coped if my mother had landed in on top of me in my final year at school," Jane admitted frankly. "Though now that I think about it, she did come into the school once to give a talk. She was a psychiatrist in child-care and a very good one too. I realise that now."

Claire had not known this.

"I wish she were still alive," Jane said, her face suddenly shadowing. "She would have been so good with Ruthie."

Claire was silent.

"If only it hadn't happened," Jane said suddenly. "Before the holidays Ruthie was just beginning to gain confidence for the first time since . . ."

She was unable to finish, but Claire understood. She nodded, feeling a little choked herself.

Despite her resolution to call more often and play with Ruthie, Claire did not find it easy to make time. She was studying hard now that her Mocks were so close at hand and short breaks were all she could afford. Barely time to share coffee with Jane and a game of Ludo with Ruthie.

One evening Jane greeted her with a wan, distracted smile. Ruthie was in the garden with Sheena, pegging clothes on the line, and her querulous demands could be heard in the quiet kitchen. Claire sat down and waited. When Jane had made coffee and placed the mugs before them, Claire felt able to ask, "Is anything the matter?"

Jane sipped her coffee before replying.

"I got a call today at the clinic to go to Ruthie's school." Claire set down her cup and studied her face gravely as Jane began to speak. "Sister Dunphy says that Ruthie has become a disruptive element in the classroom. Recently she played one or two unpleasant tricks on her classmates . . ." Jane paused and sighed.

"What kind of thing?" Claire prompted.

"Oh, tacks in another little girl's sandals, a ripped painting. She said that Ruthie's written homework is skimpy and untidily presented, and her form teacher suspects her of cheating at a vocabulary test. You know what emphasis the nuns always put on cheating." Jane shrugged tiredly. "'Simply not done!' is how Sister Dunphy put it."

"But doesn't she know what happened in the summer?"

"Yes, she does . . . and so do all the teachers. Oh, they're prepared to make great allowances for Ruthie. She has always been popular with them and they are all very sympathetic. In fact, I think they would gladly have turned a blind eye to her naughtiness if they didn't believe it signalled great inner distress." Jane met Claire's eyes soberly. "The nuns believe she'll ultimately require referral to a child counsellor."

They were silent, both viewing this prospect.

"Of course I agree with them," Jane broke the silence. "Only I don't want to take the step just yet. I feel if I can hang on until after the twins do the Leaving Cert, I'll be able to think more clearly." Claire nodded, well able to understand this. She was reminded of the time and got to her feet.

"Won't you wait until Ruthie comes in?" Jane asked.

"Well . . ." Claire looked helplessly at her. "I still have trigonometry to do."

"Off you go then," Jane said, giving her a pat. "Don't worry. I understand."

As Claire returned home, her relief was mixed with sadness. In the past she had loved being with the little girl. Now it was taking on the aspect of a chore. Claire told herself that any child's personality would be adversely affected by all Ruthie had been through. With love and understanding she would soon be restored to herself.

Sometimes Claire wished there was someone she could talk to about Ruthie. Her mother sometimes enquired after the little girl, but she could not bring herself to speak to her about what had happened. Anyway she knew that Annette had enough on her own mind. Ever since Jim had told her that Marissa was expecting a baby and he had begun annulment proceedings, she was acting in a slightly deranged manner.

Annette seemed to think it was diabolically calculating of

Marissa to become pregnant, as though she had deliberately planned it to sink her hooks deeper into Jim. Claire got the impression that Annette felt somehow threatened by the impending birth, as though it effectively relegated her to the role of dowager princess, while Claire and Christopher, one time heirs-apparent to some mythical throne, would now be declared bastards.

This was taking it a little bit far but in essence seemed to sum up Annette's attitude. She accused Marissa of bewitching Claire's father, whom she described as not entirely to blame, just weak and easily led.

"She has a lot to answer for," Annette said bitterly. From what Claire had observed, however, her father was equally enamoured with Marissa.

Claire thought the news that she would soon have a half-sister or half-brother very exciting and wished they lived nearer, so that she might babysit for them. Only she supposed that her mother would regard it as a betrayal.

Austin told Annette that he had moved in with his friend of the walking tour and said he would call over some night for his things.

Annette was out when he came, and beyond telling Austin he could go upstairs, Claire had no conversation with him. Later he rang complaining in an aggrieved manner that half his books were missing. Annette stormed into Claire's bedroom where she was revising history.

"Why didn't you tell me Austin was here?" She took an angry turn about the room. "Not that I give a hang about him or his books," she muttered. "I should have thrown him and them out long ago."

Claire knew Christopher had been lending them to his classmates but she kept silent, knowing she would be next in the firing line if she said the wrong thing.

"I suppose you think I'm an idiot too?" Annette said unfairly, and went downstairs to pour herself a drink. God knows how many she had got through during the summer.

Before long Annette got herself another lodger. Plump

and separated from his wife, Thomas was a journalist in his forties. He moved into the spare room in February on St Valentine's Day, around the same time that Marissa gave birth to a baby boy.

Claire wished that she could go and live with her father and Marissa and the new baby. Even if the baby cried it would be less distracting than the sound of Thomas' stereo playing long and late in the next room. Night after night, hour after hour.

And now it was starting up again.

Claire lifted her head from her history book and sighed in frustration. She turned back the pages to read the chapter again but her concentration was broken. Her head felt light and insubstantial as bog cotton. She decided to take a break and call over for a chat with Sheena.

Jane thought the girl was looking paler than usual and noticed how often she rubbed her eyes when reading to Ruthie.

"Have you a headache, Claire?" she asked her at last.

"A bit of a one," Claire admitted. She had a pain over her left eye and felt a little sick. Sometimes there was a shimmer before her eyes and when she tried to read a line, part of it seemed to be missing.

"Mmm. Sounds like migraine," Jane diagnosed. "I'll give you something for it." Then she remembered that it wasn't her place to treat Claire without her mother's knowledge. "If it doesn't get any better," she amended.

It got worse. One day in class Claire was unable to make out the figures on the blackboard. Her head ached from the effort of trying to read the maths teacher's squiggley writing. The next class was English, usually her best subject. She found she couldn't make sense of Macduff's speech. Birthdoms? Foisons? Each word seemed coded, with no cipher. When she stood up to recite, she heard her voice echoing in her head as if it belonged to someone else. It was a terrible effort trying to explain to Sister Whelan what was wrong with her. The words came out all funny. She flushed and was silent.

Jane felt it was time to have a chat with Annette.

"Migraine?" Annette said. "Oh, is that all? I thought it was something serious."

"It is serious." Jane sighed and averted her eyes from the overcrowded clothes horse, on which a man's outsize black and gold silk underpants hung, partially obscured by a white lace bra. "Claire's studies could be affected."

Annette wasn't listening. "Tea okay for you?" she asked, and not waiting for an answer, swiftly dunked a teabag between mugs.

Jane left hers untouched. Surely Annette realised that her daughter was doing a very important exam in less than two months and, if she didn't do really well, had no chance of getting into any decent third-level educational course?

"Look Annette," she said, suppressing her annoyance, "There's a safe, effective tablet for migraine. What I'm suggesting is putting Claire on it for a month and see how she goes."

"That's fine with me," Annette said.

"One other thing. An important factor with migraine is diet. I can give you a list of the right foods, but it's equally important for Claire to avoid long gaps between meals."

Annette sighed. "It's not that simple, Jane. I'm out all day and so is she."

"I understand that," Jane said patiently. "Just so long as she gets a meal when she comes home." She began jotting down the kind of nutrition she was talking about.

Annette nodded obediently. Jane wondered how much, if any, of her advice would be followed.

The daily tablet had the desired effect. Claire had no more migraine attacks and was able to take the long hours of study in her stride.

The Mocks turned out to be tougher than anyone expected. Even the brightest girls in the class looked doubtful when they congregated outside the exam room to compare notes, sighing and clutching their foreheads. Poisonous

181

and lethal were the adjectives used. Claire was in despair over the English paper. She had been fairly confident, she told Imelda, until she saw the literature section. Question after question on *Saint Joan* which she had barely covered. She had been really counting on Friel's *Philadephia, Here I Come!* She easily identified with Gar's pain over his father's inability to express affection.

With the Mocks behind her Claire felt able to accept her father's invitation for the weekend, if he didn't mind her bringing her schoolbooks with her. Her father said that was fine with him although maybe a complete break would do her good. Anyway, he left it up to her.

Marissa's baby – for that's how Claire had come to think of him – was almost three months old. David was tiny, with beautiful grey eyes and a silky thatch of dusky hair. Claire could not decide who he looked like, but he had her father's eyes, which, of course, were hers too.

Claire was fascinated by the sight of her tiny half-brother clinging limpet-like to the mountainous Marissa. Before marriage she had not appeared overly stout but now she was a solid mass of flesh, with none of the expected ins-and-outs. She was still wearing tent dresses. She was philosophical about her lost figure though and sometimes said with a laugh, "Oh that this too, too solid flesh would melt." When she put David into Claire's arms, Claire loved the sensation of the baby's dewy skin against her, although she was terrified of dropping him.

Her father smilingly watched them as he turned eggs in the pan, cheerfully calling Marissa and herself 'his girls'. He had opened a bottle of wine in honour of Claire's visit, although in reality the wine was for Marissa. Jim touched very little drink himself. He didn't need it, Claire thought. He had Marissa.

Claire sometimes pondered on Marissa's attraction for her father. She was so much plainer than Annette, yet her father obviously loved her. Claire came to the conclusion that Marissa might be without physical beauty but she was straightforward and undemanding. On the other hand, Annette was ambitious, devious and capricious. Marissa probably never thought of her work except as a job. Jim obviously found this restful. Claire could understand why. At the same time, Annette was clever and even witty. Marissa would never stand up in front of a class full of sixth year girls, challenging their preconceptions, or blatantly discussing the perils of unprotected sex. Not Marissa. And that's what her father liked about her.

Claire did not open her books in the end. The atmosphere in the tiny flat was not conducive to study. Apart from a brief walk with her father along the seafront on Saturday evening she never left the flat.

When she went home Annette did not ask her about her weekend. Anyway, she had other matters on her mind. Thomas had decided to reunite with his wife and had left suddenly, without paying his rent. Annette regretted not getting the money in advance and swore she wouldn't be so foolish again. She said that everyone thought she was a soft touch. Well, she was going to toughen up. And about time!

Her mother was on her third whisky by the time Claire said goodnight and climbed the stairs to bed. She could not help contrasting the two households: the one she had just left, which had been all laughter and love, and the one she had returned to, full of bitterness and recrimination.

She got out her books to give them a quick glance over before school next day and was all at once struck by how quiet the house was. No stereo blasting out Chris De Burgh or Billy Joel. She felt overwhelming relief that their lodger was gone.

Exam fever mounted. Claire kept wishing it was all over, that she had done a brilliant exam and got more points than anyone else in her class. Jane laughed when she said this. Not that she needed all that many points to do an arts degree, but it was what she wanted to do. The only thing she hadn't decided on was her subject. English or history? Naturally Annette felt English would be best and Jane agreed

183

with her. At the same time, Claire's best mark in her Mocks had been for history. It was all very confusing.

Jane laughed and got up to pour more coffee. Sheena was displaying the McArdle talent for portraiture and had been awarded a scholarship to the Art College. Jane sounded a little sad when she said this, perhaps thinking of Hugh.

Jane said that the letter had arrived from the Art College over a week ago but she still hadn't told Sheena. If she knew, Sheena wouldn't do another tap. Anyway, she asked Claire to keep the secret. Claire felt glad for Sheena, but a bit envious too. It must be great to have your career all decided.

A few days later Claire bumped into Terry as she was going into Sheena's bedroom, and learned he was practically fixed up too.

"Heard the latest, Claire? I'm going to be a pilot."

"Since when?" Claire asked.

"Ages. Right, Sheena?" Terry turned to his twin who nodded.

"You never said anything before," Claire pointed out as she perched on a stool.

"Nothing to say until I get my okay from the Air Corps," Terry said cheerfully. "But I've done a few good interviews and now it depends on my Leaving results."

"He has to pass Irish," Sheena said, making a comical face at Claire, who grinned in sympathy. It was Terry's worst subject.

"I think I can just about scrape through if I work my head off," Terry admitted. "I only wish I'd started earlier."

"Me too," Sheena admitted. She cast a hopeless look at the book in front of her.

Claire thought it seemed a shame not to tell her about the scholarship. Still, she supposed Jane knew what she was doing. Terry ripped a page from Sheena's rough copy and began folding it to make a paper plane.

"So long as my height isn't against me," Terry worried. "Might be if I opted to become a fighter pilot."

Claire had thought height would be an advantage.

"Are you sure?" she asked.

Terry nodded. "You could get tangled up with the instrument panel when ejecting, and leave your knee-caps behind." He grinned at her dismayed expression.

"Yuck!" Sheena said. She had given up trying to study and was making herself a paper plane. "Not like that." Terry refashioned it and dive-bombed it back at her.

Claire absently watched them. He would make a very dashing pilot, she thought wistfully.

Claire knew from Sheena that Terry was using his charm overtime on the clinic assistants on the nights he called to drive Jane home. Gráinne, the busty dark-haired one, was mad about him, Sheena said, but whether Terry had actually gone out with her, she didn't know. Gráinne was at least twenty-three, Sheena said. Claire wondered if she realised just how young Terry was but Sheena said, probably not. He looked older than eighteen. Acted older!

This was true. Claire blushed when she thought of herself and Terry doing very adult things. To think the pair of them had been like that! She had relived these moments in her dreams many times, in different guises, and thought that even if Terry had forgotten, she never would.

Terry hadn't forgotten, but when he looked at Claire, sitting there so cool and seemingly unaware of him, he found it almost impossible to believe they had ever been so intimate, although the mere memory of it brought him out in a sweat. He thought that if he lived to be ninety he would never forget the sensuous feel of her, the sweet response to his love-making, her near surrender. He wondered if he would ever get another chance with her and swore to himself that if he were so lucky, he wouldn't mess it up next time.

Claire and Sheena were making plans for the last day of school. "Some of the class want to bring in eggs and flour and mount an assault near the teachers' common room," Claire was saying.

"Sounds feeble," Sheena grimaced. "Can't anyone think of anything better?"

"Only to Vaseline the blackboards and put glue on the teachers' chairs."

"Big deal," Sheena sighed.

"We have a great gag planned," Terry said, and they turned to look at him. He took a piece of paper from his pocket and waved it in their faces. He laughed provocatively. "Wouldn't you like to know what it is?"

"Come on, Claire," Sheena cried, jumping up. "We won't let him out till we get it." She dived on her twin and tackled him about the knees. Terry laughed and easily bowled her back. Sheena ran at him again, breathlessly exhorting Claire to come and help her.

Claire hesitated, watching as Terry easily held Sheena off, his eyes alight with laughter, white teeth flashing against the tan of his face. He's so attractive and sure of himself, she thought. If only I could get him out of my mind.

She met his smiling gaze over Sheena's madly bobbing head and felt her face suddenly grow warm as the amused expression faded from his tawny eyes and was replaced by the intent look she remembered so well from the summer. They stared wordlessly at each other across the room.

"I've got it." Sheena fell back triumphantly clutching the paper, pleased at her easy victory. "Now we'll see what the great gag is." She scanned it eagerly and her face fell. "Well honestly! It's nothing but an old bus timetable."

The other two were aware only of each other and did not hear her.

Terry really did have a great gag planned.

The night before their schooldays ended he and three others from his class returned to the school, dressed in black jeans and balaclavas. They carried walkie-talkies and a rolled-up canvas flag, painted with the skull and crossbones. Their intention was to rig it up on the clock tower, a building strictly out of bounds to the boys and requiring skill and nerve to scale. They successfully rigged it so that next morning, just before the eleven o'clock break, they had only to climb on to the school roof, pull a cord they had left conveniently dangling and a sinister-looking Jolly Roger flapped into view as if by magic. The juniors went crazy, dancing and pointing. The masters, hearing all the commotion, came dashing out to investigate. A search of the tower discovered nothing but the gently flapping flag. When the furore had died down and the flag been removed, the masters admitted that it was a pretty good rag.

"As a matter of fact, the best in years," Terry informed his family that evening with a satisfied grin.

"I wish I'd been there to see it," Ruthie said wistfully.

"Me too," Claire agreed, smiling at her, thinking that Ruthie looked like her old self since her hair had grown again. She was touched when the little girl came and rested her arm along her shoulders in the old fond manner.

Sheena frowned. "As usual, the boys have all the fun."

"Oh now, sour grapes," Jane chided with a laugh.

"So how did you make out?" Terry asked the girls.

"Really well," Sheena said, after a quick conspiratorial glance at Claire. "We're not at liberty to say exactly what," she went on mysteriously, "but it was rather daring."

"Yes," Claire loyally played along with her. "It really was."

Actually, Sister Whelan, knowing what to expect from other years, had released them an hour before their usual time and urged them to go straight home. The girls had quickly taken up position outside the school door and begun filling plastic bags with flour. Nothing short of a cylinder of tear-gas could have deflected them.

A kind of madness seemed to possess everyone. Even girls renowned for their gentle dispositions became spitefully aggressive as soon as the teachers emerged, and when one or two hapless first-years were caught in the cross-fire and fled, drenched and screaming, there was unkind laughter. Sister Whelan was framed in an upper window but she was too far away for anyone to read her expression. Claire couldn't help feeling uneasy as she watched the Irish teacher retreat weeping down the driveway. Poor thing, she thought, meeting Imelda's half-shamed glance. Some of the girls excitedly went in search of fresh prey, but Claire and Sheena went home. Although they had half-heartedly joined in the fray neither were in favour of the gag, considering it too childish and messy.

"The nuns put a stop to it at once, rotten old spoilsports," Sheena was saying. "I suppose they just considered it too daring."

Claire nodded loyally.

"Daring, was it?" Terry asked with an evil grin.

"More risqué, wouldn't you say, Claire?"

Again Claire nodded. Terry doubled over, howling delightedly. "Flourballs and eggs, wasn't it?" he asked, calming at last. "Boy, oh boy, how daringly risqué can you get!"

Compared to his brilliant gag, theirs couldn't have appeared more feeble.

With her exams only days away, Claire sat in her room hunched over her work table, reading the same passage of prose over and over without registering any of it. She sighed and pushed away her books.

Two nights before she had allowed Sheena to persuade her to go with Terry and herself to the Wolfhound Bar to celebrate the end of their schooldays. The pub had been packed out with sixth-formers from St Catherine's, St Gabriel's and other schools in the area, and everyone was drinking pints and intent on having a good time. One of the sixth-formers from the Dominicans had made a real set for Terry and lured him away to join her group. To Claire's secret delight, he had come back to Sheena and herself and suggested that, as soon as the pub closed, they should head into town to a nightclub. But then the fun had grown rowdier. Someone lurched into Rory, who fell against an ornamental stone flowerpot, gashing his head. Terry had called an ambulance and gone off in it with Rory, promising that the pair of them would meet up with Sheena and herself in the Grey Lizard just as soon as Rory's head was stitched. Only they had never turned up.

Claire felt again her acute disappointment at the way the evening had ended. In the urgent expression in Terry's eyes when he'd said goodbye to her she had seen how much he had wanted to meet her. So what could have happened?

Claire heaved another frustrated sigh, and as her gaze wandered down to the street below, she glimpsed a flash of red coming in the gate. Sheena. She got to her feet and ran downstairs.

"Hope you've got graph paper," Sheena said, coming into the hall. "I'm all out and haven't time to go and buy any."

"Sure," Claire said, leading the way up to her room. "I've plenty. You're welcome to it." She bent and rummaged in the bottom of her wardrobe.

"Listen," Sheena was saying, "I'm sure you'd like to know what happened the other night."

An understatement if Claire ever heard one. Dying to know would be nearer the mark. She straightened up, paper in hand. "What did happen?"

"Well, it seems the boys were kept waiting so long at the hospital that Terry decided to bring Rory to Mum's clinic," Sheena told her. "Mind you, it was late by the time she stitched him up, nearly one o'clock, but we were at the club till well after two."

"Why didn't they come?" Claire asked, feeling disappointed all over again.

"Terry never really said but he was out all night, so I think it had something to do with Gráinne. She was on with Mum and you know how she's been after him for ages."

Claire felt her spirits sink. And to think she had been jealous of the girl in the Wolfhound! A mere sixth-former like herself. She gave Sheena the graph paper and walked downstairs with her.

"Don't work too hard," Sheena said gaily, and went back across the road to her own house. She was going to a play that night with Rory.

Claire's feet dragged as she went back upstairs. So Gráinne had got what she was after. If Terry had stayed out all night, he'd obviously gone home with her without a thought for any of them, waiting like fools. Claire felt like crying.

Then she was angry with herself. Was she going to die the death every time Terry McArdle went with a girl? Why allow him do this to her? He probably wasn't even aware he was doing it. She sighed and doodled aimlessly on her chemistry notes. Terry was Terry. He wasn't going to change. People never did. But he wasn't people, Claire thought sorrowfully, he was Terry.

She stabbed her pen into the paper, making crazy zigzag patterns. Better cut off now before he ruined her life. But her life was already ruined, Claire thought. She had already accepted this. So what difference did it make what she did?

The end of May and beginning of June passed in a blur of exhaustion. Claire was in danger of collapse before the exams and felt so bad that she took Jane's advice and eased off the few days beforehand. She would do well anyway, unless she messed up the papers through exhaustion or nervousness.

Claire wrote good papers and made no slip-ups.

Nothing major anyway. Not the kind of mistakes which would pull her down to a C in weaker subjects or rob her of an A in her best ones, like English and History.

When the whole ordeal was over Claire no longer cared whether she did brilliantly or not. She felt flat, as if the prize she had slaved her guts out over wasn't really worth the winning. Sheena said she understood how she felt, but Jane had given her the good news about her scholarship to the Art College.

It was a terrible anti-climax having nothing to do.

When her exam results were out in August Claire would find that she had done not just well but very well: As in English, History and Physics; Bs in her other subjects. Annette took Claire out for a meal in her own favourite Italian restaurant and shared a bottle of wine with her. In the meantime Claire went on holidays to Spain with the McArdles.

During the year Jane had decided to sell the holiday bungalow. She got a good price for it, even more than she had hoped for and, feeling the need of a relaxing holiday in the sun, booked a fortnight in Spain for them all. On the day she told them the good news she had the flight tickets in her bag.

"Yippee!" Sheena cried when she heard. Even Ruthie was excited, a flush staining her pale cheeks.

"There's a ticket for Claire too," Jane said with a smile. She had deliberately waited until Claire was there with them before breaking the news. Claire blushed with shock, unable to believe her ears.

"M . . . me," she stammered. "Oh but you shouldn't . . . I mean I really couldn't . . ."

Jane went over and hugged her. "Of course you could. It's what we all want, isn't it?" she asked, looking about at her children. Sheena and Ruthie gave an eager assent. Terry was struggling with something that had to be said.

"Mum," he said with a frown. "Don't think I'm not grateful or anything but . . ."

"Yes?" Jane prompted.

"The fact is, I can't come with you." It was out in a rush and Terry looked grimmer than ever.

"Not come," Sheena burst out. "Don't be mad, Ter. Of course you're coming."

"Sheena!" Jane motioned her to be quiet. "Why, Terry?" she asked him.

"I'm going to America for the summer." Terry looked embarrassed. "I've promised some of the other chaps. I can't let them down."

"Well, of all the scabby things," Sheena burst out. "Here Mum goes and books us a terrific holiday and you want to go to America. I've never heard anything so rotten in my life." Sheena's expression was so disgusted that, despite her own disappointment, Jane had to smile.

"It is a pity," she agreed gently. "It would have been nice, all of us together. A really decent holiday in the sun. In the past your father and I sometimes talked about it, but

191

somehow we never got beyond the planning stage."

"Don't make me feel bad now, Mum," Terry pleaded. "It's all arranged. I've booked through the student travel bureau and even got my J1. I can't change it now."

"Well then, I suppose I'll just have to try and see if I can get a refund," Jane said lightly, but there was a pained look in her eyes. She had so looked forward to telling them all.

"Really rotten," Sheena repeated with a disgusted glance at her twin. He glared back at her, then went out banging the door after him.

Sheena looked at Claire, "Thank goodness, you're coming," she said. "Terry really is a pain, isn't he?"

Claire smiled weakly, reluctant to take sides. When she examined it later she would be both disappointed and relieved that Terry wasn't going, but now she was still trying to take in the fact that she would be going abroad. A whole fortnight in Spain. She had never even been out of Ireland before. She was actually reading a book at the moment, all about Spain and bullfighting. It suddenly seemed astonishingly appropriate, she told them.

"Will we go to a bullfight?" Ruthie asked suddenly.

"Bullfights are shockingly gory," Sheena teased. "Bet you won't like it, Ruthie. She spent most of *Bonnie and Clyde* under the couch when it was shown on television," Sheena told Claire with a grin.

"I did not," Ruthie said indignantly.

Claire laughed. "Don't mind her, Ruthie," she said. "I kept my eyes closed most of the time, too."

"So there!" Ruthie said triumphantly to Sheena.

"Okay, go to a bullfight," Sheena said. "Just don't say I didn't warn you."

"Gosh!" she said a moment later. "I can't believe we're really going to Spain."

Neither could Claire. She felt she simply had to tell someone her wonderful news and, letting herself into her house, ran into the kitchen where Annette was at the stove frying hamburgers.

"Guess what, Mummy?" Claire cried. "I'm going to Spain with the McArdles."

Annette stared. "I suppose she wants you to help out with Ruthie," she said at last.

The glow faded from Claire's face. "I don't mind if she does," she said stiffly.

"From all she tells me that child is quite a handful," Annette went on. "You'll earn your holiday looking after her."

Claire turned away and began laying the table for the tea, thinking whenever she found herself getting on with her mother a little better, Annette always went and said something that grated on her.

"Some people have all the luck," Annette was saying. "He must have left her very well off if she can take the whole family abroad like that, while here am I with hardly enough to pay our television rental." Deftly, she turned the burgers and added sliced onion to the pan. "How long are you going for?"

"Only a fortnight," Claire said. "Usually I'm away much longer."

"You'll need new clothes. Well, don't expect me to tog you out on the money your father allows me. Let Mr Family Man contribute towards his daughter's holiday wardrobe."

As if she could ring her father and ask him for money.

"I suppose I should be thankful having so much time to myself," Annette broke the silence. Christopher was spending most of the summer with his father.

"What will you do?" Claire asked, refusing to feel guilty.

Annette laughed mirthlessly. "Let me see. I've a huge range to choose from, haven't I? Honestly, Claire. What a question." She sounded scornful. "I'll do what I always do when you're away. Sit here on my own and read."

And drink. Claire was ashamed of her thoughts. She banished them and gave herself over to the delightful contemplation of two weeks in the sun with the McArdles.

The girls were instantly enamoured with Hotel El Murillo.

It was a family-run hotel with an unpretentious entrance and magnificent gardens overlooking the sea. There was one swimming pool of respectable proportions, with a shallow section for younger children and a tiny play area concealed within a flowery arbour. The food was very good, but best of all was the genuinely friendly atmosphere.

Ignacio, the manager, was plump and smiling. He made a pet of Ruthie and when she became friendly with his little daughter, Adela, he encouraged them to come to the bar for free Cokes and limonada. The girls joked about her drinks on the house – they had to pay for theirs! But in reality Sheena and Claire received a flattering amount of attention from the waiters, who brought them tit-bits on the sly and blew them extravagant kisses behind Jane's back. Sheena regally accepted their homage as her right. Claire did not have such a high regard for herself and was just as happy to let Sheena have the limelight.

She fished in her bag for a book and contentedly turned the pages. Close by, Ruthie splashed about in the shallows with Adela and some other little Spanish girls. Claire reflected that on this holiday so little was needed to keep Ruthie amused. She seemed happy to play in the water all day with her new friends, and their excited cries mingled with the shouts of swimmers as they tossed a red beach ball to one another in an endless game of *Burro*.

Claire glanced over to where Jane was dozing under an umbrella, the most relaxed Claire had ever seen her. Of Sheena there was no sign. Claire suspected she was dallying with one of the young waiters. Now that Sheena had a whole range of handsome young Spaniards to captivate, the lads back home had been quickly forgotten.

With everyone, especially Ruthie, happily occupied, Claire felt free to start working her way through the pile of novels she had brought with her. She brought her feet back up on to the metal rung of her sun-chair and, gently rocking, was soon absorbed in her book.

Ruthie giggled in high glee as the beach ball shot past

Adela and landed with a soft plop on a snoozing sun-bather.

"Butterfingers, Adela," she reproved her friend and the other little girls fell about laughing uproariously.

"Buttherfeeng-airs," they cried joyously.

Jane opened her eyes and propped herself higher to watch their antics. Wonderful to see her so happy, Jane thought with gratitude. It had been a good decision to come away like this to the sun.

The trip had worked out expensive, almost double what a camping holiday in France would have cost them, but remembering the summer holiday she had once shared with Annette Shannon while still at college so many years before, she had opted for Spain. She had even chosen the same area in Nerja, near El Balcon de Europa. This return trip was in the nature of a pilgrimage to the scenes of her youth.

She suddenly decided she would take a stroll through the town. Once there, she might stop at an open-air café and sip a leisurely *café con leche.*

She swung her legs off the sun-bed and, crossing to where Claire sat by the pool, asked her to keep an eye on Ruthie while she was gone. "You can tell her I won't be long."

"Yes, of course," Claire answered, angling her sun-chair so that she could more easily see and be seen by the little girl. "Enjoy your walk."

Jane nodded. Always so conscientious, she thought with a pang as she moved on. Not like that scamp Sheena. She looked for her older daughter but she was nowhere to be seen. Off flirting, no doubt!

Jane strolled through the cool, plant-laden lobby. Ignacio was on the telephone and he nodded and smiled at her. Jane acknowledged his greeting with a wave of her hand and passed out into the sunshine again. She stood and adjusted her sun-hat, then set off down the hill towards the town.

It was siesta time and the shops were closed. One or two people sat outside the cafeterias finishing plates of *calamares* and salad. Jane wandered past them in the direction of El

Balcon de Europa, the area that she and Annette had frequented most during their time in Nerja.

She crossed the road and stood looking down on the small cove. At first glance it seemed as though time had stood still. If it were not for the advertising billboards it could have been twenty years earlier. Groups of Spanish matrons sat on mats near the water; young children played on the sand; a cat poked its head out from behind an upturned fishing boat, one of a fleet of boats drawn up beyond the high water ridges.

Jane let her eyes travel across the beach to where the waves foamed high against the rocks. This tiny cove had been their favourite swimming spot, but it was years since she had swum in a foreign sea.

On impulse Jane started down the sandy steps, removing her sandals as she went. The sand was almost too hot to tread on barefoot and she hopped the last few yards, relieved to be so close to the water's edge.

The sea was, as she remembered it, like tepid milk. She slowly paddled up and down, arms swinging, letting the memories wash over her like the waves gently lapping her ankles. It was to this beach that she had come with an attractive Spaniard late one sultry night after an evening spent dancing in a nightclub. They had slipped naked into the water to cool off and floated, fingertips touching, buoyed up by the deep swell about the rocks. That night had been a mixture of pleasure and pain.

Jane's expression grew serious as she remembered how she had slipped away from Annette, secretly hoping that Antonio might declare his feelings for her if they were on their own. She had known him barely three months and knew very little about him, just that he owned several restaurants and came from somewhere north of Cadiz. Yet in spite of that and the difference in their nationalities and outlook, she would have said yes if he had asked her to marry him. Instead, that night he had broken it to her that he already had a wife and child.

Jane hugged her arms to her chest, reliving her feelings of heart-break and shock. She couldn't remember exactly what had sparked off the confession. Perhaps it was some half-formulated wish as they had come running out of the sea, laughing and shivering, that she need never go home but might remain in Spain, sharing such moments for ever. In a few brief words he had taken away her hopes. Jane could still remember her feeling of disillusion, of being badly used, for she had given him her virginity only one short week after they had met.

Yet, in all honesty, Jane was forced to admit that in her besottedness she had enticed Antonio to the point where he could not resist her. In the beginning when he had hung back, she had mistaken his reticence for inexperience and deliberately kept alight the flame of his passion. She saw again his heavy-lidded eyes observing her with controlled ardour, until finally beyond all control, he had allowed the storm of his feelings master him, and she had been swept with him to a place no man had ever taken her since. Not her husband or any other man. Their affair had lasted until the night he had confessed that he was married. Two weeks later she had returned home, miserable and distraught. It had taken her months to get over him. Jane could still remember her feelings of sorrow and let-down after all this time.

Now she scooped up water in her hands and splashed it on her hot face, remembering how she had allowed Annette to think she was not in love with Antonio and had turned him down. Annette had been scornfully incredulous, and more than a little jealous. Funny how she hadn't seen this until years later, Jane thought, not until the summer Eddie died and Annette came to stay at the cottage.

Jane walked back across the sand, her earlier light-hearted mood replaced by a crushing sadness, so deeply enmeshed in her memories that she did not even feel the scorching sand beneath her tender feet and was at the top of the steps before she recollected her sandals. She pulled them on and began walking almost dreamily in the direction

197

of the tree-lined square, where she vaguely recalled Antonio's restaurant had been. There was, as far as she could remember, an antique shop on the same side. Not, of course, that either would still be there, Jane told herself.

Jane strolled past closed shops, their awnings fully extended to shade the buildings from the hot afternoon sunshine. Music came from an open doorway of one of the few *tapas* bars open at that time of day. She turned down the other side of the square and had walked almost the length of it when she suddenly came upon the antique shop. She gazed in the window, not too surprised to find it unchanged for its charm, after all, lay in its antiquity.

At a kiosk she bought postcards, before continuing on, intent on laying old ghosts. She had traversed the third side of the almost deserted square, passing a ceramic shop and jeweller's store, and decided to have the *café con leche* she had promised herself.

She stepped up on the pavement and there, right in front of her, was Antonio's restaurant. Of course, Jane thought on a long sigh. It wasn't on the same side as the antique shop but opposite. Her memory had been playing her tricks.

She went closer and deliberately pressed her forehead to the thick glass. Gradually her eyes adjusted to the dim interior and she sighted the expected rows of tables, adorned with snowy napery. In the background, a fish tank bubbled iridescently, speckled crabs heaped in a crustacean Laocoön against the glass wall. She pulled back and with a last glance at the signboard overhead, crossed to the café and sat down. When the waiter approached she changed her mind and ordered a brandy instead of coffee. She sat sipping it slowly, her eyes fixed on Antonio's restaurant without really seeing it, her thoughts full of the past.

She lingered there writing her postcards. The sun had sunk low in the sky and the girls were on the look-out for her by the time she returned to the hotel.

Annette read Jane's postcard twice. So she had gone back to

El Balcon de Europa. Annette was visited by a rush of envy so strong that she almost got weak.

She picked up Jane's postcard and read it again, trying to make out her physician's scrawl. 'Went on a tour of old familiar spots,' Jane had scribbled, and 'Saw Antonio's restaurant.'

They were back together again!

Annette put the card down and gazed sullenly into space. Her mind began to fantasise a situation where Jane and Antonio got married and returned in a flurry of orange blossoms to live in the house across the street.

Jane had always been luckier than her.

Annette told herself it was ironic that women like Jane got men like Eddie and Antonio, while she got Jim and then couldn't even hold on to him. It was so bloody unfair. Was Jane, who was over forty and no beauty to begin with, to be the one to get another husband while she, a spurned wife, was left to grow old alone?

Although that week Jane made several trips back to the restaurant at times when she might expect it to be open, she never even got a glimpse of Antonio. Once she thought she recognised him standing in the doorway, looking up the street, but when she nervously approached she saw that it was a much younger man, hardly more than twenty-five or six. His dark eyes settled on her face coolly, impersonally and she was seized by confusion. She hurried on past.

Further up the street she turned abruptly and paused to stare into an estate agent's window to allow her heart time to slow down. She looked, without really seeing the coloured photographs of villas and apartment blocks, then her gaze focused and she thought how lovely it must be to own an apartment right here in Nerja and have a legitimate excuse to come away ever year to bask in the heat and beauty of Spain.

Jane shrugged and turned away. It would cost the earth.

"Mummy, you're not listening," Sheena scolded.

"Sorry, love," Jane apologised. The truth was she was distracted by thoughts of owning an apartment in Spain. The idea had begun to take hold and now she couldn't stop dwelling on the pros and cons of it. With so many people wanting to retire to the sun, it would make a very sound investment, besides ensuring a great family holiday each year.

With an effort, Jane shelved her thoughts and set about soothing Sheena's feelings.

In the shallow end of the pool, Ruthie was swimming her first strokes under Claire's careful tutelage. The little girl could do a width now and was learning rapidly.

"Ready, folks," Sheena shouted from the diving board.

"Go on!" Jane urged. "We're watching."

Sheena paused to ensure maximum attention, then launched herself in a graceful somersault into the sparkling depths.

"Well done," Jane praised as her daughter's head bobbed up, sleek and dripping. Sheena grinned and waved, delighted with all the attention she was getting.

"Look at me, look at me," Ruthie begged, anxious for a share.

Jane watched and enthusiastically applauded her younger daughter's efforts before returning to her thoughts. She had not seen Ruthie so tranquil since the sudden deaths of her father and her brother. All her children had been deeply affected by the tragedy, Jane acknowledged, but Ruthie perhaps most of all. Ever since then she had been on an emotional see-saw and after the trauma of her kidnapping Jane had despaired of her ever pulling out of it. But here in Spain Ruthie was a different child, she thought. Sunny, like the weather, and joyously receptive to any proposal that was made. Clearly, her growing friendship with Adela and the other little Spanish girls was a sign she was emerging at last from the horror of the previous summer.

An answer to prayer.

Jane felt gratitude so intense that tears sprang to her eyes.

What had been a wistful longing to return again to Spain crystallised into a burning desire to make it happen. She would give any money, she told herself, to ensure that Ruthie stayed well and happy.

Claire found herself dreading the end of the holidays. She loved Spain and everything Spanish and she might never come back again.

She had no presents to bring home and was glad on their second last day when Jane suggested that they all go shopping for souvenirs.

"If we head off before it gets too hot," Jane told them after breakfast, "we'll be back in good time for a swim before lunch."

"I must get something for Terry," Sheena said, plumping down on her bed and laying all her money out on the coverlet. "Do you think he'd like a leather belt, Claire? I saw some lovely ones in the town."

"I'm sure he would." Claire thought she might get one for Christopher and, perhaps, a brooch or scented soaps for her mother. She still hadn't any idea what to buy for Marissa's baby.

"I'll go halves with you on Terry's present, Sheena," Ruthie offered. Like her sister, she was laboriously counting out her money.

"Okay," Sheena dismissed her and turned back to Claire. "He's not returning until the middle of September. When Mummy rang him yesterday, he said he was having a marvellous time in Maryland."

Claire nodded soberly. He was bound to be very sophisticated when he returned from America, she thought wistfully. Only another month. Not so very long now.

"Ready, girls?" Jane asked, coming back into the room. She was wearing a Kelly-green blouse and a floaty skirt in some fine material, an exotic swirl of colours in peacock blue and green which she had bought in a boutique during the week.

They set off, Sheena walking ahead with her mother,

Claire and Ruthie just behind. Ruthie was bubbling over with delight at the shopping expedition.

"I hate the thought of going back, don't you?" she confided, slipping her hand into Claire's. "I wish we could stay here for ever and I could go to school with Adela."

Claire was surprised at her vehement tone.

"It would be nice," she agreed cautiously, "but wouldn't you miss your home?" She thought of the McArdles' lovely house which she had always admired. Ruthie shook her head.

"I wouldn't care a bit. Not if I could live here." Jane glanced back.

"Would you like it so much, darling?" she asked.

"*En absoluto,*" Ruthie said, sounding so like Ignacio they all laughed. She pranced along, pleased with herself.

They reached the bottom of the hill and walked along a street thronged with people. There was an open-air market in progress and they lingered at the laden stalls, gazing at the pyramids of oranges and almonds until Jane urged them on.

"Don't forget that swim," she reminded them.

Claire glanced into the windows they passed, seeking inspiration. As Sheena had said, the leather belts were good value. She would almost certainly buy one for Chris. But what about baby David? When Claire had seen her half-brother before coming away, he was cutting his first tooth and saying Dada. The latter had really jolted her. In the window of a haberdashery she noticed a furry brown monkey, hanging by one paw.

"Oh look! Isn't he lovely?" She pulled Sheena back with her.

"Fab!" Sheena said enthusiastically. "Let's find out how much he is." Without waiting for a reply she dashed into the shop.

The other two had gone ahead. With a quick glance at their disappearing backs, Claire followed her friend. They would soon catch up with them.

Jane and Ruthie walked on, unaware that the girls were no longer following. Ruthie had transferred her hand to her mother's and she skipped along, chatting energetically. Jane couldn't get over the difference in her.

She guided the still-chattering Ruthie across the street to look in a property developer's window. If she were to go ahead with her plan, Jane decided, the apartment must be situated as near El Balcon de Europa as possible. Now to her delight she saw a notice prominently displayed, advertising a newly erected apartment block in exactly the right area. The siting was perfect, the amenities impressive. If only the price was right, Jane thought, pushing open the door.

A plump, dark-haired woman sat behind a desk working at a computer. When Jane explained what she wanted, she smiled and nodded.

"*Sí, Apartamentos Las Cicadas.* Please sit down."

She waved them towards seats and leaned across her desk to press the intercom switch.

"Fernando," she spoke into it.

"*Un momento, por favor.*"

Jane looked towards the door as a fair-haired young man emerged into the small vestibule. For a moment she thought she had met him somewhere, then the impression faded.

"May I help you, Señora?"

Jane was relieved that he spoke English. She nodded and said that she was interested in purchasing property in Nerja, preferably near El Balcon de Europa, and thought they had just what she required.

"In the window," she prompted.

"Ah, yes," he nodded. "If you wish I can arrange for you to view it."

Suddenly Jane wanted that very much.

"That would be fine but I'm returning to Ireland the day after tomorrow, so I don't have a lot of time." She smiled at him. "Would it be possible to see it today . . . right away?" If she liked what she saw she wanted to leave herself enough time for a second look before making up her mind.

The Spaniard glanced at his watch. "I have another appointment around midday, Señora, but if we go at once I do not see why I cannot manage both." He smiled disarmingly back at her, and Jane suddenly found herself liking him a lot.

"Let's go then," she said, almost gaily.

"Excuse me while I get my car key." He disappeared into the other room. Jane could hear him talking to someone, another man by the sound of it, through the half-open door.

"Mummy, are we buying an apartment?" Ruthie was almost bursting with excitement.

"Shush! Not a word." Playfully, Jane stopped her mouth. "Our secret. Okay?" Over the masking hand, Ruthie's eyes were enormous.

Fernando came out and beckoned them to follow him outside to where a white Séat was parked at the kerbside. He assisted Ruthie into the back, then politely motioned for Jane to get in. Very courteous and gallant! Jane smiled to herself as she tucked her skirt about her. Everything but click his heels! Within seconds they were pulling out into the traffic.

Fernando brought them on a quick tour of the showapartment and then retired to the courtyard to allow them time to view on their own. Jane wandered back through the tastefully furnished rooms and out on to the tiny flowerbedecked balcony. The pungent smell of geranium filled her nostrils and below, in the distance, the waves endlessly tumbled and broke on pale sand.

"Mummy, it's so beautiful." Ruthie came to stand beside her, and together they absorbed the scene.

A tiny tortoiseshell kitten clambered over the apartment wall and toppled into a flower pot, where it clung mewing pitifully. With a little cry, Ruthie extricated it from the tangle of leaves and cuddled it to her chest.

"You little dote," she breathed, and looked up at her mother with shining eyes. "Oh Mummy, this makes it just about perfect."

In that moment Jane made up her mind.

Jane was by no means rich, but Eddie had left her comfortably off. In addition to his pension, there was her salary from the clinic and her own thriving medical practice. She owned her house and had the money from the sale of the holiday cottage, as well as a few other sound investments her husband had made in the years before he died. She had never been extravagant herself. Her biggest expenditure was on her home and her children's education. If she wanted to buy an apartment now in Spain, there was nothing standing in her way.

She glanced down at Ruthie's entranced face. "You really like it?" she softly enquired.

"Oh Mummy!" Ruthie sighed, her eyes like twin stars.

"Come on then," Jane said, feeling suddenly as hopeful and excited as a young girl. With a last fond pat, Ruthie returned the kitten over the wall and followed her mother out of the apartment. They pulled the door after them and ran breathlessly down the stone steps leading to the courtyard.

The Spaniard turned to look at them as hand-in-hand they came hurrying towards him, their faces radiant.

"You like it," he stated, his naturally grave countenance suddenly swept by a smile.

Jane nodded happily. "Very much. Can we go back to your office? I think we can do business."

"Very good, Señora." Fernando moved with alacrity to open the car door.

"Mummy," Ruthie whispered, tugging urgently at Jane's arm.

Jane looked down at her. "What is it, Ruthie?"

"Claire and Sheena," Ruthie prompted. "They'll think we've been kidnapped."

"Oh my goodness!" Jane was horrified. She hadn't given them a thought in the past hour. Whatever would they be thinking! She bundled Ruthie ahead of her into the car.

"My girls," she explained to Fernando's mystified face, "I'd forgotten all about them. Perhaps we can telephone the hotel when we get to your office."

"But of course." He turned his eyes back to the road and rapidly weaved his way through the traffic.

By five o'clock that afternoon Jane had signed the conveyancing document on the Spanish apartment. The one she had picked was on the same side of the building as the show apartment, and had a prime view of the beach.

Earlier, she and Fernando had gone to a solicitor together and arranged the financial details. Jane had already telephoned her own bank in Dublin and asked the manager to send the solicitor her deposit of one million pesetas – the balance would be paid on completion of the apartment, in approximately three months' time – and all that remained was to sign the *escritura* which was sent off at once to the Registro de Propriedad.

Now they stood outside the property developer's office and shook hands.

"May I drive you to your hotel?" Fernando enquired. "It would give me much pleasure to do so."

Jane shook her head. "Thank you but I think a walk is what I need." She gave him a tired smile. Her head was aching from the events of the past few hours and she wanted time to be alone and think over what she had done. She had telephoned the hotel and asked the girls to come and collect Ruthie. They had arrived, agog with curiosity, but she had dispatched them with a promise to fill them in later on. Doubtless by now Ruthie would have told them. Just now she badly needed a stroll in the air.

"*Sí. Comprendo,* Dr McArdle." Fernando gave her professional title with quiet courtesy. "I look forward to our meeting tomorrow."

"*Hasta luego.*" Jane smiled and turned away. There were one or two alterations she would like in the kitchen and main bedroom, which Fernando assured her could easily be done. Now was the time to do it before the apartment was completed. Second thoughts were always the most expensive, Jane knew. She sighed, feeling as if she had run a marathon, and set out wearily for the hotel.

Fernando watched Jane walk away, a smile in his dark eyes. He had been infected by her excitement and got almost as much fun out of her buying the apartment that afternoon as she had herself. He had been greatly struck by the Irish woman. *Una mujer hermosa,* he thought approvingly, as she vanished around the corner. Although perhaps on reflection, he mused, not in the strictly physical sense. It was her mind and spirit that was truly beautiful, like that of his own mother. Interestingly enough, Fernando further mused, the doctor's hair was very similar in colouring to what his mother's rich auburn hair had once been, though sadly now streaked with grey. He smiled again and went on into the building.

There was no one in the outer office. He went straight through to the inside room.

"Congratulations, Father," he told the man seated behind the desk. "You were not here when I returned earlier, but I am happy to tell you we have sold yet another of our apartments."

Antonio Gonzalez looked at his son affectionately. "So Consuelo told me. But you are the one to be congratulated."

Fernando shrugged and laughed. "Perhaps," he conceded. "However, I think the lady herself deserves much of the credit. She came to us knowing exactly what she wanted and by good fortune we were able to supply it." He shook his head and whistled softly between his teeth. "Ayee, she took one look and decided it was for her. *Olé.*"

"If all our customers knew their minds so well we would not be able to build apartments fast enough," Antonio said wryly. "Still, we are not doing so badly. We shall soon have more than half of *Las Cicadas* accounted for." He swept some papers into a drawer and locked it. "You know," he said thoughtfully, "it might be worthwhile keeping that advertisement in the newspapers until the end of the tourist season."

Fernando frowned. "That is a good idea," he agreed politely. "But I must point out, Father, that it was not our advertisement in the newspapers, but in our front window, that drew Dr McArdle's attention."

Antonio pondered this a moment. "All the same," he decided, "keep the other advertisement running another few weeks."

"Very well." Fernando took a silver pen from his pocket and made a memo. "By the way," he went on more enthusiastically, "the lady is coming again tomorrow to discuss the one or two small changes to the interior of her apartment. I thought we might throw in a few of the optional features as a mark of goodwill." He looked questioningly at his father. "Such as the vanity unit in the main bedroom and perhaps the glass shower door in the bathroom."

His father looked surprised. "If you think so, Fernan. I leave it entirely to your judgement."

Fernando smiled. "You are thinking that the lady in question is young and beautiful and that I'm hoping to impress her with my generosity?"

Antonio laughed. He came around the desk and clapped his son on the shoulder. "Why not? You are young and have been enamoured before."

"Undeniably. But Dr Jane McArdle is not a young *irlandesa guapa*, Father," Fernando said reprovingly. "She is a medical doctor and almost of an age to be my mother."

Antonio said nothing.

"She is not young and beautiful," Fernando went on, "but – *qué alma! Qué espíritu!* I feel sure when you meet her you'll agree."

Antonio had gone to the window and was looking out on the small patio at the rear of the building, seemingly entranced by a lizard darting in and out of the flowerbeds. If it weren't for the pulse throbbing in his forehead – always a sure sign that he was agitated – Fernando might have thought he had not heard. What his father might be upset about he could not for the life of him understand.

Sheena went into raptures when she heard her mother had bought an apartment in Spain.

"But you never let on," she kept saying. "How ever did you keep it so quiet?"

"It all happened rather suddenly," Jane admitted. "I still can't get over it myself."

"Our own apartment in Spain," Sheena gloated. "Doesn't it sound grand, Claire?"

Claire nodded, feeling a little left out of it. A little inner voice kept reminding her that it was nothing at all to do with her. It was wonderful, yes, but only for the McArdles.

Jane laughed. "Sounds classier than a cottage in County Waterford," she agreed, catching Claire's eye and smiling at her. "What do you think, Claire?"

"I think it's great," Claire said, her mouth wobbling.

Jane felt stricken by their insensitivity. The poor child, she thought contritely, having to listen to the lot of them rhapsodising about the wonderful time they were going to have and never a mention of herself.

"Of course you'll be coming to Spain with us often," Jane hastened to reassure Claire and was touched to see the girl flush with pleasure. "Our holidays wouldn't be the same without you, my dear," she added quietly. "You must know that!"

Claire cast her a grateful look. "You've been so good bringing me away. I don't know how I can ever repay you." She was on the verge of tears. "I'll never forget it."

"Well, it has given us a lot of pleasure too, don't forget," Jane said kindly. "Now let's all go downstairs or Ignacio will believe we've deserted him and gone elsewhere for our dinner."

Jane re-read her copy of the purchase agreement and pondered on how quickly she had made up her mind to buy the apartment. Well, she couldn't rescind the agreement now without considerable financial loss, so she hoped she would never regret her decision. Somehow Jane didn't think she would.

Fernando was in the outer office next morning. When they all trooped in the door, he advanced with a smile and outstretched hand. *"Buenos dias, Señora . . . Señoritas"*

Jane smilingly indicated the girls. "Ruthie you've met and this is my daughter, Sheena, and this," she continued warmly, putting an arm about her, "is Claire, who is like another daughter to me."

Claire blushed rosily at the compliment and Fernando looked at her with interest. He was his usual urbane self and, starting with Jane, gallantly shook hands with each of them. Sheena couldn't take her eyes off him, Jane noticed, with a mixture of amusement and resignation.

"If you will come into the other office I will show you the plans," Fernando said, leading the way.

When they were grouped about him he discussed the changes Jane wished to make and suggested a few improvisations which would enhance the property. He really knew his stuff, Jane thought, unsurprised to learn he had a degree in architecture from Barcelona University. A very impressive young man, she thought, not for the first time.

The outer door opened and Antonio Gonzalez entered. At once Fernando jumped to his feet and extended his hand towards Jane saying, "Father, I would like you to meet Dr McArdle, who has just purchased one of our apartments."

Jane turned with a polite smile, which quivered and faded as she saw who it was. A lot older, his black hair streaked with grey, but unmistakably her Antonio Gonzalez. Her chest felt as though it had been struck by a bullet.

"Señora," Antonio murmured, his dark expressive eyes, so like his son's, meeting hers as he bent over her hand.

"We are just about to pay a visit to the show apartment," Fernando was saying. "Dr McArdle wishes her family to see it before returning to Ireland."

Antonio's eyes strayed from Jane to the girls and back again. "When do you leave, Señora," he politely enquired.

"We fly home tomorrow," Jane said, feeling as if she were in a dream. She automatically answered the other questions he put to her. When did she intend returning to Spain? And would she consider coming back in the spring for a short visit when the apartment was completed? He waited for her reply, his head on one side, eyes half-closed, regarding her inscrutably.

As she spoke Jane was struggling to cope with the shock of seeing Antonio after all these years. Then, to her relief, they were all standing up and chorusing their goodbyes as Fernando cheerfully led the way to the outer office, clearly pleased she had met his father and happy at the prospect of showing off the apartment to the girls. She heard him answer something Consuelo said and then he ushered them onto the street to where his little car was parked. Jane was acutely aware of Antonio standing in the doorway gazing after them as they drove away.

While Fernando was showing the girls over the apartment Jane stood on the balcony, thinking how much Antonio's appearance had changed over the years and his voice not at all. She found herself remembering little mannerisms, like his way of pinching his forehead when puzzled, and his sleepy, heavy-lidded way of listening. She had not thought of these things in years. Other memories came to her. She seemed to hear his murmuring voice in her ear, uttering little Spanish love words, and her face grew suddenly warm, making her glad she was by herself on the balcony.

Jane had immersed herself in her work in the years following her husband's death and had been hardly aware of men or the lack of them. But since meeting Antonio, her libido, inert even prior to Eddie's passing, had received a reviving jolt. She had never expected to feel this way again and had believed herself to be immune.

She heard the girls trooping in and out of the rooms, questioning Fernando and sounding the praise of everything they saw. She could not hear his replies but every so often there was a merry burst of sound, suggesting that they were highly amusing.

She took a deep breath and went to join them.

"The young ladies have seen and approved of it all," Fernando announced, his dark eyes meeting Jane's with amusement in their velvet depths.

So like his father's. Jane banished the thought and smiled back at him. "So what's your verdict?" she asked the girls.

"*Estupendo*," came the chorus, followed by a burst of laughter.

"See how quickly they learn." Fernando beamed. "Before you know it they will be speaking like Spaniards."

Jane felt pleased. He was really quite charming, she thought, and just the person to befriend the girls when they returned often to Spain. What a very satisfactory son-in-law he would make. She was appalled at herself.

Oh God, matchmaking already! thought Jane in horror. She grimaced and vowed never to think this way again. Yet in spite of her good intentions she found herself watching Fernando for signs of preference as he led the girls outside to point out the view.

By the time they had seen everything and returned to the car Jane had come to the conclusion that while Fernando was extremely courteous to each of the girls and treated them impartially, if his eyes ever rested overlong on one of them it was always upon Claire.

They were all a little sad as they sat over dinner that evening, their last in Spain for some time. What made it bearable, however, was the thought that this was not really goodbye, for they would be returning often now.

On the way back to the hotel Sheena had said that she looked forward to bringing her easel with her on their next trip abroad and to capturing the Spanish scene on canvas. Ruthie expressed her intention of inviting Adela very often to play with 'her' kitten, and Claire spoke lyrically of the view from the balcony and the heady scents perfuming the air. Only Jane had remained silent as she tagged along behind them, her thoughts taken up with the conversation she had had with Fernando.

"My mother has a natural gift with colours," he had told her with pride, when she admired the decor of the show apartment. "At one time she was a very successful interior designer, but these days her health is not strong and she confines her talents to our apartment blocks."

Jane had been startled to hear him mention his mother. Now sitting with the girls she wondered at herself. Why wouldn't Antonio still be married to her?

Jane made an effort to put thoughts of Antonio out of her mind but, in spite of herself, he kept creeping back in again. That she still found him extremely attractive was painfully evident. She sighed and decided she would have to discipline herself with regard to him. Now that she had bought one of his apartments she could expect to bump into him regularly. She would soon grow accustomed to it.

Very well, she wouldn't, but she wasn't the inexperienced, besotted girl she had once been. She was a grown woman and a widow to boot, and whatever fate decided to throw her way she could confidently handle. She lifted her glass and happily proposed a toast. "To many more holidays like this one."

The girls solemnly clinked glasses and regarded each other over the rims.

"Next time we'll visit the caves," Jane promised.

"And see a bullfight," said Ruthie, still disappointed at missing it.

"And see a bullfight," Jane agreed, nodding to the waiter to take away their plates. He did so, his eyes fixed yearningly on Sheena. She was flirting with all of the waiters. They took their cues from her and held their hearts behind Jane's back, or sighed over the *gaspacho* they carried to the table.

As the evening advanced Sheena's mood became progressively giddier. When José, her favourite, comically mopped his tears with a linen serving cloth, she went into paroxysms of laughter. The mood quickly spread, and soon even Ruthie was shaking, crimson-faced, behind her napkin.

Jane watched their high spirits with a tolerant smile. She silently made another toast: that although the strong bond of friendship between the girls must inevitably weaken during the coming year while they pursued their different careers in their different colleges, it would continue to strengthen and grow on Spanish soil.

Claire was well into her second term at Belfield before she settled to college life. The buildings were so big and sprawling and it seemed to take half a day to get from one place to another. The library was miles from the sports centre and another long distance from the students' canteen. Although they were initially supplied with a plan of the college she found it difficult to put it into context and for the first few weeks wandered late into lectures because she had been too shy to ask the way.

She had decided to take an Arts degree and in the first year chose for her subjects English, philosophy and classical studies. Her English class was split up into tutorial groups. Her tutor was an American woman in her forties, thin and slightly witch-like, who was never in her office although she was meant to be available for consultation during college hours. When, in desperation, Claire rang her home number it was invariably busy. Now she had given up expecting help and resigned herself to spending even more time in the library.

One evening as she got off the bus, she saw Sheena ahead of her and called to her friend. Sheena turned around and waited for her.

"Hi, Claire. Were you downstairs? Just wait till you hear . . ." Sheena was lugging her portfolio and was dressed warmly against the crisp March weather in a blue duffle coat and a black felt hat pulled right down over her ears, hiding most of her glossy dark hair. She chatted away full of her news. "What do you think? Mum got word this morning the apartment is ready for occupation. Isn't it great?"

Claire nodded, infected by her excitement. She felt her heart lift at the thought of returning to Spain. She was living for the moment.

Claire had seen little of the McArdles since the summer. Although Sheena always invited her in for a chat whenever they met, like this, on the way up from the bus, she seldom took up her invitation. Apart from being genuinely busy studying, she felt that her lines of communication with Sheena had become somewhat blurred. Sheena had taken to speaking in an ultra-modern kind of jargon and she herself, through her contact with classical literature, seemed to have taken a step back in time. 'Prithee, sweet maid' as opposed to 'Move it, baby'. Besides, these days Sheena was mixing with an older, more liberated crowd and spoke and dressed differently from the way she had before. Claire missed their old easy relationship but consoled herself with the thought of the summer when they would all be heading off again to Spain.

"Mum's going over for a quick visit some time after Easter," Sheena was saying. "She's waiting until Terry can go with her." Sheena flashed her a sly grin. "Aren't you going to ask how he is?"

Claire blushed. "Of course."

"Well . . . he's flying solo now and doing all kinds of dangerous things . . . not sure what . . ." Sheena wrinkled her brow in concentration, "but really dangerous. He almost crashed a load of times."

Claire looked anxious. "Is he all right?"

Sheena laughed. "Oh yes. Terry has nine lives. Hey, I've got a great video. Want to come over tonight and watch it?"

"Wish I could but I have an essay to hand up tomorrow," Claire told her with regret. "I expect I'll be up late finishing it."

"Pity," Sheena said. "It should be good. Robert de Niro and Meryl Streep."

"I'll come over another time."

"Sure." Sheena went through her gate then impulsively turned back. "What's wrong with right now? Come on in and say hello to Mum. She's always saying how seldom we see you."

"Okay." Claire followed Sheena into the house, her mind still distracted by this latest bulletin on Terry. She wondered how Jane was feeling. She must be out of her mind with worry.

"Claire!" Jane looked around with a welcoming smile. "Come in and sit down. This is a nice surprise." She rose to pour coffee and soon placed mugs of milky brew in front of them. "How's college treating you?"

"Great." Claire sipped the hot liquid gratefully. Now that she was into her second term she was gaining more confidence, felt less timid about speaking up at lectures.

"I suppose Sheena told you we were down in Baldonnel last month for Terry's ceremonial parade," Jane said. "It was a beautiful cloudless day and the Air Corps' acrobatics team provided a marvellous air display. You really must come to his Wings in May, Claire."

"Thanks. I'd love to." Claire was glad of an opportunity of asking the question that was bothering her. "Don't you worry at all about Terry flying?"

Jane deliberated for a moment. "Look at it this way," she said at last. "Terry is the kind of person who needs the excitement and variety of a physically demanding job. I have no doubts that the Air Corps is just right for him and will teach him the discipline he badly needs."

"Sheena says he nearly crashed . . ."

"Oh Sheena exaggerates as usual," Jane frowned. "It was all part of their routine training . . . recovery from spins and forced landings type of thing." She met Claire's sceptical gaze. "Of course, I'm aware of the danger, Claire, but statistics prove there are more deaths on the road than in the air, you know."

Claire suspected Jane was protesting too much. She knew just how emotionally involved Jane was with her children. How could you not feel concerned about your only son becoming a military pilot?

The conversation became more general and Jane spoke of Ruthie and the improvement in her since she had taken her to a child counsellor.

"Sister Dunphy says she's so much better this term the

teachers can't get over it," Jane said. "I think the Spanish holiday really did wonders for her, Claire."

Claire grinned. "She's not the only one. I loved every minute myself." Over the months her memories had kept her warm as she battled in and out of college in the cold and damp of yet another typically Irish winter.

When Jane began preparing the evening meal, Claire ran upstairs to chat with Sheena, not at all convinced by the older woman's apparently calm acceptance of her son's perilous career. It just didn't ring true somehow, Claire thought. When she said as much to Sheena, her friend lowered her paintbrush and nodded vehemently.

"That's just it, Claire," she said. "Mum cares so much that she deliberately keeps aloof to protect herself. She worries dreadfully, you know."

Claire saw that Sheena was working on a water-colour of a flowering cherry tree with a blurry black and white penguin in the foreground. It was rather good, Claire thought, like the work of the Impressionists.

She noticed that there was a new snapshot on the bedside table. The man was slightly older than Sheena's other boyfriends and rather arty looking, with long hair and an engaging grin.

"Did I tell you I've got a new boyfriend," Sheena said. "I met him at a party. He's a sculptor and has a fabulous motorbike. Wait until you see it, Claire. Does a ton! Sean's really nice," Sheena went on. "Takes me to lots of parties. Some night we'll bring you with us." Claire was too much of a stay-at-home and Sheena was fully determined on shaking her out of her rut.

Claire liked her rut.

She didn't stay much longer. She still had that essay to do. She stuck her head into the kitchen to say goodbye to Jane, and let herself out.

The following week Claire crossed the campus, her books gripped tightly under her arm, and entered the arts building. She was relieved to find her tutor's room empty and sat down to take a last look over her essay before she had to stand up and read it to the class.

She would be glad when this ordeal was over. And then there would be another, for she had agreed to go with Sheena to one of her arty parties that night. She didn't really want to but she felt the need to get out of the house. The sight of her mother's drinking was beginning to get her down.

Annette had taken to spending her weekends before the television with a book in one hand and a glass in the other. Once or twice Claire had crept down during the night and thrown a quilt over her mother's sleeping body, only to find her still lying there in the morning. She found the situation disturbing and depressing. Even thinking about it now was enough to cast her down.

The classroom door opened and Claire moved over to make room as, chatting and laughing, her fellow students sat into the seats alongside her. She hated these group sessions. While the majority of students were avid for the limelight, Claire disliked drawing attention to herself. She had got away with this until the second term, but only the previous week Rothman had cottoned on to the fact she hadn't yet read a paper and ruthlessly winkled her out: "Okay, Shannon, your turn to dazzle us next week." And now the time had come.

Blushing, Claire rose to her feet and started to read her paper, which explored the influence of colonialism on the writers John Millington Synge and Jean Rhys. The fact that she knew practically nothing about Synge had greatly added to her task, and she greatly regretted not paying more attention to him in class. Fortunately she was already familiar with Rhys, having read and enjoyed her novels the previous summer. She knew it was quite a good paper. She had spent the whole weekend on it and been fairly satisfied until now. But it was one thing reading in the quiet of her bedroom and another before this mob.

"Okay," the tutor told her at last. "You can sit down."

Claire retreated gratefully to her seat, her face burning and her throat dry.

"So, any comments?" the tutor asked.

This was the worst part, when other students felt free to tear your precious paper to bits. Claire waited in trepidation with her head down.

There were surprisingly few comments, mainly because few people had actually read Jean Rhys or Synge, nor indeed knew much, if anything, about either one of them. The focus quickly shifted to Joyce, about whom everyone had some opinion.

Claire sighed with relief. She leaned tiredly back in her seat and concentrated all her remaining energy on willing the session to end early so that she would get home in good time to get herself ready for the party.

Except for a few candles stuck in bottles the cellar was in darkness. Music thundered from twin speakers. It was mostly men, Claire could see as she came down the steps after Sheena and was effusively welcomed by Sean. He introduced her to his friend Phil and bore Sheena away.

Phil took Claire's hand. "Come and have fun," he suggested.

"Yes, of course," said Claire. She did not in the least expect to.

They were immediately drawn into the group on the floor. Everyone linked hands behind each other's necks and swayed to the music like they were about to go into a rugby scrum. Claire felt a bit silly. She smiled a lot to show she was enjoying herself, but the girl opposite her frowned at her through her curtain of hair.

More women and one or two men spilled down the cellar steps. It was too dark to make out their faces, but when the light from the candles fell on the face of one of the men, Claire, with a jolt, recognised Terry. She supposed the girl with him was Gráinne. She was wearing a low cut dress and looked a lot older than twenty-three. Very sophisticated, Claire thought, with a dipping of spirit.

"Let's dance," Phil said, putting his arms about her.

Claire was aware of shouted conversations going on about her and caught the whiff of various scents: turpentine and sweat, heated wool and flesh. Her mind felt very alert, perhaps because she had practically nothing to drink. Some had already over-imbibed and were crashing into other dancers, but she was shielded from the worst of it by her partner. She raised her eyes to find Terry staring at her. She was too taken aback to even smile. She couldn't remember when it was she had seen him last – October . . . November? He quirked his eyebrows at her and flashed his white-toothed grin. Claire was cheered at this silent exchange and the noisy cellar seemed a friendlier place.

The music stopped and Phil went in search of a drink, got waylaid by someone and forgot about her.

"Enjoying it?" Sheena asked.

Claire nodded. She wasn't, but then she never felt at ease at parties. Everyone was far too intent on having a good time

"What do you think of Phil?"

"He seems nice, if a bit forgetful."

Sheena laughed. "Watch out! His girlfriend is lurking somewhere."

The girl with the hair, Claire supposed.

"Terry is here with Gráinne." Sheena made a face. "He has a weekend pass."

Claire nodded and looked about for him. She saw him coming through the gloom, carrying a drink in each hand. He sat down cross-legged on the floor beside Gráinne and the girl whispered something in his ear. Laughing provocatively, she pulled him towards her, pressing his face down against her nearly naked flesh. Shaken, Claire looked away.

Gráinne's laughter was beginning to jar on Terry. He was glad of the covering darkness, which concealed the embarrassing way she was poking her fingers in his pants. He twisted away from her on the pretext of making himself more comfortable and wondered why he had given in to the impulse to bring her with him tonight. He supposed he had wanted to boast a bit about the Air Corps. He had taken his first flight on a jet that morning and, still caught in the euphoria of jet-powered flight, wanted to tell everyone.

Terry would never forget the sense of power as the Fouga had gone screaming into the sky, turning onto its back at the top of the climb before rolling right way up again and diving earthwards through the cloud with dizzying speed. They had repeated the manoeuvre, climbing almost vertically into the sky every time. He had climbed out with the other pilot and gone unsteadily back to flight operations for debriefing still soaring and diving.

He had been given a weekend pass and come up to town with his friend, Con, and some other cadets from his squadron.

Dropped at his mother's clinic, he had lingered to chat with Gráinne. Lately, he had cooled off her a lot and they only met very occasionally, but she had hung on his words, telling him she had always known he would be a wonderful pilot. When she had begun dropping heavy hints about finishing work early, he had asked her to come with him to the party.

Seeing Claire there he had realised his mistake.

"Isn't that your sister over there?" Gráinne was asking.

Terry nodded and took another sip of Coke. He would have liked beer but he was driving.

"Let's go over and talk to her."

"Who?" Terry stalled.

"Your twin. I'm dying to meet her and see if she's anything like you. They say identical twins have the gift of telepathic communication. Did you know that, lover? Comes from sharing the same ovum." Gráinne gave her provocative laugh again.

"We're not identical twins," Terry said. "Telepathic communication!" he mimicked. "Who spelled that one out for you?"

Gráinne sulked. "Okay, be like that!" She pushed herself to her feet and made her way through the shifting crowd.

Terry frowned and went after her, afraid of what she might say in front of the girls.

"I knew you'd change your mind," Gráinne crowed, moving over to make room for him. She laid her hand on him as she talked, suggestively rubbing her fingers up and down the inside of his thigh. He shifted away from her.

Terry noticed the way Claire was eyeing Gráinne's sagging décolletage. In different company he might have enjoyed the sight, but now he was conscious only of embarrassment and decided to leave.

"I'm off," he whispered to Sheena. "I have to drive Mum home. Don't let on I'm gone." He cast a significant glance at Gráinne, now flirting with an entranced Phil.

"Sure thing," Sheena said, only too pleased to join the conspiracy. Claire leaned over and asked him for a lift.

"Of course," he agreed, surprised. It wasn't midnight yet. "Give me a minute and I'll meet you outside."

Claire nodded and watched him slip adroitly through the crowd about the stairs. Despite herself, she couldn't help feeling a little sorry for Gráinne. Terry was so charming and so fickle, she thought soberly. Heaven help any girl caring too much for him. She was still a little dismayed by her own jealous reaction earlier.

Claire almost shivered with pain as she remembered how deeply smitten she had been two summers before and how quickly their growing intimacy had been shattered. The pain of it still lingered. However, there was no trace of it in her manner as she sat into the car beside him.

"I think you've got clear," she reported with a grin.

Terry shot her a glance.

"You must think I'm a real bastard," he said, as though actually caring for her good opinion.

"Not really," Claire said, after consideration. "I would say Gráinne gives as good as she gets."

Terry laughed. "She has that reputation," he agreed. He spun the wheel between strong, capable fingers and aimed the car fast down the street, pressing the accelerator to the floorboards. "I had to leave early, but you could have stayed on. Weren't you enjoying it?"

"It was all right, I suppose," Claire said doubtfully.

"You don't sound too crazy about it."

"I was afraid I wouldn't get a lift home," she lied. "Sean could hardly take both of us on his motorbike."

"I could have come for you," Terry offered.

"Thanks, but I didn't know you'd be there," Claire pointed out. Probably wouldn't have gone if she had.

Terry nodded. It was ages since he had been alone with Claire. He couldn't remember the last time.

Yes, he could. It was the night Rory cut his head in the Wolfhound pub and they had gone to Jane's clinic to have it stitched. And Gráinne had made a grab for him, Terry thought, and started up a sexual relationship which had been hot and furious until he went to America. Which about described how she would be tonight when she found out he'd ditched her!

He glanced at Claire. "I flew a jet today," he said. "It was like nothing in the world. You've got to believe it, Claire. Fantastic!"

"I do," said Claire sincerely. "So you're really glad you joined the Air Corps."

"Yeah," Terry said. "It's great. I wouldn't want to do anything else. No point!" He found himself opening up and telling Claire things closest to his heart, in a way he had never told anyone else. "I suppose I always wanted to fly since I was a kid," he confided. "Dad took me over to Hendon to see the air show. I was only about nine at the time but I suppose that's what got me hooked on flying."

Claire felt a pang as she wondered if Eddie had ever taken Hugh on an expedition which might have shaped his future, had he lived.

Claire had a vision of herself and Terry soaring skywards, twin souls possessed of a love like in 'Song of Songs', that no flood could quench, no torrents drown. They were almost at her house when she remembered Jane. "Aren't you going for your mother?" she asked.

"It's too early," Terry said, slowing. "Say, Claire. I'm starved. What would you say to hamburger and chips?"

Claire laughed. "Chips maybe. I don't think I could eat a hamburger."

"'Course you could. I'll eat it if you don't!"

She laughed and gave in. "Okay. Whatever you say."

They parked in Terry's driveway and ate their midnight feast. Claire would have liked to invite him into her house for coffee but was put off by the thought of her mother lying collapsed on the couch.

Terry licked his fingers and screwed the empty bag into a ball. "Hadn't a thing since midday," he admitted. "I was too churned up to eat much. My stomach felt like it was still upside down at thirty thousand feet. Hey, aren't you going to finish those?" He eyed her chips hopefully.

Claire laughed. He'd already eaten most of her hamburger. "I think I can spare you one," she teased.

"Mmmm. Nice." He ate it from her fingers and waited expectantly.

She fed him another and then another.

"Hey, don't let me take them all," he cried remorsefully.

But Claire only laughed and continued to feed him, one chip at a time. "All gone," she said with regret, withdrawing her hand.

Terry thought he had never felt so relaxed with any girl as he felt with Claire. By this time with any other girl Terry McArdle would have been on the back seat, launching an assault on her virginity. Now, however, he felt content to just sit and chat. Not that he wouldn't have liked to kiss Claire and gone a lot further, he admitted, but he wasn't going to risk spoiling the intimacy of the past few hours. 'Play it cool,' he told himself with unusual perception. 'This is too important to ruin.'

"I'd better go and get Mum," he said at last, reluctant to make a move.

"Yes," agreed Claire guiltily, seeing the time. "She'll be

wondering where you are."

He packed everything tidily into the McDonald's bag and opened the window wide to let in air.

"Let's do this again," Terry suggested, his hand falling naturally about Claire's waist as they walked to her house. "We could go bowling or maybe take in a dance?"

Claire smiled up at him. "I'd really like that," she said with husky sincerity. In the glow from the street lamp her eyes had a sheen like grey mother-of-pearl and her lips were rosy and full.

Terry stared down at her, his senses stirred by those sweetly parted lips. He imagined what it would be like to kiss them and go on kissing them until his ardour was satisfied. For the first time in Terry's life his will was in direct opposition to the urges of his body and, for the first time in his life, will triumphed over desire. He stepped back.

"Be seeing you." He gave her a little military half-salute and strode back to the car. Feeling absurdly happy, he roared past her on his way back to the clinic to pick up his mother.

In a trance Claire went into the house and walked through the living-room, where her mother was sipping whisky and watching a film. Without hearing her query as to how she had enjoyed herself, Claire went upstairs to her room.

Was this happiness? she wondered. Was this what it felt like?

She lay listening for the sound of the returning car and when she heard it crunching into the driveway across the street gave a small sigh and fell into a deep dreamless sleep.

All week the thought of his date with Claire filled Terry with delight and a strange humility, adding zest to everything he did. He couldn't get over how he had bared his soul to her.

He had rung her midweek to arrange a meeting-place and had thrilled to the sound of her eager, slightly breathless replies. Since then she had completely taken over his thoughts. Normally when flying, any stray thought, however pleasant, was a dangerous distraction, but this time Terry found to his surprise that he experienced an acute sense of well being, which resulted in heightened timing and perception and more skilful handling of the controls. He seemed to have an additional supply of fire in his veins.

Terry was caught napping when Captain Monahan unexpectedly reduced speed and threw the aircraft into a bad stall. Terry struggled to regain control, putting all his newly acquired skills into action. He remembered his training – in an emergency summon full power – and managed to regain control of the Marchetti. For a few bad moments it looked as though they might end up splattered all over the Naas dual carriageway.

Terry grinned at Dinny's remark as he wiped his sweaty forehead: "Terry, lad, you've thrilled us enough for one afternoon. Take us back to the base." But immediately after debriefing, he found that he'd done very well, for Monahan had given him the good news that he was ready to do his familiarisation on jets.

Now added to Terry's euphoria at the prospect of meeting Claire that evening was the heady knowledge that he would almost certainly be the first in his group to fly jets. He grinned from ear to ear as he thought of Con's disgusted expression when he heard, and he hurried into the mess.

"Didn't you hear?" One of the cadets from Terry's group strolled to meet him.

Grinning, the other pilot told him how Con had failed to pull out of a spin and, on instructions from his training instructor, had bailed out over Saggart.

"So where's Con now?"

"Hoofing it back from Saggart, I reckon."

"Poor sod." Terry grinned in sympathy. "He'll be like a bloody lunatic." He strolled to the door of the mess and looked out. Suddenly he gave a great crack of laughter. "What do you know, but here's the man himself."

Other cadets hurried to merrily watch Con's plodding

approach. Even at a distance he was a sorry sight, red-faced and sweating in his full flying kit, with his parachute untidily bundled under his arm. When he spotted them doubled over in the doorway, laughing and hooting, Con shook his fist at them and grinned sheepishly.

"Hard luck, Con." Terry, the first to reach him, slapped him affectionately on the back. "Better luck next time. Looks like you're down a fiver, old son."

"Oh, my sweet sainted aunt," Con groaned in disgust. "Listen, McArdle. Would you ever do us a favour? Go eff yourself."

Terry chuckled. "Come and drown your sorrows and be thankful you're all in one piece." He placed his hand on Con's shoulder and turned him back towards the mess.

They sat thirstily downing pints, joking and laughing. It was good to be alive. Terry looked about him in satisfaction at the flushed and laughing faces of his friends, savouring the moment. But the best was yet to come. In another few hours he would be meeting Claire and seeing those grey eyes light up at the sight of him.

Earlier that Thursday afternoon Jane arrived into the clinic and spent her first ten minutes opening the post which had accumulated since her last visit. She sorted through the results of smear and pregnancy tests, putting them to one side for her secretary to type up, and reached for her appointment pad.

Her first patient was due shortly. Mary McCann. Originally from South Africa and married to an Irish man. Mother of four, all under eight years and the youngest child nearly two. Jane glanced over her file. Mary was in her forties and prone to high blood pressure and she also suffered from porphyria, a rare urinary disease. The disease was extremely unusual in this part of the world – Jane had never had another patient with it – but in Mary's own country, amongst the white population, its incidence was estimated at one in four.

Jane had not seen Mary McCann in almost two years, not

since her six weeks' check-up after the birth of her last child. Let's hope she wasn't pregnant again! Jane went to the door and called Gráinne.

"Be a dear and bring me in a cup of coffee?" she said. To be friendly, Jane chatted about her busy morning and last minute dash to the clinic.

Gráinne listened with a slightly veiled expression and murmured something.

Jane sighed and went back into her room. She hoped Gráinne's moodiness of late had nothing to do with Terry. She had seen the way Gráinne made a set for him whenever he visited the clinic and, knowing her son, was prepared to believe he had taken full advantage of what she had to offer. Gráinne, as well as being far too old for Terry, was not at all what she had in mind for her son. But alas, Terry had his father's passionate blood in him. He was also headstrong and too much opposition invariably spurred him to do the forbidden. Jane had refrained from outright condemnation of the friendship and hoped and prayed that the restrictions of army life would soon break up the liaison.

Gráinne came in with the coffee and, a moment later, showed in Mrs McCann.

"How are you, Mary?" Jane put aside her cup and watched the woman as she sat down.

"My period is late, Doctor," Mary said happily. "I think I'm pregnant."

Jane regarded her soberly. Mary doted on children. Against Jane's advice, she had gone ahead and had the last two. Irresponsible, Jane considered, in view of Mary's age and medical history, yet she couldn't help feeling a sneaking sympathy with her. She had so wanted more children herself.

"Well, let's find out for sure," Jane said. "Did you bring a specimen?"

The woman shook her head. "Sorry, Doctor. I should have known."

"Never mind," Jane said kindly. "Lie up on the couch and

I'll take a look at you,"

Jane turned away to wash her hands. "It's a bit early to say but there are certain changes," she agreed.

"I knew it," Mary gave a joyful sigh. "We are hoping for a girl this time, Doctor. Wouldn't it be marvellous after four boys!"

Jane nodded and smiled, unable to remain disapproving in the face of Mary's enthusiasm. "Now, Mary," she gently cautioned her, "save the raptures until we know for certain."

As she reached in her drawer for a sterilised container, Jane thought that it might be no harm to have the laboratory run a few other tests at the same time. It would be helpful to know whether, in the interim, the disease had progressed.

"Take this with you," Jane said, handing her the container, "and drop me in a fasting specimen in the morning. I've a mind to have a few other tests run at the same time."

"I will, Doctor."

Jane squeezed her arm sympathetically. "You're really taking on rather a lot at . . ."

"My age!" Mary cheerfully finished for her. "Well, I'll take my chances.' She struggled into her blouse and buttoned her cardigan. "I'll bring it in first thing in the morning, Doctor. And thanks. I know you're only speaking for my own good. It won't be easy and John will be worried sick about me for the next nine months . . . Oh, but we both do so want this baby."

Jane smiled and saw her out with a lightened heart. So many times in her work she came across women, like Mary, generously struggling to cope with the burden of each successive pregnancy, despite failing health and a small income. At least in Mary's case she had a good supportive husband and was thoroughly contented with her lot.

Jane saw a dozen patients that afternoon and when the last one had departed, lay down on her couch before tackling the drive home. She had no sooner begun her breathing exercises when a knock came on her door. She was tempted to ignore it but while she was still in the clinic she was officially on duty, and padded in her stocking feet to the door.

Gráinne stood outside.

"What is it?" Jane asked, controlling her impatience. She was tired, her back ached and she was anxious to get home before the traffic built up.

The girl stood with downcast expression. "I need your advice, Doctor," she said.

"Of course, Gráinne," Jane widened the door and went to sit behind her desk.

"I don't know what to do," Gráinne began. "I'm late with my period and I think I may be pregnant."

"When did you have it last?" Jane asked automatically.

"Eight or nine weeks ago . . . I'm not sure."

"So you've missed twice."

Gráinne nodded.

"Have you had a pregnancy test?"

Gráinne shook her head.

"All right," Jane said quietly. "First thing is to make sure." She reached in her desk for a sterilised container. "If it turns out to be positive what are your feelings about having the baby?"

"Well, it wasn't planned," Gráinne admitted ruefully. She fidgeted with the belt on her coat, avoiding Jane's eyes.

"So what are you going to do?"

"That's what I was hoping you would tell me."

"My dear," Jane said, wishing she could summon up more sympathy for the girl, "that's something entirely between yourself and the father."

"I haven't told him yet. I thought I'd better come to you first . . . in the circumstances." Gráinne lifted her head and looked straight at her.

Jane felt a sudden shock. Oh dear God, no! Her heart sank as the girl told her that Terry was the father of her baby and how much she loved him and wanted to do whatever was right and best for all of them. As she broke down and snivelled into a Kleenex, Jane thought that there was something not quite convincing in Gráinne's manner.

"Very well," Jane said, her mind still cloudy with shock. "We'll talk of this again." She rose and Gráinne looked at her in consternation.

"But aren't you going to speak to him?"

"Eventually," Jane said.

"When will that be?"

"When I have a positive result to your test."

"But that won't be for at least another week," Gráinne said dismayed. "Perhaps longer. "By then it may be too late . . . if . . . if . . ."

"You mean too late for an abortion?" Jane asked coolly.

Gráinne hung her head.

Gráinne went towards the door, but before she reached it she turned back and faced Jane defiantly.

"If he says there were others I suppose you'll believe him," she challenged her.

"If it's true," Jane agreed.

When she was alone Jane slumped at her desk and put a hand to her eyes.

Jane tried to analyse her feelings and was ashamed that she felt so little sympathy for the girl. But it takes two, she reminded herself. Terry is to blame every bit as much. But he may love her, in which case there is no real problem. Jane did not invest too much hope in that. Like father like son, her unhappy thoughts echoed. The girl returned and, with a defiant look, placed the specimen on the table.

"Don't worry, Gráinne," she felt constrained to say, sorry for her earlier hostility. "I will help you whatever you decide to do."

The girl mumbled her thanks and went out the door. Jane watched her go then labelled the specimen and went to put it in the fridge. It would go across in the morning with Mary McCann's to the laboratory.

Despite what she had said to Gráinne Jane decided she would speak to Terry as soon as she saw him. He had rung earlier to say he would be home later. "Don't wait up, Mum," he'd said. "I don't know what time it'll be." But as she walked across the mucky ground in the rain to where her car was parked Jane decided that she would wait up and have it out with him.

Ever since she had received Terry's phone call the previous evening Claire's thoughts had been wandering in a most uncontrollable fashion. She found herself looking forward with an almost unbearable delight to seeing him. He had suggested they might go dancing and she had happily agreed, but just to be with him was enough.

At her tutorial she was unable to concentrate on anything that was said and as soon as the group broke up, she set off immediately down the long road to the bus stop. Claire pulled up her collar, fretting that the light drizzle would turn her hair limp and frizzy. She became aware of a car pulling in at the kerb and heard a familiar voice calling, "Claire, get in quick."

It was Jane. Thankfully, Claire ran over and got into the Rover. Jane pulled out again into the traffic and increased speed. "What a terrible night," she sighed. "Lucky I saw you. You must be drenched. Have you no hood to your anorak?"

"I was just about to use my drama notes," she confessed with a giggle. Sitting comfortably in the warm car she felt suddenly elated. She chatted away gaily, unlike her usual shy self. Jane, however, seemed preoccupied.

"Sorry, Claire. What were you saying?"

"Just that it's great to get the lift," Claire repeated. "I'm going out again tonight and don't have a lot of time to get ready."

Jane said pleased, "You've got a date? Is he nice, this boyfriend of yours?"

Claire hesitated, loth for some reason to admit that she was meeting Terry.

"It's all right, Claire. I'm not nosey." Jane laughed. "Just glad you've found someone you like. You do like him a lot, don't you? Somehow I can tell."

"Yes I do," Claire admitted, and felt a warm rush of delight at the thought of Terry.

Rain beat continuously on the windscreen. Jane flicked the wipers to high speed and peered through the cloudy glass. "I can't see too well," she said after a moment. "I think the rubber on the wipers needs replacing. I must get Terry to check it when he comes. I'm hopeless with anything mechanical and so is Sheena."

Claire felt somehow deceitful remaining silent, as though her meeting with Terry would seem wrong in Jane's eyes. But really, hadn't Jane always been most kindly to her, treating her like another daughter?

Strangely, Jane's kindness was at the root of Claire's unease, for she recognised that it wasn't something she could ever take for granted, like a true daughter could. She stared out at the lashing rain, and the old fear that Jane might some day discover what had taken place between Eddie and herself returned to haunt her. With an effort she turned her thoughts away from this bleak possibility and tried to recapture her earlier euphoria at meeting Terry.

They met as arranged inside the gates of Trinity College.

"Hi, Claire," Terry said as she walked up to him, his eyes glowing with the pleasure of seeing her. "How do you look so smooth and unruffled in this weather?"

She thought he was looking pretty smooth himself in a leather flying jacket with sheepskin lining.

"You look almost too perfect," he said, running his hand teasingly over her hair in an effort to break the shyness between them.

"Hey, you're undoing the work of hours," she joked, twisting away from him. Her hair hung to her shoulders, straight and silky. They walked out on to the street and his hand reached for hers as they had continued on close together towards Grafton Street.

Terry seemed charged with energy. One minute hurrying her forward, the next pulling her back to look at the window display in Brown Thomas.

It was filled with the latest spring fashion, clumps of fresh daffodils everywhere.

"You'd look good in that, Claire." He pointed to a suit. Long jacket, short skirt. "Huh! Blondes look good in red. You sometimes wear red, don't you?"

He began singing "The Lady in Red". "You know what I feel, Claire?" he broke off to ask.

"What?" She waited.

"Like I've been just let out of school. I feel I've been missing out on life and now I've got a heck of a lot of catching up." He laughed. "C'mon. Let's get a drink."

He brought her into a pub and got them beers. He drank fast, urging her to keep up with him, making her laugh out loud with descriptions of his life with the Air Corps.

"Bloody bugle lifts us out of it in the morning," Terry sighed comically. "Then the drill sergeant crashes in the billet door like something out of an old Boulting Brothers comedy. Effing and blinding and shouting his head off."

Claire laughed. According to himself, he and his friend Con were the best pilots in his squadron. Nerves like iron and stomachs to match. Con had flown solo almost as quick as him. She was beginning to know a lot about Con, and feeling a tiny bit jealous too. Terry was so great with him.

"Pete's a pretty nifty flyer too," Terry was saying. "We're all three of us hoping to go solo on night flying soon." Claire watched him, smiling faintly. He was showing off dreadfully but she liked it.

"Ah, Clairey, don't look at me like that," he said suddenly, "or I'll have to kiss you."

She blushed. "Look at you like what?"

"Like the ace pilot I'm cracking myself up to be."

After they finished their drinks they wandered back on to the street. The rain had quite cleared away and the night was mild.

Terry said: "Mum's going to Spain soon and I'm going

with her."

"Wouldn't I like to be you," Claire said wistfully. "I can't wait to go back."

"Perhaps I'll get down to join you for a few days this summer. I really hope so."

"You'll love the apartment," Claire told him. "It's beautiful and it has a great view of the beach. That's what I liked best." She was silent remembering the waves breaking on pale sands and the warm, geranium-scented air on the balcony. How lovely to go back again. She only hoped Jane would invite her.

"Sheena never stops talking about the guys you met out there." Terry glanced down at Claire. "I suppose you're equally besotted with the Spaniards?"

"They were very nice," Claire said cautiously.

"And this Fernando?" Terry asked impatiently. "I'm always hearing his name."

"He's one of the property developers. His father owns the apartment block. Fernando showed us over it." Claire smiled at the memory. "Sheena was really crazy about him."

"What about you?" Terry asked jealously.

"I liked him," she admitted.

Terry scowled. "I suppose I'll be meeting this guy when I go over. Have you any messages you'd like me to convey?"

Claire looked up at him demurely, almost coquettishly. "Tell him I'm looking forward to returning to Spain."

They were walking up a darkened side street.

Terry suddenly gripped Claire's arm and swung her round to face him. He stared urgently into her eyes, his expression softened and blurred, bent his head and kissed her. It was a deep slow kiss, more like a seal of ownership than the suddenness of passion. When he lifted his mouth from hers, he smiled down at her and his teeth were large and square and very white in the darkness. A little shakily she smiled back.

They stood for a moment, not kissing or speaking, just holding each other. They were so close that Claire could feel his breath warm on her face and the buttons on his flying jacket pressed against her bosom.

"Gosh!" He spoke at last, sounding awed and very young. "I know this sounds stupid, but I've never known a kiss like that. It was so . . ." Words failed him. "Was it . . . did you find it . . ."

"Yes, I did," Claire said simply.

He took her hand and they started walking again, going along streets leading away from the town. They stopped once to have a drink in a pub, another time to buy cod and chips, sitting up on a wall outside the chipper to eat it, before walking on.

"Is this too much for you, Claire?" Terry asked her at one stage. "I mean you aren't wearing shoes that hurt, or anything?"

Claire shook her head. She loved him for thinking of that. She could have walked for ever.

They talked until they reached the street where they lived. At least Terry talked and Claire listened, asking a question now and then. He couldn't keep off the subject of flying, describing the squadron and the guys and his flying instructor, Captain Dinny Monahan. Claire got the impression of a big, good-humoured man, but with a hot temper and razor sharp wit. She did not think she would fancy army life herself. She could see, however, that Terry, rather than resenting the toughness and discipline, actually revelled in it. Jane had been right, she thought, feeling excluded by Terry's new way of life and his close friendship with Con and Pete. He didn't need her, and she longed to be needed.

They slowed outside her house. Without a word, Terry drew her across the road and down the side of his house. He led her into the garage by the small side door. As they stood pressed together in the musty darkness, Claire felt a deep unease, thinking of her thirteen-year-old self crouching in the darkness, listening to the sound of Eddie's voice and his footsteps crunching past on the gravel outside.

Why did you bring me here? she wanted to cry out, but then as Terry pressed his lips down on hers, she pushed away all thought of anything but him and returned his kisses with equal fervour.

Jane came out of her bedroom at the sound of the front door closing and went downstairs. Terry turned from hanging up his jacket. He looked happy and smiling and was humming under his breath.

"Why aren't you asleep, Mum?" he demanded with concern. "I told you not to wait up."

Jane opened the door of her surgery. "Come in a moment, Terry" she said quietly, "I have something to say to you".

"Oho! What have I done now?" Confidently, he followed her inside. He threw himself into a chair, legs sprawling, and regarded her quizzically.

Jane sat down behind her desk. He looked so mature, she thought with a pang, glancing away from his amused, handsome face. He's almost twenty, old enough to take responsibility for his actions.

"Today at the clinic Gráinne came to me," Jane launched straight into it. "She thinks she's pregnant."

She saw the smile fade from his eyes. He eyed her warily. "What's it to do with me?"

Jane frowned. "Please don't make things worse with lies."

"Mum!" Terry protested. "You're assuming I'm responsible without even asking me." He attempted to laugh.

"Are you, Terry?"

"I'm damned sure I wasn't the only one," he said with a scowl.

Jane acknowledged this with a slight nod of her head. "She seemed to think you might say that."

"But it's true, Mum," Terry protested. "She's been around. Some of the fellows . . ." he broke off.

"So you thought it was enough to leave everything up to her?" She eyed him sternly. "Don't you realise what selfish and irresponsible thinking that is? Apart from the risk of bringing a child into being, you are leaving yourself open to all kinds of trouble."

He winced at the scorn in her tone.

"I realise that now," he said lamely. "I didn't look much beyond having a good time."

Jane felt a sudden rush of love for him. She wanted to wipe the expression of shamed misery from his face, assure him that she understood and loved him. Instead she said coolly, "Well, until we get the result of the test we'll just have to wait and see." She stood up. "You'd better go to bed now."

"I'm sorry, Mum." He went to her contritely. "I'm sorry I put you in this position."

"Goodnight, Terry." She hesitated then inclined her cheek for his kiss. "Maybe it will be a good lesson to learn that you can't indulge your passions without paying some price."

"Goodnight, Mum." With a last wretched look at her, he went out the door and she heard his footsteps sounding heavily on the stairs. As soon as he was gone the rigidity left her pose and Jane went back to sit at her desk. He had been so happy and glowing when he came in, she thought regretfully.

Jane felt old and tired and unbearably vulnerable. If only she had someone to advise her, she thought, someone strong who would love and support her.

She leaned forward in her swivel chair and picked up the photograph she kept on her desk of her husband. She stared at his sombre, handsome face and wished desperately she could go back in time and somehow prevent what had happened. "Oh Eddie," she whispered, "I've tried to bring them up well. I've tried my best but . . ."

She went to the window and stared out at the darkened driveway. The bulb in the porch had burned out and in the street too the lamp was dead. She shivered thinking, Terry must take responsibility for what he had done, at least offer his support to Gráinne so that if she genuinely wanted it, she might have her child. But if she didn't . . .

Jane's spirits sank lower as she remembered her promise to help the girl. She had all along supported women's right to freedom of choice, but the thought now of an abortion was utterly distasteful to her.

Terry lay motionless in his darkened bedroom, unhappily staring at the dim outlines of the football posters on his wall. Normally he loved being back in the comfort and privacy of his own room after sharing a billet with fifteen other flying cadets. But tonight bitterness lay like silt upon his soul. He had been at the threshold of a wonderful life and now it was spoiled before it was barely begun.

What wounded him most was the memory of Claire's soft farewell to him. "No more misunderstandings, Terry."

Those gently whispered words had touched him deeply, filling him with hope for the future. And now it could never be! By his stupidity he had jeopardised his chances of happiness. He turned his head into the pillow to smother the groan of despair which rose in his throat.

Gráinne's love for Terry was genuine. She would even go ahead and have the baby, she told Trish, if only she could have him too. Three years of an age difference was nothing. Some men were still juvenile at forty. Terry, at nineteen, was as masculine and mature as ever she wished to find.

"You seem to have handled it well," Trish said approvingly. "But stick out for marriage, Grá. There's a limit to the amount of terminations anyone can have."

Gráinne had been pregnant before, five years earlier. She had solved her troubles then by crossing the water.

"He'll probably try and slither out of it," Gráinne said glumly, still smarting over the way Terry had ditched her the previous week. "What'll I do then?"

Trish shrugged. "Depends on how his mother feels. She might be just as glad for you to get rid of it. You might even get some money out of it."

"I don't want money. I want Terry." Gráinne began to cry. She had felt awful all day. She knew in her heart that she didn't want to have a baby or an abortion. She just wanted to be happy again, without pressures of any kind. She clutched her stomach. The cramps were really bad. Maybe she was having a miscarriage.

"Are you sure you're pregnant?" Trish asked suspiciously.

Gráinne did not bother to reply. Of course she was pregnant. She had known just as soon as she realised that the guy hadn't used a condom. That was the trouble with one-night stands, she thought resentfully. Men on the booze all night and no conscience about doing it to you unprotected. She had been too far gone herself to notice until it was too late. Yes, of course, she was pregnant.

Only she wasn't. She woke up the next morning to find her period had come. It was heavier than usual so it might have been an early miss. Her first feeling was relief, her second dismay. Now she would never get Terry to come back to her.

Gráinne went into the clinic with a long face. How was she going to face Dr McArdle? She grew hot just thinking of the things she had told her about all the times Terry had come to her flat and the things they had done.

Then Gráinne remembered that Jane was not due into the clinic until the following week. She felt weak with relief. She went to the fridge and was about to take out her specimen and dump it when she heard the outer door of the clinic opening and went out to the reception desk.

Mary McCann stood there looking tired and flustered. "My little boy was sick all night or I would have got here earlier," she explained. She took a tonic bottle filled with liquid out of her bag and thrust it down on the desk. "I lost the container the doctor gave me but I gave this one a good wash."

"Fine, fine," Gráinne said, hiding a smirk. Enough piss, she thought, to do fifty tests.

"You'll ring me as soon as you get the result?" Mary asked anxiously.

"Yes, of course, Mrs McCann. The very minute we hear," Gráinne said smoothly, and waited until she was gone before going back inside. So the woman was pregnant again, she thought.

Gráinne hunted in a drawer for a sterilised container.

She labelled it with the woman's name and poured in a small amount of her urine. She was about to jettison the rest of it when an idea took hold. Why couldn't she still have Terry? She stared at the bottle thoughtfully. Right! So McCann was almost certainly pregnant again. What could be more convincing?

Gráinne's emotions were still raw from Terry's rejection and her recent fright. She picked up her own container, labelled in Jane's handwriting, and filled it with the overflow from Mary McCann's specimen, then put both containers back in the fridge. She was only just in time, for the messenger was at the door to take them away to the laboratory.

Claire thought of little else but Terry. He had said he would ring her before the end of the week, but she was sure he would not wait that long. She wished it were possible for her to ring him as Monday and Tuesday came and went without a word. She told herself that it wasn't easy for him to contact her. After all there must be hundreds of people in Baldonnel using the public payphone.

Terry did queue up for the phone a number of times that week but each time it was his turn to make his call, shrugged and let the guy behind him have it. He tortured himself with visions of Claire's growing impatient at his silence and, in retaliation, starting to date some other guy. When the strain became too much for him he rang her number merely to hear her voice but, as soon as she spoke, hastily replaced the phone.

"What am I doing?" he asked himself in anguish. "Am I crazy?" He felt a little crazy. All week he had carried the burden of Gráinne's pregnancy around with him. The only time he could shuck off his anxiety was when he was in the air.

Now the squadron was engaged in formation flying during the day and each evening, once darkness fell, he and Con were putting in a lot of practise at night flying. Both manoeuvres demanded precision and close concentration and kept him from brooding too much. Soon they would begin their gunnery course. All these exercises provided a distraction from his unhappy thoughts, but as soon as he was back on the ground Terry felt swamped by his dilemma.

"So what if she is pregnant? I don't have to marry her," he told himself, but the thought of Claire's disgusted reaction sent him into the miseries again. She would never look at him once she knew. Terry groaned.

On Wednesday Claire was convinced that this was the night Terry would ring and she declined an invitation to go to a French film with some of the girls in her class. She sat in her room all evening, gazing absently at her books but with an ear cocked for the telephone.

It rang twice that evening. The first time she picked it up there was a pause and then she heard the engaged tone, the second time her mother answered it and laughingly replied. Disappointed, Claire went back along the landing to her own room. It was only Wednesday, she reminded herself. Still early yet.

She did not give up hope of hearing from Terry until the new week had started. When she could bear it no longer, she went across the street to talk to his twin. Claire couldn't believe that Terry would treat her so casually. She swallowed hard. There had to be another reason.

Sheena avoided her eyes. "I'm not allowed to say," she whispered at last. Say what? Claire began to be worried. Had he crashed, was that it? Her thoughts leapt in alarm.

"Oh Shee, he's all right, isn't he?" she cried. She had visions of him lying in a heap of smoking twisted metal, his back broken, his face disfigured. Her voice rose almost to a scream. "Please, Sheena, you've got to tell me."

Sheena glanced at her in alarm. "Stop it, Claire. It's not Terry . . ." Now she was embarrassed. "It's Gráinne."

Claire stared. What had Gráinne got to do with anything? She had seen for herself how Terry had ditched her at the party. Since then he had told her that the affair had been purely physical and he had never loved her. So how could it be Gráinne?

"She's pregnant," Sheena whispered, staring at Claire. "You must promise not to let on you know. Mum will have a fit if she finds out I've told."

Pregnant? Claire felt her cheeks flush.

"Mum's waiting for the result of the test," Sheena said, looking at Claire pityingly. "She doesn't know about you and Terry."

Claire nodded and turned away. She felt cold and sick and wanted more than anything in the world to bury herself somewhere so deep she would never come to surface again.

Two days into their gunnery course Terry and Con were top boys of their unit once more. Terry's dash and verve were matched by a similar lighting reaction in Con, and what had started out at the beginning of the cadet course as a kind of friendly rivalry between the two young men to attain first place, had deepened into strong friendship.

All week the sorties had kept Terry fully occupied but when not engaged in artillery practise, he was haunted by visions of being tied in a loveless marriage to Gráinne. Con never pried or took offence at his moodiness, just supported him tactfully with an infectious grin and an encouraging word.

Not that Con was having an easy time of it himself, Terry thought, as he successfully fired his quota of SNEB rockets and went into a tight climbing left hand turn, his participation in the sortie finished for the day. Con's gunnery captain had read his impressive dossier and, ever since, had been intent on cutting him down to size. Fireballs Brennan hadn't got his nickname for nothing. All week the man had been harassing Con, never letting up on his views on 'today's brash young pilots.' Even more disturbing to Terry was the gunnery captain's fixation with holding Con off from firing his machine-gun, or releasing his rockets, until the very last minute on the firing run. Scary, Terry thought, remembering how, early in the course, they had all been warned of the danger of pulling up at too low an altitude, not to mention the risk of ricochets and bombs so near the ground. Only that Con was such a damn good pilot, Terry reckoned, he would have been in trouble. He knew from his own experience just how much skill it took, heart pounding and muscles aching, to pull up the nose of the Marchetti and climb back into the sky. Terry did not think he would ever forget the shock he had experienced earlier in the week, when finding himself almost below 800 feet, the outer limit for safe recovery.

Now Terry flew in a holding pattern with the other Air Corps' aircraft and doubtfully watched Con's plane go zooming down for the last time on the target. Con was disturbingly low. Terry heard his own gunnery captain making this same observation on the radio to Con's captain, but Brennan had replied curtly that they were no lower than usual.

As Terry watched the exploding shells glint and sparkle against the circles traced on the sand, he was uneasily aware that the blast was dangerously close to the underbelly of the aircraft. He turned his head and saw that Captain O'Driscoll was watching the Marchetti with a preoccupied frown.

Their earphones crackled suddenly and Captain Brennan's irascible voice erupted in their ears. "The bloody fool! I warned him he was past interception point." And seconds later a frenzied, "Pull up, man. Pull up!"

Terry froze in his seat and stared through the rain-spattered windscreen as Con's aircraft fell sheerly away, its power spent, like a child's discarded toy tumbling out of the sky.

"Good Christ!" Liam O'Driscoll's gasp startled Terry and he sucked in his own breath in dismay, as the aircraft continued its slow dive earthward. Next on the radio transmitter was a confused babble of voices and, seconds later, the sound of impact.

Watched by the appalled eyes of the airborne unit, the aircraft hit the ground and exploded in a bright, blossoming flash.

Terry felt the impact of his own shock and his throat was

244

dry with horror and grief. His friend who had been closer to him than his brother was dead. Terry wanted to cry out at the unfairness of it and in his mind kept soundlessly repeating the same protest, until it broke from his lips in a groan. "No! Oh God no, not Con."

Below, moving fast along a track between postage stamp fields, an ambulance and two fire engines screamed towards the pall of smoke ballooning out over the crashed aircraft.

"Nothing anyone can do now," Captain O'Driscoll said heavily.

He hardly heard the terse command to regroup and return in formation to the base. After a look at his face, Captain O'Driscoll took over the controls, still stunned himself by the disastrous end to the sortie.

Jane had waited anxiously all week for the results of the pregnancy tests, but due to a go-slow at the hospital it was not until the following week that they were posted. They arrived at the clinic on the day after the funeral of the two crashed airmen. By this time Mary McCann was throwing up each morning, and Gráinne had fully regained her spirits and was out again with Trish every night, enjoying herself.

Jane read the result of Gráinne's test with dread. So she was pregnant. Her slight hope that it might have been a false alarm withered and died. She sat with her head bowed, swept by waves of hopelessness. Terry's life was spoiled. If only he had loved the girl, but she knew he did not. She found she was weeping and brushed aside her tears. A child was the sign of life, of hope, Jane reminded herself. Her first grandchild should be an occasion for rejoicing.

She picked up the report again and glanced at the result of Mary McCann's test. Positive, as she had expected. Running her eye over Mary's other laboratory tests Jane saw that her condition had worsened. There was a marked increase in coproporphyrin as well as delta-aminolevulinic acid. And this time the report showed that slight leukocytosis was present. Her eye swept further down the page and was arrested by a footnote.

"N.B. Accompanying urine specimen corresponds to an amazingly identical degree to McCann specimen, even down to typical colour changes within specified time. Could it be a case of duplication or an error in labelling?"

Another symptom of porphyria was the gradual change from normal-coloured urine to dark brown, red or even black. How could Gráinne have porphyria? It seemed highly improbable!

Jane tapped the report thoughtfully with her biro. She reached for the telephone and rang the laboratory.

When she put down the phone there was no doubt in her mind that both specimens had been produced by the same woman.

She went to the door and called Gráinne. When the girl entered Jane told her to sit down, then handed her the report. "I would like you to take your time and read this," she said. "I think you will grasp the significance of two urine specimens testing out identical in every way."

Gráinne saw her face and burst into tears.

"This is very serious," Jane said quietly. "I am not sure if interfering with a patient's specimen and falsifying tests is a criminal offence. If, however, you are still insisting that you are pregnant, I will arrange for you to be admitted to the hospital where full tests and checks can be carried out under supervision." She waited. In answer, the girl sobbed louder.

"But you don't really want that, do you?"

"N . . . no."

"Very well then. Of course, there is no question of your staying on here. I would like you to leave the clinic at once." Jane crossed to the door and opened it. "Whatever is owing to you will be sent on. Goodbye, Gráinne."

The girl went snivelling through the door and Jane closed it after her. Her legs felt suddenly unsteady and she went to sit behind her desk. "Thank God," she whispered. She had always prayed she would never be required to sanction another abortion and now she was spared this agonising dilemma. The telephone rang. Slowly, she picked it up.

"Mum! I can't go on like this.' Terry's voice cracked with misery. "I've got to see you."

"Yes, of course, Terry." She heard the shaky tone of her voice and firmly cleared her throat. "It's time we had another talk."

"See you at the weekend," he said, and rang off.

Jane slowly replaced the receiver. Her first instinct had been to give him some indication that he was off the hook, but she decided not to tell him until after they had returned from their trip to Spain. Jane sighed. It seemed cruel to prolong his distress, especially after the tragic death of his friend, but this was one lesson she wished to drive well and truly home.

Claire was a little taken aback when Jane asked her to sleep in the house while she was away in Spain. Her feelings about meeting Terry were very mixed. In a way Claire wished Sheena hadn't told her about himself and Gráinne, although it had undoubtedly softened the hurt at not hearing from him. She realised that it was shame, not indifference, which prevented him from keeping his promise. Each time their relationship showed signs of developing, she thought, something always happened to drive a wedge between them.

On the day of departure she went over early to the McArdle's house, knowing from experience that Jane would have lots of instructions to give Sheena and herself. Jane had written everything down on two foolscap sheets and Sellotaped them to the fridge door, but she still took time to go over it all with them again while Terry was out putting their cases in the car.

"I doubt the telephone in the apartment has been connected yet, so I'll leave the estate agent's number in case you need to get in touch," Jane concluded at last. "Liz here will help out in the evenings with Ruthie if you both have to go anywhere." She glanced at her receptionist and the girl grinned back.

Liz was the latest of the sprawling Murray family to work for Jane. She was pretty and easy-going and devoted to Ruthie.

Liz said earnestly, "Mammy said she'll be glad to do any shopping while you're away."

Jane nodded at her in a distracted fashion and turned to the girls again, "Now don't forget, Spain is one hour ahead of us. If you need to get a message to me be sure and ring before six in the evening."

"Mummy," sighed Sheena, "please don't worry. Nothing is going to happen. You're the one going away, not us. We'll be fine. Off you go and enjoy yourselves."

Jane nodded. She supposed she was fussing a bit but if she didn't get it all off her chest now knew she would spend the entire time away worrying about what she might have omitted.

"Now you won't forget to read my instructions?" she reminded them.

"No, we'll throw them in the bin the minute you're gone," Sheena said with a grin. "Of course, we'll read them, Mummy. What do you think! Anyway, you know well that Claire has everything off by heart already. She'll keep us on the straight and narrow, like she always does."

Jane chuckled. "Thank God for Claire. If I was relying on you, Madam, I don't know where we'd be." But she gazed affectionately at her daughter. She knew that Sheena had matured enough in the past year to take her responsibilities more seriously. She bussed Sheena's cheek and pulled Ruthie into her arms. "Bye, darling."

Ruthie tightened her arms in stranglehold about her mother's neck. "Tell Adela I was asking for her."

"If I see her."

"And give Fernando my undying love," Sheena said wickedly.

Jane ignored her and kissed Claire. "Keep an eye on these monsters," she joked, "there's a love."

Claire smiled back, acutely conscious of Terry watching

248

their farewells. He wore a scowling expression which she correctly divined as embarrassment. She met his eyes but he gave no sign that he was in any way thinking of her. He had made no apologies for not ringing her and she sensed he was tightly holding himself in check, lest he say too much. He strode out to the car without a backward look.

"Four whole days on our own," Sheena gloated. "Let's make the most of them."

Claire nodded absently, her heart with the disappearing car. She told herself that she was mad to care so much. Terry probably couldn't help flirting with every girl he dated. It was second nature to him. She swallowed her hurt and turned back into the house.

Terry got his first view of the apartment block peering out of the rear window of Fernando's car as it turned into the parking lot in front of *Las Cicadas*.

The Spaniard had met them because there was a one-day taxi strike at Malaga Airport. Jane was touched by Fernando's thoughtfulness and doubly glad she had telephoned early in the week to say they were coming. When he warmly inquired about *las tres princesas* Jane had to smile at this description of the girls and told him they were all well and sent their regards.

He's a good-looking bastard, Terry thought grudgingly, his eyes fixed on the back of Fernando's well-shaped head as the Spaniard swung the car into the roundabout and filtered into the flowing traffic. He noted the heavy gold watch on Fernando's wrist and the way his dark blonde hair fringed the collar of his cream silk shirt. Terry ran his hand defensively over his own freshly cropped army stubble. So this is the guy Claire likes, he thought.

Clearly his mother liked him too, judging by the way she was chatting and laughing. Almost flirting, Terry thought in amazement. He hadn't seen her so animated in years.

Fernando came with them to the door of the apartment. "I think everything is in order," he told Jane. "I made it my special concern. However, if there are any changes you would like made, please do not hesitate to ask."

"It's beautiful," Jane said, looking around. "I love it."

"Then I am satisfied." Fernando smiled at her enthusiasm. "I wish you many happy moments in Spain, Señora." He bowed over her hand.

What a smooth talker, Terry thought in disgust as he carried the cases inside. To think women actually fall for that line.

Then suddenly it didn't matter any more. Terry had walked through to the balcony and was confronted by the view of the sea. He stared at the pale sands and billowing waves. It was every bit as beautiful as Claire had said.

Next day Jane and Terry went shopping and walked back to the apartment, heavily laden down with carrier bags full of household articles, ranging from crockery and cooking pots to tea towels and electric light bulbs.

It took them the best part of an hour to put everything away and by the time they were finished, the sun was low in the sky.

"Want a drink, Mum?" Terry asked, going to the fridge.

"Mmm . . . that would be nice." Jane lifted a cushioned cane chair on to the balcony and lowered herself into it.

Terry poured chilled orange juice for himself and wine for his mother and they sat sipping their drinks and admiring the view.

Now would be a good time to tell him his worries are over, Jane thought, but a reluctance to spoil the afternoon with mention of Gráinne stopped her. Her mouth twisted in distaste. Not now, Jane decided. She found the whole subject too painful and distressing. Some time before they returned home she would carefully choose her moment. She put the matter out of her mind and gave herself over to enjoying the sun and the wine and the soothing sight of the sea. She began to yawn.

She was awakened by a light tapping on the apartment door and heard Terry get up to open it. There was a murmur of voices in the background and she struggled against the tide of weariness.

"No, please don't disturb her," she was dimly aware of a voice saying and then the door of the apartment closed.

"Who was that?" she asked as Terry came back.

"That Spanish guy," Terry answered shortly.

Jane was awake now. "I hope you were polite to him."

"Of course, Mum," Terry's expression was scornful. "I did everything but kiss San Fernando's hand."

"Now, Terry," Jane warned but she had to smile at his exasperated expression. How painful it can be, when young, to come up against someone as good-looking and well-off as Fernando Gonzalez.

Terry said sulkily, "He brought an invitation from his father to have dinner with him tonight."

That evening Jane dressed with extra care, choosing to wear a filmy blue dress which matched her eyes and fastening about her neck a gold and sapphire pendant, which had been a present from Eddie on their tenth wedding anniversary. She was not a beautiful woman or even a strikingly good-looking one, but she had a certain presence and there was about her a glow of goodness and gentle authority that was beautiful in itself.

Terry also dressed with care. He wasn't going to appear at a disadvantage. He knotted his tie and eased down the collar of his shirt and regarded himself critically in the mirror. Maybe not as flash as pretty boy Gonzalez, he thought sardonically, but at least he was taller than him by an inch or two. As Terry attached his flying emblem to the lapel of his blazer he wished his hair was not cropped quite so close. Short cuts were all very well back at the barracks, he thought. He was unaware how well the military clip suited him, moulding the fine bones of his head and accentuating his cheekbones. He thrust out his jaw at an uncompromising angle and went out to join his mother.

It was only a short walk to the restaurant and they arrived just after eight-thirty. At the sight of them Antonio left the group of people he was with and came forward, his dark, sorrowful eyes lit by a welcoming smile. Jane thought that his whole face changed when he smiled and became youthful, less melancholy. She smiled shakily back at him. She involuntarily dug her nails into the palm of her hand.

"Señora." He took the maltreated hand and bent over it. "I am very glad you could come. I was afraid you might have to hurry back to your children. Fernando tells me that in your absence they are on their own." At the concern in his deep voice Jane quickened with pleasure. She looked up at him and felt herself drowning in his dark eyes. To break the spell she said:

"My youngest is the only one I worry about, but she's in good hands. Sheena, my older girl, is well able to look after her." She studied his appearance and saw that his hair was shorter than it had been in the summer and consequently the grey not so evident. His skin was still fresh and, for a man of his age, he had very few lines. Then she realised with a start that he was still holding her hand. Jane had to ease her hand gently from Antonio's grip, and to her dismay felt the blood rush to her cheeks.

"My son speaks often of these young ladies," Antonio told her. "I can see they have made a big impression on him." He turned toward Terry. "This young man is another of your children?"

"He is." She realised that her reply was brief almost to the point of gaucheness, but her mind felt like jelly. She was standing there like a teenager, blushing and staring at him. She became suddenly aware that one of Antonio's party, a rather striking woman with beautiful dark hair coiled on the nape of her neck, had turned her eyes soulfully upon them as if willing him back to the group. His wife? Jane became suddenly self-conscious.

"Come and join the rest of my party, Señora." Antonio placed his hand at her elbow and pressed her forward.

A waiter approached with menus. Jane took one and ran her eye down it as Antonio poured wine into their glasses.

There was a ripple of laughter as someone told a joke. All of them, with the exception of Jane and Terry, were Spanish but, out of politeness, some English was being spoken at the table. Jane caught Terry's eye and he gave her a slow wink. She could see he was entering into the spirit and attempting a conversation in halting Spanish with the lady on his left.

"You are glad you have come back to Spain?" Antonio suddenly asked her.

Jane nodded. And you, she wanted to say, are you glad? "I look forward to spending a lot of time here," she said. "You have such a wonderful climate."

"Ah, so it is only our climate you are enamoured with," a man accused with dolorous inflection. "Are you not at all interested in our architecture, Señora? The wonders of Seville or Granada?" He flung up his hand. "Sun is all very well but art considerably more enriching."

"But surely one can enjoy both?" Jane suggested, her droll look invoking sympathetic laughter from her audience. "I can only say that if you were forced to endure our wet Irish climate for twelve months of the year, you might not be so high-minded." She laughed to take any sting out of her words.

"I have often thought of making a trip to Ireland," Antonio addressed the table thoughtfully, "but now I wonder would that be wise . . . With so much water," he gestured in mock dismay, "I might well be drowned."

A burst of laughter greeted this observation.

As the conversation switched into other channels she sipped her muscatel and mused on the fact that she was seeing a side to Antonio she had never seen before. She raised her eyes and found him regarding her intently.

"I never thought to see you again, Jane," he murmured suddenly. It was the first time he had called her by her name and his Spanish inflection made it sound as Spanish as José or Juan, causing her a sudden sharp pang of recollection.

"And now there is the miracle of your reappearance," Antonio went on in the same low intimate tones as if they were the only ones at the table, "and that golden world of which you were the sun, sleeping all this time with my memories, is fully awakened."

His voice husky with feeling rose the hairs on Jane's neck. She reached for her glass in defence, needing to occupy her shaking hands with something. She raised her eyes and met his over the rim of the glass. She saw the doubts and fears and the anguish of wanting that seethed behind those dark eyes and she waited with joyful resignation for what else he might say. Before he could speak the door of the restaurant swung open and Fernando entered, his eyes seeking those of his father across the width of the room. Antonio rose at once and went to him.

The two men manoeuvred a wheelchair between them through the doorway. Obviously some aunt or close friend, Jane thought, as the frail elderly woman put up a hand to pat Fernando's cheek, and Jane was impressed by his kindness in delaying his meal to bring her.

Jane smiled at the woman as Fernando lifted her on to a chair at the other side of Antonio. Menus were presented but the woman redirected the hovering waiter towards Fernando and accepted a glass of mineral water from Antonio.

'*Nada*,' Jane heard her say in a low voice. She sat hunched in the chair as though her back ached and she was missing the support of the wheelchair. The doctor in Jane felt curious as to her malady and was pondering this when Antonio turned to her and said quietly. "Señora, I would like you to meet my wife, Elena."

Jane automatically glanced towards the beautiful woman beside Terry, then seeing that Antonio was indicating the frail woman at his side, felt a flare of amazement. This was his wife! She had to take a deep breath to steady herself.

"How do you do," Jane whispered, and forced herself to extend her hand. The other woman pressed it between thin, wasted fingers.

"I am very happy to meet you, Dr McArdle. Fernan tells me that you are pleased with your new apartment." Elena's voice was sweet and gentle and very slightly accented.

"I am thrilled with it, Señora Gonzalez," Jane enthused, while inside she was torn by grief and dismay. Oh the poor, sick woman, she thought. She remembered how Fernando had mentioned something about his mother's health but none of it had prepared her for this.

Elena Gonzalez lifted a shaking hand to her lips and pressed it there as though troubled by a fleeting spasm of pain. Her eyes were huge and tragic in her sallow face and her body thin and wasted in the velvet dress. Antonio bent towards her and whispered something. Elena shook her head and fluttered her hand at him. When she turned away from him Antonio watched her with such a fond, sorrowing expression that Jane was overwhelmed by a terrible wasting pity. For Antonio's wife and for herself. She knew she had no choice but to put aside all thoughts of him and to keep well away, lest she be betrayed into an action for which she would never forgive herself.

Thoughts of Eddie and Hugh had somehow returned to haunt Claire since coming to sleep in the McArdle's house. She seemed to feel them all around her and, at every turn of the stairs, it was as if they had either gone up or down before her and were always just out of sight.

Claire was not upset, merely grieved by these shades from the past. She found herself wondering if, in the weeks following the tragedy, Terry had ever been similarly affected, then rejected the notion. Although not insensitive, Terry did not have a lot of imagination in the way that Ruthie and Hugh had. Perhaps that was why Terry had such an iron nerve when it came to flying. Claire remembered on the two occasions she had gone on board an aeroplane her imagination had run riot, so perhaps there was something to be said for the lack of one.

She was preparing for bed and crossed to the window in her blouse and tights to look out of the window. What was Terry doing right now? she wondered. Somehow staring into the dark, starry heavens made her feel closer to him. The moon hung full and low in the sky and she wished she could use it like a satellite to carry back images of him.

"What are you doing, Claire?" Ruthie asked, coming into the room.

Claire turned from the window with a start and laughed a little self-consciously. "Just looking at the moon. It's beautiful tonight, isn't it? So luminous and full."

Ruthie came to stand beside her. "Yes," she agreed, "like a huge blob of yoghurt. Do you look at it every night?"

"You can't always see it," Claire said, "but yes," she admitted. "Certainly, I look for it every night."

They stood in companionable silence staring out. Of all the McArdles Ruthie was perhaps the most imaginative. Claire had thought Jane was being fussy when she had lined up Liz to sit with the little girl in the hour or two before she and Sheena got in from college, but she saw the wisdom of it now. Ruthie was exhibiting signs of stress since Jane's departure and was nervy and disinclined to sleep on her own.

Claire indulged her, although she did not sleep half so soundly as on her own. But then she had not expected to sleep well. Not here in this house which held such forbidden memories. Across the landing where more than once . . . She glanced away, refusing to release that particular dragon.

Ruthie jumped into bed and pulled the duvet snugly around her. Claire finished undressing and went down to the bathroom. On her way back she saw through her open door that Sheena had left on the powerful light over her drawing board. Claire bent to look at the exquisitely detailed sketch. Sheena was really talented, she thought wistfully. She only wished she had been endowed with such a satisfying, tangible gift. She switched off the lamp and returned to her room.

Ruthie was asleep. Claire got into bed, careful not to waken her. She lay listening to the shifting night sounds, the gurgling of pipes, then closed her eyes and allowed herself the luxury of dwelling on Terry, doing so with a mixture of more pain than pleasure and finding it not quite the antidote she had hoped for.

Jane and Terry spent a very leisurely Sunday and were ready to go sight-seeing on their last day. Jane hired a car and rather adventurously decided to make the 170 kilometres trip to Almeira, for the sole reason that she had gone there years before with Antonio. She saw this trip in the nature of a farewell to certain impossible hopes and dreams she had been unconsciously entertaining and which, after meeting Elena, she realised could never be. There had been mention over dinner the previous night of Frigiliana, which was approximately an hour's drive inland and another example of Moorish village architecture, but Jane was moved by nostalgia to make the longer trip. "You've been there before, Mum?" Terry asked, looking curiously across at her. He had the road map open on his knee and was plotting their course with moving finger.

"Yes, I had a romance going with a rather attractive Spaniard and he brought me." Jane flashed him a quick smiling glance. "Oh, years ago. Long before I met your father." Actually, she could recall very little about the place, but as soon as she saw the huge fortress, with turreted ramparts looming high above the city, it all came back to her.

Jane planned to stay in the city just long enough to eat, buy a few souvenirs for the girls, and to visit the *Alcazaba*. They had a long journey back, and she had already picked out the part of the coast where they would stop and swim.

She went into the cathedral for a quick visit but it was the fortress which exercised the strongest pull on her. She climbed the steep hillside a few yards behind Terry and reached the top breathing hard. Looking back down the way they had come she was visited by a flash of memory: Antonio and herself pausing on the hillside to kiss and then later, arms entwined, gazing out over the city and the sea. She remembered him telling her that the *Alcazaba* was the haunt of thieves and not a safe place for people to come to on their own, especially at night. She shivered and looked about for Terry. She saw him clamber energetically on top of a ruined wall and balance there, looking downwards, a hand shading his eyes.

"Let's go," she called, suddenly wanting to be gone from this place. "I think we should be moving."

Jane was glad of his supporting arm as they descended over the sloping, rough ground but, even with it, she stepped incautiously and wrenched her ankle. Her face contorted in pain.

"No! I'm all right," she cut him short when he tried to insist that she sit down and rest. "Don't fuss! I'm not an octogenarian."

"Okay, okay," Terry said, throwing up his hands. He had been enjoying the protective feeling of helping her. Poor Mum, he told himself. After all she's over forty. This kind of thing is all very well at my age but too much for her.

They went on down the hill in silence. Jane was annoyed with herself for her irritation and even more for not watching her steps. She had been thinking of the look in Antonio's eyes when he'd said, "That golden world of which you were the sun". Oh my God, she thought tiredly. Poetry and romance at my age. What a fool!

She drove fast on the road back to Nerja, taking risks in her determination to cover the distance. In record time she pulled up a few miles short of Motril and parked in sight of the Calahonda beach. With more than half the journey behind them she felt she had earned her swim.

An hour later, feeling much restored, she sat on the beach and combed her damp hair back from her face. Terry patted himself dry and stretched out beside her, letting the sun dry his swimming trunks. They spoke little, content to relax and enjoy the tingling aftermath of their swim. It had been fun, if exhausting, pitting themselves against the high waves.

"Thanks, Mum," Terry said suddenly. "I mean for bringing me with you on this trip. I was really low after what happened to Con. God, it was awful. I mean, right in front of our eyes." His voice shook and he rubbed a hand over his eyes.

Jane watched him sympathetically. As she gave him time to recover his composure she thought how good it was to hear him expressing gratitude for the holiday.

"I'm glad you've enjoyed it," she told him now. "Having you along makes it a lot more fun for me."

Terry grinned. "Thanks, Mum, you can hardly say anything else." But he was pleased. He genuinely wanted to make his mother happy and sometimes wished fiercely there was something he could do to make up for the difficult time she had endured in the years since his father's death. She had been given a rough deal yet she had managed to survive and make a good living for them all. They had never wanted for anything and now there was this terrific apartment in Spain. He was really proud of her.

He felt sudden shame at what she must have endured as a result of his fling with Gráinne and his smile faded at the thought of what might await him on their return.

"Mum," he began tentatively, feeling reluctant to broach the subject but desperately needing to air his fears. "About Gráinne. Look, I know I was wrong . . ."

"Terry!" Jane put a gentle hand on his arm. "I have a confession to make. I intended telling you when we got back, but now seems as good a time."

He listened and overwhelming relief showed on his face. "I hardly dared to hope," he blurted. "In fact I was sure there was no way out of it. Oh, Mum, it seems almost too good to be true."

He is so touchingly young, Jane thought, and he has a conscience and sensitivity. She let him run on before raising her hand and saying seriously.

"This time it worked out, Terry. But what if it hadn't, or if you had got some teenage girl pregnant and her family insisted you stand by her? You are far too young at nineteen to take on such responsibilities. Apart from anything else you don't have the money to support a family," Jane pointed out. "When the time is right let it be with someone you really love and want to spend your life with. Promiscuity does not lead to happiness."

Terry nodded his head, prepared to believe her.

"Here endeth the lesson," Jane said lightly, but with a tired smile. She squeezed his arm affectionately. "Let's get back on the road while I'm still awake."

"Mum, why don't you let me drive?" Terry suggested. "I'm a good driver. You've always said so, and you look tired."

"But you're not used to driving on the right hand side of the road," Jane said. "And you haven't got your licence with you. I mean, what if we're stopped by the police? They have a name for being very strict here, you know."

"We won't," Terry said firmly. "C'mon, Mum, let me. You know you want to."

Jane was tempted. Perhaps I'm fussing too much, she thought. "Okay," she agreed. "But mind you take it easy. No tail-gating or overtaking. We're not in a rush, so just concentrate on keeping on the right hand side of the road."

"Sure thing, Mum."

They walked over the hot sand and climbed the steps to the road. Jane threw their towels in the boot of the car and handed Terry the key. He took it and sat jauntily behind the wheel.

"Blast off!" Terry said, and gunned the car down the road.

"Don't forget what I said," Jane murmured. She opened her mouth and let a yawn take her. It was good to lean against the seat and feel her aching muscles relax.

They were on the narrow, winding switchback which followed the shoreline into the thriving port city of Motril. Terry slowed behind a convoy of lorries laden down with the day's harvest of sugar cane. Beside him, Jane blinked, giving only a fraction of her attention to his chatter about some marvellous girl.

"She doesn't know about Gráinne of course," Terry said.

Who was she? Jane wondered sleepily. He seemed very keen on her. Youth, she thought in resignation. Barely rescued from the perils of one dubious alliance before leaping headlong into another.

"I can't wait to get back and make it right with her," Terry was saying. "But she's not the kind to hold a grudge. That's what I like so much about her, Mum. She's great to talk to. I mean she listens and makes intelligent remarks. Not like some girls with nothing between their shoulders."

He sounds over the moon about this girl, thought Jane uneasily. She forced herself to listen.

"I think I always liked her. Even before she came away with us on holidays," Terry admitted with a sheepish laugh.

"Give me my sunglasses, Mum," he said suddenly. "This sun is getting me right in the eyes. On the back seat," he directed her. "Under the map."

Jane unfastened her seat-belt and reached into the back. It was Claire he was talking about. Terry was in love with Claire. Distractedly she handed him the sunglasses, as she tried to grasp the significance of what he was telling her. When had it all started? Jane wondered in dismay. And how far had it gone? She wanted, yet didn't want to know.

As her son chatted on, Jane told herself it was incredible and yet not so incredible. She was amazed that she hadn't cottoned on to it earlier. Right there in front of her eyes if only she had seen it. She felt a strong compulsion to let Terry know something about Claire's past. Perhaps warn him that all wasn't as uncomplicated as it seemed. But what could she say?

Your father made her pregnant when she was thirteen years old and I destroyed the child in her womb.

Jane shuddered. Who should be warned against whom? Her handsome headstrong son or the girl who had already suffered enough at their hands? Only one thing was clear. Terry should be made fully aware of the situation before he committed himself further. Otherwise, Jane believed there might be even greater difficulties to face in the future. But how to do this without seeming to discredit Claire?

"Terry," Jane began, "There is something I feel I must tell you, but I don't quite know how to say it."

"What about, Mum?" Terry frowned in concentration as he carefully rounded the corner. He had hardly time to straighten out when he was faced with another steep bend. "Bloody awful road," he muttered, as the lorry in front braked and skidded out of sight on dusty wheels, loose pieces of sugar cane working free of the slackened ropes and littering the road.

Jane began, choosing her words carefully. "Claire is a lovely girl – please don't take amiss what I am about to say – but certain events took place in the past which make it unwise."

"Mum!" Terry interrupted, taking his eyes off the road to glance at her. "I know all that! Dad fancied Claire's mother, is that it?" He shot her a glance that was both pained and defiant. "I know all that!"

Jane was taken aback but carried on. "I think not," she said quietly. "There was rather more to it than you imagine." She broke off, recollecting where they were, negotiating torturous bends in the shimmering heat. Involuntarily she glanced out the window. The least little distraction, she thought with a shiver.

"You can't just leave it like that," Terry protested, two bright spots burning in his cheeks. He drove faster, his hands painfully gripping the steering wheel. "Come on out with it, Mum. Whatever you have to say won't make me feel any less for Claire." He caught his breath painfully. "I can't believe you're doing this. I always thought you liked her." He was almost panting in his distress. "I really did. Now you're trying to make me think badly of her." He choked, unable to go on.

"No, no that's the very last think I want," Jane cried, distressed beyond words herself. Hardly aware of what she was doing she put out her hand to reassure him that he was wrong. Terry jumped nervily at her touch and swung fast round the narrow bend without slackening speed. As he did so, a huge bale of sugar cane broke free from the lorry in front and somersaulted into his path. Instinctively, Terry swerved to avoid it and his tyres skidded out of control on the loose, sappy canes, sending him speeding into the path of an oncoming car.

"We're going to die," was Jane's last horrified thought before the two cars slammed together. She felt agonising pain in her head and chest, then everything was blotted out as she lost consciousness.

The ambulance arrived within a half-hour. Terry heard the wailing siren as he slumped in the seat beside his mother and listened in anguish to her shallow breathing. A highway patrol man stood in his green uniform directing traffic past the two crashed vehicles. The other driver had been wearing a seat-belt like Terry and was dazed but unharmed.

Why wasn't Mum wearing hers? Terry wondered, then remembered her reaching into the back for his sunglasses. Damn! She must have forgotten to fasten it again. He averted his eyes from the angry red gash on her forehead where she had been thrown forward into the windscreen.

Terry felt a deep sense of guilt. Fine fighter pilot he would make if every time the going got rough he allowed himself to be distracted.

He got out of the car, dazed and shocked, but apart from an aching hip and shoulder where the seat-belt had cut into his flesh, he didn't think he was injured. The ambulance had halted a little way off and the orderlies came with a stretcher. They checked Jane's pulse and made a quick preliminary examination before carefully lifting her on to the stretcher.

She stirred and moaned softly as the doors slammed shut and the ambulance moved forward.

Terry bent over her. "You're all right, Mum," he told her. "We're on our way to the hospital."

She opened her eyes. They were dazed and unfocused. She rolled her head on the pillow from side to side and muttered his name.

"Don't try to speak," Terry begged her.

Her lids fluttered and closed. As the ambulance swayed and bumped its way over the narrow twisty roads into Motril Terry sat tensely beside her, his eyes trained anxiously on her face.

About the same time that the ambulance was speeding into Motril, Claire was standing in front of the stove poking bubbling spaghetti with a fork. Sheena came noisily into the kitchen and flung down her satchel.

"I'm starving," Sheena cried. "When will tea be ready?"

"About ten minutes."

Sheena sat down at the table and began pinching pieces out of a loaf and stuffing them into her mouth, as Claire turned back to the stove.

Terry would be home in another few hours, she thought, but he'd be so late she wouldn't see him. By the time he got up in the morning she would have already left for college. With Jane due home, this was her last night. All too soon she would be back in her own house.

Back to Annette and her endless drinking.

Claire sighed. "Sheena!" she called behind her. "Will there be enough in this for three of us?" holding up the family-size jar of pasta sauce. "Loads," Sheena said absently. She had already made herself a cup of tea and was munching her way through cheese and crackers. "Bung it in and let's get started. I'll die if I don't eat soon."

Claire heated the sauce and drained the spaghetti. Another four hours and they'll be leaving for the airport, she thought. It occurred to her that even if she missed her nine-thirty lecture in the morning and hung about the house she still mightn't see Terry. Miss a lecture and her exams in less than two months! She must be mad where Terry was concerned.

She hadn't done much studying over the last few days and rationalised her idleness with the excuse that Ruthie and Sheena needed her. Now she heaped spaghetti on to plates and generously ladled tomato sauce on top.

"Tea's ready," she called. "Come and get it!"

Terry strolled restlessly up and down the hospital corridor, acutely aware that in a matter of hours their flight would be departing from Malaga.

He sighed and rubbed his bruised shoulder, regretting that he had made light of his own injuries when the doctor wished to examine him. His hip too was throbbing painfully.

"Señor McArdle!" he heard someone calling and swung round. He saw a nurse beckoning to him and followed her eagerly into the curtained cubicle. His mother lay propped up in bed and, to Terry's relief, her eyes were open.

Jane smiled wanly at him, her face pale under the huge sticking plaster on her forehead, and put out her hand to him. Terry moved close and gently took it.

"Mum! Thank God." He gave a shaky little laugh. "You gave me a real fright, you know."

"Sorry," Jane whispered. "I suppose we are lucky to be alive." She was in a hospital gown and he saw that under the white material her chest was bulkily bandaged. Terry swallowed hard. He found himself trembling and sank down on the chair beside the bed.

"Are you all right?" Jane asked in weak anxiety. "You look very pale."

"I'm fine, Mum. Just a few bruises, that's all."

She nodded in relief and her eyelids began to droop.

"The doctor has given her a sedative," the nurse told him quietly. "She will be very uncomfortable for a while."

"But we are flying home in another few hours," his voice tailed away. Now what was going to happen?

The nurse suggested that he might like to speak to the doctor and Terry nodded and followed her out of the cubicle.

"Your mother has suffered three broken ribs and is concussed," he told Terry. "It will be some time before she will be well enough to leave the hospital." He glanced into the young man's anxious face and decided not to tell him that one rib had pierced a lung.

"But we are due to fly home tonight." Somehow he had been hoping for a miracle to get them to the airport. He saw now that this was out of the question.

The doctor looked at him sympathetically. "Your mother needs rest and care," he said gently. "She will be in good hands here."

Terry did not doubt it, but how could he go off and leave her on her own like this in a strange country? Yet go he must, Terry realised. He was due back on duty at Baldonnel next day. Then he had an idea. He would ring Antonio Gonzalez. The Spaniard would advise him what to do.

Terry searched in his mother's bag and found the property developer's business card. His residence was listed.

Señor Gonzalez responded at once to Terry's plea for help.

He was really decent, Terry thought as he replaced the receiver, thinking of the Spaniard's offer to drive him to Malaga Airport. He had been very concerned about Jane and was making plans to visit her. As Terry hurried back to where his mother lay, he felt immensely relieved at having someone so reliable to take care of her.

An hour later, Terry sat in the front seat of the Mercedes beside Fernando, as the powerful car sped along by the darkened coast. He had been a bit taken aback when he came out of the hospital to find not Antonio but his son waiting at the entrance. The young Spaniard had regarded him unsmiling and clicked open the passenger door, without getting out of the car.

"Ah, so San Fernando isn't the paragon Mum thinks," Terry told himself, amused. He grinned and relaxed back in the seat.

They had less than ninety minutes to get to the airport.

"Think we'll make it?" Terry glanced at the Spaniard's aloof profile.

"Naturally," Fernando replied haughtily. He rested his hands lightly on the wheel, exerting no more pressure than was needed to keep the powerful car speeding through the night. He drove exceedingly well, Terry grudgingly admitted. The car was a beauty, of course. He would love to drive it himself.

As though tuned into his thoughts Fernando asked, "Your mother was driving at the time of the accident?"

"No . . . I was," Terry admitted reluctantly.

"Aah, you were."

Terry felt the blood warm his cheeks. "A cargo of sugar cane dropped its load right in our path," he said.

"You swerved to avoid it, eh?"

"Something like that," Terry agreed.

"You were going too fast?"

Terry frowned. "Not really."

"Perhaps you are not used to driving?"

"Yes, I am," Terry answered shortly, resentful of this interrogation. Who the hell did he think he was!

"It must have been a great shock," Fernando said, suddenly becoming more human. "I am sure you are very concerned about your mother."

"Naturally!" Terry sounded every bit as haughty as the Spaniard.

They stopped by the apartment to pick up Terry's bag and drove swiftly on. No words passed between them on this final lap of the journey, but when Fernando stopped the car before the airport terminal building, he turned to Terry and said gently, "Please believe we will do everything in our power to ensure that your mother makes a good recovery." He smiled warmly and held out his hand. "*Hasta luego.*"

"So long!" Terry shook it briefly and smiled in return. "Thanks for the lift."

"*De nada,*" Fernando said graciously.

When he was gone Terry glanced at his watch and saw that they had made the airport with eight minutes to spare. Naturally! Despite himself he had to grin. He took the remaining few yards at a painful run and arrived panting in front of the check-in desk. As he passed his ticket over the counter his jauntiness left him and he was suddenly hit by a wave of loneliness. How happily he and his mother had arrived in Spain only a few short days ago. He swallowed past the obstruction in his throat, unable to rid himself of the feeling that he had deserted her.

Claire was late going to bed. She wanted everything to look just right when Jane returned and, as soon as the other two had gone yawning up the stairs, began cleaning the kitchen, doing a thorough job of tidying presses and mopping out the floor. One thing seemed to lead to another. The cooker hadn't been cleaned in weeks and detracted from the overall effect. When at last she turned off the kitchen light and wearily climbed the stairs to bed, it was after one o'clock.

The bath beckoned invitingly and she gave into the temptation to run the hot water and have a long soak. There was never enough hot water at home to do more than just shallow-bathe. She mingled in some of Sheena's lavender bath essence and lowered herself into the scented water.

She lay there letting the hot water wash over her, drawing the ache from her tired muscles. Her hair spread out like a pale, silken fan, dark gold where it dipped the water. The occasional lazy stirring of her limbs was the only sound to break the silence.

Gradually she became aware of sounds below: a car stopping, doors slamming, footsteps in the hall. Surely they weren't home already!

She stepped on to the floor, wrung out her wet hair, and wrapped the towel about her damp body. She opened the bathroom door and was about to go quickly to her room when she heard footsteps on the stairs. Claire turned her head and saw Terry step on to the landing.

For a moment she froze, the sight of him seeming to deprive her of all movement.

Terry checked, tiredly, and his bag dropped on the carpet. Framed in the open doorway he saw a slim girl, the snowy whiteness of her cotton towel and the dark gold of her long, wet hair accentuated by the light falling on them. Then the haze of tiredness cleared from his eyes and it was Claire.

They stared at each other for a long moment, and then Terry moved forward as Claire came to meet him. He put out both his arms to her and she felt them going about her and he held her close to him in a desperate grip.

"Mum's not with me," he spoke against her wet hair. "We . . . she . . . had an accident." His voice shook. "She's back in Spain in a hospital in Motril. I had to come home on my own. Oh Clairey." He looked down into her face with such a look of misery that her heart caught in her throat.

Forgetful of her towel, she raised her hand and gently stroked his face. How pale and exhausted he was. His eyes in the dim light had an odd, blind look. She drew him with her through the open door of the nearest bedroom – Jane's – and his arms lifted her and pushed her down on the bed. He pulled aside the thick cotton towel, and laid his tired face between her small firm breasts. Her skin was fresh from the bath, cool and sweet, and he kissed it lingeringly, moving his tired face and aching neck against it, holding her closer. Then he raised himself up and his mouth burned kisses on hers and his arms about her drove the breath from her body.

"Oh Clairey," he told her softly, his voice breaking huskily in his throat, "I've missed and wanted you so much." When his hands moved again Claire felt a fleeting fear which she quickly banished. This was not Eddie. This was Terry . . . Terry . . .

There was a great physical hunger in Terry's touches and kisses, as though he were trying to lose himself in her firm, smooth body, to recover from the tremendous strain of the past hours. She was glad to be able to give him that.

Jane was injured – maybe badly. Tomorrow enquiries would have to be made and the others told. But now in the quiet, sleeping house there was only herself and Terry, his hands and his mouth, kissing and caressing her, and needing her. To think he might have been injured. Killed! But he was alive and in her arms. Nothing else mattered.

At last he shuddered and was still, his arm thrown possessively across her body, in a deep sleep. Claire eased the duvet out from under him and drew it snugly about the pair of them. There was a faint light under the bedroom door and the usual shifting, creaking night sounds of the McArdle's house. Once an ambulance wailed past in the distance and once, close to the house, some feline prowler noisily overturned a refuse bin, but Terry did not stir. Claire held him closer, her cheek against his hair, and was not fearful of anything any more. Presently she grew drowsy herself, lulled by his breathing into a sleep as sound as his own.

Towards morning Claire awoke and felt Terry stir and pull away from her. After a moment she opened her eyes sleepily and turned her head to look at him. He was gazing at her and he smiled and pulled her into his arms. Then he winced and Claire saw his eyes darken with pain.

"What's the matter?" she whispered.

"My . . . shoulder . . . it hurts like hell."

"Let me see." He was wearing only a shirt and she gently eased it across his chest and bared his shoulder. She drew in her breath sharply. A livid bruise ran from his collar bone down along the left side of his chest and across his right hip bone. With gentle fingers she stroked the bruised area and then stooped her head to brush it with her lips.

Terry felt as if something had flopped in his stomach. His throat tight and dry, he reached for her, desperate to make love to her again. When Claire came readily into his arms he read the same hunger in her eyes.

Later, lying in each other's arms, with the early morning light creeping into the room, Terry told Claire what had happened on the road to Motril and what the doctor had said about Jane and how Fernando Gonzalez had driven him to the airport.

"It's getting late . . . the others may wake up." She sat up hurriedly in the bed then looked in confusion at her naked breasts. Terry laughed at her expression and tenderly wrapped his arms about her, covering her shoulders and breasts with tiny kisses.

"You are so beautiful," he kept telling her.

Weakly, Claire pulled away. "I'm afraid Ruthie will come looking for me."

"No, she won't. It's too early." Terry tried to pull her back to him but Claire resisted. She held the duvet against her.

"Close your eyes," she told him and seeing that she was serious, he reluctantly obeyed. "Keep them shut," Claire ordered, and reached for the crumpled cotton towel on the floor . . .

Terry closed his eyes but as soon as she slipped from the bed he opened them again. He watched her bend and pick up the skimpy towel and wrap it about her slim body. He could not get enough of looking.

The days that followed were a mixture of unease and delight. Claire's anxiety about Jane was compounded by feelings of guilt at having slept with Terry in his mother's bed. At the same time, she felt loved and cherished as never before.

She came home from college each evening hoping he would be there before her. He always was. He had Jane's car to travel from the barracks, and a genuine excuse for the late passes on the grounds that he must take care of his sisters in his mother's absence.

Sometimes he stayed the night and got up very early next morning to drive back to Baldonnel before the bugle sounded reveille. The long hours before bedtime they spent in the kitchen, sitting apart, touching only fleetingly when she handed him a mug of coffee or he passed behind her chair as she was helping Ruthie with her homework, but stroking each other with their eyes and their thoughts until the tension was almost too much to bear. Later when Ruthie was asleep he would be waiting for her and they would come together in a frenzy of lovemaking. It was as if the accepted standards of behaviour were temporarily suspended and

271

they lived in a curious kind of erotic limbo, enjoying the solace of each other's bodies with an almost pagan sensuality and deliberately blocking out everything but themselves.

After lovemaking, lying in each other's arms, they talked about things closest to their hearts. Terry told her how Con had died. He did not go into details about the crash for the memory was still too raw and painful. Claire lay on the pillow watching him and fondling the tendrils of hair on his neck with a gentle hand as he spoke. And then of his own accord Terry brought up the subject of Gráinne.

"When Mum told me I was off the hook I was bowled over," Terry confessed. "I couldn't take it in at once. I felt . . . I dunno . . . like it must feel before a firing squad and at the last minute someone comes dashing up with a reprieve. Like a bloody miracle!" He laughed softly. "I knew I didn't deserve it. Oh Claire, the worst part was not being able to see you or ring you like I wanted. You must have wondered."

"Yes I did."

"I was sure you would despise me. I despised myself. God! I felt so trapped. I kept worrying about the mess I was in, even when I was flying, and that's really stupid. You need every bit of concentration or you could end up in bits. I found myself hating Gráinne, which was unfair, and myself for mixing Mum up in it and letting her sort out my mess. Squalid!" His voice shook.

Beside him in the dark, Claire shuddered. She thought she would want to die if Terry ever felt like that about her. Despite herself, her sympathy went out to the unfortunate Gráinne. But although she felt her own heart would break if she lost Terry, she knew she would never resort to tricks to keep him. She would rather give him up. Their relationship could only endure, Claire told herself, just as long as he loved and wanted her, not because of any sense of obligation.

Antonio Gonzales rang twice during the week, reporting favourably on Jane's progress, and then at the end of the first week a letter arrived from Jane addressed to them all.

Sheena read aloud to the others, her voice quivering with suppressed tears.

'My dear children, I am getting better every day so please do not worry. I think of you all the time and look forward to the moment when we can be together again. I wish you could visit but that is the drawback of having an accident abroad. I should have planned it better! Everyone here is being so kind. Fernando came to see me today. How lucky we are to have such good friends. I know I can trust you to take care of each other. Claire, don't allow Ruthie to have all her own way and please insist that she take her vitamins. *Mucho amor* and a thousand kisses, Mum.'

Sheena laid down the letter. "It's not in her handwriting," she said worriedly.

Ruthie had taken the news of her mother's accident surprisingly well, better than Sheena who had wanted to fly at once to Spain to be with her. Now rereading the letter, Sheena was not entirely convinced that Jane was recovering.

"I can't understand how Mummy couldn't scrawl even a line," she said.

"Perhaps she didn't have any note-paper," Claire tried to reassure her. "Surely the fact she could dictate a letter shows she's not too bad. Anyway, we have Antonio's word for it that she's getting better."

"Yes," agreed Sheena doubtfully. "Still, I wish we knew for sure."

When Terry arrived later in the evening Claire told him how upset Sheena was and he suggested that they ring Antonio and get the number of the hospital from him so that they could ring it directly themselves.

Sheena cheered up at this and they all grouped about Jane's desk while Terry gave the Nerja number to the operator. Terry was relieved when Antonio rather than Fernando answered.

"I am happy to say your mother continues to make good progress," Antonio's deep voice resounded in his ear. Terry nodded and glanced encouragingly at the girls to signify the news was good. "Today we heard that she is being moved to a convalescent hospital in Nerja towards the end of this week. You will find it easier to visit her when you come."

"Thank you, Señor," Terry said politely. "Please give Mum our love and tell her we're managing fine. I'll ring again when I know for sure when I'm going." His CO held out hopes that he could arrange to get Terry a cockpit seat on a jet carrying diplomats to Spain in another week or two. Literally a flying visit – a couple of hours at the most – but it would be long enough to visit her.

Terry got the number of the hospital and put down the phone feeling a lot happier, as was Sheena when she heard what he had to tell her. She decided to wait until the following evening to ring and find out more about the new hospital her mother was going to. In the meantime she ran upstairs to hunt up some notepaper and, with Ruthie hanging over her shoulder, sat down on her bed to write a long letter back to Jane.

Terry had said they were managing fine in their mother's absence, but secretly he was concerned about their lack of money for day-to-day living expenses. The money he had brought back with him from Spain was almost gone.

Suddenly remembering that Jane always kept cash in her desk to pay bills, he rooted around in the drawers and was relieved to find almost one hundred pounds. He stuffed the notes in his pocket and went to tell the girls, and then they all drove to the supermarket and bought enough food to last them another week.

Jane was not used to playing the passive role of patient. Except for an occasional bout of 'flu she had never been sick in her life; like all doctors she was better at administering post-operative advice than taking it herself, and found it hard to accept her dependent condition.

For the first few days she was unable to raise her arms and everything had to be done for her. She was reliant on nurses to wash her and feed her and change her dressings, even clean her teeth for her. She was lonely too. The nurses were busy and could not linger to give anything more than nursing care to *la médica irlandesa*, so Jane was grateful when Fernando came to see her. She was also more receptive to Antonio's attentions than she might otherwise have been, when he too visited her later that week.

Antonio was shown in after the nurse had settled her down for her afternoon nap. Quite unprepared for the sight of him as he came around the door, Jane tried to struggle upright and gasped with pain at the effort it cost her.

"No . . . please do not disturb yourself," Antonio beseeched, his expression concerned. He took a step forward then stood where he was, helplessly gazing at her.

Jane sank back on the pillow, weak tears stinging her eyes. "I'm not as recovered as I thought," she whispered forlornly.

Antonio laid the flowers he had brought her on the washstand. He drew the chair to her bed and sat down.

"Your son telephoned my house last night . . ." he began.

"Terry rang? Tell me how they all are," she begged. "Are they managing all right? Did they get my letter? Do they know I am being moved to Nerja?"

Antonio laughed. "So many questions." He crossed his knees and sat back regarding her serenely. "Which will I answer first?"

"My letter, did they get it?"

"Yes, but they were troubled because it was not in your handwriting."

"I could not write myself," Jane said simply, relieved that Terry was so practical. Antonio smiled. "Terry hopes to fly out and visit you very soon," he went on, watching her face. "Perhaps next week."

Jane stared. "But how? He has no money."

Antonio shrugged. "I do not know exactly. The Air Corps are arranging it for him. He seemed hopeful it could be done and said he will ring me when he has all the details!"

How wonderful to see Terry. My son, she thought with a rush of emotion. They had shared those lovely few days together and then for it to end like it did. Remembering his courageous little farewell wave, tears sprang to her eyes. To her dismay they overflowed and poured down her cheeks. Antonio's smile faded and his dark eyes brimmed with concern.

"You are overwrought," he said gently. "I did not mean to upset you." He got to his feet. "Forgive me! I have stayed too long."

'No, don't go,' she wanted to say but only cried all the harder. She felt him stoop over her and his lips brushed fleetingly against her forehead. Then he pressed his hand-kerchief into her hand and with a murmured, *"Hasta luego, mi preciosa,"* he was gone.

Jane mopped her eyes with Antonio's handkerchief and cursed her weakness. Her tears dried and she lay very still. Had he really called her his *'preciosa'*? The crumpled piece of linen lay forgotten in her hand. Oh please God, let him come again.

She lay in the sun-filled room and gazed for a long time at the sheaf of crimson carnations he had brought her before pressing the bell for a nurse to come and put them in water.

These days Claire was in a state of perpetual bliss. She felt she was experiencing happiness at last. Terry was a vigorous but tender lover and he told her that she was beautiful, that he was crazy about her, that he had never been happier himself.

She still felt guilty about sleeping with him in his mother's bed. While his was nothing like so roomy, she felt happier there and the narrow divan was an excuse to cling close together. She was careful to launder Jane's sheets and make up her bed again. Although Terry's room was at the furthest end of the landing from his sisters' rooms, Claire was tortured by fears that Sheena or Ruthie would surprise them in bed together and made a point of getting up early each morning and returning to her own room, to be there when Ruthie awoke. Terry felt that Claire was making too much of it, but when he saw how upset she was, he agreed to keep their lovemaking concealed, in so far as they were able, from his sisters. Claire realised very soon, however, that Sheena knew what was going on. Although she never actually put it in words Sheena made it clear that their liaison had her full approval. The only oblique reference Sheena ever made to Claire's affair with her twin was one as they sat in the kitchen one evening.

"I always knew Terry was your type, rather than Hugh," Sheena said, apropos of nothing. "Hugh was far too sensitive and introspective for his own good. That's why he did what he did, you know."

Claire stared at her. Her friend had never once mentioned that grim time in all the years since it happened.

"I remember when Hero had her pups and you were so matey with Hugh," Sheena continued. "Terry was always grumbling to me about it. He was as jealous as hell and he couldn't hide it."

Claire felt a rush of delight and stored away the information to examine later. She returned to her studies and sat with her head bent, her hair touching the page. She tried to analyse a passage of prose but her mind kept returning to Terry and the night he had returned from Spain and made love to her. He had never once mentioned the fact that she was not a virgin but he must have noticed. It wasn't as though he were inexperienced, Claire thought. Far from it. She blushed behind the screening curtain of hair at the memory and her flesh tingled and she felt a warm shivery feeling in the pit of her stomach.

Claire had seen the first signs of the immense power of Terry's physical attraction for girls in her early teens, when she was away on holidays with the McArdles and observed Susan Deveney waylaying him every chance she got. Later, when Sheena had told her that he'd made Gráinne pregnant, Claire had felt relief rather than shock. It made it easier for her to contemplate some day confessing what had burdened her own soul for so long. She wondered if, indeed, she would ever find the courage to tell Terry about Eddie and that dark area of her life.

Since she had experienced an untrammelled and mutual love, Claire clearly saw that Eddie had taken from the near-child she had been what she had hardly understood or valued at the time. But in Terry she had found the mate who matched her soul's craving. She had experienced with him what she had only read about in books, but what would he think if he knew of her past?

She could never tell him. He would not . . . could not . . . understand even though he had voluntarily revealed the skeletons in his own past. Claire wished there was some way that she could so easily clear her own conscience with a similar confession, but she was not willing to chance it. Her eyes grew sad as she recognised that there could never be a true blending of spirit while anything remained hidden between them.

When they met one evening in town Claire saw at once that Terry was bursting with news. First he insisted on going into St Stephen's Green and the pair of them sitting down on a bench overlooking the duckpond.

"Go on," Claire prompted urgently, and unable to contain his elation any longer, Terry laughed and told her.

It seemed there was a shortage of trained pilots for the Dauphin helicopter and the Air Corps were offering a brilliant chance for three young pilots to circumvent the normally slow and restrictive regulations and to gain promotion, all in one go.

"Dinny Monahan is recommending three from our squadron and just guess who one of those lucky pilots will be?" Terry asked, hugging Claire to him jubilantly.

"Can't for the life of me think," Claire teased. "Could it be you?" she asked with seeming innocence.

"None other, Miss Shannon. You see before you a future rotary pilot, soon to be ranked as Flight Lieutenant McArdle." He dropped his lofty pose and jumping up, swung her round and round, oblivious of staring onlookers.

Claire laughed breathlessly and shyly tugged him down on to the bench again.

When he got his own breath back he said eagerly. "The minute we get our wings we start training on the Gazelle. Dinny says it has the most sophisticated flight instrumentation for fixed-wing pilots making the transition to the Dauphin. We went aboard her today and she's a real neat little job."

Claire listened with her eyes fixed attentively on his face, trying to share his enthusiasm, but as always when he spoke about flying, she felt distanced from him.

It was the beginning of May and a sudden mild spell was encouraging everyone to behave as though it was already summer. Terry was wearing Bermuda shorts and a denim shirt opened at the throat. Claire had cut off the sleeves of an old poplin blouse and knotted the ends at her waist, showing bare midriff above blue jeans. She glanced down at herself as they wandered back on to the street, regretting the fact she had nothing new and summery to wear.

"What do you bet this is every bit as hot as Spain?" Terry said, changing the subject at last.

"Did you hear yet when you're going?"

"Nope. Should know in another few days," he grinned. "Like to come with me? You could stow away in the hold. I'd smuggle you on board in a hamper."

Claire looked askance. "On a government jet! Think what the penalty would be."

"Only kidding." Terry protested, intrigued to see she was serious. "Little Miss Perfect," he teased.

Claire was troubled. "Please don't think so well of me," she said. "If you only knew, I'm not good at all. Quite the opposite."

"Oh yeah." Terry rumpled her hair fondly. "Listen to her! A real baddie-waddie." He kept her hand in his as they swung along by the park railings. Since becoming her lover he was more tender, more tolerant, less moody. "You would have me believe you're a real femme fatale – a right little raver without a heart – when I know you to be the most tender-hearted creature alive."

Claire blushed and looked away.

"You mightn't like me quite so well," she began, casting a sideways look at him, "not if you knew everything."

"Everything! Now that sounds really sinister." Terry laughed. "Like you had chopped up your mother and hidden her under the bed. Come to think of it I haven't seen her lately," he added thoughtfully.

Claire was forced to smile. "Well, maybe nothing quite so drastic," she conceded, pinching his hand to get his attention. "But years ago when you were all away on holidays . . ."

"Go on . . . really . . . years ago," he intoned melodramatically.

"No but listen . . ." she interrupted him. "I . . . I was in your . . ."

Claire's breath quickened.

"Okay . . . you were in my . . . what?"

"I used play in your garden when you were away on holidays and pretend it was mine."

"So – why should that make me like you any less?"

"I was trespassing. I shouldn't have been there."

He laughed.

"What a funny girl you are. Do you really think any of us would have minded if you had? Must have been years ago. I can't remember a time when you didn't come away with us."

"I didn't come the first year."

He pulled her close to his side. "And this was the dread secret? You pretended you were little Claire McArdle playing in her family garden. Disgraceful!"

Her courage had deserted her at the last moment.

"Claire McArdle," Terry repeated gently. "I like the sound of it. Do you think we'll get married, Claire? I hope I've got the good sense not to let you get away from me."

Claire was silent. Marriage? The thought filled her with joy and terror. But how could she ever marry him with this obstacle between them? And what if she lost him because of it? It was too painful to contemplate so she tried to make a joke of it.

"Hey! You've just had a lucky escape from Gráinne. You surely don't want to become involved with me."

Terry frowned. "Don't mention yourself in the same breath as her," he said. "Anyway, I am involved with you."

Claire flushed and looked away. She was very quiet as they finished their walk and went into a pub.

A couple of fellows coming out jostled past them. Terry recognised Stephen Rigney whom he hadn't seen since they had graduated the previous year. Terry noticed Stephen look at Claire and was outraged when he heard him mutter to his companion that Claire might look like butter wouldn't melt in her mouth but she and her mother were a couple of tarts.

"That bastard was just begging for a belt in the gob," he growled, putting his arm protectively about Claire, but she was so deeply enmeshed in her own unhappy thoughts that she did not notice the incident.

As she followed Terry into the pub she was wondering why she hadn't been able to tell him about the past. If he really cared for her he wouldn't think any the worse of her. She sat beside Terry, feeling slightly depressed. If only she'd had the courage to speak out, she thought, only half hearing what he was saying, vaguely aware that he was talking about helicopters and the Air Corps again.

Jane travelled by ambulance to Nerja, arriving late in the evening. When she awoke next morning in the new hospital she had momentary amnesia until she saw Antonio's carnations on her sidetable. Then it all came back to her.

Hospital Belen was privately owned, small and exclusive, with about eighty patients, most of them recovering from surgery, as well as two or three semi-invalided old ladies with broken brittle bones, who permanently resided in the nursing home wing. Jane would come to know them all in the weeks of her convalescence.

Sarah Lewis, the nurse on duty, brought Jane's breakfast tray and lingered to chat as Jane drank her juice and nibbled toast. Jane felt an instant rapport with the friendly Yorkshire woman and began telling her all about the accident and about her children too. She was missing them all and felt hungry for conversation.

Jane found herself looking forward more and more to the times when the English nurse came on duty. The other nurses were all Spanish, and although pleasant enough, were too young to have much in common with her. Sarah was in her late fifties.

One morning she came in early with a letter for Jane. "Maybe it's from your son," she said. "Didn't you tell me he'll be coming to see you soon?"

Jane nodded wistfully. "I'm almost afraid to hope in case it doesn't happen. This is an invitation to his Wings." Jane sighed. "I was really looking forward to being there."

"Aye, that's a shame," Sarah agreed. "Oh now I can tell he's the apple of his mother's eye." She laughed comfortably. "And a good looking young scamp too, I'll be bound."

Jane smiled and nodded, thinking of Terry's darkly handsome looks. "You should see him in uniform. He's very dashing altogether. I intended taking photographs at the ceremony, but I'm afraid he'll never think of it himself. Pity," Jane shrugged. "It would have been nice."

"Can't he dress up again and have his picture taken?" Sarah suggested.

"Of course," Jane agreed. "Anyway Sheena loves being photographed and might even remember."

"Well, there you are," Sarah said. "You can be sure she won't forget. Twins are very close. And the younger girl. Who does she take after?"

"Ruthie isn't really like either one of them," Jane told her. "She's more like another of my children . . . Hugh died when he was eleven." She fell silent, knowing she was talking too much, but she was really missing her children and talking about them helped to ease her loneliness.

Sarah asked no more questions and tactfully withdrew. But she was back five minutes later with some yellow blooms she had gathered from the garden and a cup of Earl Grey tea to cheer Jane.

"There now! There's nothing to compare with a drop of our own."

She was really a dote, Jane thought. She'd be lost without her.

A few more days and Jane was allowed out to sit in the garden behind the hospital. She took a book with her and wandered down the path, enjoying the feel of the sun on her skin after so long indoors, and the sight of the brightly massed flowerbeds. How lovely to be up and about again. It felt good to be on the mend at last.

Jane was sitting with her face uplifted to the sun, when a little way off came the sound of voices. She glanced towards the hospital building and saw, with a sense of shock, Fernando coming towards her pushing his mother before him in her wheelchair.

"Dr McArdle!" Elena's sweet low-pitched voice was barely audible against the tree-top chatter of birds in the drowsy afternoon sunshine. "I was sorry to hear of your accident. I hope you are making a good recovery."

Jane forced herself to smile. "Yes, thank you. I'm much better now." If Elena had come of her own accord, was it merely a good Samaritan act or was there a deeper reason?

"It is good to see you out in the air," Fernando said warmly. "Now you will get well very quickly."

"Nothing like sun and air to effect an instant cure," Jane lightly agreed.

Fernando smiled. Jane thought how like his mother he was, with his fair colouring and gentle manner. Elena said nothing, but whenever she met Jane's eyes she smiled wanly. They seemed interested in what Jane was saying but didn't say anything themselves, so she kept talking. She spoke about the accident and her children. How she didn't really worry too much because she trusted them. How responsible

Claire was and what a loyal friend. This for Fernando's benefit. She felt he was listening for the sound of Claire's name and his expression did indeed lighten at the sound of it.

"She . . . Claire . . . will be visiting you soon?" he asked.

Jane shook her head. "I expect it will be the end of June before Claire and my girls come to Spain." Jane glanced at Elena and said, "I hope that I'll be gone home long before then."

"I am quite certain of it," Elena said quietly. "Broken ribs are painful but heal quickly I am told."

"Very true." Jane was aware of the complication of her punctured lung but she did not wish to speak of her health to Elena, who looked even frailer than when Jane had last seen her. Jane wondered again what her illness might be. The Spanish woman had difficulty raising her right arm and her left hand lay useless in her lap. Hardly from a stroke. She would not be so wasted. More like a muscular dystrophy or motorneurone disease, Jane decided pityingly, and was aware of Fernando standing up.

"We must go," he said. "My mother tires easily these days."

"Of course." Jane stood up too and extended her hand to Elena. "Thank you for coming, Señora. It was most kind of you." She looked curiously into the other woman's eyes and saw only compassion in their dark depths.

"*De nada, Señora,*" Elena said gently. "If there is anything you need or anything we can do for you . . ."

"Thank you," Jane said again. Elena glanced up at her son and at once he turned the wheelchair back on to the path.

"I will come to see you again very soon," Fernando promised Jane.

Jane watched them until they were out of sight then sank down trembling on the bench. Antonio's wife had visited her out of common humanity, no other reason. Jane had divined in Elena's compassionate glance one woman's support of another in a strange land. She was touched and, at the same time, ashamed when she thought of her overwhelming desire for Antonio.

On the day of his Wings Terry called for the girls early
and they drove down to Baldonnel in plenty of time for the
ceremony. They were all looking forward to it, especially
Claire, who felt as though she would burst with pride and
excitement.

Sheena had described the style at the last parade as stun-
ning – all floppy hats and designer suits – and Claire,
realised with dismay that there was no way could she appear
in such company in jeans and sweater. For once Annette had
risen to the occasion when Claire steeled herself to ask for
new clothes. On returning home from shopping with
Annette, Claire tried on the new outfit and raptly twirled the
silky pleated skirt between her fingers as she stood before
the mirror.

Her mother stood watching her. "Happy now?" she asked.

"Oh yes. Thanks, Mummy." Claire was moved to hug her.

"Oh you really must be happy," Annette said with sarcastic
inflection, then softened it with, "My little girl is well and
truly grown up. You look very nice, darling." Just before
Claire went back across the street she saw tears in her
mother's eyes and was surprised.

Claire dressed herself and turned around to help Ruthie.
The trouble was, the little girl had grown so much over the
year that everything she owned was way above her knees.
Claire was almost in despair until Sheena rummaged in her
closet and brought out a pretty rose-coloured gingham skirt
edged with broderie anglaise and an embroidered peasant
blouse with a scooped neck, both long outgrown but kept
out of fondness. When the girls ripped off the broderie
anglaise, the length of the skirt was just right. The delicate
pink suited Ruthie's fair complexion and the mid-calf skirt
made her look more like a teenager than a child turned ten.
Ruthie jumped up and down with delight at her changed
appearance.

The excitement remained with them as they piled into
the car and drove down the country. Claire did not quite

know what to expect from the day. Sheena and Ruthie had tried to describe it to her, but the reality far surpassed Claire's expectations. It was colourful and moving and a lot more besides.

Claire felt a constriction in her throat as Terry marched past, arms swinging, cap dead straight over his eyes. He's mine, she thought with a jealous shiver as she heard girls near by speaking admiringly about him. He's so terribly attractive, was her next despairing thought. How could he possibly love her? The old conviction that she wasn't worthy to be loved, and which had dogged her for years, returned now to dent her happiness.

Sheena's saying, 'All the girls are swooning over Terry. Better watch out they don't try and swipe him, Claire,' did nothing to boost her confidence. Sheena herself was in a state of high excitement over some cadet marching alongside her twin.

Captain Monahan strolled over to join them and was introduced to the girls. He was a ruddy-complexioned man with a big beaky nose. Dinny shook her hand and smiled into her eyes.

"You look like a nice normal young woman," he said in a wondering voice. "Now how in the name of Albert Reynolds did you ever become involved with this fellah here?"

"Looks can be deceptive," Claire smiled back at him, liking him at once.

"Hey, Dinny," Terry said with a wink at them all. "How many kegs of Guinness have you lined up for us then?"

Dinny scratched his nose and drawled. "Guinness is for men, Cadet McArdle. Didn't you know?"

Terry grinned. "Only know it's bloody good for you, Skipper."

Dinny laughed and turned courteously to Claire. "A pleasure meeting you, Miss Shannon. Don't let this lot corrupt you now."

"I'll try," Claire promised, and he walked away to join another group.

"Pity Mum isn't here," Terry said suddenly. "And Con." His expression grew broody and sad. Claire reached for his hand and felt the tension in his clenched knuckles. Suddenly he pulled her fiercely against him and nuzzled her ear. "But you're here," he whispered. "That's the important thing."

In Hospital Belen, whenever her eyes rested on the gilt-edged card from the Air Corps, Jane rejoiced in the thought that in just another two days Terry would be arriving in Spain. So gradually over the months had he graduated from a beloved, if irresponsible, teenager to a manly son, whose company she enjoyed and whose judgement she valued and trusted, that she had hardly been aware of the transition. It had taken her accident and the long weeks of separation from her family to bring home to her just how much she had come to depend upon him.

As she lay there, her thoughts drifted back to the conversation they had been having at the time of the accident and her own appalled reaction on realising how deeply infatuated he was with Claire. Since his early teens she had seen him too many times in this ambivalent state over some girl or other to call it love. Since Gráinne there just wasn't time for it to have developed into anything more serious with Claire.

Jane had a mother's natural reluctance for her only son to become romantically involved too early in his career. Nineteen was ridiculously young. She also hated the thought of Claire perhaps falling for Terry and then being cast off when he grew tired of her, for Jane believed this to be inevitable. Not for a moment did she think her restless, spirited son could remain constant to one woman for long. Terry always got devotion too easily to value it.

Jane believed that Terry needed time to wear off some of the raw impetuosity of youth before he would be mature enough to take on the responsibility of answering for another's happiness. Very likely the whole thing was just a teenage crush, she assured herself, and would die as quickly as it had flared.

Nothing she could do about the situation until she returned home, she told herself. Then she would have a chat with Claire and see if she was as deeply committed to Terry as he appeared to be to her.

Jane was so deeply taken up with her thoughts that she did not register the gentle tap on the door until it was repeated.

"Come in," she called, resenting the intrusion.

The door cautiously inched open and Antonio looked round it with an expectant smile. Jane's displeasure gave way at once to intense delight at the sight of him. "Y . . . you," she stammered in her surprise. "I thought it was the nurse coming to take my temperature."

Antonio drew a chair close to the bed. "I am very sorry to disappoint you, Dr McArdle," he said with a droll shake of his head. "The best I can do is inspect your tongue." He pretended to look at it very seriously and Jane giggled. She was amazed at herself. She hadn't giggled in years. Antonio seemed unsurprised at the girlish sound. His answering chuckle made her feel wickedly light-hearted and young again.

"I see that our patient is a good deal better," Antonio pronounced. "Although I think in a somewhat melancholy mood when I arrived." His eyes strayed to the invitation card. "Ah, *el piloto!*" He looked at Jane with sudden realisation. "Today he is being decorated and you are naturally downhearted to be so far away."

"Just a little," Jane said.

"He is coming soon?"

"Monday."

"Ah, that will bring back the smiles to your heart. See, you are smiling already." Antonio beamed himself.

Jane couldn't tell him that she was smiling at his English and felt another urge to giggle. She repressed it and said, "I suppose I was feeling a little sad but then I have only one son and I miss him quite a bit since he joined the Air Corps."

"Understandably," Antonio agreed. "Now I have three sons but no daughter. When I see your little girl I wish it had been otherwise."

Jane nodded in sympathy. Suddenly she wanted to tell him about Hugh and how he had been such a lovely boy, sensitive and affectionate.

"I did have another son . . . but he died tragically when he was eleven years old." Seeing Antonio's sympathetic glance she added with a gulp, "By his own hand."

"*Querida,*" he murmured sincerely. "I am so very sorry." His hands reached for hers and held them comfortingly in his strong grasp. "To lose a beloved child is the most tragic of all afflictions . . . and in the way you describe even more so. We have had our share of sorrow, Elena and I. Many years ago we lost a little one when he was only a few months old."

Jane looked at him dumbly, the mention of his wife bringing back to her the impropriety of being alone with him and the danger of heightened emotions. Still, she could not move or take her hands away.

"Elena is a brave and uncomplaining woman," Antonio went on softly. "I love and respect her and wish to make her days happier, but I wish . . ." He broke off and stooped his head to kiss Jane's hands passionately.

Jane looked down on his bent head and her own heart was full of yearning. By a great effort of will she remained silent but inwardly she was answering him just as fervently. Yes, my darling, I wish it too with all my heart. When he raised his head and met her gaze her tender thoughts showed plainly on her face as if she had spoken them and he groaned softly in his throat and abruptly released her hands. She had only time to register her deep sense of loss before he had taken her fiercely, almost roughly in his arms, and pressed his mouth on hers with the anger and desperation of an honourable man who is no longer able to resist the temptation of his over-riding desire. She held him just as fiercely and, as if under a similar compulsion beyond her control, her mouth was soft and yielding beneath his.

He released her at last and got to his feet. He stood looking gravely down at her. "What had to happen has happened," he said with quiet finality, and she heard him without contradiction. "*Te quiero mucho, mi querida* Jane."

"Toni." She whispered her old name for him and all her heart was in the look she gave him. His face was swept by a smile at this reminder of the past and with a last murmured endearment he went away and left her with her joy and guilt and with the small consolation that she had not sought or anticipated any of it, merely accepted what was inevitable.

When Claire and Terry reached home around midnight, having wound up the Wings celebration dancing in the Grey Lizard, they both agreed it had been a wonderful day but all they wanted now was to get into bed and relax.

The evening had been marred by a small incident. As they were making their goodbyes and about to head off, Terry had noticed Stephen Rigney in a group of young men coming in the door of the club. Who did Rigney think he was, casting aspersions on Claire because of some rumour circulating years ago? Well, just let him try it again and he'd be chewing on his teeth. Terry turned to face him.

"Hey, McArdle. You're everywhere these days like a bad smell," Stephen said offensively, his eyes flickering to the emblem on Terry's lapel. "See you've taken to wearing jewellery like a bloody poof."

For a moment Terry failed to get his meaning, then his fist shot out and connected with Stephen's jaw. Women screamed and tables overturned as the two men went crashing across the small space. A group of cadets surged to join the fight and the bouncer appeared almost as quick and proceeded to drag Terry off Stephen. Within minutes they had all found themselves out on the road and, with a last muttered insult, Stephen and his gang drifted away.

Later, as they lay close together, spent and relaxed in the aftermath of lovemaking, Claire thought to ask, "What started the fight?"

"Didn't like the look of his ugly mug." Terry looked so serious, almost brooding, that despite his facetious answer Claire felt uneasy. She suddenly remembered that Stephen Rigney was the elder brother of Mark, the boy who had made Hugh's life a misery at school. She felt a return of her earlier disquiet.

"Clairey . . ." Terry said slowly. "You know I've never asked you anything about guys you knew before me. I mean I know I'm not the first man you made love to . . ."

Claire stiffened in the crook of his arm. She didn't feel surprised, only very tired, as though she had been travelling for ages along the same dusty highway hoping to reach home and had finally arrived to find her house deserted and the door barred against her.

"No more than you were my first girl," Terry continued slowly. "I haven't exactly been an angel myself. I've told you all about Gráinne – anything else was just kid stuff – so you know it all while I . . ." He sat up higher in the narrow bed, bunching the pillow behind his head and watched her face expectantly.

"What do you want to know?" Claire asked tonelessly.

"Well . . . not his name or anything, just what he meant to you and when it was. Stuff like that." He reached for her hand. "I suppose it was since you went to college . . . was that when it happened?"

"No."

He gently stroked her face. "Tell Terry all about it. You know we agreed on no secrets."

Had they?

"C'mon, Clairey," he prompted. "I've bared my soul; now it's your turn."

What had sparked this off? Claire wondered wearily. "Okay," she said, accepting the inevitable. "If you really want to know it was while I was still at school."

Terry went very still.

"Look," she said almost angrily, "He was an older guy . . .

291

a lot older. Can we leave it at that?"

Terry got out of the bed and went naked to the window. He stood for a long while staring out. Claire sat hunched forward, watching him.

"You loved him?"

"At the time I thought I did."

He turned suddenly and came back to her, and she saw that he was aroused. He caught her fiercely to him and kissed her lips with bruising force, all his possessive jealousy in the kiss, and his hand fondled the nape of her neck and pushed caressingly upwards through the warm weight of her hair.

"Claire . . . Oh Claire." His voice was like a caress, and at the sound she melted against him. He pushed her back down on the bed and covered her naked body with wild kisses as though he wanted to reclaim every inch of skin and make it all his own again. And when he took her he did so quickly, almost roughly, as if no other way could satisfy his aching need of her.

Terry lay awake long after Claire had fallen asleep, her head on his chest, her arm trustingly curved about him. His thoughts kept returning to the little she had told him. An older man. To a school-girl anyone over twenty would seem old. It had to be one of the various men lodging in Claire's house over the years, he thought. How else could it have happened? He grimaced, hating the thought of her losing her virginity in this way. In reality he hated her losing it to anyone but himself.

Two days later Terry flew out to Spain on a government jet. The captain, a friend of Dinny Monahan, had agreed to take on Terry as a supernumerary member of the crew. His first words to Terry were: "Keep your effing carcass out of my way like a good chap and we'll get along like sweethearts."

Terry grinned and nodded, a bit disappointed. He had seen himself in the right hand seat, if only for part of the journey. At least the co-pilot was friendly.

"Relax and enjoy the trip," he told Terry cheerily, tossing

him a newspaper. "The old man's bite is worse than his bark, but he's already had his lump of flesh today. Some poor sod had the temerity to fill in the Simplex crossword and got his balls torn off. Depend upon it, the skipper will be all sunshine from now on."

Terry grinned and put away the paper to read later, enjoying the familiar feeling as they roared powerfully down the runway and lifted smoothly into the air. They climbed rapidly and soon emerged above cloud, levelling out at 30,000 feet.

Terry sat back as the co-pilot advised and enjoyed the trip. The hostess came in with coffee and he eyed her appreciatively. Claire came unbidden to his mind. Usually he liked thinking about her, but now his pleasure was marred by the constraint between them since the night of the Wings. He had rung her from the barracks the next night, having first rung Spain and learned from Antonio that Jane was making good progress and hoped to be discharged from hospital in another week, and Claire had promised to tell the others. They had said little else to each other, and Terry had put down the phone feeling depressed. He knew he shouldn't have tried to delve into her past. He blamed Stephen Rigney and his sly insinuations. What did he care if Claire had been loved by another man. He had distributed his own favours to plenty of girls before her. Terry scowled and shifted in his seat, thinking he had been a right knucklehead. He would have been much better off not knowing.

"Hey back there," the captain swivelled in his seat and lifted his earphones on his balding head to bellow back. "Want to sit in while I go aft and spread a bit of cheer amongst the diplomatic corps?"

"Sure." Terry eagerly unclipped his harness as the man struggled out of his seat and reached for his braided cap.

The co-pilot looked up as Terry jauntily took up position beside him and donned headphones. "Don't get too comfy," he laughingly warned. "The old man soon tires of licking assholes. You've got about nine . . . ten minutes at the most."

Terry settled down to get the feel of the vast panel of instruments. With any luck, he thought, the old man might trip in the aisle and break a leg!

Terry followed a dark-haired nurse through the hospital corridors and thanked her absently as he stepped out again into the sunshine.

Jane was sitting on a bench in the sun and as Terry drew near he saw she was not alone. Her companion was Antonio Gonzalez and from the way the man was leaning close to her they were obviously having a very serious conversation.

As Terry approached it seemed to him they moved hastily, almost guiltily apart. Was it his imagination or were they holding hands? Jane got up with rosy cheeks and came slowly to meet him.

"Terry!" She put her arms about him and kissed him on both cheeks, then turned to Antonio. "Isn't he smart in his uniform?" She caught sight of her son's new wings and gave a little crow of delight. "Congratulations, my dear." In her affection and excitement at seeing him she gave him another fond hug. Terry laughed and urged her to sit down.

"Please don't tire yourself, Mum." He put his arm about her and guided her back to the seat where Antonio sat watching them with a smile. As Jane sank down, breathless and smiling, Antonio got to his feet.

"I will leave you together," he said considerately. "Until later, Jane." He smiled at her, then nodded at Terry and walked away down the path. Jane watched him go with a thoughtful, smiling look.

Jane! Those two have got very matey, Terry thought. He saw the expression on his mother's face and how she started in surprise when he spoke to her, as if she had already forgotten his presence. And then it dawned on him. Those two are in love! Antonio Gonzalez is the man Mum knew all those years ago . . . the one she said she was in love with before she met Dad. "No wonder he was so upset when he heard about the accident," Terry told himself. "It's because he cares . . . Gosh! Why didn't I see it before?"

Then he forgot all of it in the pleasure of telling Jane about the Wings Parade and everything that had happened to him since he had left her that night in Motril. Well, not quite everything. He did not tell her about himself and Claire. He didn't know how she would react. Some things were better kept hidden, Terry decided, even from one as broad-minded as his mother.

"How long have you got, Ter?" Jane asked, her eyes glowing and her face flushed with the excitement of having him with her again. "You can have no idea of how much I've looked forward to your coming. I've missed you all terribly."

"We've missed you too, Mum," Terry said huskily. "The girls have been really great and old Dinny was decent about giving me overnight passes so I could get home often and see they were all right."

"And Ruthie?" Jane asked anxiously.

Terry quickly set her mind at rest. All too soon the time ran out and he got up to go. He had to be back in Malaga for nine o'clock take-off.

"Could you call into the apartment on your way?" Jane asked him. "I intend spending a few days there when I leave hospital."

"Sure." Terry calculated he would just have time to make himself a cup of coffee before heading for the airport.

"Terry . . ." Jane looked at her son uncertainly. "There's something bothering me . . ."

Terry, wondering if she were going to speak about Antonio and herself, felt suddenly embarrassed and hoped frantically she wouldn't say any more.

"You may remember what we were discussing just before the accident happened," Jane began.

"Yes, Mum," Terry said reluctantly.

"Something you said at the time rather surprised me. Something I thought no-one but myself and Claire knew anything about."

"You mean about Dad and her mother?" Terry hazarded.

Jane nodded, not meeting his eyes. "Well . . . as I said at the time, there's a lot more to it than you imagine."

Terry felt a sudden urge to go now before he heard anything unpleasant.

"If you are fond of Claire . . . as I think you are," Jane continued slowly, "you should go very gently with her. She has been hurt badly in the past and I would hate if she were to suffer any more because of us."

"Us?"

Jane chose her words carefully. "I mean if you were to treat her casually in view of . . . Well, no matter." Jane stopped short and looked uncomfortable.

Terry thought he knew what his mother meant. "You mean the older man she was involved with while she was still at school . . . she told me all about it."

Jane looked concerned. "She told you?"

"Yes," Terry said. "Only recently. I suppose in a way I forced her . . . something was said . . . well, anyway I wanted to clear the air."

"Did she tell you everything?" Jane looked startled.

"I think so . . . she didn't go into detail but I know she got sort of led into it and was too young to know better."

Jane was amazed and relieved he was taking it all so calmly. "And you don't think any the worse of him?" she asked, wanting to make quite sure. "I mean he did something that was a criminal offence in view of her extreme youth."

Terry was all at sea. Why should he care about the man? Suddenly all the careful questioning sank in and with a feeling of horror he realised who the older man who had abused Claire had been as certainly as if his mother had come straight out and named him. A wave of nausea hit Terry and he felt his brain darken and grow dizzy.

"Are you all right?" Jane put her hand on his neck and pushed his head down between his knees. After a moment Terry sat up shakily and pushed her off.

"For God's sake, Mum," he said in a strangled voice. "You can't mean who I think you do."

The colour ebbed from Jane's face leaving it pale and sickly. "You said she told you," she whispered.

"Not his name," Terry said weakly, her aghast expression confirming his worst suspicions.

Jane began to cry quietly, making no sound. "Oh what have I done?" she said brokenly. "I would never have – I thought you knew. Oh the poor child. I wouldn't have betrayed her for the world."

"Mum!" Terry cried agonised, "Why didn't you stop him? How could you let him . . . ?

"I didn't know anything until she became . . . pregnant." Jane breathed the word so low that Terry had to strain his ears to catch it. He stared deeply shocked at his mother. Oh God! He couldn't take any more in. It was like a nightmare. He got up and looked at her despairingly.

"I've got to go or I'll miss my flight."

She reached her arms to embrace him but he brushed past her and rushed away down the path without looking back at her. Jane sank down weeping on the bench and her shuddering sobs tore painfully at her newly healed ribs. Antonio was appalled to find her in this state when he came moments later into the garden.

Terry climbed the hill behind the apartment, his breath coming in jerky gasps. He had walked at top speed back from the hospital and stopped only briefly at the apartment before going out again and climbing to the promontory overlooking the sea. He was breathing hard when he got to the summit.

He threw himself down on the grassy knoll and stared down at the waves licking the rocks below, his thoughts thundering in his head. He was aware of a searing pain over one eye. All the events of his childhood, every family holiday appeared in a different guise in the searchlight of this terrible new revelation. Seemingly innocent gestures took on hideous connotations and half-remembered phrases and scraps of overheard conversations became impregnated with new sinister meaning.

Terry rolled on to his stomach and buried his burning face in the cool grass. Now the meaning of Hugh's actions became clear. A seemingly demented deed was a carefully carried out execution. With new respect for his dead brother, Terry saluted his unflinching courage. Poor Hugh. He had loved Claire too and defended her in the only way he could.

Terry rested his head on his arm and gave way to his grief. He cried for a long time: for his brother, his father and himself, and although he did not quite realise it, for lost innocence. When he finally shuddered to a stop it had grown late and the light had faded in the sky. Down below shadowy figures dragged a boat high on the sand.

Terry got to his feet, brushed grass from his uniform and, conscious of the passing time, made his way quickly down the hillside. Across the street from the apartment block was a line of taxis. He approached the first one in the rank bearing the sign "*libre*" and climbed into the back.

"*El aeropuerto, por favor . . . rápido!*"

As they careered along, Terry, his face strained and white, felt as though he had aged by one hundred years in the space of a single afternoon.

It was three days before Terry got an overnight pass and went home. They were, without a doubt, three of the grimmest days and nights he had ever spent. Not even the grief and horror of Con's death had had the devastating effect of his mother's revelation.

"Off gallivanting again," Dinny said good-humouredly as he signed Terry's pass. "Isn't it great to be young?" I suppose it wouldn't have anything to do with that charming young lady you introduced to me last week?"

Terry forced himself to return Dinny's roguish grin but any mention of Claire these days was like acid on an open wound. As he drove towards the city his thoughts were gloomy. He longed to have it out with Claire and, at the same time, felt terribly afraid. What could she tell him that would ease the sick ache of disillusion? As the miles fell away under his wheels his spirits sank even lower and he was tempted to go back to the barracks and continue to uselessly sweat it out. Yet he had to hear it from her own lips.

Sheena and Ruthie were delighted to see him. They urged him to tell them everything about his trip but Terry could only think of Jane's face when she had revealed what she knew about Claire and his father, and he returned sparse answers to their questions.

"You are in a mood," Sheena said at last. "Claire is at a lecture and won't be home until late."

"Didn't you hear what I said?" she demanded, a moment later. "Claire's not here."

"Okay, so you've told me." Terry went to turn on the television.

Sheena stared after him. "Have you two quarrelled?" she asked curiously.

Terry said nothing, just sat frowning and grimly flicking through the channels.

"Honestly, Terry. I sometimes wonder about you," Sheena exploded. "Claire could get anyone and here she is hanging about every night waiting for you, and when you do show you don't even want to know where she is!"

'So she's eager to see you,' an unpleasant inner voice said. 'Going to get a hell of a shock then, isn't she?'

He was standing in his mother's surgery looking out the window, long before he saw her turning in the gate. Then he went out to the hall with a grim expression and waited for her.

The key turned in the lock and Claire hurried in, her face glowing. "Terry! Terry!" she cried. "I saw the car. Oh if only I'd known! To think I've wasted the whole evening at a stupid old lecture."

She dropped her books on the floor and ran to him laughing, but he held her off. She faltered and hung back, staring at him uncertainly.

"Let's go upstairs where we can be private." In silence, Terry led the way up to his room. But although the questions which had troubled him since then still remained to be answered, he found that as soon as he was alone with Claire and the door closed behind them, he could only stare dumbly at her, not knowing where to begin.

"What is it, Terry?" Claire whispered, frightened by his silence.

"The older man," Terry said, without preamble. "Who was he?"

Claire trembled. During the week she had gone over their last conversation many times in her head and only wished she had been braver and more honest with him, yet she still attempted to stave off the moment.

"You said you wouldn't ask his name," she said forlornly.

"I need to be sure."

He knew. Somehow he knew. Her heart felt like a piece of heavy lead. "How can you be so cruel as to ask," she cried pitifully, "when you already know the answer."

"So it's true." Terry gripped her arms and shook her. "You and my father . . . Oh but it's sick, really sick. A man more than three times your age." Terry looked pretty sick himself.

"I . . . I was only thirteen," Claire gabbled. "I didn't know what I was doing,"

"Go on," he grimly prompted.

"In the beginning I was drawn to him," Claire admitted with painful honesty. "I couldn't seem to help myself. It was a kind of hero worship. I hung about hoping he'd notice me and when he did it quickly became physical. Later when I tried to get free of him he always came after me." She swallowed with difficulty and continued bleakly, "Maybe if I'd been older I might have had some defence against him but I was lonely and he was nice to me."

Terry seemed to be gathering himself for some great effort. "Are you saying you did with him what we do together?" He spoke slowly and painfully, "Not just let him kiss and fondle you . . . but the whole shebang?"

Claire nodded miserably. He had moved as far away from her as was possible in the small bed.

"How could you, Claire?" Terry said in a dazed voice. Disgust and horror blended in equal proportions. Claire began to tremble. How could she have thought he would ever accept it in the same light as his confession about Gráinne.

"How long?" he asked harshly. "How long did it go on for?"

"Almost a year," Claire whispered.

"How did it end?" His voice shook. She could almost feel sorry for him if she did not already feel so desperately sorry for herself.

"I became ill . . ." her voice tailed away. This was something that she had not allowed enter into her mind until now.

"You didn't have a baby . . . you couldn't have. You were never away in those years except you came away with us."

So he knew about that too. "I was . . . I had . . ." She couldn't say the word but she saw from his face that he was appalled.

"Oh God!" Terry buried his face in his arm and groaned aloud. When he raised his head and looked at her she saw despair there and something else she was convinced was contempt. She put out a hand and touched his face gently, moved close to take him in her arms.

"Try and forget," Claire pleaded. "What's past is done with. Make love to me. I've missed you so."

Terry allowed her to hold him and even kissed her a few times, but when he tried to make love to her, he couldn't. "It's no good." He turned miserably away from her. "I can't do it." He removed the condom and flung it from him in disgust.

"Do it without the condom," she begged. She felt desperate to have him love her with his body, racked by a terrible dread that otherwise he would never do so again. She couldn't explain to him how she felt or her certainty that she would never get pregnant. That the things done to her had left her sterile.

"No," he said shortly. Not since that first unguarded night had he done it unprotected. "It's too dangerous." He looked down at her moodily. "Anyway that's not it . . . My own father," he said, unable to let it alone. "For God's sake, Claire, why didn't you tell me yourself instead of letting me hear it the way I did?"

"You told me you didn't need to know his name," she reminded him brokenly. Only one person could have told him. Claire was shocked to think that all along Jane had known about herself and Eddie. Oh but how could she have betrayed me? Claire thought in anguish, remembering all the older woman's protestations of affection.

"I thought it was some guy in his twenties," Terry said sullenly, "some crud that didn't matter . . . that I needn't . . ."

Claire pulled herself away from his side, shaken by the shock of sudden revelation.

"You're jealous of him. Jealous of your own father," she cried. "You don't love me at all. You are just using all this as an excuse not to make love to me . . . to make me feel guilty." Her voice broke on a sob. "Oh . . . I never want to see you again." She had turned and run from the room before he realised her intention. He heard the muffled sound of her bare feet thudding on the carpet and the sharp click of her bedroom door closing after her.

Terry lifted his hand and rubbed it slowly across his eyes. It was true. He was jealous of his father, jealous as hell. Jealous of a corpse, he thought bitterly. He sat down on the edge of the bed and dressed himself with careful concentration, shoved a change of underwear and socks into his kit-bag, and went downstairs and let himself quietly out of the house.

When the headlamps of the Rover swept the front wall of the house, he thought he glimpsed a pale blur at the upper window. Then he was scorching down the road in the direction of Baldonnel.

Claire turned from the window with a stricken look. He

was gone. He hadn't even waited until morning to try and make things right with her. She climbed blindly into bed beside Ruthie and her eyes brimmed and overflowed in hot sorrow. It was the first time that she and Terry had slept apart since they had become lovers and she felt as bereft as any widow after a lifetime of sharing.

She got out of the bed again and, shaking with suppressed grief, crept along the landing to Terry's room and slipped between the still warm sheets. With the scent of him all about her, her control finally broke and she let her sorrow take her and carry her. She lay half-buried beneath his pillow and sobbed with terrible abandon.

Jane came home the following weekend. Terry met her at the airport and drove her to the house where the others were waiting. Claire stayed long enough to greet her and then slipped quietly back to her own house. She did not speak to Terry more than to nod hello, and though he stared at her as she turned away, he did not come after her.

Claire felt battered and dejected, her spirit bruised beyond healing. Now beyond tears, she felt as though every drop of moisture had been squeezed out of her. How could Jane have done what she did? She felt she could never trust another human being again. If Jane had set out to do it she could not have more effectively blighted her hopes of happiness. In all the years of her association with the McArdles, Claire had never blamed them for any of the misfortunes that befell her. Now for the first time she felt sorrowing resentment.

Claire kept herself busy. She had more than enough work to get through for her June exams. She was aiming for a first-class honour in English, but because of the extra reading her migraine had returned. She was eventually forced to cross the street and ask Jane to renew her prescription. In her present state begging favours from Terry's mother was the last thing she wished.

"Of course, Claire. Nothing simpler," Jane smiled at her

earnest request. "But where have you been hiding all these weeks? I really wanted to thank you for staying here while I was away. You'll never know how much it meant to me."

"I was glad to," Claire said woodenly. "You were always good to me." Until you betrayed me. Oh how could you, how could you? Jane had been closer to her than her own mother.

"Are you all right?" Jane's concerned voice reached Claire through the fog of misery surrounding her.

Claire nodded, unable to speak.

"Oh you poor thing. Let me get you something." She gently drew Claire towards her surgery. Claire wanted to throw off the encircling arm and, at the same time, cling to the comfort it offered. All the misery she had felt on the night that she and Terry had broken up, returned to swamp her and she had difficulty keeping back the treacherous sobs gathering in her chest.

"You are in a bad way, aren't you?" Jane said gently, and sat down with relief behind her desk to write the prescription. "This bandage I'm wearing makes me walk like a robot," she joked. Claire tried to smile but failed miserably. She wished she hadn't come.

"I suppose now is as good a time as any to talk about our plans for the summer," Jane said, when she had handed Claire the slip of paper. "I can't get away to Spain until August but when I explained my dilemma to my cousin Anne she kindly agreed to go with you all. So there's really no reason why I shouldn't book the tickets now and then you and the others can head off the minute the exams end."

Claire stared blindly at her hands, not knowing what to say.

As the silence lengthened Jane added, "That is, of course, if you still want to share our summer holidays, Claire . . . but we consider you one of our family and really want . . ."

"I wonder you can say that after what happened," Claire cried in a strangled voice.

Jane looked startled. "My dear, what do you mean?"

Now the tears could no longer be held back. "You know

what you did."

"Claire . . . sit down." Jane came round the desk and gently pushed her on to a chair. "Perhaps we had better clear the air. Please tell me what's troubling you?"

Claire gulped miserably. There was no way of avoiding a confrontation now.

"Terry hates me after what you told him."

Jane was too honest to prevaricate. "Oh, my dear. I never meant to betray you," she cried in distress, "but when Terry said you'd told him everything I assumed . . ."

"You didn't set out to tell him?" Claire asked uncertainly.

"Of course not!" Jane was vehement. "Why would I try and discredit you, love? You know I've always cared for you like one of my own."

It was true.

"You believe me, don't you?"

Claire blinked away tears, convinced by her evident distress. Jane had shown her more kindness and understanding that anyone else, even her own parents. She nodded.

"Well, thank goodness for that," Jane said in relief. She looked at Claire gravely. "I've never talked about what happened before, not because of any bad feeling towards you, merely because I believed it was best to try and put it behind us."

Claire silently assessed her words. It was true that Jane had clearly demonstrated the lack of any ill-will towards her.

"You must remember it came as a great shock to Terry," Jane was saying. "He obviously cares very deeply for you. In the beginning I was inclined to think it was just a teenage thing but I see now that it goes far deeper. For you both. Try and give him time to adjust, my dear. It may sound like a cliché but time does sort most things out." Jane looked suddenly tired. She came closer to Claire and put her arms gently about her. "It will all work out for the best, believe me."

No, it won't, Claire thought. How could it? She shuddered when she remembered the horror and revulsion in his eyes. He would never come back to her.

"Claire . . . Claire," Jane called her attention back from the dark pit she was wandering and gazed at her in concern. "You mustn't allow yourself to brood. Right now the most important thing is to put it out of your mind and finish your exams." She hugged her gently. "I'm so glad we're friends again. I care far too much ever to allow anything to come between us."

Claire felt like crying again. For weeks she had been existing in a cold, loveless vacuum. Now by some miracle she had been drawn back into the warmth and magic of the McArdle's circle. She pressed Jane's arm shyly. It was a moment before she said, with a little catch in her voice, "You don't know how much it means to hear you say all this. I thought . . . I believed . . ."

"Enough confessions for one day," Jane said briskly, but kindly.

Claire smiled tremulously. She went home, feeling reassured that the misunderstanding between them had been cleared. While the loss of Terry's love and respect was devastating, there was consolation in knowing that none of it had been deliberate on Jane's part. Claire blamed it upon the nemesis which had shadowed her from early childhood and from which she believed there was no real escape.

Jane was relieved too that the misunderstanding was cleared up. In Spain she had resolved to have a chat with Claire just as soon as she returned home, but she had been caught up in her work straight away. Even now she was spending long hours at the clinic, trying to make up for her weeks of absence.

Jane had been genuine when she'd said that she did not harbour any bad feelings towards Claire, not since the first irrational madness had passed in the troubled weeks after the tragedy. Now she was only sorry for the distress she had caused the girl. She would really try and make it up to her.

Jane had been surprised at how exhausted she felt since returning to work, even though her physical injuries were nearly healed. Somehow she did not seem to have much energy to cope with anything but the most straightforward of cases. Even routine examinations and the necessary follow-ups to clinical tests seemed to take her an inordinate amount of time and effort. Now there was an extra problem to sort out.

Soon Sheena and Ruthie would be going away to Spain for the summer and there were still all the arrangements to be made. Jane at last stirred herself to ring the travel agent and book their tickets. Once it was done she felt better. Next thing she would start shopping for their clothes. There was so much they needed. But before she could even begin she received a letter from her cousin saying that she was really sorry, she knew just how much Jane was depending on her but she could not, after all, accompany the girls to Spain.

Jane bit her lip in dismay and read on with sinking heart. In her thin upright script Anne explained that she had been admitted to hospital for tests and it now appeared that she would have to undergo a hysterectomy at once. What a time she had to go and pick, was Jane's first unfeeling thought. Poor Anne, she thought contritely, but there was no denying it left her in a spot. She couldn't go herself and she couldn't let the girls go on their own either, so what on earth was she to do?

It was the Murray family as usual who came to her rescue. When Liz heard how Jane had been let down, she offered to ask her mother's advice. "I wouldn't mind volunteering for the job myself if you didn't need me here. What I'd do for a few weeks in the sun!" she laughed.

Jane grinned in sympathy. Actually, she thought, there were very few people she would be happy to let chaperone her young family and they away in another country. But when Liz returned after her lunch break happily she was the bearer of good news.

"Mammy says if you're stuck she could go with the girls herself. She'll be dropping in later to see you and when does it suit?"

"Tell her I'll be here all evening." Thank God for Teresa. Jane would never forget how supportive her former receptionist had been when Eddie and Hugh died. She would be just right to go with the girls, and what was so important, Ruthie liked her.

When Teresa arrived it was clear from her manner that she was delighted at the prospect of a few weeks in the sun. "Not often I get away, I don't mind telling you," she admitted cheerfully. Jane could well believe it. Teresa's own brood numbered eight, the youngest of which was not yet twelve years old. In addition she had a steadily increasing number of grandchildren whose young parents made constant demands upon 'Granny's' time and energy.

"The only thing is, I've promised to mind the kids for Babs when she goes in to have her baby. If she was to come before time . . . Ah forget it!" Teresa dismissed the possibility with a wave of her plump hand. "That'll be the day. The other three had to be coaxed out into the world and do yeh think they've changed?" she snorted in derision. "If they were any more laid back they'd be horizontal, just like their mother. That one is never on time for anything."

Jane smiled in sympathy.

"If she's right with her dates Babs isn't due till the middle of August, so we're away in a hack."

"By then I'll be able to get away myself," Jane assured her. "So it's all settled then."

Next day Jane rang the travel agent and changed the fourth ticket to Teresa's name. At the same time she took out travel insurance for all of them, Claire included. She did not imagine that Annette would think to make provision for her daughter.

Since returning home Jane had valiantly tried to put Antonio out of her mind but he continued to dominate her thoughts. As she packed the girls' cases, she often caught herself with a half-folded garment on her lap, dreamily remembering, especially that last evening when he had called to the apartment to say goodbye. They had sat on the balcony in the evening sunshine, the air about them scented with the fragrance of datura. She had found herself telling him about the years since Eddie's death and how she had been driven by the need to work long hours at the clinic to support her small family.

"It was a tough and lonely time," Jane said, without self pity. "When my husband and son so tragically died, I learned there was no-one I could rely upon but myself. I suppose I have become used to the battle."

"Ah, Jane. I only wish it were different."

She gazed at him candidly. "I wish it too."

In her mind's eye Jane saw again the great dangling trumpet flowers behind his head as Antonio took her in his arms. She had tightened her own arms about his neck and fervently returned his kisses, but all the time, like an unseen watcher, was the ailing shadow of Elena. When she had drawn back and looked into his eyes and seen the urgent need in them, Jane had ached to give him what he so clearly desired, but felt she would be dishonouring herself and him too. She had, besides, a superstitious conviction that by selfishly brushing aside all thoughts of the sick woman and giving in to their passions, they would forfeit each other for ever.

In the following weeks Jane often wondered if she shouldn't have loved Antonio when she had the opportunity. In her lonelier moments she sometimes bitterly regretted depriving herself of the solace of his body, but then she remembered the strength of her feeling at the time and knew she had made the right choice. Jane had come to know and love Antonio again in those leisurely afternoon visits to the hospital when they spoke freely of the years they had been apart, and now she was conscious of an aching loss that had not been there before.

Sometimes Jane felt there was a fairy tale quality about her finding him again after so many years. Now like Sleeping Beauty she was hungry, not just for food but for life and love, and in a way she had not been for most of her married life. With each letter that arrived, she experienced a sensation of excitement followed by depression, for it only served to increase her feelings of frustration and guilt which the memory of Elena's gentle goodness had left with her.

Sarah Lewis also communicated frequently with her. "Don't forget there's a shortage of good doctors here should you ever decide to work in Spain," she wrote half in jest, but Jane found herself seriously considering the idea. The women's clinics had a great need for qualified doctors and Jane had to admit that she was greatly drawn to the notion of working in sunny Spain. And to being near Antonio? She quickly banished the thought, knowing that while Elena lived she would not even contemplate such a step.

Another person Jane badly missed was Terry. He had been home only twice since completing his initial thirty-seven hours training to become a rotary pilot. Now he was engaged in further emergency training in troop carrying into confined areas and low-level tactical flying.

As Jane packed beach towels on top of her daughters' summer clothing and closed the lids of the cases, she found herself dwelling on Terry's last visit. It had been brief, less than two hours, and barely time for him to do more than outline his activities. When she had steeled herself to ask how things were between Claire and himself, he had frowned and turned away without replying.

"Terry, it wasn't her fault," Jane felt constrained to say. "She couldn't help what happened, you know."

"Don't say any more, Mum, or I'm going," Terry warned her, his voice thickened by disgust and outrage. Jane realised in dismay that he saw himself as the injured party and, in his blind, unreasoning pain, was unable to summon up any pity for the true victim of the unhappy affair.

Remembering, Jane sighed with regret and her heart grieved for the pair of them. But perhaps it was better, she told herself. They were both so young and still had their careers to make. Maybe time would prove kind to them both and they would come together again. She genuinely hoped so.

The afternoon post brought her weekly letter from Antonio and she had just finished reading it and was feeling lonely and dispirited, when the phone rang. Jane picked it up and found her son at the other end. He told her with an underlying current of excitement in his voice that he had an overnight pass and would be home later in the day.

Jane looked up expectantly from her desk when she heard Terry's key in the lock. He was in uniform with the airman's peaked cap set at a jaunty angle and he was carrying his army kitbag. He dropped it with a thud in a corner of her surgery and came round the desk to kiss her.

"Hi, Mum. What do you know? I'm on my way to Shannon to do my ship-borne conversion in the Atlantic." His golden eyes sparkled. "We'll be involved in sea and air rescue. Might even pick up a D.S.M." He was more animated than she had seen him since his break-up with Claire and she guessed he welcomed the change of scene as well as the chance to see some action.

"For how long?" Jane asked, her heart sinking. Helicopters really scared her. Unlike planes, helicopters were only kept in the air by forces and controls working against one another. If anything went wrong they could not gracefully glide to earth but just fell out of the sky. She wouldn't have a peaceful moment while he was away.

"About three months," Terry said.

"When are you going?"

"A detachment from the Air Corps leave Baldonnel in the morning. Pete will be with me. You remember him?"

"Yes, I remember." Jane felt an icy foreboding. Oh God, she thought, please bring him back to me. Don't let him be taken too. She stayed awake most of the night praying and bargaining with God to spare her only son, but none of it showed in her face when she held Terry in her arms next day and kissed him goodbye. "Take care, love," she said, and kept her tears until he had gone.

That same weekend Claire went to stay with her father and so knew nothing about Terry's departure for Shannon, not until it was too late. On the night before he had gone away she had been sitting on the bed, sorting through the books she would need for college in October, when she thought she heard a ring at the front door. She had waited, not wanting to go down herself because she was in her night things. After a moment, she heard Christopher going heavily along the hall and absently listened to the rumble of voices in the distance. When the front door closed curiosity compelled her to glance out of the window and, with a painful lurch of her heart, she recognised Terry's tall figure crossing back over the road. She hadn't seen him since the day Jane had returned from Spain. She hurried downstairs to find that Terry hadn't left any message.

"Why didn't you call me, Chris?" she asked, her voice rough with disappointment and the longing the sight of Terry had inspired.

"Didn't think you were in." Christopher was watching sport on television and barely turned his head to answer.

"You could have called me . . ." What was the use? He wasn't even listening.

She had gone back up to her room and stood looking out her window. The McArdle's door was just visible through the branches of the silver birch. Perhaps he would call over again later. But she had known in her heart that he wouldn't.

She quite enjoyed her weekend away. At sixteen months baby David was a chubby little boy, taking his first unsteady steps. Marissa said he was slow to walk because everything was given to him before he cried for it. Claire had brought him a wind-up bear with a tin drum slung about its neck. David squealed with pleasure and loved it to death. Although she feared it would not outlast her visit, the bear was stronger than it looked and was still beating its drum when she left two mornings later. She was on the point of departure when her father told her that Marissa was expecting another baby.

"We're delighted." Jim beamed all over his face. "And glad for David's sake too. We can't seem to help it but we're spoiling the little chap rotten." Claire, remembering how badly her mother had taken the news of Marissa's first pregnancy, resolved to keep the news to herself.

But when she arrived home her mother already knew and had another cause for grievance. Jim had applied for an annulment and in that morning's post she had received notification of the date they were both due to attend a hearing in the Bishop's Palace.

"How could he?" Annette sobbed, showing Claire the letter. "Denying his own children as though they'd never been born." Claire glanced quickly at it, unable to take it in. She felt embarrassed and saddened to see her mother so reduced.

A week later, her mother's new lodger moved into the house. Claire did not like this new man any more than she had liked Austin or Thomas. He went out of his way to pay her fulsome compliments, and whenever he tried to detain her as she passed through the living-room, Annette always found some excuse to send her out again. Claire found her mother's insecurity embarrassing and pitiful. She could not know the mental anguish Annette suffered on seeing herself alongside her daughter's delicate beauty. It was no longer an equal competition. Annette had once been a good-looking woman and still dressed smartly, but she had not worn well. Since turning forty her skin had taken on the texture of coarse orange peel and had a faded, patchy look. In her obsession with remaining youthful, she slavishly adopted special diets and health fads. She could not hide her relief at the end of June when Claire kissed her goodbye and flew off to Spain with Sheena and Ruthie for the whole summer.

Fernando Gonzalez stood at the window watching Pepe, his father's chauffeur, hose down the Mercedes. Since receiving news that the family of *la médica irlandesa* would be flying into Spain that afternoon, Fernando had cleared all appointments in order to leave himself free to meet the girls and their chaperone at the airport. Anxious to make a better impression on them than was possible in his small Séat, he had instructed Pepe to prepare the Mercedes.

The water gushed in a silver jet, drumming on the glass and fountaining over the curved fenders. When at last Pepe stepped back to survey his handiwork, the black saloon car gleamed like anthracite in the sunshine. Fernando nodded approval. It was fitting that the car should look its best when he picked up Señora McArdle's daughters and their so beautiful friend, Claire.

Fernando was equally concerned about his own appearance and had already changed his shirt three times that morning and discarded as many ties before selecting the navy silk with the emblem of the exclusive Andalucian golf club, of which he and his father were members. He was contemplating dashing up to his room to try yet another ensemble when Pepe raised his hand to signify that he was almost finished.

Fernando nodded at him and turned back into the room. "Another five minutes, Mother, and we'll be on our way."

"Thank you, Fernan." Elena Gonzalez gently smiled at her son as she sat in her wheelchair, rosary beads in her hands, her mantilla covering her greying auburn hair. She had grown very frail over the months, but despite the disease that was slowly ravaging her nervous system her spirit remained as indomitable as ever. Each morning she struggled out of bed and, with the help of her maid, Christina, washed and dressed herself. Then, after breakfasting lightly on coffee and a fragment of her favourite powdery almond croissant, she allowed an hour to elapse before attending mass at the local church of *Santo Tomás*.

Fernando knew how much these daily visits meant to his mother but, lately, he had found himself wondering about the wisdom of leaving her there on her own. It was true that Don Jaime, the parish priest, was not very far away but, by the time the missal was removed from the altar and the candles extinguished, it was close on siesta time and if Elena were suddenly taken ill . . . Fernando frowned and decided that this time he would bring Christina with them. Elena would consider he was fussing but better safe than sorry.

He placed his hands on his mother's wheelchair, smoothly turning it in the direction of the cool, tiled hallway, and parked her within sight, smell and touching distance of the potted azaleas, her favourite plant. Elena smiled and gently caressed the glossy leaves between the fingertips of her left hand, her useless right one lying bunched and knotted in her lap.

"One moment, Mother," Fernando whirled about as though just getting the notion, "I will see if Christina can accompany us."

"There is no need," Elena protested, preferring the quiet and peace of the cool church on her own, without the distraction of Christina's fidgeting and barely suppressed sighs. Then seeing the anxiety in her son's eyes, she closed her lips again, knowing how he worried about her.

Fernando ran up the stairs in search of Christina, glancing hurriedly at his watch as he went. The Iberia flight was due to land at Malaga Airport in another forty-five minutes and he must be there, waiting for the girls when they disembarked, as they were not expecting him.

He strode along the landing and rapped briskly on Christina's door, a little smile tugging at the corner of his lips as he pictured the girls' surprise at seeing him or, more particularly, Claire's surprise, for she was the one who primarily interested him. Since meeting her the previous summer Fernando had been unable to get her out of his mind. He wasn't sure but he thought it was a case of love at first sight.

Fernando Gonzalez, good-looking and assured, was in his twenty-sixth year and had often been in love before. Since completing his first term at the University of Malaga there had been a succession of affairs with pretty Spanish girls of good family. Although not as instantly successful with the female sex as his younger brother Alejandro, who possessed the kind of dashing good looks associated with romantic nineteenth century novels of duels and love trysts, Fernando's good bearing and impeccable manners were enough to attract the interest of the most discerning of young Spanish ladies. In addition to his personable appearance there was his extreme wealth. The marriage of Antonio, the only son of Ferdinand Gonzalez, to Elena, the only daughter of Mañuel Lopez, had resulted in the amalgamation of their vast vineyards in the Jerez region to the north of Cadiz, where the fertile *alberiza* soil of their combined crops produced a plentiful supply of the fine Palomino grape. Besides this, there was Antonio's investment in real estate and the successful and rapidly spreading number of their *Las Cicadas* apartment blocks, which stretched as far east along the coast as Almeria and as far west as Marbella. As eldest son Fernando stood to inherit the greatest share of this accumulated wealth. Given the prospect of such an inheritance it was greatly to the young Spaniard's credit that he was virtually unspoiled.

He went downstairs again to begin the process of transferring Elena and her wheelchair to the car. By the time Christina came panting out the door and heaved her cumbersome bulk into the rear of the Mercedes beside her mistress, Fernando was seated in the driver's seat, drumming his well-manicured fingernails on the steering wheel.

Fernando slipped the car into gear and drove rapidly between the ornate gates bearing the Gonzalez crest and down the twisty road to the church. There he deposited his mother with a dutiful kiss and a promise to return for her within the hour before speeding off again along the road to Malaga.

An Iberian DC9 aircraft, with its distinctive red and gold colouring, was coming in low on the skyline as Fernando drove into the airport. As he paced up and down in the arrivals area, his gaze trained expectantly on the narrow exit channel, Fernando was shaken by a sudden presentiment that the young girl, soon to emerge, would some day come to mean more to him than any other woman he would ever meet.

They came quickly through the customs area and their mood was light-hearted and gay with anticipation of the months that lay ahead.

Sheena came first, easily pulling her soft-topped leather case on its trolley behind her. She wore faded blue jeans and a striped navy and white poplin waistcoat over a white cotton shirt. There was a pair of sunglasses pushed to the top of her head and a sparkle in her eyes.

Claire wore jeans too and a blue denim shirt open at the neck. Her fair hair was tied back in two pigtails and she looked no more than seventeen. She held Ruthie's hand and bent her head to chat encouragingly to the little girl, while guiding her own case on its nose-wheel. Ruthie pulled a slightly smaller version of her older sister's case. Two steps behind her charges, breathing hard, Teresa Murray struggled to correct her case's tendency to overturn while all the time puffing encouragement after their disappearing backs.

Fernando stepped forward into Claire's path and relieved her of her case.

"It's Fernando," Ruthie cried in recognition.

"*Buenos días*." Fernando's wide welcoming smile lit his rather sombre features and he held out his hand to Claire. As she shyly shook it, Sheena noisily came back inside to find out what was keeping them and broke into exclamations of delight at the sight of the Spaniard.

"Hey, this is great. Mum never said a word." She led the way outside, chatting confidently. Fernando looked back at Claire with a helpless shrug before strolling on with Sheena to where he had parked the Mercedes.

"Isn't it great Fernando came to meet us," Ruthie said enthusiastically.

Claire nodded, still a little overwhelmed by the welcome he had given her. He was such a good-looking, sophisticated man, she thought, feeling clumsy in his company.

317

"Look at Shee flirting like mad with him. Bet she means to add him to her list." Ruthie gave Claire a wise look.

Claire sat into the back of the gleaming black Mercedes with Teresa and Ruthie. Fernando had motioned her towards the front seat but Sheena got there first. The Spaniard, too polite to show his feelings, listened with a slightly bewildered smile to Sheena's chatter, straining to hear what was being said behind him. Sheena, who could not envisage that a young man might possibly prefer anyone else to her, gaily chattered on, confident that she was making a hit, as the big car easily covered the miles to Nerja.

When Fernando had deposited them at the apartment block he placed their cases on the ground and turned and shook hands with each of them, politely bestowing a smile on Teresa, who was plainly bedazzled by the assured young Spaniard.

"I hope you will not hesitate to call upon my family if you are ever in need," he told them formally. He looked at Claire as he spoke, and she felt that he was somehow singling her out and felt sudden disquiet. Oh God, Claire thought in despair, she was here to enjoy herself. Didn't she deserve to, like anyone else?

Soberly, she returned the Spaniard's farewell and turned away. She was very quiet as she went in out of the sun and lifted her case up the stone steps.

"What a hunk," Sheena said, taking the steps at a run and carelessly bumping her trolleyed case after her. She passed them all out and arrived breathlessly at the apartment door before them. She delved in her bag for the key and went ahead of them inside.

"Wow!" her voice floated back to them. "This is great . . . really something."

Although Jane and Terry had enthusiastically, and at length, described the furniture and decor, none of them was prepared for the sumptuousness of the apartment, from the richness of the glowing teak in the living-room and bedrooms to the tiled perfection of the bathroom. They clattered about looking into the presses and exclaiming over everything. Teresa just stood inside the door and looked about her with her mouth dropped open. "Never in all my life!" she kept repeating. "By God! This is better than the Gresham Hotel."

Sheena laid immediate claim to the biggest bedroom, Teresa having assured her that she was just as happy to sleep in the small room, and plonked her case on the woven matting before bouncing boisterously on the wide bed. "Who knows?" she joked. "I might get lucky."

Claire grinned dutifully with a desolate, hollow feeling inside. Would she never stop aching for Terry? Even now the thought of him brought a lump to her throat.

"That reminds me," Sheena looked at her thoughtfully. She snapped open her case and burrowed beneath her underclothes. When she turned around she was holding an envelope in her hand. "Terry asked me to give you this. Never thought of it till now."

The letter lay in Claire's hip pocket while she unpacked her clothes and put them away in the louvred press. While Sheena and Ruthie went out to buy milk, Teresa bustled about the kitchen, exploring her territory. After the girls had returned and boiled water in a saucepan for coffee and the four of them sat on the balcony sipping the hot liquid and nibbling crusty rolls, Claire was conscious of it all the time against her hip.

She toyed with the idea of never opening it, because then she would be no better off but certainly no worse. When she had given full rein to her imagination and exhausted every possibility, both good and bad, she went into her room and extracted the letter from the envelope. It was written on a piece of jotter paper and folded in half.

'Dear Claire, I'm off to Shannon tomorrow where I'll be stationed for the next couple of months. I called the other night but you were out. You can contact me for the first week in the evenings between 7 and 8 o'clock at Crowley's pub. Number below. I know what you said the last time we met . . .'

She heard Ruthie calling her name and quickly turned over the paper. Halfway down the page it was signed, 'Love, Terry.'

She felt herself growing dizzy and light-headed.

She glanced back and read, '. . . but I hope you'll ring. Otherwise, I'll believe you really meant it when you said you didn't ever want to see me again.'

Had she really said that?

Ruthie came in the door and Claire saw that she was wearing her swimsuit and carrying a shrimp net she had bought earlier. Sheena must have received this precious letter over a week ago and left it all this time, lying in her half-packed case. She felt herself getting dizzier and sicker.

"Clairey," Ruthie cried. "You're not listening! We're all going down to the beach for a swim and would you please hurry up and get a move on."

The clattering roar of the Dauphin filled Terry's head and he moved his left hand up and down, twisting it to control the collective and throttle, while his right hand moved in small circles, controlling the cyclic. Below, the slaty waves of the Atlantic lashed the bow of the patrol ship, and above the sky was equally grey and ferocious.

For a moment it was like his first time in a helicopter and all parts wanted to go their own way, but gradually Terry got control, and the machine gently rose and fell in the same spot. He pressed his feet on the spongy pedals, turning the machine back towards the patrol ship and held it in a hover fifty feet above the main deck.

"Okay, bring us down lower and keep us pointed at the mainmast," the instructor's nasal voice sounded in his headphones.

"Yes, sir?" Terry grabbed the collective stick in his left hand and at once the helicopter shot up to sixty feet. He knew he was making a poor showing but his concentration kept wandering. Claire hadn't even bothered to answer his letter or make contact with him. Every night in Crowley's, waiting like a dope, Terry thought, feeling his anger swelling again.

He panicked and overcontrolled as the deck of the ship rushed up. Damn! He had pulled up too hard, causing them to pop back up in the air.

"Try and keep us over the same spot, laddie."

"Sorry!" Terry grunted, the sweat running down his neck. The instructor took over the controls. "I've got it," he said. The machine drifted down twenty feet and pointed towards the mast of the ship again. Terry felt a fool.

"Okay, it's all yours. Think you can take us down?"

Terry nodded grimly. He would or die in the attempt. He looked for a place to approach, then aimed the machine into the wind, to reduce groundspeed on touchdown. When they were thirty feet from the chosen spot on the main deck and the instructor had not taken over the controls, Terry knew he was going to let him go the whole way. He glided down in autorotation and concentrated on landing straight ahead, into the wind. He hit the deck, skidded a few yards and came to a halt.

"Great bloody man, McArdle," the instructor was smiling openly.

"What do you mean, sir?"

"I thought you handled that like an ace."

"But I was all over the place, sir."

"That's what I mean . . . an ace arsehole."

Terry flushed and turned his head away to complete his landing checks.

Claire walked up and down the cool aisles of the *supermercado* carefully selecting items from the well-stocked shelves and placing them in her trolley. It was a job that had invariably fallen to her in the fortnight since they had arrived in Spain and one she secretly relished. Sometimes Teresa Murray went shopping with her and, for the sake of politeness, Claire pretended to be glad of her company, but really she preferred to be on her own. Teresa was kindness itself but she kept up a continuous flow of conversation, mostly about her extended family and the amazing doings of her grandchildren. Claire found it exhausting and was just as glad whenever Teresa admitted to feeling 'a bit lazy, love.' There was no denying her presence saved Claire a lot. Normally in Jane's absence, she was lumbered with most of the housekeeping chores but with Teresa doing the cooking and cleaning Claire's only duty on this holiday was the difficult task of budgeting their allowance to pay for their food. She had even managed to make it stretch to a train trip to Barcelona on the previous weekend to see the Picasso exhibition and was hoping that soon they might all attend a bullfight in Malaga. This was something she had taken responsibility for since the days of their summer holidays in the seaside cottage. Claire told herself she didn't really mind and accepted that in Spain Sheena's prime consideration was to achieve an all-over tan. Her bottom was already '*muy tostado*', and when she was not on the balcony sunbathing nude, she spent her time on the beach in a skimpy sun-dress, lazily sketching or making pastel studies of children and animals. Teresa was fond of sunbathing too and she often shared the balcony with Sheena. Some days Claire and Ruthie would leave Teresa to her sunning and stroll down to join Sheena on the beach. When the sand became too hot to sit on, the three of them would climb the stone steps to sit under the coloured awnings of a beachfront cafe and sip *naranjada* or *café con leche*.

Now as Claire popped a jar of apricot preserve into the trolley, she reflected that she had got out of the habit of counting on Sheena to do anything other than eat the food she bought. She was the one who accompanied Ruthie to visit their old friends at Hotel Murillo and, while the little girls played happily together, lingered near them in the pool or lay dreaming under the trees. Ignacio was as doting as ever and insisted upon Ruthie and herself, and Teresa when she accompanied them, staying to lunch or tea. He was always urging them to sample different dishes on the pretext of requiring their opinion. Claire had indulged herself so much with his delicious *tortillas* that she feared she must have put on at least a half-stone weight since coming to Spain.

Claire took her place in the queue behind a Spanish matron who was checking through what looked like her week's shopping. Leaning on her trolley, she glanced about her, enjoying the foreignness of the scene and the attractive scents wafting her way. She loved the way Spanish people smelled as though they had stepped straight out of a delicately perfumed bath. As she was thinking this a stout, middle-aged man, carrying a basket of groceries, stood in front of her.

She debated whether or not to say anything. After all, she was a stranger in this country. But something deliberately arrogant in his manner offended her however, and although she was usually so gentle and accepting, she found herself taking issue.

"Excuse me," she said, the words coming out almost of their own volition, "but I was before you."

He stared at her haughtily, then tried to bluster his way out of it, but she stood her ground and after a moment he sullenly withdrew to the end of the queue. That'll teach him, Claire thought, moving into his space. She looked around and met the amused eyes of a young Spaniard standing behind her.

"You are to be congratulated," he told her with an infectious grin. Claire self-consciously returned his smile, as she packed her groceries into bags.

"Please allow me." He was at her elbow, taking the two weightier bags from her. "Contrary to your experience the Spanish are not an inconsiderate people."

"Thank you," Claire said doubtfully, wondering if she should try and take them back. She preceded him out of the store and began walking quickly towards the apartment.

"Guapa," he said approvingly. He walked beside her and quietly studied her. "You are English?"

She shook her head. "Irish."

"Ah yes . . . *Irlanda*."

As they arrived at the entrance to *Las Cicadas*, Claire looked for Fernando's car, but there was no sign of it. The Spaniard went on into the building and, ignoring the lift, began climbing the stairs. There was nothing else Claire could do but follow him. He was about to continue on to the next floor when she called him back.

"This is it. Now may I have my bags?"

"Certainly." He laid them carefully on the ground and stepped back with a smart half-salute, causing Claire's heart to lurch painfully. The military action was so reminiscent of Terry she could have wept. She bent her head and rummaged in her bag for the key. When she raised it again the Spaniard was regarding her curiously.

"My name is Alejandro," he was saying. "And yours?"

"Claire."

He smiled, showing even white teeth then turned and ran lightly down the steps. She moved to stare down the stairwell and, after a few moments, saw his dark head appear briefly. She stepped back hurriedly as he twisted his head to look up. Then he was gone. She shrugged and went into the apartment.

The following afternoon Claire and Teresa came down the hill from Hotel Murillo with Ruthie and Adela. The little Spanish girl carried a soft leather duffle bag over her shoulder. Ignacio had readily given permission for his daughter to stay overnight and now the two little girls skipped along, delighted at the proposed treat.

"Would you look at them," Teresa nudged Claire. "Happy as Larry, the pair of them."

Claire nodded and smiled.

"That little Adela is the spittin' image of my Sara's eldest girl," Teresa went on affectionately. "Stand to look at her you would."

Claire was amused. Teresa's grandchildren were her favourite topic.

"Please let me hold Carmencita," Ruthie begged now. The huge rag doll was attired in Spanish national costume and the children were taking it in turns to carry her. The two of them collapsed into fits of the giggles at the way the doll's head-dress flopped over her eyes.

"She is drunk!" Adela said in glee. "Too much *sangria.*"

"Poor Carmencita," sighed Ruthie. The minute the children got in the apartment door they ran to prepare her for her siesta. Adela pulled out an embroidered lawn nightie from her bag and, clucking fondly like two little mother hens, she and Ruthie robed the doll and laid her tenderly on a pillow.

"Shh . . . she is sleeping." Adela put her finger to her lips as she backed out of the darkened room. "Tonight she will dance flamenco."

Claire smiled at the pair of them, glad to see them in such good spirits. She had been a little worried in case Adela might be bored without the distractions she was used to in her father's luxurious hotel, but Adela was a sunny, unspoilt child and was thoroughly enjoying the novelty of the visit.

"Come and see my kitten," Ruthie proudly invited her and, while Teresa was busy getting out the iced *limonada* and fancy biscuits, they went on to the balcony. To Claire's relief there was no shortage of cats visiting the apartment to succeed the tortoiseshell kitten from the previous summer.

As Claire sat on her bed and picked up a book, there was a ring at the door. She opened it and found Fernando outside.

"Ah, Claire." Fernando's face was transformed by smiles at the sight of her. "I cannot stay long. I came only to invite you to tea at my house tomorrow. My mother intended you should visit before this but she has not been well. So! It is arranged. You will come?"

Claire nodded.

"Can Adela come too?" Ruthie asked eagerly. The little girls had come running at the sound of the bell.

Fernando bent towards the Spanish child. "You would like

to come, Adela?"

"*Con mucho gusto, Señor.*"

"*Muy bien.*" Fernando turned smiling back to Claire. "So, I shall call for you at three o'clock." He smiled mischievously. "All of you. Your chaperone too."

"*Hasta luego.*"

"Ah, you are learning fast. *Hasta luego.*" Fernando gave them a small wave and was gone. Claire closed the door thoughtfully after him.

"Let's go and meet Sheena," she suggested to the little girls and they ran to get their swimsuits and towels.

Calling goodbye to Teresa, who was dozing in the sun with her feet up, they set off for the beach. Sheena was waiting for them, her sunbathing and sketching done for the day. She was amused by Fernando's invitation.

"What did I tell you," she chuckled. "He wants you to meet his mother."

"All of us," Claire stressed, but Sheena laughed and said that was only camouflage.

They sat chatting while the little girls played on the sand and swam, and then they all left the beach and went to their usual café for drinks.

Sheena gave their order to the waiter, who grinned and eagerly went to do her bidding. As always, she had lost no time in enslaving the male population. She had been disappointed but philosophical when Fernando had plainly showed his preference for Claire, and although she still practised her charm on him, it was merely a reflex action.

"Will you make me a picture of Carmencita, please," Adela asked her politely. Sheena good-naturedly took up her sketch pad and obliged.

She was engaged in shading in the costume and assuring Adela that the next would be in colour, when a shadow fell across the table and the girls looked up to see two Spaniards smiling down at them.

"*Hola*, Claire," one of them said.

With a start, Claire recognised the young man she had

met at the supermarket. Whereupon Alejandro indicated the chairs about the table, and Claire had no choice but to invite him and his companion to sit down. Sheena regarded them both with bright, interested eyes.

"You are an artist?" Alejandro bent to look at her sketch. Sheena grinned and nodded.

"Are portraits very expensive?"

"Special rate for good-looking men," Sheena said cheekily.

Alejandro's companion was slightly older than Alejandro, perhaps in his early thirties, tall and well-built, with black hair spiking across his forehead. He murmured something to Alejandro and when the younger man responded with a laugh, he fell silent again and stared so intently at the girls that Claire was embarrassed. To cover her confusion she turned to Alejandro.

"It's a portrait of Carmencita," she explained, holding up Adela's doll, "who, by the way, dances flamenco."

"Ayee, I have always wanted to meet such an accomplished young lady." Alejandro took hold of the doll's hand and solemnly shook it, much to the delight of the two little girls. "And speaking of flamenco," he turned to Claire, "would you and your friend care to accompany us to a show?"

"We'd love to." Sheena accepted excitedly. "We've been longing to see flamenco, haven't we, Claire?"

Claire nodded, but with less enthusiasm. "Yes, we have."

"But you do not know anything about us," Alejandro said astutely, "and you are not sure if it is correct to accompany two Spaniards to a show without being formally introduced?"

Claire smiled reluctant assent.

"*Comprendo.* So what is to be done?" Alejandro sighed and turned to his companion. "Should we ask Señora Carmencita to make the formal introductions?" He glanced back at Claire with an understanding smile. "Would that meet your requirements?" Claire found her objections melting under his charm. Perhaps she was being silly.

"Of course it would," Sheena said, impatient of such scruples. "Don't pay any attention to Claire. She worries about nothing."

Still Alejandro hesitated, his eyebrows quirked.

Claire smiled and nodded.

"Estupendo," Alejandro said in relief and leaned towards the rag doll. To the amusement of the little girls he began, "Señora Carmencita I would consider it a great honour if you would introduce me to your charming friends."

Sheena grinned and mimicked through the doll's headdress. "I would be delighted, Señor," pointing first at the little girls and then herself, and pronouncing their names.

"And now," Alejandro's companion drawled, "won't you introduce me?"

Alejandro laughed and clapped his shoulder. "Miguel Delgado is a very good friend of mine," he told them. "I am most happy to present him to you."

"Señoritas." Miguel bowed, and resumed his lazy watch on the girls again.

Alejandro ordered wine and said, "Tonight we will go to La Hacienda, the best in town. But first we will take you to a friend of ours who owns a bar with the most delicious *gambas*."

There was a relaxed feeling between them now although Claire was still not at ease with Miguel. He seemed to her coarse and full of suppressed energy. Maybe it was only in her imagination, but she felt distinctly uncomfortable in his company. Before long she stood up and said they must go. Sheena was reluctant to say goodbye and there were many farewells before she could drag herself away.

Between the attention of two good-looking young men and the wine Sheena was on a high as they walked back to the apartment, brimming with plans and ideas for further meetings with the two Spaniards.

"Let's see how tonight goes first," Claire suggested cautiously. She was more concerned with leaving Ruthie and Adela.

"Are we right to go?"

"Oh, they'll be all right with Teresa," Sheena said carelessly. "Anyway we won't be late. Alex says the show only lasts an hour."

Claire allowed herself to be persuaded. So often lately hers seemed to be the only dissenting voice. She was tired of being the conscience for everyone.

At the appointed hour the Spaniards were waiting for the girls in the courtyard and they walked to the bar where the *gambas* were every bit as good as Alejandro had promised. Miguel had been replaced by a young man called Luis, and no explanations were offered. Claire suspected that Sheena was disappointed but she was just as glad.

At La Hacienda they were shown to a table and ice-cold glasses of Coke laced with white rum were placed before them. Claire drank slowly but Sheena, as she did everything else in life, tackled hers vigorously, airily opining that *Cuba Libres* were not a whole lot different from Coke. Except for the kick, Claire thought.

Talking was difficult with all the tempestuous dancing going on so close at hand. Another round of drinks was brought, and then another. Alejandro seemed to be paying for everything.

When the flamenco finished the Spaniards invited the girls on to the dance floor. The song that was playing, "You'll Never Stop Me Loving You", had been popular the previous summer when Terry and Claire danced together. She felt such a wave of longing that she tightened her grip on Luis's narrow shoulder and he glanced down at her in surprise. After a moment he thrust himself hard against her and Claire felt so moved by desire and all the rum she had drunk that she almost turned faint. She had not thought that she would ever feel sexual awareness again, nor had she wanted to.

When they arrived back at the apartment she said goodnight at once and ran up to join Ruthie and Adela. She found the little girls sitting with Teresa stretched out on the couch, who raised a red suffering face as Claire came in the door.

"Poor Teresa isn't well," Ruthie said, jumping up at once and running over to her. "Her head is aching and she says she feels dizzy."

"I'm afraid I overdid it," Teresa admitted. "Too much blooming sun. I should have known better, lying on that balcony for hours."

"Poor Teresa," Claire commiserated with her and went to get her a cup of tea and two paracetemol. By the time Sheena had said goodnight at last to Alejandro and come dashing up the stairs, it was clear to Claire that unless by some miracle Teresa recovered from her sunburn before morning she would never be well enough to accompany them to Fernando's house next day.

Fernando sat behind the wheel of the Mercedes looking cool and relaxed as he drove the short distance into Nerja to pick up the girls. He wore light, stone-coloured linen slacks and a short-sleeved shirt with a button down collar and a bronze silk tie. His arms were dark from the sun and contrasted strongly against the soft pearl. He went the length of the street and turned into the parking lot before *Las Cicadas*. He had told Claire to expect him at three o'clock and it was now ten minutes before the hour.

It was deeply satisfying to Fernando's punctilious soul that he was early despite the many preparations needed to ensure that everything was in order for this afternoon's tea-party.

His first priority had been to ensure that Elena should take her afternoon nap undisturbed in the cathedral-like quiet of her bedroom, so that she would be rested and at her best for the visit. Leaving Christina to wake her mistress at the appointed time, Fernando had gone downstairs and supervised the laying out of the china and silverware bearing the Gonzalez crest, nodding his approval of the trays of sweet confectionery that Pilar had been preparing all morning and taking it upon himself to check that the *limonada*, as fresh and fruitily delicious as only Pilar knew how to make it, was keeping cool in big earthenware jugs on the marble shelves of the larder. All that remained was to shower and change into casual clothing before driving into the town.

As Fernando parked the Mercedes he glanced in the mirror, his attention was caught by the sight of his younger brother jauntily crossing the concrete forecourt. He stared in surprise, for he had believed Alejandro to be far away in his military barracks in Cadiz.

"*Hola*! Alex!" Fernando called through the window and his brother checked and looked behind him.

"Fernan. What are you doing here?"

"I might ask you the same question," Fernando said with a smile, noting that Alejandro was out of uniform and carried no kit. "When did you arrive?"

"Not long ago." His brother's reciprocal smile was wide but his gaze was almost furtive, Fernando thought, frowning at the vagueness of his reply.

"Does Father know you are here?"

Alejandro shrugged. "There wasn't time to tell him. I got the chance of a lift home and felt like coming."

"So we'll see you later?"

"I'm not sure. It all depends . . ."

"I thought you said you felt like coming home."

"Yes I did . . . but you know how it is, Fernan," Alejandro smiled disarmingly. "Naturally I want to see my mother, but I am meeting friends and may decide after all to stay with them rather than inconvenience anyone at home. Anyway it is merely a flying visit . . . there may not even be time to go home."

Fernando regarded his younger brother gravely.

"Are you in trouble, Alex?"

"Of course not! What a suspicious mind you have. It's just that if I go home it will only upset mother. You know how fussed she gets. She'll want me beside her every minute and when I go she'll miss me like the devil so perhaps . . ."

Alejandro looked uncomfortable.

"Very well." Fernando took pity on him. "I will say nothing, but only for her sake. She will be even more upset if she knows you are here and she doesn't see you."

Alejandro looked relieved. "Thanks, Fernan. I'll be home for a week in September and then I will be a model son, I promise."

Fernando suddenly recalled his purpose in visiting *Las Cicadas* and clapped his brother absently on the back. Alejandro was a selfish little beggar, he thought, but there was no real harm in him. He got along better with him than he did with Federico, who took himself far too seriously for his taste.

"Make sure you do!" With a last rejoinder Fernando turned away and ran lightly up the steps to Claire's apartment. He forgot all about his brother the moment she opened the door.

Señora Gonzalez, sitting on the patio, shaded from the sun by a huge parasol, stretched out her hand in welcome. She greeted each girl in turn in a low, sweetly accented voice and expressed polite regret that their chaperone had not been well enough to accompany them.

"I am sorry to hear she is suffering from sunburn," Elena said. "It is so easy to underestimate the strength of the sun. I hope she will soon be recovered." Then, turning to Fernando, she said, "Fernan, my dear, pour drinks for the girls. They must be thirsty."

"Certainly, Mother," Fernando replied, as he bent to kiss her, "but not until I have rung for your iced tea. I notice you have not had it yet."

As Fernando made himself useful, pouring glasses of chilled *limonada* and cheerfully handing them about, Claire took hers and went to sit near Elena. She was drawn to the frail figure and, observing Fernando's tender care for his mother, was struck by the deep affection between them.

Sheena, glass in hand, wandered off across the smooth lawn to admire the flowerbeds massed with salvias, carnations and begonias. In one place they had been planted out in a striking arrangement to represent the Spanish flag. Fernando walked beside her, content to leave Claire with his mother.

"Gosh!" Sheena said in awe. "I bet that took someone hours of back-breaking toil."

"A fair amount," Fernando agreed, amused. It had taken their two full-time gardeners, along with some outside help, ten hours to produce the effect.

"This place is enormous," Sheena said admiringly. "Just how big is it?"

"About four acres." Fernando smiled.

"Wow!" Sheena was suitably impressed.

Fernando looked back and saw that Claire was holding a book and leaning close to his mother's chair. Elena was a great reader. He knew Claire was taking an Arts degree at college, which increased his interest in her. He was full of admiration for learning and, in addition to his architectural degree, would liked to have taken a degree in languages. He hoped some day to put this right. As it was, he was fairly fluent in German and French. He looked around at the sound of excited laughter and saw Ruthie and Adela frisking with his black Labrador.

"What a friendly, beautiful dog," Ruthie gasped. "She licked my face."

Fernando laughed. "Stella is very fond of chocolate," he told her, eyeing the marks about the little girl's mouth.

Sheena shoved a tissue at her sister and said disgustedly: "Wipe your face, silly".

"I much prefer Stella," Ruthie said, thrusting her face close to the dog's muzzle and Stella obligingly used her tongue again to great effect.

"Honestly, Ruthie," Sheena scolded. "You can't be taken anywhere. What would Mummy say if she were here?"

"Mummy would approve," Ruthie said serenely. "She's always telling us to use natural rather than artificial resources."

"Isn't she incorrigible," Sheena laughingly appealed to Fernando with such affectionate pride that he grinned back at her, liking her a little more than he had formerly.

Claire was oblivious of them all as she chatted to Elena. She discovered that Elena was almost as great an admirer of Charlotte Brontë's novels as she was herself.

"I cannot decide which I like better," Claire confessed after some thought. "*Jane Eyre* or *Villette?*"

Elena smiled. "I have no hesitation in deciding upon *Villette*," she said. "I think if you have ever had to leave home and live for a time in another country you would share a fellow feeling with poor Lucy Snowe."

Claire considered this. At present she was away from home but she supposed that she wasn't really qualified to judge since she wasn't entirely amongst strangers. Oddly, she felt more at home here in Spain than she had anywhere else in her life, and had done so from her first day on Spanish soil.

"Have you had such an experience, Señora?" she asked shyly, wondering if she should be so personal.

Elena nodded and sighed. "When I was eighteen I lived one whole year in England. Ah, but how I missed Spain. Alas, I did not have the consolation of Doctor John or Monsieur Paul Emanuel to alleviate my loneliness." She laughed gently. "But, of course, I cannot complain having by that time already found my *novio*."

Claire remembered Fernando's father, a big untidy man with bushy eyebrows and curly black hair.

"Sadly these days I do not read as much as I would like," Elena was saying. "I get tired easily and find it difficult to support a book for long."

Claire had noticed how twisted the woman's hands were and how restricted her movements. She had an idea, but hesitated to express it for fear of seeming presumptuous. But when Elena leaned back, looking ill and exhausted from all the effort of talking, Claire offered to come to the house and read to her.

"Any time you want me," Claire said earnestly, her own eyes meeting Elena's with such a look of concern that the older woman was startled.

"I would like that very much," Elena said slowly, and was surprised to find it was true. There was something about the girl's look that went straight to her heart. From the first moment Elena had felt an immediate rapport with her and now, watching her son's eyes fixed ardently upon the young Irish girl as he strolled across the grass to join them, she perceived with a slight sense of shock that his interest in Claire was more like that of a lover than the family friend he claimed to be.

Jane put down the phone and with a sigh reflected on how little she had learned from her phone call to Spain. Her daughter might have a great gift with a pencil and manage to pin a scene on paper, she thought, but with words Sheena failed miserably. She should have spoken to Claire, who would have supplied her with the kind of details she craved.

With interest Jane had heard of the afternoon visit to Señora Gonzalez. She was sorry to learn that Teresa had not been well enough to accompany the girls. Poor Teresa, she thought. Jane could well imagine how disappointed Teresa had been to miss the outing and the chance of impressing her family later on with an account of how the wealthy Spaniards in Nerja lived. Jane would have loved to see the place for herself and could only guess from Sheena's excited description of the beautifully furnished mansion and well-kept lawns just how sumptuous Antonio's house had been. Sheena had hardly been aware of Fernando's mother, except as a sickly old woman. Jane sighed, knowing Sheena's capacity to successfully block out unwelcome details, aware too that her daughter had not Claire's instinctive empathy. It wasn't really surprising that Sheena had nothing to say about her hostess, Jane acknowledged ruefully, that she had not already observed for herself when Elena visited her at Hospital Belen. Yes, Jane told herself, it was undoubtedly Claire, having spent so much time with her hostess, who could have told her the type of thing she wanted to know, such as the state of Señora Gonzalez' health and what she was interested in. Jane, although curious to know if Antonio had been present that afternoon, had not been able to bring herself to ask. Now she wished that she had asked Sheena to fetch Claire to the phone too, because she realised she was missing her adopted daughter every bit as much as her own children. At her last meeting with Claire, she had been struck by just how much their relationship had strengthened and developed over the years. Now, feeling her absence, Jane crossed the street to give Annette the latest news of her daughter.

Annette was on her own and invited Jane out to the garden, where she was soaking up the last rays of sun.

"I've had a few postcards from Claire," she said, pulling out a deckchair for Jane. "She seems to be enjoying herself."

"Hard not to in Spain," Jane joked, and wondered whether to mention the visit to Antonio's house. Better not, she decided. Annette would only read too much into it.

"I wonder if my daughter realises just how lucky she is," Annette was saying. "But then Claire always did have the knack of landing on her feet."

Jane wondered that Annette could say such a thing but repressed the retort that sprang to her lips. Annette had always been blind where Claire was concerned. She thought Annette did not look very well. The bruises under her eyes seemed to suggest she was suffering from insomnia and the doctor in Jane noticed a tremor in her friend's hand as she poured them wine.

"I believe Teresa Murray went to Spain with the girls," Annette said suddenly. "I must say, Jane, I was very surprised when I heard." There was an aggrieved note in her voice.

"Surprised and hurt," Annette went on. "Really, I would have thought after all the years we've known each other you might have asked me."

"The thought never crossed my mind," Jane said truthfully, knowing that if it had she would have rejected it at once. She felt amazed that Annette could expect anything from her, not after the way she had betrayed her with Eddie.

"After all I've been through I could do with a few weeks

in the sun," Annette said plaintively. "I wouldn't mind if I could afford to go abroad myself, but I can't, not in my circumstances. The irony of it is my teenage daughter gets to go twice, it's so terribly unfair."

"I'm sorry you feel that way. My own circumstances are not ideal either," Jane said coolly, refusing to feel bad. Privately she considered that if Annette had not drunk so much she could have risen to the price of a cheap charter. "I only wish I could have gone with the girls myself, but it was out of the question to be away from the clinic again so soon." She paused. "As it is I'm planning to take my holiday sometime in the middle of August and maybe stay on in Spain until late September. It will mean Ruthie missing school but, at her stage, it doesn't matter too much. The girls can stay on with us too – college doesn't open till October."

Annette frowned. "Well, Sheena may for all I care," she said, "but I expect Claire home long before that."

Jane was taken aback. "I merely meant . . ."

"I suppose you've heard Marissa is pregnant again. Not losing any time, are they?" Annette's voice was bitter. "He never bothered to make time for his own children and now look at him."

Jane forced herself to meet her friend's gaze. "And what about you? Have you thought of marrying again?"

"You mean when Holy Mother Church wipes out my marriage as though it never existed?" Annette laughed mirthlessly. "Why should I bother? If they can so easily abrogate marriage vows entered into in good faith, then the whole thing is meaningless. Quite frankly I'd much prefer an illicit relationship without their blessing. At least there's no humbug about living with a partner and taxwise I'd be much better off."

Jane stood up, a little shocked by Annette's bitterness and said, "If there's anything you want me to bring out to Claire when I'm going . . ."

"There won't be."

Annette did not see her out, clearly still angry. She sat sipping wine, her face set in a cold, hard mask. Jane shivered as she let herself out the side gate. She thought she had never seen anyone deteriorate so fast as Annette.

Jane was barely inside her own front door when the telephone rang. She was delighted to hear Terry's voice.

"What a coincidence," she told him happily. "I was just thinking about you. How are things working out on board ship?" He had suffered in the beginning from sea sickness and had been furious with himself.

"Fine. We're being kept pretty busy," Terry said, sounding very far away. Jane could hear voices and music noisily competing for supremacy in the background.

"Not working too hard, I hope."

"Not at all. Anyway it's all a bit of a breeze."

Jane took that with a grain of salt. He had told her in an unguarded moment about the hours spent in emergency training while engaged in what they called the black hole – the dreaded hover at night. Taking off and landing from a patrol vessel, pitching and rolling in heavy seas, was also a lot more difficult than from a stationary helipad ashore, and required the highest degree of discipline and safety consciousness. She was touched, however, by his regard for a mother's feelings.

"How are Sheena and Ruthie getting on in Spain?" Terry asked.

"They are all well," Jane said, suspecting that Claire was the one he really wanted to hear about. "I was only speaking to Sheena about two hours ago and she filled me in on all they are doing." She went on to describe the afternoon visit to Fernando's house. He was silent so long she thought they had been cut off.

"Terry? Are you still there?"

"Yes, Mum."

"Sheena tells me that Claire does all the shopping and gives them so many tomato salads the stuff is coming out of their ears." Jane laughed. "I told her to stop complaining and take her share of the housekeeping."

"Is that Spanish fellow chasing after Claire?" Terry asked

abruptly.

"Well, if he is," Jane replied spiritedly, "I'm sure he's not the only one."

Terry gave a strangled grunt. "I've got to go, Mum. Someone here wants to use the phone. I'll ring you again."

"Couldn't you find somewhere quieter?" Jane cried, but the phone clicked off. She replaced the receiver with a thoughtful expression. He would need to take care, she mused, or Fernando could very well end up cutting him out.

Claire went to Elena's house and read to her as she had promised. In the beginning she was careful to keep the sessions short, fearful of tiring the sick woman, but she soon found that Elena could be relied upon to say when she had had enough.

Fernando insisted on driving Claire, although she had assured him she was quite happy to walk. Once there, he would escort her to where his mother sat and ring for *limonada* and iced tea. Sometimes he lingered in the room while Claire was reading, sitting so quietly that she forgot all about him until Elena addressed him. Claire had not thought it possible to be so unselfconscious in his presence.

Each afternoon Claire closed the book with the greatest of reluctance and went to replace it on the shelf. At the end of the first week when she held out her hand in farewell Elena clasped it and said in heartfelt accents,

"*Muchas gracias, mi querida.* I look forward more than I can say to your next visit."

As though, Claire thought, she had never read *Villette* herself and couldn't wait to find out what happened. When she said as much Elena smiled and nodded, "Yes, Claire . . . because you are making it come alive for me. In truth, I feel as though I am hearing it all for the very first time."

Claire had experienced this herself when reading a favourite book again after a long time, seeing nuances she had missed and gaining new insights into the workings of the characters.

The following day she was ready again for Fernando when he called. Ruthie and Teresa were planning to walk to the hotel and take a swim in the pool with Adela. Once she knew that the little girl would be looked after for a few hours Claire found herself eagerly anticipating her visit to Fernando's house. Influenced by Elena's keen analysis of the vagaries of Lucy Snowe's mind, Claire was coming to a new appreciation of *Villette* and no longer had any doubts as to which of the Brontë masterpieces she liked best.

And so the afternoons repeated themselves, and it was turning out to be one of the most enjoyable periods of Claire's life. She felt as though she had always been making this daily trip to this Spanish house. She was reminded too of how she had felt years before when she had happily read her favourite childhood stories to Ruthie. In time she was moved to share this memory with Elena.

"Ah yes, but now, *querida,* I am the fortunate one," Elena said. "Your coming here puts an entirely different complexion on my day and gives me so much joy." There was a flush on her normally pale cheeks and she was more animated than Claire had ever seen her. "Where before there was so little now there is so much," Elena told her with tremulous sincerity.

Claire's own eyes misted with tears. She felt both moved and embarrassed. "It means a lot to me too," she said gruffly. And felt it was a gross understatement.

One afternoon, as Claire sat opposite Elena in the shaded room and removed the bookmark from the spot she had left off reading the previous day, Elena said gently, "Would you mind if we talked for a bit?"

"Of course not. I'd love to," Claire readily agreed.

"Tell me some more about your life in Ireland," Elena suggested, relaxing back in her chair. "You have a younger brother and are friendly with the doctor's children, that much I know . . ."

Claire gladly chatted away about her friendship with the twins and Ruthie, stressing how good Jane had always been to her, including her year after year in their holiday plans and treating her like one of the family.

"She is kind, the doctor, and clearly you are very fond of her."

Claire nodded and went on to talk of Sheena and Terry. She did not know it, but whenever she mentioned Terry's name her expression was full of yearning. Elena watched her quietly.

"And the children's father?" she asked. "He died some time ago, I believe."

"Yes." Claire dropped her eyes.

"I can see you are very fond of them all," Elena smiled, "but I think you have an especially soft spot for your friend's twin brother."

"Well, yes," Claire admitted, meeting Elena's eyes reluctantly. "Terry is in the Air Corps and he's a terrific pilot. He and I . . ."

Elena waited.

Terry and I were lovers, but he cannot forgive me because he found out that when I was thirteen I became pregnant by his father.

Her mind sealed up again. She avoided Elena's eyes and, changing tack again, began speaking about Ruthie.

"She can be so funny at times and says things far older than her years. She's really great because . . . something happened a while back, but she seems almost over it now."

"Something bad?" Elena enquired gently.

"Yes . . ." Claire faltered. "She was tormented by some boys and they cut off all her hair. She was only eight at the time and she was terrified."

And I was only thirteen but Eddie was always kind to me . . . he never hurt me physically but he hurt me in other ways . . .

"Can we read now," Claire whispered, "before you become too tired?"

Elena looked at Claire with a blend of curiosity and compassion, but she nodded.

341

"Yes . . . please do."

Terry left by the side door of Crowley's pub, glad to be out in the air again. He bent to tie his shoelace before setting off at a jog down the road that led to the quay. He had spent the past hour sitting at the counter chatting to the publican's daughter and when she had gone to the other end of the bar to pull pints, he had seized his opportunity to slip away.

Terry had taken the girl out a few times. Her company had kept him from brooding overmuch on Claire, but he could see that she was becoming too attached to him and it would be wiser to end the relationship. She was a nice girl, Terry told himself, but there was no future in it. Next thing old man Crowley would be putting questions to him and he'd be lucky not to find himself one of the family. He shuddered between amusement and horror at the thought.

There was a moon, partially obscured by cloud. Terry gazed at it as he jogged along and wondered if Claire were looking at it in Spain. As always when on his own he found himself retracing the circumstances leading up to her confession on their last night together, and agonising afresh over the whole sordid story. He was conscious of a niggling unease that he had been grossly unfair to her.

Terry kept a wary eye out for potholes while inwardly engaging in further analysis and heart-searching and was, at last, able to admit that what it all finally came down to, what had upset him most, was not the unsavoury aspect of the affair but the fact that Claire had obviously loved his father. Terry couldn't understand this at all. The man had despoiled her innocence and yet she didn't hate him for it. Every time Terry thought about it he felt a rush of helpless anger and found himself hating Eddie even more.

Troubled by the thought of his own intractability, by strong memories of Claire, and by the sadness of his father's betrayal, Terry slowed to a stop. Below where he stood the sea held a dark, opalescent shine and even as he watched he saw reflected in its depths a spreading blob of silver as the moon broke free of the restraining cloud and majestically rode the high heavens.

Terry stared upwards, entranced by the sight and was taken by the sudden fancy that if only he could bounce a message off that shining orb it would bounce right back at Claire. What would he say? That he missed her like hell and wished he'd never been so stupid as to let anything come between them. No, he wouldn't!

Terry's heart hardened when he remembered that she had gone away without making contact with him. Right now she was probably in the arms of that smooth-talking Spaniard. He was passing a warehouse and he bent and picked up a rock and hurled it with all his strength, hearing it smash into the corrugated roof.

Sadly, Elena's health was deteriorating, and the readings were frequently interrupted. Often it was the doctor coming to take Elena's blood pressure or Christina with her tray of pills and lotions to tend to her mistress's needs. There were times too when the sick woman dropped into a doze or became too exhausted to concentrate, and Claire was learning to recognise and anticipate these moments. But although much of the time was spent waiting about and the hours passed in the stuffy, darkened room were undeniably trying, Claire never regretted making the offer to come and read to Elena.

Despite intrusions and delays Claire began to have an idea of the fortitude and intellectual scope of this uncomplaining woman. She grew very fond of her and felt it a privilege to be allowed help her. Elena had the mind of a poet and a sweet generosity of spirit which was particularly inspiring in a woman who had known so much suffering. She felt no bitterness for her ill-health and allowed it as little space in her life as she was physically able. She was deeply spiritual and put the welfare of others before her own comfort or desires. In some ways Claire was reminded of Jane, whom she was missing deeply.

One afternoon Fernando came in at the end of an unusually prolonged session and waited quietly until Claire had stood up and made her farewells to Elena. On the drive back to the apartment he spoke little and seemed in low spirits.

At last he asked, "How was my mother today?"

"She slept a lot," Claire admitted. Elena had seemed devoid of energy and unable to concentrate for long. They were making so little progress with *Villette* that Claire was now convinced they would never finish it.

"She has become very frail," Fernando agreed soberly. "I think my father will see a great change in her when he returns . . . and my brothers also."

Antonio was in Almeria, where he was supervising the completion of their newest apartment block. In the two weeks since he had gone away Fernando had been kept exceptionally busy at the office and Federico was seldom at home, completely taken up with running the restaurant in his father's absence. Claire had met him only once and thought how unlike Fernando he was. In looks, he favoured his mother but his speech lacked Elena's sweet, humorous inflection. He took life *muy seriamente*, according to Fernando, and was very different from his other brother who was away in some military academy. About this potentially more interesting sibling Fernando furnished no details, not even his name. But then Fernando did not talk much about his family. Claire was learning what a private person he was.

"It is a great relief knowing you are with her," Fernando was saying. "It is a debt I can never repay. If it wasn't for you . . ." Sadness swamped him and he could not go on.

Claire laid a gentle hand on his arm and softly repeated that she was only too delighted to do it and that it gave her a lot of pleasure too.

The following day Claire had hardly begun when Elena's head dropped suddenly forward on her chest and she slept. The chiffon scarf she used wrapped about her wrist, to lift her paralysed hand, slipped from her grasp and slid to the floor.

Claire read on for a minute, but when it was clear that Elena was not just dozing, but deeply asleep, she relaxed back in her chair and fell to thinking about her mother. Lately, she was troubled by vague feelings of guilt that if only she had been a different, better kind of daughter or made more of an effort, they might have succeeded in closing the widening gulf between them. But the rift, which had started with the death of her little sister, had deepened with her parents' separation, and now Claire was convinced that, even with good intentions on both sides, it was beyond their power to heal it. She sighed and turned her thoughts instead to Jane.

Since coming to Spain Claire had been missing her adopted mother to an astonishing degree. Perhaps this was partly because Sheena, with whom she normally felt so much in accord, was spending all her time with the attractive young Alejandro. Some nights Sheena did not return to the apartment at all. She worried about her friend and only hoped that Alejandro was as decent as he seemed. Thankfully, Miguel Delgado seemed to have completely faded from the scene.

The door opened and Fernando entered. He gazed sorrowfully down at his mother and Claire was deeply touched by his expression.

"What, sleeping again?" he said, gently laying Elena's scarf back in her lap.

Claire closed the book and stooped to pick up her bag, knowing that there would be no more reading today. As she straightened up she felt suddenly sick. She thought it might be migraine from sitting so long in the darkened room with just the one lamp directed in a blob of light on the page.

The attacks were occurring with disturbing regularity, which was puzzling now that the strain of the exams was over. Claire put a trembling hand to her hot forehead and swallowed dryly.

"What is the matter?" Fernando moved forward in concern, and gently helped her up. Claire stood dizzily for a second while he supported her without a word, patiently waiting until she had regained her balance.

"I was feeling a bit light-headed," Claire confessed, conscious of his arm about her as he helped her out into the air. She pulled away from him and sank into a chair, a hand to her eyes, and concentrated on not bringing up her breakfast. As she gratefully sipped the glass of mineral water he brought her, Stella came bounding up and covered her bare ankles with affectionate licks. Claire stroked the Labrador's smooth head, feeling ashamed of all the fuss.

"I'd better go," she told Fernando, "but I'll come again tomorrow if your mother wants me."

Fernando nodded, his sombre expression softening in gratitude. As he walked with Claire to the car, unspoken between them hung the fear that there might not be many more such visits, and they drove the short journey to the apartment in silence.

While Claire spent her afternoons in a shaded room reading to Elena, Sheena spent hers in bed with Alejandro. Two days after the *flamenco* show, when Sheena had returned from sketching on the beach and found Alejandro waiting for her outside the apartment, she had gone with him on a round of the local bars where the young Spaniard seemed to be known and well-regarded everywhere. They had finished up the evening dancing in a night-club and afterwards he had brought her back to what she believed was his apartment, but later discovered belonged to his friend Miguel, who had lent it to him in his absence. Miguel had helped him out in various other ways too, it seemed. Once when he was drunk Alejandro had laughingly admitted to Sheena that he owed a lot to the man, too much maybe, grinning sheepishly when she questioned him and murmuring vaguely about gambling debts and other matters.

Alejandro gave her a spare latch-key and they met there each afternoon. They had a pre-arranged signal – two short rings followed by one long one – and Sheena, who was usually there first, felt very daring as she slipped out from the shower to open the door wearing only the briefest of towels, and pulled him giggling inside.

Sheena had thought she was in love before, but had never felt quite so helplessly besotted as she felt about this vital young Spaniard. Since she had lost her virginity to Killian three summers previously, Sheena had experimented with a succession of schoolboys, but never any mature men. Sean, her sculptor, was the most sexually experienced of anyone she had known, but he did not even come close to Alejandro.

In the slumbering heat of the Spanish siesta they made love on rumpled sheets, behind shuttered windows, and Sheena was willingly initiated into the art of the orgasm. Each time she would think that nothing could surpass her sensation of excitement and satisfaction, and then Alejandro would surprise her again. "*Bebé, princesa, bebé,*" Alejandro moaned contentedly. He leaned over the side of the bed and reached for his wine glass, feeding Sheena little sips as if she were the infant he called her. Supporting himself on his elbow, he looked down in approval at her smooth tanned body. He slopped a little wine into her navel and chuckled at her squeals as he bent his head and neatly lapped it up.

"You are just like a cat," Sheena praised, loving his firmness, his flat belly and swelling manhood. She held him to her and sighed, ready for love again.

With a perceptive chuckle Alejandro disengaged her arms and rolled off the bed in one smooth movement. Pouting, Sheena turned over on to her front and rested her chin on her arms to watch him.

"Ah, what perfection." Fondly, he smacked her plump brown bottom. "*Espléndido..incréible!*"

He lifted a lock of her hair and looked deep into her eyes. "And, of course, you do not sunbathe nude, Señorita," he chuckled.

Sheena threw a pillow at him and snuggled deeper into the bed, reluctant to get dressed, her senses satiated by wine and lovemaking. Alejandro seemed to have cast a spell over

347

her mind, as well as her body, and when she was with him she was incapable of thought or action. There was only him. She grew heavy with sleep and barely registered his murmured goodbye and the slam of the outer door before she drifted off. She was not conscious that someone had entered the apartment until she felt hands stroking her buttocks and thighs. There was a dreamlike quality about it and she lay there unresisting until she felt herself being pulled gently, but firmly, to the bottom of the bed. Behind her, the skilful fingers continued to stroke and caress and, as her pleasure increased, she seemed to have no will or shame. The seductive touch moved to her breasts. With difficulty she opened her eyes and she glimpsed slim brown fingers with unusually long nails, before she began to gasp and shake out of control. She felt her hips lifted and she moaned and instinctively arched her back. Her body heaved and shuddered in response to the thrusting from behind. When Sheena opened her eyes again she was on her own in the room and the sun had gone down outside the window.

In Spain in the last week in July the temperatures were in the high nineties. Claire could hardly draw a breath. It was warm and close in the apartment during the day and if she forgot to close the heavy curtains before midday, the rooms became unbearably hot.

One morning early there was a phone call for Teresa. "I don't believe it," the girls heard her whoop. "You're having me on," and then, "Go on, she never did. I don't believe you." When she put the phone down Teresa reached for her cigarettes and tottered into the kitchen to make tea and recover from the shock.

"Twins! Would you believe it! Babs has gone and had twins and they nearly three weeks early," she told the girls, still amazed. "Two little boys. One five pounds and the other seven and a half. Now where in the world did they come from?" she wondered, bemused. "There's never been twins in the family, not that I heard tell of."

Claire and Sheena exchanged sleepy, amused glances before hastening to congratulate her.

"I'll have to go at once," Teresa said, "I gave her my word. She has three little ones waiting on her at home, God help her." And in the next breath in a doomed voice, "Oh dear, what am I going to do about you and your Mammy counting on me to stay with you till she comes."

"We'll be all right," Sheena said. "Why wouldn't we be?" And Claire murmured in agreement.

"What about little Ruthie?" Teresa nodded towards where the little girl was still asleep. "I could take her back with me. Maybe that's what I should do."

But Ruthie refused to leave Sheena and Claire. "Don't send me away," she begged. "Let me go and stay with Adela."

"But you'll be back again with Mum in a few weeks," Sheena reminded her.

"I don't care. I want to be here now. Oh, it's not fair," Ruthie began to weep noisy pitiful tears.

"Ah, the poor lamb. Don't take on like that." Teresa stroked Ruthie's hair soothingly and looked helplessly at the girls for guidance.

"Maybe she could stay with Adela," Claire said hesitantly. "Why don't we ask Ignacio and his wife? We can ring Jane and find out what she wants us to do."

Teresa looked relieved. "If you think it will be all right." Ruthie, sensing that the battle was nearly won, sobbed more quietly.

Suddenly, Teresa became conscious of time passing. "Oh my! I'd best get myself packed and be on my way."

The girls rushed to help her. Claire got her case out of the cupboard and Sheena made her a pile of toast, which Teresa gratefully nibbled while hurriedly piling clothing on the bed. Thirty minutes later she was ready to go. The girls helped her with her case to the taxi rank some yards up the street.

"We'll ring Mum," Sheena promised her, as with a last fond hug all round Teresa heaved her plump bulk into the back of the taxi and leaned out the window.

"Are you girls sure you'll be all right?" Teresa asked, yet again.

"Yes, of course," Claire reassured her. "You mustn't worry about a thing."

They all waved and Ruthie, hopping on one leg, happily blew a kiss after the departing taxi. They had just time to see Teresa, misty eyed, return the kiss, and then she was gone from their sight.

Claire brought Ruthie to the hotel later in the morning. Sheena said that Claire would do better on her own. Otherwise, Ignacio might get the idea that they were all pushing to be taken into the hotel. At any rate, she needed to buy a new sketchpad and it would save time if she got it while Claire was away.

Clare thought how much she would have appreciated Sheena's support. For all she knew Ignacio might not be that keen to take responsibility for the little girl. But she need not have worried. Ignacio seemed more than delighted to have *la hermanita* to stay with them. He called his wife out from the dining-room where she was setting tables for lunch, and as soon as she heard they both insisted that since the chaperone had left all the girls must come and stay at the hotel. Claire was touched by this generous gesture, but assured them, however, that for the time being they would be fine in the apartment. Ignacio and his wife threw up their hands in protest but gave in. Claire left saying she would be in touch with them as soon as she had spoken to Jane.

When she returned to the apartment Claire found a note from Sheena saying that she had gone to the beach to sketch and would be back later. Why couldn't she have waited while she rang Jane? Claire thought, It wouldn't have killed her to wait. She felt daunted at the prospect of having even more explaining and apologising to do. Oh well, she would just have to manage as usual without her.

Feeling thirsty again, Claire went to the fridge. These days she made a point of boiling water first thing in the morning to cool in the fridge. *Limonada* left her feeling bloated and faintly sick. But that morning in the rush she had forgotten. She would have to make do after all with the fizzy drink.

Claire grimaced as she sipped the sweetish liquid. How nice, she thought rather wistfully, to have been able to take Ignacio up on his offer and stay at the hotel. Already she was finding it quiet at the apartment with Ruthie gone and Teresa no longer bustling about. Right now, she told herself, Ruthie was probably splashing about in the pool, having a great time and undoubtedly cooler than she was. Nevertheless, Claire was conscious that she had neglected her on this holiday, but once Elena had become dependent on her visits, she had felt obliged not to disappoint the sick woman. At any minute now Claire expected Fernando to collect her so that she might make her daily visit to his mother.

She went out to sit on the balcony and work out what she would say to Jane when she rang her. Now was a good time to get her while she was still at the clinic. Claire only hoped that Jane would approve their decision to keep Ruthie with them. When she heard how terribly upset Ruthie had become at the thought of leaving Spain, she would surely understand.

As Claire sat there putting off the moment she suddenly realised that Fernando was late. She was just beginning to wonder if he was coming at all when there was a prolonged ring at the door. She jumped to her feet and ran back through the apartment. As she released the door catch she felt suddenly dizzy and leaned against the wall until her head cleared. Fernando stood outside, looking hot and dishevelled himself, and he stepped quickly inside with none of his usual polite greetings.

"Ah Claire . . . *mi madre* . . . my mother . . . is very ill," he stammered. "She has been taken to the hospital."

Claire felt the shock of his news. Although Elena's condition was clearly worsening, there had been no indication that she was so dangerously ill. Listening to Fernando she realised that her death was only a matter of days, if not hours, away.

"Oh Fernan! I'm so sorry," Claire cried, unconsciously using his mother's name for him. Fernando winced, then reached wordlessly for her. He held her close to him, his cheek pressed against her hair. Claire stood startled and unmoving in his embrace. After a moment she felt the tension go out of him and he said tiredly, "Will you come with me to the hospital, please?"

"Of course." Shyly, she squeezed his arm and stepped back. Fernando stared solemnly at her and, on a long drawn-out breath, repeated shakily, "Claire . . . Claire. *Mi preciosa.* What in the world would I do without you!"

Elena was conscious but very weak. She held Fernando's hand but kept her eyes fixed on Claire. A nurse whispered to them not to stay long.

Unable to reach his father, Fernando left a message for Antonio to ring home. Federico had come at once from the restaurant and sat outside his mother's room, awaiting his turn. Too many visitors would tax her waning strength and they were terrified she might not live until Antonio arrived.

Fernando gently released his mother's hand and got up from the bedside. He had still to make contact with his youngest brother.

"I'll send Federico in," he whispered to Claire. "Please stay while I go and ring Alejandro."

Claire heard him and yet didn't hear him. She was watching Elena's face intently, conscious of the pulse beating feebly in her temple and superstitiously afraid to look away in case it stopped.

Fernando rang the military academy and was put through at once to his brother's commanding officer. When he replaced the receiver, he wore a stunned expression. Alejandro had been away without leave and was facing a court-martial when he returned. Now Fernando cursed his stupidity in not following his instincts and insisting that Alejandro come home at once, when he met him near the apartments.

Fernando's features set in even grimmer lines as he went to join the silent figures grouped about his mother's bed. His father would have to be informed of the situation, he told himself, and his wayward brother would have to be found. This was not the first time that Alejandro had been AWOL and he was on his last chance, so his commanding officer had crisply pointed out. Fernando sighed. This time Alejandro would almost certainly be expelled from the academy.

All that evening Claire and Fernando sat at Elena's bedside. Federico had departed earlier with a promise to return when the restaurant had closed for the night. Elena was on a drip and lay with her eyes closed, pale and unmoving. When it grew late Fernando drove Claire back to the apartment. She wanted to stay the night with him at the hospital but he would not allow her.

"You must get some rest," he said, looking pale and weary himself. "I will come for you in the morning." And with that she had to be content.

Next day Fernando picked Claire up early. Elena had passed a fairly good night and, thankfully, seemed to have grown a little stronger.

Claire sat with her, feeling a bit sleepy after the late night and early rising. She had managed to speak to Jane before Fernando arrived. When Sheena had not come back to the apartment the previous night and was still not home by the time Claire got up, she had considered it was high time someone told Jane that Teresa was gone. Jane was taken aback. Although news normally travelled fast in the neighbourhood, she had not heard that Babs had given birth. She had been working late at the clinic, she said, which probably accounted for it.

"You say she had twins?" It was a bad line and Claire found herself having to say everything twice. She gave Jane as many details as she could remember.

"But how are you managing on your own. What about Ruthie?"

Claire reassured her that Ignacio and his wife were taking great care of the little girl. She held back the bit about Elena being so ill. She was worried that Jane might not approve if she knew that she was not spending much time with Ruthie. It would only worry her unnecessarily, Claire eased her conscience.

"Get Sheena to ring me. I'll need to talk to Ruthie often. She may get homesick away from the pair of you."

Claire said that she would tell Sheena while, at the same time, mentally resolving to leave her a note in case they missed each other again.

"Mind yourselves and be sure and keep in touch." Jane finally rung off.

During the morning Claire used the hospital telephone and finally spoke to Sheena, who was grumpy at being woken from sleeping off her late night. Sheena promised, however, to ring her mother and Claire put down the receiver satisfied.

By midday Elena had rallied enough to ask for Antonio.

"He will be here soon, Mother," Fernando assured her with a helpless look at Claire, who returned his look sympathetically. Despite repeated telephone calls to the site office in Almeria, there had been no word as yet from Antonio.

"He must have gone to one of the other sites," Fernando fretted in an undertone. "I cannot understand why he has not telephoned the office. He is usually so punctilious." He went to the window and stood there, staring out. Claire noticed the way Elena's anguished brown eyes followed his every movement and wished with all her heart there was some way she could find and bring Antonio to her.

Just before midday a nurse came in to tell them that Señor Gonzalez had telephoned to say that he was on his way. Fernando's face brightened and he looked as if a great load had been lifted from him.

Claire was conscious of the immense strain he had been

under, trying to cope on his own and unable to trace his brother. She thought of Sheena's recent admission that she was deeply in love with Alejandro and wondered if there could possibly be any connection between the two Alejandros. Claire could not quite say why, but she was beginning to be convinced there was.

Antonio arrived within the hour and took his son's place at Elena's side. Fernando waited just long enough to greet his father then left for his office, hoping to get in an hour's work before coming again to the hospital. When the door closed behind him Claire stood up.

"I'll come back later," she whispered.

Antonio nodded blindly and she left him holding Elena's limp hand between his two strong ones, his unruly dark head, shot with grey, bent close to his wife's pillow as he listened anxiously to her frail breathing. Thank God he had arrived in time, Claire thought, as she slipped away.

Sheena turned into the familiar alleyway that led to Alejandro's apartment and entered the building. The memory of what had happened there, her utter abandon filled her with hot shame and a tingling of excitement. She had not seen the face of the man, which had somehow made it even more decadent. She would not recognise him again but he would know her.

She was standing under the cool spray, lathering her hair, when she heard Alejandro's two short rings followed by one long. She grinned in relief and reached for the towel to pat her eyes, before running to let him in. The key scraped the lock and the door swung open.

"Alex," she cried, then stopped in confusion when she saw who it was.

Miguel stepped smiling inside the door and closed it after him. Sheena blushed in dismay, then backed away, conscious of his eyes boldly taking in her nudity.

"Where is Alejandro?" she gasped, grabbing backwards for a towel and draping it against herself. She felt mortified,

355

yet strangely exhilarated.

"He asked me to say he would be late."

Sheena stood, water dripping down her neck, her hair a mass of cooling suds. Something in Miguel's eyes, some arrogant awareness, told her that this was the man. She trembled, and almost of their own volition her fingers released their grip on the towel and let it fall. She stood naked and helpless before him.

"You do not want Alejandro," he murmured, stepping nearer. "You want me . . . is that not so?"

Elena hung on to life with a tenacity that pained but did not surprise those who loved her. She had always had a great zest for life and she was loth now to release her hold upon it. She was moved to Hospital Belen, where she would get the expert nursing care needed to make her comfortable until the end came. Sarah Lewis was engaged to be with her and Elena could not have had anyone kindlier or better qualified to care for her in her last days.

Claire came often to sit by Elena's bedside. Once Nurse Lewis realised that Claire was the great friend of Dr McArdle's family, she couldn't do enough for her. She brought her tea throughout the day and persuaded her to take breaks from the sickroom to walk in the garden. Although Fernando and his father took it in turn to come to the hospital during the day whenever they could be spared from the office, their visits were understandably short and only for the nurse Claire would have found the day long and lonely. In Sarah she felt she had found a true friend.

Eventually the sick woman was unable to speak or move any part of herself except her eyes, and was being fed intravenously. Claire thought hard and long to devise some means of communicating with her. Eventually she came up with the idea of using a child's alphabet. Fernando immediately went out and purchased the *abecedario*.

Claire held Elena's hand and quietly explained to her that she was going to ask her questions and wanted Elena to try and answer them with the help of the plastic alphabet.

She would hold up letters in front Elena's eyes, and Elena was to blink when Claire reached each letter of the word she wanted to say.

Claire demonstrated this and then asked Elena to blink to show that she understood. Although painfully slow to begin with, it was to prove a good method of communication between them. At first, Elena was only able for very short sessions but as they grew more accustomed to their 'game' Claire found a way of speeding the process by asking first if the word began with a vowel. Claire became so astute at anticipating Elena's needs that even before she got to the letter 'i' of drink she realised Elena was thirsty. Elena was unable to swallow and if anything was put into her mouth she was in danger of choking, but Claire got the idea of wrapping an ice cube in muslin and Nurse Lewis agreed to try it.

"We are taking a risk, lass," she said quietly, "but if we are very careful I think it will work."

Claire held the ice against Elena's lips and the drops of moisture seeping through in tiny quantities afforded the sick woman a measure of ease.

"You are so good with her," Fernando whispered gratefully as he sat watching them. Claire turned her head to smile at him, relieved that he was present not Antonio, as she felt slightly in awe of the older man.

Elena soon dropped into an exhausted doze and Claire leaned tiredly back in her own chair to rest.

"I cannot thank you enough for all you are doing," Fernando told her, and his mouth wobbled and he blinked away tears.

Claire looked away uncomfortably, and wished he would not make so much of it. She considered she was only doing what any caring person would do, and did not require thanks. From the start she had felt a deep affinity with his mother. She couldn't say what it was that had drawn her to Elena that first day; she only knew that she felt a deep affection for the Spanish woman. What she did for her stemmed from love not duty.

Sheena was only vaguely aware that Claire was spending a lot of time with Fernando's mother and that Elena was seriously ill. Most of what Claire told her went over her head for she was caught up in her obsession with Miguel, and all reason and restraint had been washed away. If Alejandro had not gone off without a word and left her so totally on her own, Sheena might have recovered her balance, but in his absence she could not keep away from the apartment.

All that week she had gone there, drawn by the lure of the other man. Miguel was a strange mixture, rough and gentle by turns. He was a man who was slow to climax and never seemed to tire of bedding her. He used her for his pleasure and that in itself made her excitement more intense. Sheena was a little frightened of him but then fear was half the attraction

Sometimes he made her do things to him that she did not understand, like tying a scarf about his neck until he almost lost consciousness. When he wanted to do it to her she was afraid, but the strange languorous feeling it inspired greatly excited her. Sometimes he slapped her or denied her orgasm, but this too only served to increase her desire for him.

And all the time he kept her on leading strings of hope, telling her Alejandro had sent messages that he was missing her and would soon be back. One afternoon when she came to the apartment she found Miguel putting clothes in a case.

"Are you going away?" Sheena asked in dread.

"*Sí* . . . and you too, my little bimbo," Miguel murmured, intent on his task. "Alejandro has sent word you are to come. He is waiting for us in Gibraltar. We must leave at once."

Sheena's heart leapt.

"I'll go pack my things," she offered eagerly.

Miguel frowned. "No, there is no time. We must start at once."

"But I've nothing with me."

"I can give you everything you need. Come, let us hurry."

He snapped the catches on his case and straightened up. Sheena shrugged and allowed herself to be persuaded. She would stop on the way and buy herself shorts and a T-shirt, she thought, and maybe ring Claire at the same time and let her know where she was headed.

Ten minutes later they were driving towards Malaga, the roof of Miguel's battered '79 Lamborghini rolled fully back. As they sped along, Sheena's dark hair whipped about her face and she was filled with excitement at the prospect of seeing Alejandro again.

The evening sun was warm on her shoulders as Claire took a short break from Elena's bedside and strolled away from the hospital, glad to be out in the air. Her head ached from long hours in the stuffy atmosphere of the sick room and her back felt permanently stooped from bending over the sick woman's bed.

Elena had grown progressively weaker each day and clearly the end was very near. Claire had not left the hospital in the past twenty-four hours except to take the briefest of breaks. Tonight she was prepared for another long vigil by the bed of the dying woman.

Claire had never felt so glad of anything as Ruthie's friendship with Adela for the little girl seemed more than content in her company. Once or twice, Claire had spoken to Ruthie on the telephone. Ignacio also confirmed that Ruthie was in good spirits and assured Claire that Ruthie was welcome to stay at the hotel until Jane arrived or Claire was free to return to the apartment, whenever that would be. Claire had shivered, not wanting to be free in the way he implied. Elena's death would be a merciful release, but Claire dreaded it with all her heart. While Elena lived, so too did hope. In her exhaustion and grief, Claire could not see beyond this.

She did a circuit of the streets and went into a church on the corner of the square. She sat near the altar and began to pray, her tired gaze fixed on the ornate figure of the Madonna and child, richly attired in satins and silks. As she sat there, surrounded by tier upon tier of red offertory lamps, her senses drowning in the aura of hot wax, Claire wondered if Elena had ever come to this church to pray. She wondered too if, before she died, Elena would be able to speak again to her through the *abecedario*, and found herself petitioning Our Lady that this might be so. When she hurried back to the hospital in the cool of the evening, Fernando was pacing the corridor and his face lit up at the sight of her.

"Claire! I have made contact with my brother at last," he told her. "He has returned to his military academy and, in the circumstances, the authorities have agreed to allow him return home. So I must go at once to Cadiz."

Claire said sympathetically. "How dreadful that you have to leave now with your mother so ill . . ."

Fernando looked pained. "There is no help for it. I must go, Claire. She will want to see him and his place is at her side." He shook his head dispiritedly. "Alejandro is wayward and thoughtless, but he is not a bad fellow."

"Yes, he has great charm," Claire absently agreed.

Fernando stared. "You know Alejandro?"

Claire was confused. "I'm not sure . . . maybe not," she stammered in embarrassment. "Sheena and I met a Spaniard of that name and she has been going about with him ever since. Really we know very little about him, only that he has a friend called Miguel."

"Miguel Delgado?" Fernando enquired ominously, "*Qué sinverguenza!*"

Claire was startled by the anger and contempt in Fernando's voice.

"Delgado is not fit to associate with my family," Fernando said haughtily. "I have warned Alex against this man many times, but my brother is weak and easily led."

He was only saying what Claire herself had suspected.

Fernando's expression softened. "Ah but I cannot tell you how happy and relieved it makes me to know you will be here with my mother while I am away. You will keep her alive until I return, of that I am certain."

"I only wish I could be as sure," she admitted honestly, "but I'll gladly stay with her if that's what you and your father want."

"*En absoluto*," Fernando said with a sad smile. "In fact, I could not go if you did not assure me of your presence," adding passionately, "*Tu eres mi angel.*"

Claire blushed at the intensity of his emotion and felt a little light-headed again. She put her hand to her forehead.

"Perhaps I ask too much." Fernando looked concerned. "You have already spent so many hours with my mother. Please tell me frankly if you cannot stay."

Claire said firmly. "Of course I'll stay. There's nothing I want more."

Fernando gave her a glowing look of gratitude. "*Muchísimas gracias, mi Clara,*" he said fervently. And before she realised his intention, he had bent his head and kissed her full on the mouth

It was late evening when Elena woke up. She opened her brown eyes and stared at Claire with some deep emotion struggling in their depths. Claire leaned nearer the bed, feeling frustrated and not a little frightened. Oh, if only there was some way she could help her. She was just about to call for Nurse Lewis when she saw Elena deliberately blinking and, with a thrill of relief, understood she was saying, 'Get our alphabet.'

As she hurriedly fumbled with the pieces, Claire was all the time conscious of Elena's anxious gaze trained on her. At last she sat poised with the box on her lap and said quietly, "I'm ready, Elena."

At the beginning of their relationship Señora Gonzalez had asked Claire to call her by her Christian name. She had no daughters of her own, Elena said, but if she had been so blessed she would have liked them to address her in this way. Claire had felt both honoured and embarrassed, but in time grew accustomed to it.

Now she asked, "Is it a vowel?"

Elena gave no sign. Claire ran quickly through the first few letters, and when she reached the letter L Elena blinked. This was followed by O, which was followed by V, and Claire knew Elena meant 'love'.

The next word began with F. "Fernando"? Claire guessed. "You love Fernando?"

Elena blinked.

"He has gone to fetch Alejandro," Claire told her. 'Love' again, then it was the third letter of the alphabet before Elena reacted again.

"Is it me?" Claire asked.

It was, and then it was 'Fernando' again.

"You love Fernando and you love me?"

Elena gave no sign. Claire was puzzled. What could she mean? Then it broke upon her and she flushed.

"You mean that Fernando loves . . ." She couldn't go on.

Elena blinked and some of the anxiety eased in those painfully aware eyes. Claire spoke slowly and clearly.

"You think that Fernando loves me and you wonder if I love Fernando?"

Elena blinked again.

Claire chose her words carefully. "I am very fond of him and I would be honoured if he loved me." It was true. Any more than that she couldn't say but, there was no mistaking the relief and happiness in Elena's gaze. As they continued on with questions and answers, it became clear that Elena's main concern was that Claire should allow Fernando to take care of her. Claire stared, convinced she had somehow got it wrong.

"But why should I need anyone to take care of me?" Claire asked puzzled. When Elena indicated that she believed this would be Fernando's wish, Claire attributed it to some loss of translation, or perhaps the strange fancies of a dying woman.

"Is there anything else worrying you?" Claire gently asked her. But no. Elena was happy now and resigned to whatever would happen. Strangely she did not show fatigue but seemed powered by some tremendous inner resource. After almost an hour it was Claire who had begun to flag. She shifted in her chair and was aware of Elena watching her closely.

The next word was 'tired' and then 'Claire', followed by 'concerned'. Elena was concerned that she was growing tired.

"I am a bit," Claire confessed. She took a turn about the room and came back to sit at her bedside again.

Elena wanted Antonio.

When he came, Claire handed the alphabet to Antonio and went out into the night to get some air herself. She felt exhausted but content. Her prayer to the Madonna had been answered.

Claire sat for some time in the garden under the stars, where Jane had sat so often during her convalescence, and felt her mind go blank. After so much concentration she felt all played out. She saw Nurse Lewis bustling towards her in the gloom.

"My dear, you look poorly," Sarah said in her direct fashion. "I've brought you a cup of tea."

Touched as always by the woman's thoughtfulness, Claire sat sipping the warm liquid, feeling some of her weariness fall from her. Soon she went back inside, feeling ready now to cope with whatever the night might bring.

As she sat once more by Elena's bedside Claire hoped that Sheena would not be too worried when she was absent another night from the apartment. However, since her friend had stayed away herself all night so many times lately she didn't think there was any real likelihood of this. She had made several attempts that day to phone Sheena and got the engaged signal so often that she was beginning to think the telephone must be out of order. She yawned and resolved to try again in a little while.

As it grew late Claire began to feel hungry and slightly light-headed, but even when Nurse Lewis tiptoed into the room and laid a gentle hand on her arm, saying, "Won't you come away and have a wee rest, lass," she shook her head.

"I'm fine, Nurse. Honestly. I promised Fernando I'd stay with his mother until he returns." Antonio was snatching a nap in another room and Claire feared that Elena would be distressed if left entirely alone.

"Very well then." Sarah came back often throughout the night and tried to get her to sip a cup of tea or eat a piece of toast, but Claire refused everything but the tea.

Claire could feel Elena's eyes on her face from time to time, but there was none of the earlier agitation mirrored in their dark depths. Elena was at peace now.

Towards morning Fernando and Alejandro arrived at the hospital and with grim expressions hurried down the corridor to their mother's room. Elena was still conscious but very weak. Hour after hour, by a tremendous effort of her will, she had kept herself from slipping away until her sons arrived.

She looked at her sons long and lovingly and her eyes, the only mobile part of her, were intelligent and bright, and then she slipped into a deep sleep from which she never awoke.

"She is gone," Fernando came out to tell Claire. She put her arms about him and held him close, and he buried his face in her hair and broke into muffled, childish sobbing. When he eventually regained control he gave her a last sorrowful look and went back into the room to join his father.

Claire felt every muscle aching and her mind was floating in a kind of limbo. Elena was dead, but she could not really take it in; they were just words.

Sarah Lewis brought her into a nearby room, sat her gently on the bed and began undressing her with kindly, capable hands. "You can sleep here," she said. "You're in no fit state to go anywhere."

In her exhaustion Claire was barely aware of Sarah removing the last of her clothing before she was deeply asleep.

Sarah stared, taken aback by the unmistakable curve of Claire's belly, her swollen, veined breasts. She had been too many years nursing not to recognise that the girl was pregnant.

Sarah could not repress feelings of shock and disappointment as she drew the night-dress over Claire's head. She reminded herself that young people today looked on pregnancy out of wedlock in a very different way to older folk like herself. She had different values, she supposed, but she would never get used to it. Such a lovely young girl too. Remembering the way the young Spaniard had held Claire so tenderly in his arms, Sarah assumed that he was the father.

Claire stirred and opened her eyes. Nurse Lewis was sitting on the bed holding out a cup of tea to her.

"I thought you might like this before you get up," Sarah said quietly.

Something in the older woman's restrained tone surprised Claire. She sat up and took the cup, cradling it in her hands. She had been asleep six hours and could have slept twice as long.

"I'll bring you some toast when you've drunk that," the nurse said. Again there was that cautious intonation, as though humouring a sick person.

"Thank you but please don't go to any trouble," Claire begged. She looked down at the unfamiliar night-dress, blushed and avoided Sarah's eyes.

Sarah saw the blush and was puzzled by Claire's modesty, having already unconsciously judged her to be other than the innocent she had at first assumed. When she returned with the toast she sat down again while Claire nibbled it, and was unsurprised when the girl suddenly hopped out of bed and ran to the hand basin.

"I'm sorry," Claire gasped. "For a moment I thought I was going to be sick." She raised an apologetic face from the bowl and glanced at Sarah.

Sarah returned her gaze steadily. "Sit back into bed, child." When Claire slipped back under the sheet she said, "How long have you been like this?"

Claire stared at her uncomprehendingly. What was she getting at?

"How long have you been feeling sick?" Sarah asked.

"I'm not sick," Claire began, and then she remembered all the times she had felt dizzy and nauseous lately. But that was just migraine. She just wasn't used to such oppressive heat. She threw off the sheet, her head whirling. "I must go back to the apartment," she cried. "Sheena and Ruthie will be wondering where I am."

"Sit still a moment," Nurse Lewis said sternly. "Do you really not know what ails you?"

Claire looked at her desperately. She couldn't be what she read in the woman's face. How could she? Terry had always used a condom. Even when she had begged him not to he had always insisted. But what about the first time? Suddenly she saw herself and Terry lying on Jane's bed, both of them carried away by passion. She was filled with panic.

"I really must go," she mumbled. "I've been away too long as it is." She got out of bed and the floor rushed up to meet her. Only for Sarah's supporting arm she would have fallen.

Claire lay on the bed after Nurse Lewis had left the room and gazed down at her belly, which had always been so flat, and then higher up to her swollen breasts. How was it she hadn't noticed these changes before? She had a sudden image of herself long ago, lying on a bed in the holiday cottage with Jane bending over her, gently examining her breasts. Claire had to bite her lips hard to keep from crying out as this image was replaced with another: Elena urging her to allow Fernando take care of her. Claire burned with new shame and insight. Did everyone know what she herself had failed to see? She broke out in a sweat and grew dizzy again.

Claire left the hospital without seeing anyone. It was very hot, even hotter than the previous day, and a headache throbbed into life as she covered the two miles to the apartment. There, the rooms were hot and airless and she automatically pulled over the heavy curtains to block the burning light.

There was half a jug of water in the fridge and she drank it, then went into her room and lay on the bed. She was badly shocked. It had never occurred to her that she would ever conceive. Her head ached and she closed her eyes.

She was awakened by the sound of someone calling her and struggled through the fog of sleep surrounding her, in an effort to take in what the voice was saying.

"Claire, please Claire, wake up." Somehow Ruthie was back. How had she got there? With difficulty Claire opened her eyes and focused them on the little girl's anxious face.

"Who brought you, Ruthie?" she asked through dry lips. Slowly everything began to come back: Elena's death and her own pregnant condition.

"Ignacio drove me. He's waiting downstairs," Ruthie was saying. "Sheena rang the hotel because she couldn't get any reply here. She said to tell you she was going away."

"Going where, Ruthie?" Claire tried to take it in.

"Gibraltar."

"Why would she go there?"

"She has gone to meet Alejandro," Ruthie explained, pleased and proud to have such an important message to deliver.

"But how was she getting there?"

"She said that Miguel was taking her."

"Miguel?" Claire felt shock and dread as she remembered him and the contempt in which Fernando held the man. "Are you quite sure she said it was Miguel?"

"Quite sure," Ruthie said brightly. "*Cierto! Absolutamente!*

Sheena began to worry when they were in Gibraltar three days and still had not met up with Alejandro. Perhaps Miguel had lied to her like he had lied about so many other things, she thought. He had said they would stay in a hotel and then brought her to a cheap lodging house, where people screamed at night and threw things at the wall, and bought bread and cheap wine to consume in their room. And he had assured her he would buy her a T-shirt and change of underclothing, but she was still in the clothes she had been wearing when she left Nerja.

On the third day Sheena pointed all this out to Miguel in as light and reasonable tone as she could muster. At once he turned morose and taciturn and refused to answer her questions. When she persisted, he shouted at her and slapped her face. In their lovemaking too, he had grown more violent and increasingly knotted the scarf about her throat so that she was almost on the point of suffocation. He left her sobbing on the bed and went out slamming the door behind him and did not return until nightfall.

Left alone in their motel room for hours Sheena grew afraid. She had no money, having used her last few pesetas to ring Ignacio's hotel.

By the time Miguel returned Sheena was resentful and starving. She submitted to his caresses and when he fell asleep, desperation gave her the courage to go through his pockets. With the thousand peseta note she found there she went out to a café and bought herself a Coke and a hamburger. Men eyed her and women whispered. She knew how strange she must look with her bruised throat and clothed in the grubby dirndl skirt and sun-top she had been wearing for days, but she was past caring.

She bit ravenously into the hamburger, almost choking in her haste to get some food inside of her. Her throat hurt her but she was hardly conscious of it as she quickly cleared the last crumbs from the plate and washed them down with sips of Coke.

A little later, Sheena returned to the motel, feeling less afraid of Miguel now that she had some hot food inside her. Tomorrow she would find Alejandro, she promised herself, as she slipped quietly back into the room and gently closed over the door.

Miguel lay snoring on the bed, and despite her earlier optimism, Sheena felt suddenly downcast. What if she didn't find Alejandro? She was struck anew by the precarious state of her position, without money and far away from her sister and friends. Her chin wobbled and lonely tears suddenly pricked her eyes.

Sheena slipped out of her crumpled clothing and lay down beside Miguel. A few more tears squeezed out of the corners of her eyes and rolled down her cheeks. She choked on a sob and suddenly longed for her twin with a desperation she had not felt since she was six years old and had found herself trapped in a neighbour's loft with flames licking into the straw. Terry had come running across the yard looking for her and, hearing her frantic screams, had dragged her clear just in time. If only Terry was here in Spain now, Sheena thought longingly. Oh, if only he were, then everything would be all right.

Terry awoke with a start and lay still for a moment before reaching for the light switch over his bunk. His heart was thumping and his body was drenched with sweat. He looked dazedly about the shadowy cabin, still in the grip of the frightful dream he had been having. Christ! he thought. He shuddered and sat up.

He sat hunched over, his head in his hands, trying to rid himself of the disturbing image of his twin being slowly garrotted by some lunatic. The usual night sounds from the top bunk, instead of irritating him, gave Terry a feeling of security and, in the aftermath of the nightmare, he listened to Pete's snores, almost with affection.

Terry swung his legs to the floor and crossed to the wash hand basin, where he doused his head in cold water. Remnants of the dream still clung to him. He had dreamt it twice before. Each time his twin was pleading with him to help her, and each time he was forced to stand helplessly by and witness her slow strangulation.

Terry vigorously towelled dry his hair and went to lie on his bunk. In their early childhood he and Sheena had been very close and often experienced a similar kind of telepathy, but it hadn't happened in a long time. In the troubled years since their father's death, Terry had distanced himself from his twin and although, at the time, this first rift in their relationship had hardly been recognised by either of them, they had never been so completely at one again.

He slept fitfully until morning, and all that day he couldn't get the dream out of his mind. He resolved to go ashore and ring home. He knew that his mother was in constant touch with the girls and would be able to set his mind at rest. Terry briefly considered ringing Spain himself, but when he thought of Claire perhaps answering his call . . . His break-up with Claire was a separate issue, he told himself, and when, and if, he tackled it he wanted to be able to see her face and look in her eyes.

Later that evening he made his call from one of the pubs near the quay. Jane answered at once. She was in her surgery, she told him, going over household bills.

"When did you last hear from Sheena?" Terry asked without any preliminaries.

"She rang me the day after Teresa Murray left Spain. About a week ago, I suppose," Jane admitted. "That's right. Teresa rang me later that evening to apologise for not ringing me herself. Why?"

"No particular reason," Terry said. "Just got a funny feeling, that's all."

"I'm sure they're all fine," Jane said, adding doubtfully. "I tried ringing them the other night and got no answer, but they were probably just in late."

"Well, keep trying, Mum," Terry said, and rang off. When it had come to the point he had found it hard to explain his unease.

He arrived back on board ship to find the Dauphin being manoeuvred from the hangar to the flight deck grid. There had been an emergency call in his absence and they were under orders from Baldonnel H.Q. to join the search for two Kerry climbers, who had got separated from the rest of their party in the mist on Brandon.

"Both reserves are in sick bay with food poisoning," Captain Landy told him. "You'll have to stand in." He shot Terry a keen glance. "Have you taken a drink?"

Terry shook his head.

"Good." Landy looked relieved. "See you in the operations room on the double, McArdle!"

"Yessir," Terry saluted jubilantly and sped off to his cabin to gear up. Poor devils, he thought, but what a stroke of luck for him, his first time co-piloting a rescue mission. All his earlier anxieties were forgotten at the exciting prospect.

Jane put down the phone, more disturbed by Terry's call than she had let on. She knew how close the twins were, and if he had a hunch that Sheena might be in some kind of trouble, he could well be right. For the next few hours she rang the apartment repeatedly and got no answer. They were probably off sight-seeing, she told herself, trying not to worry.

But when she rang on and off the following day without success, Jane began to be really worried. "Nothing for it but to ring Antonio," she decided, not knowing what else to do, and wondering if she was merely using the excuse to speak to him. Then she remembered the underlying anxiety in Terry's voice.

Jane waited with her heart thumping, until the receiver was lifted.

"May I speak to Señor Antonio or Fernando Gonzalez," she asked as soon as she heard Consuelo's voice.

"Who is calling, please?"

"This is Jane McArdle ringing from Dublin."

"Ah, Dr McArdle." Consuelo's voice became less impersonal. "I am sorry but they are not here."

"I see." Jane was disappointed. She had been so certain of getting one of them.

"Our offices are officially closed," Consuelo explained. "Señora Gonzalez died some days ago and her funeral takes place today."

Jane was so startled that she forgot her reason for phoning. "I am so very sorry," she stammered. "Please don't bother them. It was nothing important." She put down the receiver and stared into space. Elena was dead. On the heels of this thought came another: Antonio was free. Then she felt deeply ashamed of herself. Poor Elena. How she must have suffered.

Jane took a distracted walk about her surgery and absently straightened a cushion, hardly aware what she was doing. For the moment all thought of the girls had fled from her mind. She could think only of Antonio and what his wife's death could mean to them both.

In the bright Spanish sunshine Claire stood by Elena's graveside as Antonio and his three sons laid roses on her coffin and sadly watched it being lowered into the earth. She stooped and laid her own offering with theirs – a spray of red and white carnations – for Elena had told her that, like the great Teresa of Avila, these had been her favourite flowers.

Afterwards Claire decided that she would not go back with the mourners to the Gonzalez house, knowing this was where she would miss Elena most. She crossed to where Fernando stood with his father, looking unfamiliar to her in his formal dark suit. Of all the Gonzalez family he had shared the closest relationship with her, and when he thanked Claire for coming, he met her eyes with such a sad, sweet smile that her heart was wrenched. Alejandro gave her his quick, ravishing smile as she politely shook his hand in turn.

"When did you last see Sheena?" Claire took the opportunity to ask him as the others walked ahead to the entrance of the cemetery. "She told us she was meeting you in Gibraltar but we haven't heard from her in ages. In fact we're rather worried about her."

Alejandro just stared at her, a flush darkening his fair skin. "I have not seen your friend for some weeks," Alejandro said. "But please tell her when you see her that I . . . that I regret my hasty departure from Nerja and I have so much enjoyed her company."

Claire nodded. She had seen him blink in surprise at the mention of Gibraltar, but at the same time something was clearly bothering him, she thought. She took her leave of him at the gate and with a last sad nod in the direction of Fernando and Antonio began to walk into the town.

Alejandro stood and watched her go, a frown creasing his forehead. He was thinking of the last time he had seen Sheena and the memory was not pleasant. Since Miguel had boasted that he had taken advantage of his beautiful girl-friend the image had returned often to shame Alejandro, and for the first time in his young life he had suffered great anguish. He had quarrelled with the other Spaniard and, during his venomous diatribe, clearly seen the other man for what he was. At the same time he could not discard out of hand Miguel's boast that Sheena had been more than willing to allow him sexual liberties or his spiteful claim that there had been other sexual encounters between him and the young Irish girl. Alejandro did not fully believe Miguel, but either way he felt his honour besmirched. The complication lay in the fact that he owed Miguel money and he had gone away to try and raise it, wanting only to be shut of the alliance – he could never have at any time called it friend-ship – that had grown thoroughly distasteful to him.

Alejandro sighed and turned away as Claire's slim figure grew smaller with distance; he walked with none of his usual swagger towards his father's car. Added to his feelings of regret and shame over his dealings with Sheena was the knowledge that he had also failed in his filial duty to his mother. With genuine sadness he mourned her passing, while all too painfully aware that by his own selfish attachment to worldly pleasures he had thrown away the precious chance afforded him to be with her during what turned out to be her last weeks on earth. He told himself that had he known she was to die so soon he would have acted very differently. He knew that no matter how he regarded all that had gone before, he had not come well out of either business and no amount of self-deception could ever persuade him otherwise.

As Claire walked slowly back to the apartment her heart was heavy too, not only for the death of Elena but for her failure to try and trace her friend. She knew that she should have at least let Jane know that Sheena was missing. But burdened by sorrow for Elena and the shock of her pregnancy, Claire had felt it was beyond her to even try and explain. The same irrational fear she had always entertained that Jane would somehow blame her or perhaps regret the many kindnesses she had shown her over the years, continued to hang over her. It had been all too much for Claire to cope with and so she had allowed the days slide past, without taking any action.

Claire was reacting to crisis as she had always done in the past. Her thoughts became cloudy and insubstantial. She would have a thought and then lose it almost immediately, only able to recapture it by a great effort of concentration. She was still struggling to come to terms with her pregnancy. At times it seemed so incredible as to be untrue; at others she was amazed she had been so long in recognising what was surely so evident. Her system had never been regular like other girls and at times of exceptional stress, like exam times, became even more erratic. This coupled with what had happened to her as a child had left her with the conviction she was sterile. Now there was something growing inside her.

Claire let herself into the apartment and went to lie down on the narrow divan in her shaded bedroom. After a while she heard Ruthie coming into the apartment. The little girl had suddenly tired of being away from her family and Ignacio, knowing that Claire was returning immediately after the funeral, had agreed to drop her over some time in the late afternoon. Ruthie wandered chattily in and out of her room, but when she got no response from Claire, soon grew bored and went to play with her kitten on the balcony.

Claire felt heavy and drugged as she lay there in the lazy heat of the afternoon. The hours were passing and still she had no energy or desire to get up and get dressed. The radio on the bedside table emitted soft strains of popular music and was strangely hypnotic. It grew dark outside and she struggled up to open a tin of spaghetti for Ruthie, and when she eventually went back to bed she slept at once.

The days and nights were running into each other and still Claire dozed away the hours. She dreamed that she and Elena were both in wheelchairs, being pushed down a corridor by nurses. Claire was holding Elena's hand and she felt very happy. And then the nurse who was steering Elena suddenly quickened her steps and Elena's hand was wrenched from Claire's grasp and contact cruelly broken. Claire began to weep piteously and her own choking sobs awoke her.

Claire lay shuddering, still in the grip of her dream. And then it seemed as though Elena was speaking directly to her and telling her how glad she was to be rid of her sickly body. 'I am so happy to be out of it,' she was saying. 'If you could only know what it's like you would be rejoicing too, dear Claire. Please don't grieve any more for me for I am free at last.'

Claire felt amazingly soothed and scraps of conversation she had once had with Elena replayed in her mind. Elena had said just before she died that Fernando was in love with her. If he really did love her, Claire thought, maybe it was the way out of her present trouble. He was a kind and caring man and would make her happy. At the same time she felt a fastidious aversion to marrying someone under false pretences.

The telephone rang suddenly, sounding harsh and discordant in the lazy hush of the afternoon. It had rung on and off that day, but in her lethargic state Claire had let it ring. Now she struggled off the bed and padded into the lounge.

"Claire!" It was Sheena's voice, terse and nervously high. "Where have you been? I've been ringing and ringing and getting no answer."

Claire swayed on her feet, the sudden exertion making her dizzy. She tried to think clearly. "Where are you,

Sheena?"

"I . . . I'm not sure . . ." Sheena sounded hurried and scared, not at all like her usual bubbly self. "We left Gibraltar yesterday and drove for miles. I think we're heading back to Nerja."

"Don't you know?" Claire asked.

"I've got to go." Now there was no mistaking the terror in Sheena's voice. "I'll ring you again."

"But Shee . . ." The line went dead.

Claire stared at the phone. She heard a sound behind her and turned round. Ruthie stood in the doorway, the kitten clasped in her arms.

"That was Sheena, wasn't it?" There was fear and doubt on the little girl's face.

Claire nodded.

"Is she all right?"

"Yes, of course." Claire forced herself to nod and speak cheerfully. "She rang to say she's staying away a little longer."

Some of the anxiety left Ruthie's expression. "I miss her," she said forlornly. "I really miss her."

Claire stared at her helplessly. "Why don't we go down to the beach," she suggested, and was glad to see Ruthie's face brighten. "Give me time to shower."

The shower helped to clear Claire's thoughts. She should have rung Jane days ago and now there was no time to waste. Clearly Sheena was in some kind of trouble and the sooner she was found the better. Claire had a sudden vision of herself and Jane searching the roads the summer of Ruthie's attack, and felt a shiver of apprehension.

Sheena replaced the receiver and faced Miguel with a frightened expression. She exhibited none of her usual bravado as he hustled her out of the shop. Her face showed traces of recent tears and there was a cut on her cheek where his ring had struck her.

"Why do you keep slipping away like this?" he demanded petulantly. "I told you I would return immediately."

Miguel guarded her as closely as a gaoler, but she had taken her chance when it came and slipped out, using her last few coins to ring Claire. Now they went back up the street, closely linked. The sun had burned Sheena's face and arms the colour of dark honey and with her black hair and brown eyes, she and Miguel looked like any Latin couple.

Once back inside the building Miguel dropped his lover-like pose and shoved her before him into the room. Sheena staggered and turned to look at him, as he went out again, locking the door behind him. She sat down on the unmade bed and stared tearfully at the small window set high in the wall, golden beams of sunshine spilling through it. Her cage, she thought dully. She felt her stomach rumble and despaired of Miguel remembering to bring her anything to eat. Since he had taken to locking her in, she never knew when her next meal would be. She stretched out on the rumpled bed and, after a while, fell asleep.

Sheena was awakened by the sound of the key in the lock and sat up, feeling hot and parched. The sun had moved round from the window and the room was no longer bathed in light. It was a minute before she saw that Miguel was not on his own. He had a young man with him.

Sheena swung her legs off the bed and got up. She felt dizzy from heat and lack of food. She saw that Miguel carried a bottle and welcomed the thought of a drink, although she knew she would only feel thirstier after the cheap wine. She wondered vaguely about his companion.

Miguel was very hearty, talking rapidly in Spanish and laughing a lot. It was clear he had been drinking. Sheena accepted the glass he gave her and sipped thirstily. He made a great ceremony of filling another glass and giving it to the young Spaniard.

"*Feliz cumpleaños*," he toasted him.

Sheena moved to make room as Miguel sat down on the bed.

"*Me permite usted?*" the boy asked, for he was no more than that, and sat at her other side.

Miguel filled their glasses again and left down the bottle. Before Sheena realised his intention he was gone out of the door, leaving her alone with the young Spaniard.

The boy looked at her then glanced shyly away. Conscious of her dishevelled appearance, Sheena ran her hands through her tangled mop and bit her lips to give them colour. They sat sipping the wine and not looking at each other. She asked him his name and his age in her schoolgirl Spanish, having gathered from Miguel's drunken toast that it was his birthday. It was evident that Pablo knew no English.

"If you could have three wishes what would you ask for? No, don't tell me. Let me guess." The wine after days of starvation was affecting Sheena strangely. She smiled and joked a lot, an edge of hysteria to her laughter. She was unaware she was speaking all the time now in English and that Pablo, although he laughed along with her, showed no sign of understanding.

They made love. In a way there was comfort in his smooth young flesh, his arms holding her close. When he admitted that it was his first time Sheena felt old beyond her years, vaguely sad too as she gently initiated him in the act of love. How long ago it seemed that she was young and free herself.

It was over almost before it was begun, and he rolled away from her and stood up, modestly tugging down his shirt to cover his lean buttocks. Sheena struggled forward on to her knees and watched him reaching for his trousers. Maybe through him she could get word of her predicament to the others. She grew dizzy with hope.

"Do you have paper . . . a pencil?" Sheena began rummaging through the pockets of the boy's jacket and, finding nothing, took the trousers out of his hands and hurriedly searched it too. After a moment's hesitation, the young Spaniard took a couple of crumpled notes from his shirt pocket and slowly held them out to her.

Sheena flushed hot with shame and despair. He thought she was looking for payment. With an inarticulate cry she turned away from him and threw herself sobbing on the bed. Through her tears she heard the sound of the door closing and she cried all the harder, with a bitter strength that drained her emotionally and left her exhausted, weeping for the loss of her self respect as much as her predicament.

Some time later Sheena was wakened out of a doze by the sound of murmuring voices. Her head ached from the cheap wine and her throat was dry. She sat up in bed, holding the sheet against her, and looked towards the door. Perhaps Pablo had understood after all and was coming back to help her?

She waited, her heart thumping hopefully as the door swung open. Then hope was replaced by fear as Sheena saw the two men coming towards her out of the gloom. As the door gently closed again and she heard the key turning in the lock, she suddenly understood the full significance of Miguel's bringing the young Spaniard to her room earlier.

Terry spent the afternoon engaged in low tactical flying but his performance fell far below what it should have been for such precise and delicate manoeuvring.

In the early hours of the morning he had woken up out of the 'bad dream' covered in sweat and with his heart pounding painfully. This time Sheena was reproaching him for not coming to help her. 'I counted on you,' she kept saying. 'Now it's too late.' Sweat was running down her face. He tried to reassure her but she turned her face away from him and lay so still he thought she was dead. He had woken up, feeling convinced that there was something terribly wrong.

Terry was so taken up with his gloomy thoughts that he almost turned the Dauphin right into some huge power lines. His instructor tapped him warningly on the arm. "Another booboo like that, McArdle, and you'll fry us."

Terry felt his chest constrict at the near miss. He turned abruptly away and found himself heading into the forest.

The instructor took control and gently turned them away from the trees.

Terry felt shaken and ashamed. "Sorry. I've got it now."

"I hope so. This is infant's stuff after that bloody good mountain rescue you did the other night. Keep your mind on the job, McArdle, and stop thinking of your girlfriend."

The mountain rescue had been spectacular. It would have been tricky enough in daylight, but at night with wind bouncing off the cliff-face the operation had been really hazardous. Terry had kept his nerve and the ship steady and afterwards the rescued climbers, two teenage girls, had thanked him effusively, tears streaming down their faces. 'Any time,' Terry had told them with an embarrassed grin. At the same time he had been mighty pleased with himself, knowing how good the report would look on his record. Remembering, he grimaced at the cretinous way he was behaving now.

With an effort, Terry put his anxieties about his twin out of his mind until they had landed and gone through the debriefing procedure. He was only minutes back on board ship when he was summoned to the telephone.

"Call for you, McArdle," the radio officer told him. "You can take it in here."

"Terry, I've just had a ring from Claire . . ." Jane sounded tense and anxious over the wire, and what she had to say only confirmed Terry's own belief that Sheena was in some kind of trouble.

"Terry, this is the strange part," Jane went on worriedly, "Claire says that Sheena has been gone over a week."

Terry was taken aback. "But why didn't Claire contact you earlier?" he demanded, thinking that it didn't sound at all like her. She was usually so conscientious. "I would have thought she would be on to you at once."

"So would I, but it appears she was away herself for few days – Elena Gonzalez has been very ill and died recently. Claire was with the family at the time."

With that smooth Spaniard, Terry thought jealously.

"I can't leave the clinic for at least another week," Jane was saying. "I really don't know what to do." She sounded tired and harassed.

"Perhaps I could get leave," Terry suggested.

"That would be great." Jane sounded relieved. "Let me know and I'll book your ticket."

When Terry approached his CO and presented his case, he found him sympathetic. "Your mother is a widow and she needs you. Very well, McArdle. Normally we don't like the training programme interrupted, but in view of the circumstances you may take a week's compassionate leave."

"Thank you very much, sir." Terry saluted and wheeled about. An hour later his bag was packed and he was waiting at the station for a train to take him to Dublin. He felt a sudden glow of excitement at the prospect of going to Spain, and even his anxiety about Sheena dimmed at the thought of seeing Claire again.

Claire sat on the hard, damp sand near the water's edge, watching Ruthie paddling in the sea. At first she had been conscious of great relief at having telephoned Jane and passed on the burden, but as the afternoon wore on, her relief turned to anxiety and guilt that she had not stood by her friend as she should have.

"Come into the water," Ruthie cried, interrupting her melancholy thoughts. "It's lovely and cool."

Claire obediently joined her in the sea. Since her figure had grown fuller, she was conscious of how skimpy and revealing her swimsuit was and had got into the habit of wearing a T-shirt instead. Floating lazily on her back she felt cool at last. She squinted up at the hot blue heavens then let her eyes wander to the women and children resting under the canvas awnings, and higher again to where the boats were drawn up on the beach. Perhaps Fernando could help find Sheena. She knew that he had returned from leaving his brother back to his military academy in Cadiz because he had called to the apartment the previous evening with a sheaf of roses for her. He had not stayed long, having only come, he said, to thank her for all she had done for Elena.

"You were wonderful," Fernando's voice trembled with

emotion. "My mother loved you, as anyone who knows you must do."

Claire blushed, a little overcome by his ardour. She felt very attracted to him but sometimes thought her own emotion more resembled affection than love.

"I'm so glad I knew her," she told him, her cheeks still tinged with colour. "She was a marvellous person."

"Ah yes," Fernando agreed sadly. "She was brave and good and now she is at rest. It would be unworthy to wish her still alive when she endured so much suffering but I cannot help it. I feel as if part of myself has died with her."

It was how Claire had felt when Terry turned away from her that last night, as if her heart had been torn from her breast, and she were only half alive. She looked at Fernando and thought if she were to marry him their marriage would be a good one for he was sensitive and loving.

He had put out his hands and clasped hers, murmuring: "Now is not the right moment, Claire, but in a little while I will speak to you of what is very close to my heart. When I do I pray your wish will be the same as my own."

Ruthie suddenly bobbed up in the water beside her and broke into her reverie. Fernando was here, now, at the water's edge. Claire touched bottom and stood up, feeling embarrassed at being caught wearing only her T-shirt and pants.

"I thought I would find you here," Fernando said with a smile, as she stepped on to the sand.

Claire picked up her shorts and turning away from him, slipped them on. The button no longer fastened and she had resorted to a large safety pin to keep the edges together. She blushed, aware of his eyes on her back, and as she turned around wondered a little anxiously if he had noticed any alteration in her figure.

"Don't you wish to change out of your wet things?" Fernando asked.

"I have nothing to change into," Claire confessed. "I went in to cool off."

"You will take cold."

"The sun will dry me." She lifted her damp T-shirt, one of Terry's, and wrung the ends, then dropped them self-consciously, glad she had worn such a loose-fitting garment.

"If you do not intend spending more time on the beach," Fernando suggested politely, "perhaps you would like to have coffee with me?"

Claire nodded. "I'd like that very much." Milky coffee was warm and filling and helped soothe her stomach, which never felt entirely well these days. She beckoned to Ruthie and they stood in silence as the little girl slipped modestly behind a boat to change out of her wet togs before the three of them walked up the steps to the road.

"Your friend Sheena is not with you?" Fernando asked, when they were sitting under an umbrella and the waiter had taken their order.

"Sheena is in Gibraltar," Ruthie chipped in before Claire could answer. "Didn't you know?"

"You did not go with her?" Fernando asked in surprise. His habit of answering one question with another was almost Irish, Claire thought.

She shook her head. "She went away while Elena was dying," she said quietly. "I didn't know she was gone until I got back from the hospital."

With a warning glance in Ruthie's direction, she added in undertone, "It seems she went with Miguel to find Alejandro."

"*Caramba!*" Fernando exclaimed in dismay. "How long ago was that?"

"Just over a week."

"Has she telephoned?"

"Twice," Claire admitted. "I spoke to her last time and she sounded frightened."

"Understandably." Fernando looked concerned. "You have told her mother, of course."

Claire blushed with upset. "Yes . . . but only today," she stammered wretchedly. "I kept hoping she would arrive back." Fernando's eyes were full of concern.

"And *la hermanita* does not know the true state of affairs." He glanced compassionately at Ruthie, happily constructing houses out of drink mats.

"N . . . no," Claire faltered, worried by his grim expression. Fernando was taking it so seriously that she became suddenly afraid. "What are we to do?" she asked him. "Jane can't come for another week or two and by then . . . Oh, will you please help?"

"Naturally. You know that I will."

At once Claire felt as though a great weight was lifted from her. She gazed at him, and her look was so sweetly trusting that he caught his breath.

"Do not look at me like that," Fernando implored, "or I will not be responsible for what I do." He seized her hand and pressed his lips to it, his own look so painfully fond that Claire dropped her eyes.

Fernando left the girls back to the apartment and drove away, his expression thoughtful. He was truly appalled to learn of his brother's involvement with the daughter of the Irish doctor he so much admired.

"*Idiota! Estúpido!*" he berated himself. If only he had insisted on his brother coming home with him that day he'd bumped into him near the girls' apartment, he thought, what a lot of pain and trouble would have been saved. Alejandro would not now be facing a court-martial and Sheena would not be in the hands of a blackguard like Delgado. What his father would have to say when he heard of this latest development, Fernando dreaded to think.

As he turned in the gates of his house and drove up the long driveway, his heart was heavy. His father would take a very dim view of this dishonouring of Dr McArdle's daughter, as well as their family name.

Fernando had hardly begun to speak when his father exploded in wrath.

"You are saying that Alejandro enticed Señora McArdle's daughter to Gibraltar and that all along you have known of their relationship and kept silent?"

Fernando stared at him bleakly. "No, Father. I learned of it only very recently, and it was Alejandro's companion Miguel Delgado who took the girl away. I do not think Alex had any part in the seduction but yes, it is true that he introduced the man to Señorita McArdle."

Antonio put a hand to his forehead. "We must do everything in our power to find her," he said heavily. "Does Señora McArdle know of her daughter's abduction?"

Fernando swallowed miserably before answering, "Yes, sir." He felt the disgrace every bit as keenly as his father.

Terry flew into Spain the following afternoon and travelled by coach to Nerja. Jane had driven him to the airport in the morning to catch his flight. She was visibly distressed as she kissed him goodbye.

"Don't worry, Mum," he soothed her. "Twins have a special affinity, don't forget. I'll find her. You can count on me."

"I know that, Terry." Jane struggled with her tears as she hugged him goodbye. "I'll finish up at the clinic and be out as soon as I can."

"I'll ring you when I get there," Terry promised her. Before he went through the sensor he looked back and saw her straining up on her toes to see him go. He waved and walked on through.

Terry alighted from the coach in the centre of Nerja and easily supporting his bag on his shoulder walked the short distance to the apartment. Ruthie opened the door and he gasped and laughed when she threw herself upon him, squealing with delighted relief.

"Hold on!" Terry protested. "It's only a few months, not years, since we met."

"Terry, Oh Terry," Ruthie cried, clinging to him in excitement. He looked eagerly around for Claire, longing to see her yet feeling a bit self-conscious.

"Where's Claire?" he asked as casually as he could when his sister was calm again.

"Fernando called for her early and they went off to look for Sheena," Ruthie told him. "I think they have gone to the police."

Terry strolled in and out of the bedrooms. He saw Claire's dresses hanging in the cupboard and was hard put not to touch them. He recognised a T-shirt of his drying on the window ledge and his spirits lifted at the sight. He got a yearning feeling in his groin at the thought of it wrapped about her.

"Did you speak to Sheena when she rang?" he asked his little sister when he went back outside. Ruthie shook her head.

"Claire was only on for a minute before she put the phone down. I think Miguel was hurrying Sheena up."

Miguel? Terry filed the name away.

"Want some coffee?" Ruthie bustled importantly about. Terry watched her with lazy affection then went out on to the balcony. He was leaning on the rail, gazing down at the distant beach, when there was a flurry of activity behind him and Claire and Fernando suddenly arrived into the apartment.

"Look who's here," Ruthie cried.

Terry turned and looked wonderingly at Claire. Her grey eyes shone and there was a roundness to her face and a bloom to her skin he had never seen before. "Terry," Claire said faintly. "I didn't know you were coming." She swayed a little on her feet and then sat down abruptly on a sun-chair.

Fernando nodded at Terry and politely held out his hand. Terry reluctantly grasped it. 'It's because of him that she's so radiant,' he thought, his heart twisting painfully. 'He's taken her from me.'

Claire looked shyly at Terry, her heart too full to speak. She thought he looked fit and well. There was some indefinable change in his appearance and it was a minute before she realised what it was. He had matured and filled out in the months since she had last seen him. Gone was the wild, restless look. His eyes held hers steadily.

"What's all this about Sheena?" he demanded, a frown between his dark brows.

Claire sighed and told him, knowing from his puzzled expression that he was wondering why she had allowed so much time elapse before ringing home. Fernando watched them in silence.

"I was away the first time Sheena rang," Claire excused herself. "Fernando's mother was dying and I was at the hospital."

"Well, as soon as you knew you should have rung Mum," Terry said sternly. "I can't understand why you didn't. Sheena is a silly eejit, but you know better."

Fernando frowned. "You have no right to speak to her in this way," he protested. "She cannot be blamed."

"I'm not blaming her," Terry growled. "Just pointing out she should have acted sooner." The two men glared at each other.

Claire felt impatient rather than grateful for Fernando's support. She got up, feeling wounded by Terry's censure, and went to the fridge for water. Behind her the silence stretched. As she turned around again Fernando was saying, "This will not solve anything."

"Point taken," Terry said coolly. "So what can we do to make up for lost time?"

Fernando shrugged. "My father is making inquiries. We should have some information very soon."

Claire sipped her water and refrained from speaking directly to Fernando.

"I suggest we drive to Gibraltar in the hope of finding some clue that will lead us to your sister's whereabouts," Fernando said. "My father's Mercedes is at your disposal."

"Thanks," Terry said shortly, not sounding at all grateful. "The sooner the better."

"I'll come too," Claire said quickly. Both men looked at her.

"Why not," Terry said offhandedly.

Fernando smiled at Claire. "Your presence will make the trip a pleasure," he said.

Terry glared. "Why don't we cut the speeches and be on

our way."

"*Claro.*" Fernando got to his feet and bowed in acknowledgement. "I will be back within the hour."

Claire accompanied him to the door. "I'm not sure that Ruthie should come," she told him doubtfully, "but she can't be left here on her own."

Fernando smiled. "No problem. She can come and stay at my home. Christina will look after her until we get back."

Claire's expression cleared. "Thanks, Fernando. That would be great." In her gratitude and relief she squeezed his arm and he responded with an affectionate kiss on her cheek.

"*De nada*, Claire. I am happy to do anything to help you."

As she closed the door after him and turned smiling back into the room she almost collided with Terry, who steadied her with a painful grip then passed on with a stormy look on his face. Her smile fading, Claire watched him go into Sheena's room and heard the angry slam of the door.

A little later, the three of them went down to the courtyard to wait in the sunshine for Fernando. Claire had packed a small overnight bag for Ruthie and did her best to reassure the little girl of their speedy return, concerned by the doubt she saw in the child's eyes.

"We won't be gone more than one night," she assured her, "And who knows, we might even meet up at once with Sheena and bring her straight back."

Ruthie said staunchly. "I don't mind. I'm looking forward to playing with Stella."

"And Stella is looking forward to your visit," Fernando overhearing, responded gallantly.

"She's a terror with that tongue of hers," Claire said, hiding a grin. "Don't let her wash your face too much, Ruthie."

"Indeed," Fernando agreed. "She may also insist on cleaning your teeth if you are eating chocolate."

"I get it," Terry pulled a face. "Stella is a hound."

"Very much so," Fernando agreed, passing through the

front gates of his house and speeding up the driveway.

"She's so beautiful, Terry," Ruthie said dreamily. "You'll just love her."

Christina took Ruthie off at once to find the Labrador. To Claire's relief, apart from an unnaturally fierce hug on parting for herself and Terry, the little girl seemed happy enough about staying the night.

"Thank you for minding my little sister," Terry said a little stiffly to Fernando as they drove away from the house. He was sitting in the back of the car, leaving Claire in the front beside the Spaniard.

"It is a pleasure," Fernando said formally. He did not speak again but concentrated on putting the Mercedes through its paces.

Jane left the clinic at five o'clock and drove home, intending to have a quick snack, before heading out again in time for evening surgery. She had not heard from Terry but told herself he had only just arrived and could have nothing as yet to report. Still, she would have appreciated even the briefest of calls to reassure her that he had arrived safely.

These days Jane was working very full hours and would have happily worked day and night if it could have speeded up her getaway to Spain.

As she pushed open the front door, she almost did not see the letter from Spain in the pile of bills and letters lying on the mat. Her heart leaped thinking it might be from Antonio but then she recognised Sarah Lewis's writing and, repressing her disappointment, went to plug in the kettle.

'Poor soul,' the nurse had written. 'She suffered a lot before the end but even then she thought only of her family. It was a beautiful and inspiring death, just like her life. She remained conscious until her sons arrived and then with her eyes fixed on them, slipped gently into sleep.'

Jane lowered the sheets and absently turned the bread under the grill; cheese on toast was all she had time for. Sarah's description of Elena's death struck her as surprisingly poetic. She could so well imagine the scene and felt pity in her heart for the unfortunate woman. When her eyes strayed back to the letter she was surprised to see mention of Claire, forgetting the toast as she read on.

'A sweet, caring young girl, although not as unsophisticated as I had thought at first. It came as quite a shock but then, Doctor, the young people of today, they are not prepared to wait nor do they seem to have the same regard for marriage like we used to have. I know you are fond of the girl and I can see how well you might love her because she is all that you said. I only hope and trust her young Spaniard will stand by her. Indeed, he does seem head over heels in love with her but the Spanish view these things differently and it would be a shame if it turned out otherwise.'

Jane lowered the letter feeling deeply disturbed. Was she imagining it or was Sarah saying that Claire was pregnant by Fernando? She felt suddenly breathless with anxiety and pressed a hand to her ribs where, since her accident, stress caused her chest to ache. Sheena in trouble and now Claire. Shocked and distraught, she went to throw the burned toast into the bin.

The sky was still light as Fernando drove through the streets of Gibraltar. Twice on the way the car telephone had rung. At first it was Antonio to tell Fernando that the police had reported sighting Miguel Delgado in Gibraltar earlier in the week, and then later, to Claire's surprise, Fernando handed her the telephone.

"Hi Clairey," Ruthie's bright voice sounded in her ear. "Toni said I was to ring you so you'd know I was all right."

Toni! Claire was taken aback. Obviously Ruthie and Fernando's father were getting on famously. "Hi Ruthie," she said. "Do you want to talk to Terry?"

"Put him on." Ruthie commanded airily, to Claire's amusement.

"Don't be a pain in the neck," Terry told his sister. "What? . . . Yes, of course, we're glad you're enjoying yourself, only don't overdo it . . . No, not until tomorrow. Okay, and remember what I said."

He replaced the phone in the cradle and laughed, sounding more like himself than he had all day. "Isn't she the limit? The hound is sleeping in her room tonight and Christina has agreed to serve the pair of them hot chocolate in bed."

Claire laughed, glad that Ruthie was captivating the household from Antonio down. She glanced at her watch. It was almost nine o'clock.

"We'll soon be there," Fernando said, observing the movement.

Claire nodded, feeling tired and faint from so little to eat all day. The trouble was when she could eat she didn't want to and when she didn't eat she felt sick.

Fernando left them in the bar of a small hotel and went to arrange for rooms. Claire wondered a little anxiously who would pay. She had very little money and was counting on not being away more than one night. She supposed she could borrow from Terry, but he was always broke.

When Fernando rejoined them the waiter brought casseroled chicken, accompanied by sticks of crusty bread and a bottle of Rioja, to the table. Predictably, Claire's appetite vanished soon after she began to eat. The chicken pieces floating in oil turned her stomach. She crumbled some bread and chewed slowly. She saw Terry looking at her in a brooding kind of way but although she greatly desired to be alone with him, she could not have taken the initiative if she had tried. She yawned and pushed her plate away.

"You are tired," Fernando said solicitously and Claire nodded, too worn out to speak. She could see that Terry was puzzled by her extreme fatigue and he frowned and shifted impatiently in his seat.

"Why don't you go to bed if you can't stay up, Claire," he said, almost scornfully and she winced at the contempt in his voice. She could not know that he believed she was using tiredness as a pretext for avoiding him – and she felt more miserable and rejected than before.

"Yes . . . go to bed," Fernando said more gently and she cast him a grateful look. "You will be fresh for whatever tomorrow brings." It was good advice but only seemed to goad Terry to fresh sarcasm. Fernando's own expression was grave as he watched Claire go.

"Why do you speak to her like that?" he asked, more in regret than anger. "She has had a very difficult time these past weeks. She could not have been kinder to my mother or done more to . . ."

"So you said before," Terry interrupted curtly. Who did he think he was! San bloody Fernando. Terry knew he was being unreasonable but when he looked at the Spaniard and thought how close he had been to Claire all these weeks, he experienced jealousy so great he could not contain it.

"Perhaps it is just as well that Claire has gone to bed," Fernando continued calmly. "We can do more easily what has to be done."

Terry looked sharply at him, wondering if he had learned of Sheena's whereabouts. But Fernando shook his head.

"No, merely a few leads to where we may find Delgado. Soon a man will come into the bar and from him we may learn something."

The man, when he came, was sharp featured and unshaven and spoke at length to Fernando, gesticulating much of the time. Terry sat across the room from them, sipping beer. He was beginning to feel tired himself. He had not slept much the night before and had been travelling most of the day. He observed the notes passing between Fernando and the man and waited until Fernando was on his own before going over to join him.

"So. Did you learn anything?" he demanded.

"Not a lot. Delgado left Gibraltar four days ago with your sister and took the road to Marbella, stopping at Estepona. There is a man there who saw them and can give us further information."

Terry exclaimed. "Good. Let's go at once. Claire's asleep and won't miss us."

Fernando shook his head. "By the time we get there it would be too late," he pointed out reasonably. "We will see him in the morning."

Terry sank back on his stool. He longed for action. At the back of his impatience was his very real anxiety about his twin and he found any delay intolerable. He pondered whether to cut loose and make his own way, then saw the futility of this without a car.

Bidding Fernando a surly goodnight, he went up to bed.

As he passed Claire's room he had a sudden, irresistible vision of her asleep in bed with her fair hair spread on the pillow. It took all his willpower to keep on going past her door.

They were on the move again. Sheena stumbled in a daze of sleep across the dark road and was shoved into the back of Miguel's car. She fell in a jumble of arms and legs, trying to protect her face, and recoiled when he reached inside and, with an oath, punched her hands free of the door.

Miguel was drunker than usual and determined on travelling that night. Sheena was not sorry to be leaving this place. Very bad things had happened here, so bad that she had not taken them out yet to look at them. She might never be able to. She had been dozing and he had come in and shaken her awake. This time Miguel was on his own and he swore long and profusely as he threw garments into a case and gathered up his few belongings.

"There is no time for that," he'd said when she tried to comb her tangled hair. He had pulled and poked her out of the bed where she was backed up like a wary cat.

As the car bumped along the road she had no idea where she might be or where he was taking her. This last stop, and the second since leaving Gibraltar, had seemed to be a seaside place. This she knew because on their first night there, when the men had ceased knocking on the door of their room, Miguel had brought her down to the water's edge to bathe. There had been only a cracked toilet at the end of the corridor, which he had escorted her to and from, and a tin bowl in the room. Sheena's skin had become coarse and dry and her eyes blinked in daylight. She had forgotten what it was like to really wash herself or apply lipstick or body lotions. Sometimes she looked at herself in the cracked mirror and mourned her fading tan. It would seem the least of her worries, but in a way, it was a relief to cling to so small a grievance when there was much that was truly sinister and frightening threatening her.

The night was hot and stifling. Miguel kept the car windows closed and Sheena could hardly draw breath. The car rocked from side to side as though on a steep, spiralling road. Once, there was the sound of oncoming traffic and powerful headlamps blossomed their car roof before blackness closed in again. She fell into a doze and her slack body no longer protected itself from contact with the unpadded contours of the bumping, straining car.

Claire woke up early next morning and came downstairs to find the two men already sitting in the dining-room. Fernando greeted her with a smile and a pleasant greeting but all she got from Terry was a curt nod. She tried not to mind as she took her place at the table, telling herself that Terry never wasted time on niceties and was probably desperately worried about Sheena.

They breakfasted on rolls and coffee and were soon making their way to the car, each of them anxious to get going and find Sheena without any more loss of time. Neither Fernando nor Terry expressed any doubt that they would find her alive and well, but Claire was not so sure. She was afraid what they might find.

Ahead of them with dramatic suddenness the coastline of Estepona came into view. Fernando slowed and nosed the bonnet of the Mercedes along the crowded streets, searching for a spot to park. It was some time before he found space in a back street.

Claire and Terry silently followed Fernando along the street that led to the beach, where he ordered beer and *naranjada*. Already into August, there was a stormy, sultry feeling to the weather and only for a slight sea breeze, the heat would have been unbearable.

Claire was sipping *naranjada* and discussing Spanish customs with Fernando when Terry suddenly pushed his empty glass away from him and jumped impatiently to his feet.

"Finish it up, Claire," he ordered, indicating her drink with a frown. Startled, she drained her orange in one gulp.

"There is no rush," Fernando said equably. "It is almost siesta time. Nothing will be done for another hour or two."

This was too much for Terry. "I don't care if half the Spanish population are comatose," he snapped. "I'm not sitting around here a moment longer. Just give me the name of your contact and I'll go see him myself."

Fernando frowned and stood up. "There is no need," he said forbiddingly. "We will go together to find your sister. It would have been better to have waited, but very well, if you must go now." His expression seemed to suggest that Terry's unseemly haste would most certainly affect their chances of finding Sheena.

Claire watched the young men's unsmiling faces and decided they would never be friends. Their natures were too much in opposition for there ever to be a corresponding chord between them, yet she had great love in her heart for both of them. If she were not carrying Terry's child she might be drawn to the idea of marrying Fernando. He was well-born and intelligent and even possessed a sense of humour, which Terry undoubtedly did not. She must be going a little mad. If she were not pregnant, she would not even be considering marriage with Fernando, let alone anyone else!

"*Sí*. Delgado was here two, maybe three nights, but he has moved on." The speaker was an elderly man, wearing a black beret aslant his bald head like Pablo Picasso. His face was brown and wrinkled and his heavily lidded eyes met theirs without curiosity, like a sleepy lizard.

"Do you know where Delgado stayed in Estepona, Señor?" Fernando asked him.

"*Sí.*" The old man jerked his head at the maze of streets behind where they stood. "They will tell you there." He went back inside, disdaining to wait for the note Fernando took from his wallet.

So not everyone is controlled by the sight of your money, Terry thought. Maybe the old man felt like he did. He felt an irrational anger at Fernando's wealth. That it might one day take Claire away from him was his real grievance, but Terry did not analyse it. He looked at the man's good suit and silk tie. Perhaps if he weren't so well dressed we would find Sheena quicker, he thought resentfully. Then Terry remembered that without Fernando's money they would never have known that Miguel had come to Estepona. This realisation only increased his frustration.

"Okay, where to now?" he demanded, looking aggressively from one to the other. He had a sudden vision of Sheena bathed in sweat, weeping and telling him he was too late to help her, and felt his spirits plummet. He had not had the dream since coming to Spain and secretly he feared it must mean she was dead.

While Fernando went off to make further enquiries Claire and Terry wandered down to the stony beach and sat some yards apart, not looking at each other or speaking. Claire reflected sadly on how once they had tripped over their tongues with all they had to say to each other.

She got to her feet and waded into the sea. She felt unbearably warm and dreaded the thought of getting back into the car without first cooling off. Her feet bumped and scuffed on the high piled rocks beneath the waves. She had not realised how stony the beach was. As she struggled to keep her balance she was carried out of her depth and gasped in the cold water, feeling the shock of it through the thin material of her sundress.

It was an enormous relief after the intense heat. Claire

turned amongst the bobbing bathers and faced back to the shore. In this heat her clothes would be dry in minutes.

Terry sat on a pile of rocks near the roadway, staring down at her, with a brooding expression so reminiscent of Eddie's.

Claire came out of the water, her sodden sundress held before her as she squeezed out the drops of sea water, the movement accentuating the fullness of her tanned breasts in the low neckline. She saw the way Terry's eyes fixed on them, and the longing to have him in her arms was so great in her that she blushed for her thoughts and abruptly turned away.

Terry saw Fernando stepping down on to the beach. So that was why she coloured up like that, he thought. He frowned and got up moodily from the rock, but forgot his grievance as he heard what Fernando had to tell them.

"Delgado and your sister were seen last night on the road between San Pedro de Alcantara and Ronda." Fernando's dark eyes shone with excitement and relief. "This time there is no mistake. The car was a 1979 sports coupé of the kind Delgado drives. There are not many to be found on Spanish roads."

"Ronda?" Terry queried. "Way up in the hills?"

Fernando nodded. "And I have it on good authority they have not come down again. The best assurance." He tapped his wallet significantly.

Instead of being angry Terry felt only relief. If Fernando's money succeeded in delivering up Sheena to them he had no fault to find with it.

"Let's be on our way then." Terry briskly assumed command. "We've wasted too much time already."

This time the Spaniard meekly took his cue from him and led the way, almost humbly, to where he had parked the Mercedes.

The road to Ronda was sharp and twisting. At times Claire felt like a fly on a wall, so steep was the incline. From the back seat, she was glad not to have too good a view as they roared around narrow hairpin bends. They had barely time to straighten out before the next one leapt at them. More than once she caught her breath as she looked out the rear window and saw the mountain drop sheerly below them.

Fernando was silent at the wheel, giving all his concentration to keeping the roaring machine on the dusty ribbon of road. Once Terry turned and passed Claire the bottle of water and when she handed it back to him and he put his lips to it, she felt as though they had kissed. The feeling was so strong in her that she wondered if Terry felt the same.

Fernando turned his head to glance at Terry. "Would you like to take a turn at the wheel?" he suddenly asked.

Terry stared. "Sure." His face broke into a grin. "Thought you'd never ask." They changed seats and Terry set off at a pace almost equal to Fernando's.

From where she was comfortably stretched Claire watched the backs of their heads and wondered at the new ease between the two men. Terry flicked through the gears, getting the feel of the stick and testing the grip of the tyres on the tight bends. Beside him, Fernando kept an impassive face and although Claire's mouth was in her throat and she frequently stabbed at an imaginary brake pedal in the floor, the Spaniard seemed quite at ease.

"You handle a car well," he told Terry, "but then you are a pilot, are you not?"

Terry was struck by something in the way he said it and shot him a glance. "You fly yourself?"

Fernando shrugged. "I did my National Service with the Spanish Air Corps and I hold a commercial pilot's licence."

Terry looked at him with new interest. "Say, that's great. It never occurred to me . . . I mean I thought . . ."

Fernando smiled. "Do not take your eyes off the road."

Terry grunted and settled his hands in a fresh grip on the wheel. They travelled on in friendly silence. Fernando nodded soberly through the window as they sped up along the road leading into Ronda. "That is the gorge where the

Republicans flung the townspeople to their death during the civil war in our country."

Claire looked out the window and shuddered as she imagined the falling figures and the screams.

"To stand on the Puente Neuvo gives you some idea of the Ronda's towering position," Fernando was saying. "It is the first thing tourists do."

"Looks jolly high." Terry spared a glance."

Fernando raised his hand. "Stop here, *por favor.*"

Terry parked the big car by the side of the Plaza and switched off the engine. He sat and glowered in silence.

Fernando glanced behind at Claire with an understanding smile. "On a lighter note, it may be of interest to know that one of Spain's greatest bullfighters, Antonio Ordoñez, was born here in Ronda."

"Oh yes?" Claire asked absently, anxiously regarding the back of Terry's head. She supposed their brief truce had been too good to last.

Fernando unclipped his seat-belt. "Actually, the Ronda school of bullfighting is held to be bullfighting at its purest. Nowhere else are matadors trained with such high emphasis on skill and courage."

"How very interesting," Terry said sarcastically. "This is beginning to sound more and more like a guided tour of Ronda."

Fernando looked at him. "You feel we should not speak of anything but your sister?"

Terry frowned. "I'm conscious of how long it is since we last heard from her. Something very bad could have happened to her. Yes," he said consideringly, "I would be happier if we could cut all this tourist crap and go find her."

Claire winced for Terry's rudeness while, at the same time, feeling a sneaking sympathy with his views.

"By all means let us not delay any further." Fernando held out his hand imperiously for the car keys.

Terry got out of the car and stalked up the street. Fernando paced after him, with his hands behind his back and his chin in the air. Claire sighed and followed them both. She wished they would hurry up and find Sheena and they could all go back to Nerja.

After a while Fernando unbent enough to tell them he had elicited the name of a person in Ronda who might be able to help them. Happily, he seemed to have unlimited contacts.

It was nearing eight o'clock that evening before they met their contact who, to Claire's shock, turned out to be a woman. The Spaniard insisted on being paid before she would speak and then revealed that Sheena was being kept a prisoner by Delgado in a room over the bar of a local hostelry.

Claire, feeling a little sick, was unable to repress a shiver of fear and disgust. All at once her arm was gripped and, looking around, she found Terry close behind her.

"The bloody swine," he said fiercely, his eyes bright with unshed tears, "When I get my hands on him he'll wish to God he'd never been born."

Claire looked up at him and nodded vehemently, a lump in her own throat. For a moment they stared wordlessly at each other, united by an overwhelming surge of love and loyalty for Sheena, and family and the past.

Later that night Terry and Claire went with Fernando to the bar in question and waited inside the door while he approached the counter. The room was full of men and in one corner a long-haired musician played a guitar, his frenzied shrieks splitting the air. Close to him another proudly postured, his heels drumming the floor. Cigar smoke hung thickly over the room.

Fernando glanced back and motioned to Terry to take Claire out again. When they were gone he ordered a beer and sipped it slowly, for he had recognised Miguel almost at once in a group of men squatting about the guitarist. Although Fernando knew the man by sight, he was reassured when he deliberately held the other man's gaze and saw him glancing past without recognition.

Miguel deliberately let his own eyes slide past Fernando. He had already spotted him in the town that afternoon, so he was not surprised to see him now. Miguel had his contacts too and been warned that Alejandro's brother was on his trail. Of Alejandro himself Miguel had neither seen nor heard anything since their furious exchange of words. The money owing to him had not been repaid, but the girl had been profitable and Miguel considered that he had already been amply rewarded by the opportunity to bring down the proud young man. As for the more senior member of that arrogant Gonzales family...

Miguel sniffed contemptuously at the naïvety of his pursuer in expecting to pass unnoticed driving about Gibraltar in his flashy Mercedes. He had seen it too often in Nerja, and even driven in it on occasion with Alex, not to recognise it at once sticking out like a sore cock on a virgin.

Miguel waited until Fernando had paid for his drink, then he got to his feet and went out to the back, as if to urinate. He paused in the shadowy passage, aware that Fernando was following him, and when the man had gone past into the open, he lingered in the gloom until he judged it long enough for the other Spaniard to have gone back inside or given up.

"*Qué imbécil!*" Miguel sneered, and slouched back along the passage congratulating himself on outwitting his stupid countryman. But as soon as he stepped back into the light he realised his mistake.

Sheena came out of a doze in the darkened room and lifted her head at the tempestuous far-off sound of flamenco, the staccato shrieks and wildly drumming heels inspiring in her a feeling of dread. The nightmare was beginning all over again. She felt hysteria swiftly rising as she anticipated the sinister shuffle outside her room and the grating key in the lock, the coarseness and brutality which inevitably followed.

She had not long to wait, and when hands fumbled the door handle, fresh tears of agony and despair slid from under her swollen eyelids and she huddled on the mattress and frantically rocked backwards and forwards. No! No! No!

"Oh God," she prayed brokenly. "Please, please!"

Slowly, the door pushed open and, despite the futility of flight, Sheena scrambled off the bed and fled sobbing to crouch in an alcove cupboard.

She clawed over the flimsy door in a feeble effort to conceal herself and as the footsteps drew nearer and came to a stop at the other side, she stuffed her hand into her mouth and chewed on the already raw and bleeding flesh to gag her screams.

Terry hovered with Claire at the entrance to the bar, undecided what he should do. "Sheena is somewhere near," he told her anxiously. "I've got to find her before that bastard moves her again."

Claire shivered and nodded. It felt good to have Terry confide in her again and see his gaze soften when he looked at her. She knew she would never be able to tell him about the baby because that would be like trying to stake a claim to him, but she was happier than she been for a long time.

Terry gripped her hand. "Claire, you'd better go back to the car. I'm going to scout about inside while Fernando keeps Delgado occupied."

Claire shook her head. "No. I'm staying with you," she said firmly. "We'll look for her together."

When he saw that she was determined, he wasted no more time. "Come on then." He led the way round the side of the pub and ducked inside a doorway. Claire peered after him. There was a stairway leading to the next floor and already Terry was going up it. She quickly followed.

Terry tried the handle on the door nearest to him and the door opened easily. He peered inside but the room was empty except for a sagging bed covered by a fringed rug. He approached another door as Claire tiptoed near.

"Look," she whispered. "There's a key in the lock."

They stared into each other's eyes on the dim landing, and then Terry turned the key and cautiously opened the door. From below came a fresh burst of flamenco singing and the rattling thud of many heels. With a warning nod for Claire to stay where she was and watch out, Terry slipped into the room.

At first, he thought there was no one there and was about to withdraw, when he heard a piteous gasping whimper in the gloom.

His nerves on edge, Terry stepped deeper into the room and glanced about him. The noise was coming from a cupboard in an alcove between the window and the bed. He braced himself and flung wide the door. At once the sound ceased. As Terry stared down at what looked like a bundle of clothing in the corner, he saw it move and was conscious of eyes in the swollen bruised face regarding him in terror. For a second he did not recognise his sister and when he did, he was horrified. He dropped on his knee and cradled her fiercely against his chest.

"Oh Shee, thank God to find you. Thank God you're all right."

She stared up at him in blind terror, and her unrecognising stare was more unnerving than her bruised and bloodied flesh. Then she began to scream and struggle in his arms and he tried to hold her while she fought him.

"Sheena!" Terry gripped her arms and shook her hard. "Stop! It's me . . . Terry!" She calmed pulled back to look up at him, really seeing him, and the mad light faded from her eyes.

"Terry!" Sheena quavered, through swollen lips. "Is it really you?" She clung to him piteously, her tears soaking his shirt. "Oh, Terry, I thought you'd never come . . . I'd given up hope."

"Well, you shouldn't have," he told her with gruff tenderness. "You must have known I'd find you, no matter what." He looked down and saw the raw mangled fingers clutching his shirt, the fresh blood leaving bright streaks on the cloth, and his anger and revulsion overcame him. What terrible things had been done to her? The thought made him shake and he forced himself to remain calm and continue to hold and soothe her, fighting his urge to rush below and vent all his hatred on the man responsible. Gradually she grew quieter, blubbering softly as she lay against him.

"Shee . . ." Terry was desperately conscious of the time. "Listen, we've got to move it. Now! At once." He pulled her gently to her feet and she staggered and nearly fell.

He lugged her across the room, half-carrying her in his anxiety to be gone before they were discovered. In the doorway he collided with Claire, who had nervously come to see what was keeping him. She gave a cry of joy at the sight of Sheena.

"Sheena, thank God. Are you all right?"

"Claire. Oh, Clairey." Sheena began to cry again, pitiful jerking sobs and the two girls clung to each other. Terry had to forcibly separate them.

"Please," he begged. "Save it for later. We've got to get out of here."

Downstairs there was another tempestuous burst of sound, followed by shouting and clapping. The eternal strumming began again. Supporting Sheena between them, Terry and Claire went out to the dim landing, avoiding each other's eyes, embarrassed and filled with aching pity. Halfway down the stairs Sheena's knees suddenly gave and she sagged between them.

"I can't . . . Oh please . . ." She looked up at them pathetically and with her damaged hand held against her bruised lips, began to weep.

Claire crouched down on the step and put her arms comfortingly about her. "It's all right, Shee . . . it's all right," she told her gently. "Take a rest. You'll be okay in a minute." She looked beseechingly at Terry, willing him to understand, and continued to soothe Sheena until she gulped and indicated she was ready to go on.

They reached the bottom without encountering anyone and made their way out of the building. Terry went part of the way up the lane with the girls and pointed out the road they must take to reach the car, then he gently detached Sheena's clinging arms and turned to go back.

"Tell Fernando to get clear of the town and wait by the roadside," he told Claire tersely. "I'll be after you just as quick as I can."

She was about to protest, but Terry gripped her arm urgently. "Please do as I say, Claire," he begged. "And get Sheena back to the car before she collapses." With a last whispered, "Good girl," he sprinted back to the pub.

Claire had to exert all her strength to support Sheena up the street. As they drew near Claire saw Fernando pacing up and down beside the Mercedes. He turned when he heard her calling him, and stared in amazement.

"*Madre de Dios!*" he exclaimed, and ran forward to help her support Sheena the last few yards to the car.

The singing in the bar had stopped and a card game was in progress. Miguel sat slumped at the counter, a glass of brandy on the counter before him. He swallowed it in one gulp and lit a cigarette, so deep in thought that he did not notice eyes watching him from the doorway. He was still thinking of his encounter with Fernando. He would have liked to have felt only contempt for this soft-featured brother of Alejandro Gonzalez, but he would not soon forget the way the man had suddenly come at him out of the shadows.

Miguel regarded the tip of his cigarette gloomily. For all his soft looks the older Gonzalez brother had dealt him a blow like iron in the solar plexus. Too late he had remembered that this was the brother who had been a pilot in one of the toughest squadrons in Madrid. When Gonzalez had threatened him with removal of his *cojones* followed by disembowelling and incarceration in a Spanish gaol, Miguel had shuddered and almost given way. Now he bolstered his flagging spirits with more brandy and decided he would ditch the bimbo and move on tonight. But first one more drink for the road. He flicked his long nails against the glass.

"Carlos Primero."

The barman laughed. "Only the best for Delgado, eh." He poured the brandy and leaned closer. "You have a customer awaiting you above in the room," he murmured as Miguel tossed it back. "A fine young Inglés," he added slyly. "Business is looking up for us both."

Miguel frowned at this reminder of his obligation and threw the barman his cut, conscious he was running very low on money. What bad luck they had been forced to leave Estepona, Miguel thought, as he stumbled up the stairs. Word had quickly spread about the *Inglesa* and there had been a knock on the door every five minutes. He could have been rich if he had not been forced to move on.

The door to the room stood ajar. Miguel smiled at such impatience. That was good. The Inglés would be willing to pay more for his satisfaction. Maybe he was already hard at it. More strength to his cock. Miguel swaggered inside.

Terry heard the footsteps on the stairs and moved swift and soundless to take up position behind the door. He stood tensed as the steps drew nearer, swamped with pity and rage at the memory of Sheena's terrified whimpers, her abused flesh. He thought of the indignities and atrocities she had endured and felt as though his heart would break.

"*Qué pasa*, has she gone into hiding again?" Miguel advanced smiling over the threshold, his gaze seeking out the corners of the shadowy room. "Do not be shy. Come out, my little whore."

A cold, murderous rage possessed Terry. He came swiftly and silently from behind the door and brought his hand down in a lethal, chopping motion on Miguel's neck. The man dropped. Terry swiftly bent over him and searched through his pockets. He took the keys to the sports car and slipped them in his own pocket then waited for the Spaniard to come round.

After a moment Miguel groaned and tried to sit up. At once Terry caught him in an armlock and forced him on to his feet. There was a look of surprise and fear on the

Spaniard's face as he looked behind at his attacker and recognised him as the young man he had seen in the town that afternoon with Fernando. Miguel was under the impression that it was to him they were now going, as Terry forced him in front of him down the stairs.

The barman looked up as Terry passed the door with Miguel and he waved and called jovial greetings at the sight of another satisfied customer being escorted off the premises.

"If time allows I will come back for you," Terry promised savagely, and prodded Miguel in front of him out the door. The Lamborghini was in an alley behind the pub. He gave Miguel the keys and kept his arm hooked under the Spaniard's jaw as he drove. When they were out the road by the ravine he told Miguel to stop the car then reached forward and took the keys from the ignition.

"Get out."

Miguel got out of the car and looked about him, fully expecting to see the Mercedes parked on the roadway. So it was to be just the two of them. Very well. This young Inglés would get more than he had reckoned. As they began the walk on to the cliff he suddenly turned on his captor with suddenness and ferocity. Miguel was strong and he tore at Terry's face with his overgrown nails.

Taken by surprise, Terry went over backwards with Miguel on top, and tried to protect his eyes. In size the two men were fairly evenly matched. If Terry was the taller by an inch or two, Miguel weighed ten pounds heavier. They were both big but Terry had the advantage on the Spaniard. He was lean and fit and in the peak of physical health. Terry's fists were hard and punishing as they smashed into the man's face.

"This is for Sheena," he panted, venting all his anger and revulsion. "And this!" Realisation dawned in Miguel's pale eyes and his bruised lips stretched in a smile.

"So the whore is your sister," he said thickly. "Let me describe to you then the clever tricks she does." A stream of obscenities poured from his split, bleeding mouth.

Terry wished he had taken a chance and brought his army pistol into Spain with him. He would have thrust it in the lewd face and blasted the vileness away. A little crazy, he pounded the face under him until it pulped red and grotesque.

Miguel's eyes in the fleshy mask stared murderous hate and he reached into his boot for the knife he always kept there. Terry caught the knife hand at the wrist, holding it low down and trying to deflect the thrust as Miguel lunged forward. But he dodged too late and the blade sliced into his neck, drawing blood in a steady stream. He was aware of the warm, wet trickle and feared his injury was bad, but he was in it now to the death.

They circled each other warily, Miguel sneering and watchful with venomous eyes. Terry steeled himself to go in against the naked blade. The wind blew on their sweating bloody faces and their feet sought for purchase on the sliding surface of the cliff.

As the Spaniard rushed him again, Terry saw his chance. He twisted sideways and, gaining purchase on the damp earth, swung his leg in a flying kick that caught the man in the small of his back, and Miguel toppled screaming into the gorge below.

Terry gasped at the suddenness of it and dropped weakly to his knees. He crawled to the edge, sobbing for breath, and looked over. It was too dark to see anything. The scream continued on in his head and then blackness rushed in and he fell senseless on the ground.

Two miles down the road the Mercedes was parked by the roadside. It had been Fernando's intention to bring the *Guardia Civil* back with them to search the bar but Claire, conscious of Terry's instructions, had persuaded him to wait. Now Fernando glanced at his watch and met Claire's eyes fleetingly. A whole hour and still no sign of Terry.

Sheena lay on the back seat fretfully tossing and crying out. She was badly shocked and most of the time seemed unaware where she was or with whom.

Claire was conscious of the smell of her friend like a bad drain in the back of the car. She felt embarrassed for her before Fernando and was glad when he tactfully kept the air conditioning running. Claire was desperately worried but trying not to show it. She shouldn't have allowed Terry go back, she agonised. If anything bad happened to him she would never forgive herself.

"We will wait another five minutes and then we will go for the *Guardia Civil*," Fernando decided. "Terry has acted with great irresponsibility. He should not have tried to take Delgado on his own."

Claire could contain herself no longer. "But all that will take too long. Oh, please let's go back and look for him now," she begged, her voice coming out in a dry croak.

Fernando looked at her startled, and without a word set the car in motion. He turned it on the narrow road and drove rapidly back to Ronda.

Terry must have relapsed into unconsciousness for he came to with a start and peered into the darkness, trying to remember where he was and what had happened. Then he felt the warm slow blood dripping from his neck and he remembered.

"The bastard deserved what he got," he whispered. He tried to struggle up but his legs were too weak to support him. He found he was lying in a puddle of blood and searched his pockets for something to wad against the sluggishly flowing wound. His handkerchief was too small to be effective, so he pulled his shirt off and wound it tightly about his neck, knotting the arms to keep it in place. He almost swooned with the effort and had to rest a moment because he felt so weak and his vision was breaking up.

"Got to get back to the road," he told himself. "They won't think to look for me out here." He tried to calculate the distance and direction but it was beyond him. "If I can drag myself nearer the road maybe I can shout . . . they'll see the car . . ." But his dizziness overcame him and he laid his head weakly on his forearm.

"Terry!" He thought he was imagining it but then his name was called again. He lifted his head and listened, his heart beginning to race at the sound of her voice.

He tried to call out but his voice was weak in his throat. He took a deep breath and with his remaining strength hollered as loud as he could then fell back waiting to see if she would call again.

"Terry, where are you?" He judged she was at the far side of the Puente Nuevo, and coming nearer. He could imagine her, slim and fair and determined, those grey eyes anxious.

"Claire!" He tried to shout, but it was merely a groan.

He imagined her giving up the search and turning back and he felt it was more than he could bear, and his heart shrivelled within him. He thought how much he hated his father and how much he had thought he hated her too – and realised he loved her far more.

"I feel he's somewhere near about. I know he is." Her voice was closer, stronger, only yards away. The softly spoken words touched him deeply, and brought tears to his eyes.

"I'm here, Clairey," he tried to say, and felt himself falling through space and darkness again.

Jane stared at the telephone, willing it to ring. It was two days since Terry had left for Spain and she could not understand why she hadn't heard from him. Now she was convinced something sinister had happened and decided to ring Antonio. Jane had never rung his house before and she was as nervous as a girl as she waited for him to come to the phone.

"Jane! Is it really you, Jane?" Her name had never been one Jane particularly liked but on hearing it now spoken in Antonio's resonant tones, it was suddenly charged with the most heavenly significance.

"Yes, Antonio." She felt suddenly shy, then hurried on lest she should just idiotically keep repeating his name. "I'm very concerned about Sheena. Terry flew out yesterday morning to try and locate her and I haven't heard from

410

him." Jane's voice faltered. "You can imagine how worried I am. I was hoping perhaps you might have heard something."

Antonio did not reply for a moment and when he spoke his voice was kindly. "I intended telephoning you, Jane, but I was waiting to hear from my son. I have been aware of the situation and arranged for Fernando to drive with Terry and Claire to Gibraltar to try and find your daughter. Until this evening Fernando has kept in touch with me, but I have not heard from him since he rang to say that they had found Sheena but regrettably lost contact with your son."

Jane began to be really alarmed. "Has something happened to Terry?" she cried.

"Please do not upset yourself, Jane," Antonio said soothingly. "I am quite sure there is nothing to worry about. It seems he parted from the others, promising to catch up with them later, only he did not show up at the appointed place."

"But surely the police in Gibraltar could help find him," Jane said bewildered.

"They were not in Gibraltar when they lost each other but had travelled on to Ronda," Antonio explained. "I am sure there is some perfectly rational explanation. Can I telephone you in one hour? By then I am certain that I will have something definite to tell you."

Jane made a huge effort to control her fears. "Very well, Antonio. No matter how late it is, please ring. I won't be asleep."

She put down the phone and went to make a soothing cup of cocoa, thinking how many crises in the past she had seen through with cups of the stuff: the searingly lonely nights after Eddie's and Hugh's deaths, the troubled months following Ruthie's attack and the worries she had gone through because of Terry's involvement with Gráinne.

Jane sighed. It was better than taking to the whisky bottle like poor Annette Shannon. She cradled the cup in her hands and blew gently on the bubbling surface, afraid to think what news Antonio might have for her when he rang back.

"He's unconscious," Fernando said quietly, on one knee beside the slumped body. He had got to Terry a few seconds before Claire and immediately felt for the pulse behind his ear. "He has lost a lot of blood. We must get him to a doctor."

Claire shuddered as she looked down at Terry's scratched and bruised face. His skin was translucent in the light from Fernando's flashlight and the bloody cloth about his neck terrified her.

"How white he is," she whispered. She held the flashlight steady while Fernando gently removed the cloth from around Terry's neck and wadded his own handkerchief over the oozing wound before retying the gory cloth more tightly.

"Claire! Fernando!" Sheena's anguished voice sounded in the darkness. "Where are you?" They had left her dozing in the car and she had woken up terrified out of her mind of being recaptured by Miguel and followed them, tripping and falling on the dark cliff.

"We've found Terry, Shee," Claire told her with more confidence than she felt. "He's hurt but he'll be all right."

"Let me see." Sheena pushed past them and threw herself down beside her twin. At the sight of the bloody neckcloth she became hysterical and rocked on her knees. "Oh God, no," she cried. "Please don't let it be. Please, God, please!"

"Take her back to the car," Fernando whispered. "I will manage him on my own."

He slipped an arm beneath Terry and lifted him to his knees, then hooked one of the wounded man's arms around his neck and hoisted him to his feet. The movement restored Terry to consciousness and he stumbled obediently along on weak legs, with Fernando bearing most of his weight.

Claire guided her weeping friend over the rough ground. Sheena was almost unhinged by her period of captivity and the events of the past hours.

They arrived at Hospital Belen in the early hours and found the emergency team ready and waiting for them, Fernando having rung to alert them. At once Terry was lifted on to a stretcher and hurried away to the operating theatre. Nurse Lewis took immediate charge of Sheena, clucking in consternation over her filthy, neglected appearance and trembling wild-eyed stare.

To Claire, racked by worry for Terry and pity for Sheena, the drive from Ronda had seemed endless though, in fact, Fernando had made very good time, completing the 148 kilometres journey in a little over an hour. He had made Terry comfortable on the back seat, gladly relinquishing him to Sheena when she insisted on sitting with her twin and pillowing his head on her lap. Claire felt greatly relieved to see her friend restored, if only temporarily, to a state of near calm and sanity.

The swing doors opened and a white-coated figure emerged from the operating theatre and hurriedly approached the nursing station to speak to Nurse Lewis. Claire started up in alarm. Apparently, Terry needed a blood transfusion.

"Please take mine," she interrupted them eagerly. She knew that her blood group, O Rh Negative, was compatible with all other groups, but Sarah Lewis still refused to take it.

"My dear, you cannot dream of such a thing in your condition," the nurse quietly reproved her. "At any rate, he needs at least three pints; it will have to come from the blood bank."

"Oh, but are you sure there's time? Oh, please, let me give you some of mine." But Sarah Lewis and turned away.

Fernando, who would have given blood himself if his had been compatible with Terry's, watched, puzzled and anxious, as Claire wept in frustration. In an amazingly short time, however, to Claire's relief, the blood was delivered to the hospital entrance and swiftly taken to the operating theatre.

Terry was given a transfusion of three pints of blood and an anti-tetanus shot, and his neck was swabbed and sutured. Back in his room, he lay drifting in a blur of pain between sleeping and waking.

His throbbing wound woke him often that night, and when it did there was another kind of pain: that of seeing Claire and Fernando sitting at his bedside and looking, somehow, so right together. Both, he considered in his fevered state, were privileged to possess that perennially summer look of fair-haired, golden-skinned people who seem to pass through life untouched by the hardships and misfortunes besetting darker mortals, even though, whatever about Fernando, Terry knew in his heart that Claire could never be so described. Once he opened his eyes and saw Fernando gently kissing Claire as she dozed in the crook of his arm, and felt again the shadow of impending loss.

Jane too was beleaguered by visions of loss as she sat waiting for the telephone to ring, and when it finally did, she hurriedly set down the mug of cocoa she was nursing and ran into her surgery.

"Yes, this is Jane," she said breathlessly.

"Jane, my dear, Terry has been found but I'm afraid he has been injured." Antonio broke off at her gasp of dismay then continued strongly, "However, please do not worry. He is receiving medical attention and his condition is satisfactory."

"Are you quite sure he's all right, Antonio?" Oh God, not my other son too, she thought.

"Yes, I'm quite sure. Fernando has spoken to the doctor and received his assurances."

"But what happened?" Jane wished to know.

"Your son was stabbed in the neck but by great good fortune the knife merely grazed a blood vessel."

Stabbed! Jane began to tremble.

"He is at Hospital Belen where you stayed after your accident, Jane," Antonio went on. "Believe me, I will personally ensure that he is given every care and attention needed to

414

restore him to health."

"I do, and thank you, Antonio," Jane told him gratefully, aware that the majority of Spanish doctors went off on holidays for the whole month of August, sometimes without leaving locums to stand in for them. "I am booked to fly out on Sunday but should I come sooner?" she asked anxiously.

"At the moment there is no need," Antonio said. "If there is any change, however, I will inform you at once. You need have no fears about that."

No, she knew that she could rely upon him totally. He was a rock of support.

"I am only too happy to be of assistance, Jane," Antonio was saying. "Oh . . . and I will make sure that your little daughter is also content until you arrive."

"Ruthie is with you?" Jane said faintly. "Oh, I do hope she's not in your way."

"Not at all. It gives me much pleasure to have her in my house. Christina is already her willing slave." Antonio's amused chuckle sounded in Jane's ear. "When I last looked in at them Ruthie and Stella, Fernando's Labrador, were sitting in bed drinking hot chocolate."

Had she heard him correctly? Jane wondered, with an overwrought giggle. But when she put down the phone and realised that Antonio had said nothing at all about Sheena, her amusement quickly faded.

Sheena lay in another room in the hospital, washed and tranquillised, sleeping the sleep of exhaustion. All that night Sarah Lewis sat beside her, witnessing her restless tossings and turnings and hearing her pitiful moans with a troubled heart.

There was a tap at the door and Claire quietly entered. Another troubled child, thought Sarah. How well pregnancy suited the girl, though. Even in her fatigue Claire had a glow about her that was arresting.

"How is Sheena?" Claire stared down at her friend.

"A wee bit restless but she'll be fine." Sarah pulled over a chair. "Sit in," she urged. "Take the weight off your feet."

Claire obeyed but kept her face averted, clearly struggling with tears.

"You are very fond of her, aren't you," Sarah asked gently, "and her twin too?"

Claire nodded dumbly, her tears falling unchecked on to the back of her hand.

There is so much love in the girl, Sarah thought. She remembered the hours Claire had spent with Señora Gonzalez when the woman was dying, never sparing herself although she was falling on her feet. Gonzalez would be the lucky young man if he got her. Aye, but she would be lucky too, Sarah told herself, for clearly the young Spaniard was out of his mind about her.

Sarah felt sudden heartache and her face grew sad, for in her youth she had known a passionate love herself. God forbid anything should happen to this lass's lover, Sarah thought with a shiver, but at least Claire would have his child to console her. She had been left with nothing but her memories.

Claire came back into the room and crossed to sit at Fernando's side. Terry was sleeping more easily and, after an anxious glance at him, she leaned wearily back and let her own lids droop.

Fernando gently put his arm about her and was pleased when she rested her head against his shoulder. She had come through the ordeal well, he thought approvingly, exhibiting courage as well as common sense in the crisis. Claire had been very upset over her friend's brother, but then, Fernando wasn't really surprised, having already seen so much evidence of her soft-hearted concern for others. He glanced across to where Terry lay with closed eyes, his features once more twisted in pain.

He was a rather brash young man but brave, Fernando conceded, and had acted without concern for his own safety. On the other hand, danger clearly excited the young airman.

Fernando was no stranger to danger himself. In his late

teens it was what had drawn him to the air force, but he had grown undeniably soft since his flying days. His great wealth allowed him access to the most rigorous and expensive of sports, which kept his body exercised and supple, but willingness to confront and overcome adversity had lessened. His decision to involve the police rather than attempt to crack Delgado's resistance when he had the man in his power showed this. Now Fernando sheered away from this unpalatable reminder of his own shortcomings and dwelled instead on Claire. She was a loyal and gentle girl, he told himself, and that was the reason he loved her.

Beside him, Claire woke and sat up with a start. She leaned forward and eyed Terry with such a look of concern that Fernando experienced an unpleasant spasm of jealousy.

"He's so pale," she whispered. "But then he has lost so much blood. If we had only found him sooner."

Fernando privately considered that Terry was lucky to be found alive. He squeezed Claire's hand consolingly and at once she turned to him and said earnestly, "I would gladly have given him my blood only Nurse Lewis wouldn't take it."

Fernando was puzzled. "But why? I do not understand."

"She knows I'm expecting a baby."

"*Caramba!*"

The strength of Fernando's reaction was lost on Claire as she recounted her own fears and feelings on Terry's behalf. She had not thought before she spoke, and, even now, she was hardly aware of what she was saying.

Fernando stared at her passionately working mouth and brimming eyes and, his earlier shock subsiding, he was struck by what a divinely beautiful girl she was, so vital and caring. He was filled with a chivalrous longing to take care of her. Her pregnancy startled but did not dismay him, living as he did in a country with a high birth-rate outside of marriage. He imagined it was a youthful mistake, something like the situation he had found himself in while still at university when he had become casually involved with a young student and she had borne his child. He hoped that Claire

417

might turn to him in her need. If he could only inspire in her an emotion that was even half as strong as his love for her, he would be satisfied.

For the next few days Claire was too concerned about Terry and Sheena to be able to concentrate on anything else. She spent all her time at the hospital. Antonio proposed to keep Ruthie with them until Jane arrived at the end of the week.

"I fear Stella is becoming a trifle heavy with so much chocolate," Fernando opined dryly, "but otherwise the love affair still flourishes."

Claire smiled, more than glad that Ruthie was in such good care. Fernando picked her up each day and drove her to the hospital, though she feared she was too distracted by her own worries to be much company. Fernando, however, bore Claire's preoccupation stoically and never referred to what she had told him as they sat by Terry's bedside, although she suspected that it was very much on his mind.

One afternoon Fernando picked up Claire earlier than usual. When he had parked before the hospital and cut the engine, he drew a sharp breath as though about to say something of importance, then dried up again as his courage failed him.

"What is it, Fernando?" Claire asked, resigned to having it out.

"Claire," he said glumly, "the time has come when we must put into words the emotions we feel for each other."

"Yes, perhaps we should talk," Claire agreed.

"You must know I love you," Fernando said without preamble. "What you told me in confidence has made no difference to my feelings for you. I think I loved you from the first moment I saw you in my father's office." He gave a despairing shake of his head and continued almost to himself, "Standing there like some beautiful angel."

The romantic speech was so like what she had come to expect from Fernando that Claire could not help smiling.

He returned the smile doubtfully, uncertain whether it boded him good or ill.

"Can you really mean it when you say my pregnancy makes no difference to you?" Claire asked slowly.

In answer Fernando seized her hand and kissed it.

"But what if I told you I still loved the man," Claire posed.

"And do you?" he asked, with a pained expression in his dark eyes.

"I don't know. Sometimes I think I do and then again I'm not sure." Claire sighed, then bravely met his eyes. "Either way, it's over."

"Forget this man," Fernando commanded. "I will make you happy as you deserve to be happy."

Claire regarded him curiously. "And what about your happiness . . . surely you could not easily give your name to another man's child?"

"*Sí.* If you were that child's mother," Fernando said simply.

Claire was moved by his answer. "Thank you, Fernan," she said, and leaned across to kiss him. His sombre eyes regarded her intensely.

"My mother loved you very much," Fernando's voice trembled with emotion.

Claire glanced away, remembering how desperately Elena had struggled, even on the point of death, to ensure that she and Fernando would marry. She felt, with a terrible impending sense of loss, that if she gave up Fernando she would be giving up Elena too. She felt cast adrift on the flood of her emotion and she turned her head and gazed helplessly into Fernando's dark eyes.

"Please, Fernan," she whispered, her voice catching and breaking. "Please give me a little more time."

Although his physical injuries were more serious than Sheena's, Terry recovered quicker than his twin and was soon able to get out of bed, although it was a while before he felt well enough to go beyond his room.

He did not expect to be discharged until his mother arrived, but his compassionate leave was almost up and he would need to supply a medical certificate to the Air Corps if he was to be away much longer. He glanced in the mirror and carefully eased aside the neck bandage to inspect his wound, wishing he knew when the doctor would pay him a visit. Usually stitches were removed after five days, Terry mused, but that wasn't until next day. He tied the belt on his dressing gown and went wandering down the corridor in search of a nurse.

"*Sí.* The doctor will be making his rounds tomorrow," the pretty olive-skinned nurse assured him warmly. All the nurses vied with each other in their efforts to look after the handsome young Irishman. They had been warned, besides, to give every care and co-operation to the good friends of Señor Gonzalez.

"Any chance of seeing him today?" Terry smiled, exerting his charm. "It's rather urgent."

"Certainly." She returned his smile and lifted the phone. She was not much older than Terry and one of his most ardent admirers. "The doctor is on his way," she told him a moment later. Terry nodded his thanks and wandered over to look at a framed print of the entrance to the Nerja caves.

The doctor arrived within minutes, his stethoscope swinging about his neck. He walked back with Terry to his room, where he gave him a quick examination and pronounced his wound to be healing satisfactorily.

"You'll need to take things easy for a couple of weeks," he advised. "The stitches can come out tomorrow, but you are not fit enough to resume flying yet. I will give you a certificate to cover you with your commanding officer."

"Thanks." Terry grinned in relief. Actually, he didn't feel all that great. His body felt as if it had been used as a punch bag and then deprived of its stuffing. He suddenly felt weak and sat down on the side of the bed after the doctor had gone and was just about to collapse back under the covers when there was a tap on the door. Terry's spirits lifted as

Claire came in.

He was relieved to see that for once she was without her faithful shadow. While he was willing to concede that old San Fernando wasn't such a bad guy in the light of all the Spaniard had done to find Sheena, as well as practically saving his own life, a little of him went a long way. He grinned and patted a space beside him on the bed.

"Come and sit down."

Claire smiled and obeyed.

"I'm getting out in another few days," he told her.

"What about Sheena?"

"We won't know until Mum gets here."

"I looked in on her just now," Claire said, "but Nurse Lewis was taking her temperature and said to drop back in a few minutes. Sheena seems a bit better," she went on doubtfully, "but I think she's still terrified of Miguel finding her."

"He won't bother her any more," Terry said at last. "Or anyone else for that matter."

Claire asked slowly, "What did happen that night, Terry?"

Terry looked away. "He pulled a knife," he said soberly. "He was saying terrible things about Shee and I belted him and then suddenly he was slashing away. We struggled and he slipped and toppled into the gorge."

Claire shuddered. "It was very deep, wasn't it? Eighty or ninety metres."

"Hope it broke his bloody neck," Terry said fiercely. "The bloody bastard deserved a lot worse."

Claire was silent, oppressed by the memory of Sheena, whimpering and demoralised, and was afraid to think what dreadful things had been done to her. She sat with mouth trembling.

Terry impulsively put his arms about her. "Oh Claire, thank God we found her," he said, his voice shaking with emotion. "Only think if we hadn't come when we did."

Claire began to cry. She lay against his chest and sobbed and he put his hand in her silky hair that he remembered so well and still dreamed about at night, and at the sweet touch of her, his body melted and became weak with desire. As she turned in his arms and looked up at him, her face desolate and streaked with tears, he was carried away by his fierce longing for her and, in desperation, pressed his mouth on hers.

For one long moment they clung together, flesh and souls in sweet accord, and his arousal was quick and strong and satisfying. Then she pulled back and stared at him, almost in horror.

"No, Terry, no!"

He stared bewildered as she ran out of the room, leaving the door swinging open behind her. He felt his excitement die and his spirit become leaden with despair.

Claire went fleeing down the corridor anxious to put distance between herself and Terry. The range of emotions fired by his touch left her dizzy and trembling, but she told herself that such physical feelings had led her astray in the past and were not to be relied upon. She found sanctuary in Sheena's room.

Sheena lay quite still beneath the sheet. She looked scrubbed clean, but there was a despairing look in her normally merry brown eyes. Claire forgot her own troubles in a rush of anger and pity. Sheena had always been so gay and carefree that this total eclipse of her bright spirit was shocking.

Claire sat on the bed and gently held Sheena's hand. It lay hot and inert between both of hers. "Are you feeling any better?" she asked shyly.

Sheena shook her head.

"Oh, but you will," Claire said, anxious to believe it. "Every day it will get easier." Sheena's eyes brimmed and she turned her head away on the pillow.

"As soon as you get back home you'll forget all this and start again," Claire told her. "There's lots of things to look forward to once college begins in October."

Sheena's mouth wobbled. "I can't bear the thought of going back and facing everyone."

Claire looked at her in compassion.

"I feel it's written all over me . . . you know . . . what they . . ." She began to cry brokenly. "I feel dirty . . . used."

"With time that will lessen," Claire said in distress. "You have to believe it."

Sheena sat up in the bed with a wild look in her eyes. "For God's sake, Claire, what do you know about any of it?" she cried. "You were always such a model girl. You haven't got the first clue about life."

Claire sat with her head bowed. Oh, but I do, I do, she thought. What if I were to tell you?

Ruthie stuffed her washbag on top of her clothes and zipped the bag shut, glad to be going home to the apartment. Though she had liked living in the big house with the fountain in the garden and the wonderful Stella to play with, she was lonely for Sheena and Claire and excited at the thought of driving to the airport in the shiny Mercedes to meet her mother.

Ruthie picked up the bag by its strap and ran down the wide staircase to where Fernando awaited her in the front hall.

"You are all packed?" he asked with a smile. He had grown fond of the little girl in the week she had stayed with them. With her shining blonde mane of hair and her wide-eyed innocent look, she reminded him of Claire.

"*Sí*," Ruthie responded, trotting out the phrase she had been practising all morning. "*Me ha dado una visita muy agradable.*" She was delighted at Fernando's exaggerated amazement.

"*Muy bien,*" he praised and held out his hand. "Come my little one, let us say farewell to Stella."

Ruthie put her hand trustingly in his and Fernando led her out to the garden. Today he was even smarter than usual, dressed in a pale grey suit which hung well on his graceful figure. And, as usual when meeting Claire, he had gone through several changes of shirts and ties before finding the combination which satisfied him. He was watching Ruthie feeding his Labrador a square of chocolate when his father came out of the house and stood on the patio, looking down at them.

Antonio, like his son, wore a light coloured mohair suit and a red carnation splashed colour in his buttonhole. He strolled across the lawn to join them and stood smiling at Ruthie's antics.

"*La hermanita* will be greatly missed," he said softly.

Fernando nodded. It was exactly what he had been thinking. All week their house had been undeniably more cheerful than since his mother's death.

"So we are on our way to the airport," Antonio said cheerfully.

"We?" Fernando enquired.

Antonio laughed boyishly. "I have decided to come with you. I feel it is fitting that we go as a family to welcome Señora McArdle."

Fernando looked at his father more closely and noticed his freshly barbered chin and the flower in his lapel. Could it be that his father's interest in *la médica irlandesa* was other than strictly business? he wondered in amazment.

Jane's tense expression lightened at the sight of the young people waiting for her as she came off the flight, and became positively ecstatic when her gaze moved on to take in Antonio, hovering awkwardly in the rear. She warmly embraced the girls and put out her hand to Fernando.

"How good it is to be back," she said, looking as if she might embrace him too. "Thank you for finding Sheena and taking such good care of my family."

Fernando bowed over her hand, embarrassed by her gratitude. "*De nada, Señora.* It was a pleasure."

Jane looked beyond him to his father and met Antonio's eyes. "You have no idea what it means to me to see you here," she told him softly. He returned her gaze with a look so charged with feeling that Jane felt like a young girl again. 'He cares for me,' her heart suddenly sang within her. 'Ah, but how he cares for me!'

Ruthie cuddled next to Jane in the back of the car, inhaling her mother's scent and possessively fingering her bracelets. She couldn't get close enough and was clingy as a monkey. Jane laughingly indulged her, while eyeing the back of Antonio's head, her ears finely tuned to catch the murmured conversation he was sharing with his son.

Claire sat at Jane's other side, making no claims on her. She had noticed Fernando's keen glance as mother and daughter had walked out of the arrivals area, closely linked. Clearly, he understood that while Claire might be like another daughter to Jane, in this instance, she must take second place to Ruthie. Claire was struck anew by how much she had to lose if she rejected him. Remembering the blaze of love in his eyes when he came to collect her at the apartment, she wondered how long it would be before he insisted on receiving an answer to his proposal.

At the hospital Antonio got out of the car and helped Jane alight, holding her hand a moment in farewell. "*Hasta luego,*" he smiled, and kept his eyes on her as she turned away with a little wave and entered the building.

The significance of the little scene was not lost on his son. So I was right, Fernando thought, and felt a pang of sorrowing regret for his mother's memory.

Sarah Lewis was waiting for them in the reception area to bring them along to Sheena's room. Terry was already there, chatting with his twin, and at the sight of his mother he slid off the bed and gave her a hug. Sheena watched them apathetically.

"Darling," Jane cried, secretly shocked at the stark misery she saw on her daughter's face. She hurried close to the bed and enfolded Sheena in her arms.

"Mummy, Mummy," Sheena's indifference suddenly melted and she clung fiercely to her mother, breaking down in a storm of tears.

When she was calmer Jane helped her sit back against the

pillows and, still holding her hand, suggested, "Terry, why don't you and Claire bring Ruthie out to the garden. You haven't seen it yet, have you, darling?"

"But Mummy I want to stay with you," she protested, as if afraid that Jane might vanish if she took her eyes off of her.

"Just for a few minutes while I chat with Sheena," Jane bargained. "There's a good girl. Then I want to hear all about Stella."

When they were gone Jane turned back to Sheena and met her glance with a reassuring smile. "Ruthie has been staying with Fernando and Antonio for the past few days and, from everything I've heard, been thoroughly spoiled."

Sheena's expression lightened, but almost at once the old brooding, unhappy look was back. Jane's heart sank. Obviously something very bad had happened. She ached to know so that she might begin to try and put it right, but wisely deciding to wait until Sheena was ready to confide in her, talked of every subject other than what was uppermost in their minds.

In the end, a light-hearted remark was the chink in the dam which eventually released all the horrors burdening Sheena's soul.

"Terry's friend Pete keeps ringing to enquire after you," Jane was saying. "I wouldn't be surprised if he has a path beaten to the door when you come back." She grinned at Sheena and was shocked to see her agonised expression.

"No, he won't, Mummy," Sheena choked. "Nobody will. Not when they know . . ."

"Know what?" Jane asked gently. She saw the shame and self-revulsion on Sheena's tear-stained face and thought that her heart might break for her. By the time Terry and the girls came in from the garden Jane knew the whole degrading story. She knew too that she would not rest until her daughter had been avenged.

That night Claire and Jane stayed up late. Long after Ruthie had settled down and gone to sleep, they were still on the balcony with the candles alight to discourage the mosquitoes.

Claire talked about all that had happened since they had first arrived in Spain, and Jane, conscious of what Sarah Lewis had revealed to her, was as patient as she had been with her own daughter and waited for Claire to confide in her. Finally, Jane gently steered the conversation to the Gonzalez family, deliberately revealing her involvement with Antonio years before

"And there's something else," Jane went on. "When I came to leave hospital after all those weeks there recovering from my accident, I found that Señor Gonzalez had taken care of my hospital bill. And, do you know, Claire, I'm convinced he intends doing the same for the twins."

"Gosh!" Claire said startled. "How generous!"

"Absolutely!" Jane agreed. "And he has been so kind keeping Ruthie at his house all this time."

Claire observed the dreamy little smile hovering about Jane's lips and wondered could she still be in love with Antonio. She couldn't help feeling shocked. Elena had been dead such a short time.

Jane said ruefully, "This seems to be the night for confidences, doesn't it? But, of course, I didn't know in the beginning that Antonio was married or that his wife was an invalid. When I did, it certainly helped to explain much of the past." She met Claire's eyes honestly. "Just why he had an affair with me when it's clear he loved her so."

Claire watched Ruthie's cat licking its paw and decided none of it was really so bad. She could not get over the sparkle and warmth in Jane's manner whenever she mentioned Antonio.

Jane caught her eye and laughed. "Oh now, I know what you're thinking, Claire. Anyone past forty is past everything else too! No, don't deny it. I would have felt the same at your age."

"I wasn't thinking that," Claire protested, but Jane only laughed the more.

Claire began to speak of her great affection for Elena and

to describe, in searing detail, the last distressing weeks of the Spanish woman's illness. Jane listened without interruption.

"She was so brave," Claire concluded with a tremor in her voice. "In a way she reminded me of you."

"Of me?" Jane was startled.

"For one thing she was so courageous . . . and for another she seemed to really understand me and think well of me, like you've always done."

"But why wouldn't I think well of you, Claire dear?"

Claire coloured. "Well . . . you know . . . after what happened years ago. Anyone else would have been angry, but you were always so kind."

Jane had a sudden disturbing memory of burning with an irrational anger and resentment towards the child her husband had wronged. She had done everything in her power since then to make it up to the girl.

"You were only a child, Claire. You weren't to blame." She squeezed her arm gently. "More sinned against than sinning."

Claire had an overwhelming urge to tell her about the baby, but still she hesitated, afraid that Jane might imagine she had allowed it happen in order to trap Terry into marrying her. She had just steeled herself to the point of confession when Jane suddenly yawned hugely and jumped to her feet. And the moment was lost.

Two days after Jane's arrival in Spain Terry was discharged from hospital. His wound was healing well and there was no reason for him to remain there any longer. He would be convalescent for almost a fortnight before flying back to rejoin his squadron.

Jane had a chat with Sarah Lewis and arranged for Sheena to be kept in for another couple of weeks. She felt that her daughter was not yet ready to resume life in the outside world and, besides, she wanted certain tests run on her. Jane confided the whole sad and sordid story to Sarah.

"Oh the poor lass," Sarah kept saying and shaking her

head sorrowfully. "Don't worry, doctor. I'll see to it that the poor child isn't troubled any more than is absolutely necessary. She has been through enough already. And so too has her twin, poor lad."

Uppermost in Jane's mind was the fear that Sheena might have contracted AIDS from the men who had abused her, and although Sheena hadn't actually put it into words herself, Jane knew that this was her daughter's greatest fear too.

Claire was glad of Jane's presence in the apartment when Terry was discharged from hospital. She both longed for and feared the thought of being alone with him, knowing she could not hold out against him if he wanted her.

On his first night in the apartment the mere thought of him, only a few yards away in the dark, made her body tremble, but she reminded herself, as she had so many times before, that their physical union would solve nothing. Her heart was pierced by the humiliating memory of Terry being unable to make love to her on the night they had split up. She knew she would never forget it or ever leave herself open to a repetition of that unhappy incident.

Terry had taken over Ruthie's bedroom and Ruthie happily moved in with Claire, an arrangement which solved the problem of space and ruled out any chance of a surprise nocturnal visit. Not that Terry showed signs of wanting one. Claire saw little of him that first week. Each day he visited his twin at a time carefully chosen not to coincide with her own visit to Sheena and, in the evenings, played pool with some English friends he had made in the local bars.

Claire invariably lay awake waiting for the sound of his return. She would lie in the suffocating darkness, listening to him moving softly about the outer room, getting mineral water from the fridge and having a snack, before retiring for the night. Then she would hear him stripping off his clothes and the tell-tale creak of the bedsprings as he lowered himself on to the mattress. Remembering the nights they had loved and lain together, her throat would grow dry and her heart would race.

It was a great relief to Claire that she had put on so little weight in the first months of her pregnancy. None but the most discerning eye could possibly have noticed the changes in her slim figure. She had an almost paranoid fear of Terry's finding out and formed a vague plan of staying on in Spain after the rest of the McArdles had returned to Ireland. She would need Jane's permission to live at the apartment, for she had no means of supporting herself and knew that any money she might get from her father, if she decided to ask him for an allowance, would be very small.

One afternoon, when Fernando had dropped Claire back to the apartment after visiting Sheena, Jane gave her the opening she was seeking.

"I suppose now that the summer holidays are almost over you'll be looking forward to college," Jane said, as they sat together on the balcony.

"As a matter of fact . . ." Claire began, watching Jane's face, "I'm thinking of taking a year out and staying on in Spain to learn the language. I wondered if I might possibly stay here in the apartment."

"I don't see why not," Jane said slowly, "although surely you would need to have given notice to the college a lot earlier?"

Claire said nothing.

"Has this decision anything to do with Fernando," Jane smiled. "I can't help noticing how very fond of you he is."

Claire found it difficult to understand how Jane could think such a thing when she had once revealed to her how much she loved Terry. Still, it was in her interests to convince Jane that it was because of Fernando she wished to stay in Spain, so she forced a smile and said, "And I'm fond of him too. Maybe not quite as much, but it might grow deeper and this is one way of finding out."

Claire was still holding off giving Fernando her answer. She was truly fond of him and considered him a real friend, but whether he would ever become her lover she could not

430

decide.

"He's a very nice young man and of good family," Jane said warmly. "But you are a very bright girl, Claire, and you have a great future ahead of you if you stick to your studies. This isn't something you should decide in a hurry."

Claire was pierced afresh by the precariousness of her position and wondered if she should be more honest with Jane. But what if she were angry and changed her mind about letting her stay in the apartment? Despite all Jane's past assurances of affection, it was such a big thing she was asking and already she owed Jane so much. Oh, but how would she ever manage to get through the next few months without her help? She had no one else to turn to.

As the silence lengthened Jane eyed her thoughtfully. "Claire, my dear, if there's something bothering you, I do hope you'll consider sharing it with me."

Claire started hotly to deny it, but there was something in the other woman's tone which seemed to hint that she already had an inkling of the truth, and meeting Jane's look of compassion Claire suddenly found herself blurting it all out. She so desperately needed someone to confide in. The words tumbled over each other and she felt such an easing of tension afterwards that she grew almost dizzy with relief.

"Have you told Terry?" Jane asked briskly.

"No," Claire shook her head. "I can't."

"But why ever not?" Jane stared at her in surprise. Surely she couldn't be contemplating marriage to Fernando while bearing Terry's child? Or worse, have slept with both young men and didn't know whose baby she was carrying?

"You don't understand," Claire said desperately. "He would only feel a sense of obligation . . . like he felt when he thought Gráinne was pregnant. I would rather die than discover he felt like that about me."

Jane was taken aback by the vehemence of her feeling.

"You don't think less of me, do you?" Claire asked, her expression agonised. "Oh say that you don't. I would feel that my last ally was gone if you, of all people, were angry or disgusted with me."

Jane put her arms about her. "My poor silly child," she said warmly, "you can have no idea of the immense joy you have given me. I love you both and to know you are expecting Terry's baby, conceived out of your great love for each other, makes me very happy."

Claire blinked, as tears scalded her eyes.

Jane hugged her. "My dear Claire, this isn't something you can possibly do all by yourself. It's only right you should tell Terry."

"I can't. I just can't," Claire repeated miserably. "Please, please try to understand."

"Believe me I'm trying," Jane assured her, "but I feel you're making a mistake. I think you should give Terry the chance to prove how responsible he can be."

"No!" Claire's response was swift and strong. "Please, promise me you will never tell him."

From Claire, Jane knew how Terry and Delgado had fought it out on the cliffs at Ronda, and she was consumed by her need to find out if the man was alive or dead. Until they knew for sure there was always the danger he might reappear on the scene.

When she at last confided her worry to Antonio, he revealed that the police had informed him that Delgado had been discovered two days after the fight with his back broken at the bottom of the gorge. Rumour had it he'd fallen off the Puente Nuevo following a drunken brawl. Amazingly, he was still alive, despite the extent and severity of his injuries. When Antonio told her that the Spanish police readily agreed to press charges, Jane felt quiet satisfaction that the man would be brought to trial. To the other counts against him would now be added the charges of abduction, rape and attempted murder. She was only surprised that Antonio had kept the information from her.

"I intended telling you soon, Jane," Antonio said with an

apologetic shrug.

There was a proviso. Before the charges could be made to stick, Sheena would have to formally identify Delgado to the police.

"I am sorry that your daughter must be put through this ordeal," Antonio told Jane regretfully, as they came away from the police station. "But I will be happy to drive you to the hospital near Marbella, where he is being confined, so that she may identify him."

Jane sighed. She supposed she should have realised that it wouldn't be simple. Nothing ever was. Should she put Sheena through this extra stress? she wondered, unhappily reminded of the years of Ruthie's trauma.

"Why don't you let Sheena make the decision for herself," Antonio suggested, his eyes full of concern for Jane's dilemma. "The act of denouncing this man might even be therapeutic and help speed up the healing process." Jane had told him how slowly the girl was recovering and he suspected that a feeling of self-hatred was at the root of it. Only by directing her anger towards the true author of her troubles, Antonio believed, could she be healed.

Jane agreed. At the clinic, she had seen women who had been raped, or battered by their partners, and knew only too well that Sheena was exhibiting the classic symptoms of listlessness and depression, as well as a general feeling of worthlessness.

While she was willing to try anything that might help Sheena to recover from her ordeal, she was firmly of the opinion that Sheena would not even begin to get better until she was back home again. Jane had telephoned one of the top women psychiatrists specialising in treating rape survivors. "Get her home and into therapy as soon as you can," she advised.

In the meantime Jane decided to do as Antonio suggested, although she did not for a minute think that Sheena would be willing to go along with the idea. When she tentatively broached the subject, she found to her relief and surprise that her daughter actually seemed to welcome the chance to confront her attacker.

"Please let me go, Mummy," Sheena pleaded. "I'm not afraid."

"Are you quite sure, darling?" Jane looked anxiously into her eyes.

"Yes," Sheena said, meeting her gaze steadily. "I'm quite sure."

On the appointed day Jane and Antonio drove to the hospital to pick up Sheena. So early in the morning there was only the hospital porter in the foyer and a maid with her hair in a kerchief washing out the front step. After a quick glance at Antonio and Jane, the porter waved them on and went back to his newspaper.

When Jane popped her head round the door of Sheena's room, she found her sitting in a chair, already dressed and ready for the journey. Nurse Lewis, who was at the handbasin arranging Sheena's washcloth and soap, greeted Jane warmly.

"All set, darling?" Jane hugged her daughter. "Sure you still want to go ahead with it?"

Sheena nodded. "Quite sure, Mummy. Please don't fuss." She was subdued but determined.

Jane said no more.

Sheena was quiet and withdrawn on the journey and sat slumped in the back of the Mercedes. Whenever Jane anxiously turned round to speak to her, she had to call her daughter to attention before she answered. Antonio gave all his concentration to his driving, and after a time, Jane relapsed into silence herself.

The nearer they got to Marbella the more nervous Jane became. All too soon it seemed they were parking in the hospital grounds.

Jane leaned into the back and patted Sheena's knee. "This is it, darling." She got out of the car and waited while Antonio went round to open the rear door. He extended his hand to Sheena.

"*Valentía*," he murmured. After a moment, Sheena accepted his hand and climbed out.

She stood looking about her in a slightly dazed fashion then, with a grim set to her jaw, walked quickly ahead of them as if anxious to get the whole thing over.

A doctor, accompanied by two police officials and a hospital orderly, brought them to the room where Miguel lay.

When Sheena hung back at the door, Jane glanced at her pale face and moved nearer. After a moment Sheena gathered herself together and, straightening her shoulders, stepped into the room. With an anxious look at Antonio, Jane followed.

Miguel lay encased from neck to toe in a plaster cast, seeming already to have passed into a kind of limbo between life and death. As Sheena stepped close to the bed his lids lifted and recognition flared in the pale eyes before the eyelids dropped over them again. At the sight of those flat eyes regarding her, Sheena took an involuntary step backwards. She recovered herself and said in a clear, hard voice, "This is the man who abducted me."

Within seconds they were walking out of the room and back down the corridor. When they were almost at the hospital entrance Sheena suddenly sagged. Jane swiftly reached out her arms to hold her daughter close and saw that she was weeping, her face contorted in silent agony.

There was less than a week left before Terry flew back to join his squadron. The situation between them was much as it had been since he rejoined them in the apartment. Terry spent most of the day in the town with his new friends and came back late at night when they were all in bed. Fernando still called to the apartment each day to bring Claire to visit Sheena at the hospital but had so far exercised great restraint on the subject of their marriage. He was usually quiet on these journeys and had fallen into the habit of sighing a lot.

Having made the supreme effort and confronted her

attacker, Sheena seemed to relapse into herself. True, for a day or two after the trip to Marbella there was a slight improvement in her spirits, so her therapist told Jane. However, following on that she had begun to have nightmares again and spoke of voices continually exhorting her to harm herself. Jane was more than ever convinced that she must get Sheena home without delay. When Claire worriedly reported this to Fernando on their way to the hospital next day, he nodded soberly.

"I am very sorry to hear it," he said, and fell back to sighing again. They drove the rest of the way in silence.

"I will call back for you in one hour," Fernando told her mournfully at the hospital entrance.

"You don't have to," Claire protested. "Really! I can walk."

"I will be here," Fernando said bleakly, and only gave her the briefest of nods when she waved and turned away. How serious he has become, she thought, becoming serious herself in turn. Today she had intended breaking the news to Sheena that she would not be going back home with her. Now she wondered if this was wise. Claire sighed and bit her lip, wishing she knew what to do.

Sheena was stretched out in a secluded part of the hospital garden and she sat up as Claire crossed the grass. She was dressed in shorts and bikini top and her skin was turning brown again from hours of sunning, surely a hopeful sign that she was on the mend. Claire wished she could believe it.

"I've been longing for you to come," Sheena confessed, slipping her arm through Claire's. Together, they strolled in the shade of the bougainvillaea tree.

As she listened to her friend's feverish chatter Claire was glad to see that Sheena could at least speak again.

"It will be good to get away from Spain," Sheena sighed. "I never thought I'd be glad to leave the sun, but now I feel as though I can't get home quick enough." She did not mention all the tests she had been given, but Claire knew about them from Jane. They would have the results of most of them in another few days, Jane had said, but it would be at least six months before they would know the result of her AIDS test. Hopefully, Sheena would then get the all clear.

"What about you, Claire?" Sheena said when Claire was silent. "Will you be sorry to leave Spain?"

"Sheena, let's sit down a minute," Claire suggested, leading the way to the stone bench. Then she said in a rush, "Actually, I'm not going back to college. I've decided to stay on in Spain."

Sheena stared and for the first time a spark of animation showed in her gaze. "But why, Claire? What will you do?"

"Jane has agreed to let me stay at the apartment," Claire told her. "I'm going to try for a year's leave of absence from college." She shrugged. "If I don't get it . . . well, I'm staying anyway."

"But you're brilliant at your work," Sheena protested. "What a terrible waste of your year at college." She paused and said doubtfully, "Although if you really hate it, I suppose there's no point in staying on."

Hate it! One of the saddest aspects of her pregnancy was the interruption of her studies.

"It doesn't have to be a wasted year," she said, hating the need for secrecy, but how could she confide in one twin and not the other. "I'll learn Spanish. I can always take it as another subject for my BA."

Sheena said wistfully, "You make me feel such a failure."

Claire shook her head, distressed. "Don't say that. I'm just a slogger, Sheena. If you had put even a tenth of the effort into schoolwork that you put into your painting you would have passed me out years ago."

"I never had the slightest interest in studying," Sheena admitted. "Remember how I was always copying your homework?" She gave the ghost of a giggle. "You used look so anguished . . . too nice to tell me to feck off."

Claire felt surprise that she had been so transparent.

"Have you thought how you'll live?"

"Waitressing, giving English lessons. I don't know. I haven't really worked it out. I only know I'm not going back." She was surprised at how determined she felt.

Sheena digested this for a moment. "What will your mother say?"

Annette wouldn't care, Claire thought. She would be just as glad to be saved the trouble and expense. Despite the three letters and two postcards she had sent her mother, she had received only one communication from her in all the time she was in Spain. Claire had been amazed at the tone of her letter, full of acrimony and self-pity and vilifying Jane for asking Teresa Murray instead of herself to accompany them to Spain. As regards her father Claire felt great regret. He would be disappointed and might even raise objections to her opting out of college.

"Fernando must be thrilled." Sheena's face clouded. "Once I thought maybe Alejandro and I . . ." She swallowed and made an effort to smile. "You and Fernando," she said. "Wow! I suppose I knew all along. It's obvious he's crazy about you."

That same afternoon Terry swam out to sea in a hard overarm crawl. The cold green water was refreshing and the exercise welcome after weeks of inactivity. By the time he swam back to the shore and touched bottom, every muscle ached and the newly healed wound in his neck was throbbing.

He limped up the beach and rubbed himself dry, then zipped on his shorts and climbed the steps to the road. He went into a café overlooking the sea and ordered coffee and a ham roll. Terry stood at the counter enjoying the snack, then paid the barman and set off briskly to the hospital.

Every afternoon Terry visited Sheena for an hour or two, striving to make the most of his last few days in Spain, and sometimes again in the evening. He felt very protective towards Sheena and was just as worried as his mother about her hearing voices. There had been a guy from his unit who went off his head that way. Terry wondered if his twin would talk about it to him, but so far she had never said a word and he felt reluctant to be the one to bring it up. But again like

Jane, he was prepared to do anything that might help her. For the first time ever, he and Sheena had begun to speak of their childhood and, with this openness between them, were discovering a new delight in each other. Only once did they touch on the family tragedy that had shadowed all their lives, and from the little Sheena revealed about that troubled time, it was clear she was in ignorance of the true state of affairs. When she sighed and said, "Wasn't Daddy wonderful? If only he hadn't died," Terry had not disillusioned her. Let her keep her unsullied memories, he thought.

He strolled through the hospital garden and was glad to find Sheena stretched in the sun. "You'll soon be the colour of mahogany," he joked, bending to kiss her. Although never physically demonstrative towards his twin, of late Terry was making a big effort to be affectionate. She was so touchingly vulnerable since her ordeal that he felt she couldn't get enough reassurance that she was loved.

Sheena acknowledged his remark with an unhappy smile. Her tan was another of the things she had lost pleasure and confidence in. Now she loved the sun only for the total relaxation she experienced when exposed to its healing rays.

"You've just missed Claire," she said, changing the subject. "She was here until a few minutes ago. Fernando was picking her up."

"Oh yeah." Terry affected indifference. Sheena often wondered what had gone wrong between her twin and Claire. They had seemed so mad about each other.

"Did she tell you that she's not going back home?" Sheena could not hide her amazement. "She's opting out of college and staying on in Spain. Fancy! Brainy old Claire. Who would ever have imagined it?"

Terry frowned. "Claire never tells me anything," he said gruffly. "She hardly speaks to me any more."

Sheena gazed at him. "Do you still care for her?" she asked curiously.

Terry stood up abruptly and walked a little way up the path, without answering. He was stunned by what his twin

439

had told him. Claire staying on in Spain! It seemed to confirm all his fears that she had fallen for the Spaniard.

When Claire had come hurrying out of the hospital she had almost bumped into Terry. She had seen him coming in the distance, striding towards her on the opposite side of the street, and quickly climbed into the car beside Fernando.

Fernando was silent on the drive back to the apartment, but Claire guessed what was on his mind. As soon as he had parked the car and switched off the ignition, he laid his hand on her arm and said with quiet intensity.

"*El amor de mi vida*, I can wait no longer. You must give me your answer now."

Claire looked shyly down at Fernando's strong wrist and finely tapered fingers. Now that the time had come she felt breathless and confused and not at all immune to the magnificence of the man.

"You must know that I'm very fond of you," she began. "You have been kind beyond anything I ever expected. I honestly believe if we married you would do everything to make me happy, and it's much more than I deserve."

She saw his face lighten at her words and felt happy for him because in that instant she had decided to marry him. All too clearly Claire saw that she and Terry had lost their chance of happiness. Even if she were capable of it there was no way Terry could ever put the past behind them. He had clearly demonstrated that what had happened with Eddie would always overshadow their lives. But with Fernando she could begin again. He would love her unconditionally and provide for her child. Claire gave a shaky laugh, overcome by the ease of it.

"And I will do all I can to make you happy as you deserve," she continued warmly. But even as she made this promise Claire suddenly felt the most extraordinary fluttering sensation in the pit of her stomach, as though her insides had been brushed by gossamer wings. She sat petrified, waiting to see if it would happen again, and when it did, knew with dizzying certainty that her baby had moved.

The change in Claire was dramatic. Her expression became ecstatic and she felt such a rush of overwhelming love for the child that she could have both wept and shouted aloud for joy. It was like nothing in her experience, this first indication of life, and it swiftly brought her to the realisation that whatever she might have believed previously, she could not now give herself to anyone, if not the father of her child.

With a poignant little twist of her thoughts she remembered "Song of Songs". She had not thought of it in a long while. How did it go?

Love no flood can quench, no torrents drown.

In her thoughts she unconsciously echoed the Spaniard's words: love of my life. And if Terry never came back to her, Claire bravely faced the prospect, then she would live out her days lonely and alone, rather than ever settle for less than the best.

Fernando was regarding her with jutting lip and frowning countenance. She saw that he was puzzled and wounded by her complete forgetfulness of him and, contritely, attempted to explain her quixotic change of feelings.

"I felt my child move inside me for the first time," Claire explained. "It made me realise that I'm not free to love you." She willed him to understand the enormity of what had happened and saw by his expression that he did, indeed, have some inkling of what it meant to her. As if in confirmation the child stirred again and Claire felt the same thrill of recognition.

"How will you manage?" His dark eyes watched her soberly. "You cannot survive without someone to take care of you."

Claire's face shadowed, reminded of her predicament.

Fernando said slowly: "I think you must still love the father of your child." And when Claire nodded, a sigh escaped him. "Ayee! I knew it!"

She watched him, helpless in the face of his despair.

"And the man," Fernando went on heavily. "Your friend's brother. I think I have known it all along."

So he'd noticed some tiny spark between Terry and herself. Despite her hopelessness, Claire was cheered to think that Terry might still retain some slight feeling for her.

"What good fortune he has," Fernando pronounced sadly, and she was stricken by the unhappiness she saw in his melancholy gaze.

Claire wearily entered the apartment and wandered on to the balcony where Jane sat relaxing in the sun, sipping wine.

"Join me in a glass," Jane suggested, and got up to fetch the bottle from the fridge. She was wearing a low-cut sun top and her skin was glowing from the sun.

Claire listlessly accepted a glass and sank down opposite her. Her head was aching and she felt inexpressibly sad. She had burned her boats and was now totally on her own. She felt like weeping. To have turned down a man like Fernando, who not only loved her but was prepared to accept her baby too, had not been easy and a fierce reaction had already set in.

"No harm in a little wine now and then," Jane said, imagining that Claire was concerned about the possible effects of alcohol on the baby. "You look tired, my dear. It will do you good."

Claire took a sip. The wine felt pleasant on her throat.

"Ruthie has gone off to play with Adela and won't be back till evening," Jane told her, adding with a grin, "so you can see I'm taking full advantage of her absence."

Claire nodded, aware how clingy the little girl had been since Jane's arrival. Only now was she beginning to relax guard on her mother. With a sigh, Claire laid back her head and closed her eyes.

Jane watched her face for a moment, then said impulsively, "Claire, my dear, won't you tell Terry about the baby. I understand you reservations but in the months ahead you are going to need all the love and support you can get."

Claire had no doubt in her mind that the future would be as lonely and tough as Jane suggested and even wondered if she could bear it without solace or support.

"If you are worried about what your parents may say when we go back, you really don't have to go on living at home," Jane hurried on, as though by sheer dint of words she could remove Claire's objections. "We'd love you to make your home with us – you have always been like one of the family and now with the baby coming it seems only right and fitting that we all be together. So long as your pregnancy is without complications, there's really no reason why you shouldn't continue in college until the spring. Why throw away a precious year of study without need?"

Why indeed? Claire ached with the effort of keeping still when she wanted so much to turn to Jane and fall weakly upon her neck in gratitude. Oh, if only she could do as she suggested, she thought. But it would be tantamount to forcing Terry to marry her. And even if he didn't feel so obliged, her presence in his home would be a constant reminder. He would only grow to hate her.

Jane watched her for a moment then added with sweet persuasiveness, "And there's another thing, Claire. I wonder do you realise just how much we're going to need you when poor Sheena comes back home. You and she have always been such friends and, without a doubt, she's going to need every bit of love and understanding we can show her."

This argument, above all others, would have swept away the last of Claire's resistance if it weren't for her deep-seated insecurity regarding Terry. She dumbly shook her head, and Jane made no further attempt to persuade her.

The sun-shade was angled between the chairs and the sky, blocking the fierce afternoon sun. The transistor radio, with its volume turned low, was on the table along with the empty wineglasses. Ruthie's cat stretched belly to the sky, occasionally rearing up to swipe a lazy paw at a darting butterfly. Jane had gone to lie down and Claire was drowsily thinking of following her example when the door of the apartment snapped open and quick footsteps passed through the lounge. Startled, she looked up to see Terry towering above her.

"What's this crap about you staying on in Spain?" he demanded. "Sheena just told me. I thought she was making it up."

As Claire drew breath to speak, he burst out again. "It's because of him, isn't it?" Bitterness salted his voice. "San Fernando of the Gonzalez millions."

It hurt that he should think of her as mercenary.

"Why else would you want to stay on in Spain only to marry him?" His voice was shaking with a mixture of doubt and pain.

Let him believe it, Claire thought wearily, trying to control the quaver in her own voice as she said, "I just don't want to go back to college, that's all. I'm going to learn Spanish and let the future take care of itself."

"The future as Señora Fernando Gonzalez," Terry said savagely. "I never thought money meant all that much to you, Claire." He turned sharply away. "Shows how wrong you can be about someone." The door of his bedroom slammed.

Claire stared down at the distant beach through a blur of tears. Nothing was changed, she reminded herself in desolation. Jane had said she was more sinned against than sinning, but Terry did not regard it so leniently. He had left her in no doubt of his feelings. Sick and perverted, he'd said. The words burned in Claire's brain. No matter how she tried to convince herself otherwise, she knew that some day he would once more fling them in her face. Out of her great love for him and the memory of the happy time they had once shared together, she was never going to give him that chance again.

Each day that was left to them, Claire stayed out of the apartment as much as she could and when she was there tried to adopt an easy manner with Terry, including him in all her remarks as if there were nothing wrong between them. But there was no reciprocation on his part, no effort to heal the split.

She had no doubts in her mind that she was right not to

444

tell him about the baby, yet there were times when she caught him gazing at her with such a pained expression in his golden eyes that it took all her strength not to break down and tell him the real reason for her decision to stay in Spain.

Fernando continued to call to the apartment, not reconciled to losing her. Despite Terry's air of brooding disapproval whenever the Spaniard appeared, Claire did nothing to discourage him for she was lonely and he was her only support. Even Jane was withdrawn, neither condemning nor approving.

One night Claire walked with Fernando through the town. When they stopped at a bar and found Terry already there, drinking with a group of young people, she forced a smile and moved on. She was aware of the sympathy in Fernando's dark eyes, but she refused to allow herself the luxury of his consolation. At such times, Claire was surprised at her own strength, but since feeling her baby move, she experienced new resilience and hope, as though nature was affording her the necessary reserves needed to maintain this precious new life developing within her.

The next day was Terry's last before returning to his squadron. As usual he went to see Sheena in the afternoon and did not return until teatime. When the meal was over and Claire had finished clearing the teacups, he said to his mother:

"Well, Mum, it was good being with you, but I can't wait to rejoin the team tomorrow and see a bit of the action. I'm getting really pissed off with the Spanish scene. Nice but deadly dull about describes it."

"I'm sorry you feel that way but you could have livened it up with a visit to Seville or Granada," Jane pointed out.

"Hell, that's the last thing I'd want," Terry exclaimed, making no effort to hide his disdain. "The Costa del Sol has been a real eye-opener. Nothing but wealthy Spaniards with their flashy hotels and apartment blocks capitalising on the gullibility of tourists."

Claire got up to go, feeling sickened by his attack.

445

"Claire!" Jane called after her anxiously. "How would you like it if we went out later for a drink?"

"Thank you but I won't be here." Claire opened the door of the apartment as she spoke. "Enjoy yourselves!" Closing the door after her, she went down the steps, unable to bear the pain of being so physically close to Terry and yet estranged.

The evening was warm with only the hint of a breeze off the sea and the sun was like a huge blood orange hanging low in the sky. Claire found herself taking the road behind the apartments, which led up a narrow trackway to the promontory overlooking the beach, which she often took in the cool of the evening. She felt angry and sad, and desperately wanted to get away on her own. Terry's scornful and unfair attack on Spain and the Spaniards had brought it home to her how far apart they had grown, and the knowledge only accentuated her misery.

Claire moved steadily over the rough ground and did not pause or look around until she had reached the top. There the wild, unspoiled beauty of the unfrequented place began to work its usual magic, soothing and renewing her bruised spirit until, gradually, her stomach muscles unclenched and her expression became less agonisingly unhappy. She sat and gazed at the sea. Only another few hours and Terry would be gone, and then she would be free to grieve in her own fashion.

The door had barely closed behind Claire. "I suppose she's gone to meet him!" Terry exploded, and began furiously pacing the room. "My last night and she couldn't be bothered staying in."

Jane looked at her son's stormy expression and wished she had not given her promise to Claire. She believed the girl was making a grave mistake, but nevertheless, she had given her word.

"For God's sake, Mum, who would ever have thought it?" Terry railed brokenly. "Claire . . . our Claire that we've known since we were kids and brought away every year on holidays. Dammit! How could she forget us and opt for that Spaniard because of his money." His hurt was palpable, so fresh and raw it bled before her eyes. Jane wondered if Claire had judged him wrongly and he might be capable of great love after all.

"Fernando has more than just money to recommend him," she felt constrained to point out. "He's an intelligent, attractive and cultured man with a strong sense of responsibility. Humorous too," she added, thinking this was a quality that Terry, so brooding and intense, badly lacked.

"Humorous!" Terry said scornfully. "That prissy little smile and those effeminate clothes. Silk shirts and shitty gold bracelets. She's out of her skull!"

Jane came to a sudden decision. May Claire forgive me, she thought, but in her present state the poor child isn't capable of rational judgement.

"Terry," she said gently. "Stop prowling about. I have something to tell you."

Terry looked at her, not really hearing her, still shocked and wounded by what he considered Claire's betrayal.

"Sit down," Jane insisted, and waited until he had obeyed.

"What is it, Mum?" he asked, shifting restlessly, imagining she was going to give him another lecture about not judging the book by its cover.

"The reason I have kept quiet until now," Jane began, wondering even as she spoke whether she was doing the right thing, "is because I promised Claire, but now I'm beginning to wonder if you shouldn't be told."

"Told what, Mum?" Terry asked tersely.

"The reason why Claire has decided to remain in Spain. You must know how shy and reticent she is and what I'm about to say isn't something she would want made public . . . even Sheena has no idea." Why am I taking so long to get it out? Jane wondered.

"Spill it, Mum," Terry said curtly. "Stop prolonging the mystery."

447

There were times when her son inspired Jane with a strong desire to smack him. She took a deep breath and said bluntly. "Claire is remaining in Spain because she's pregnant."

He was flabbergasted. She saw his expression range from shocked amazement to anger, and then sorrowing despair.

"Why didn't she say so?" Terry burst out at last. "Of course she has to stay with him now. Oh God, why didn't she tell me?" For a moment she thought he was going to cry. Then he whirled about and ran to the door.

"Terry!" Jane called urgently after him. "Listen . . . come back. It's not what you think." But she heard the door slam and realised he was gone.

Oh, God! thought Jane wretchedly, what have I done?

When she heard the peremptory knock at the door she sighed with thankfulness that he had come back and hurried to open it. She found not Terry but Antonio standing outside.

"May I come in, Jane?" Antonio waited politely until she beckoned him over the threshold.

Distractedly, Jane led the way to the balcony. She was reminded of the night he had called to the apartment to say goodbye to her after her sojourn in hospital, and how their passions had almost run away with them. Her cheeks warmed at the memory. So much had changed since then, she thought. His wife was no longer alive, the shadow hanging over them that night had been removed. And now the way was free before them.

But was it?

As Jane motioned Antonio to a chair and breathlessly sat down beside him, she could not but be aware that another shadow loomed in its place. She could not ignore that what had happened to Sheena made it unlikely that her daughter would ever want to return to the country that only months before they had all so joyfully embraced. It had undeniably put the knell on the idea she had once entertained of some day moving to Spain to work in a Spanish hospital, perhaps enrolling Ruthie in one of the day schools in the city. How could she possibly contemplate such a thing now?

So burdened was she by her thoughts and the desolate image of Terry as he rushed away that Jane almost forgot the man sitting so quietly beside her. Would she have to sell the apartment, she wondered, recalling the unhappy blend of circumstances that had compelled her to sell the seaside cottage. But surely they could not spend their lives running away from things?

She sighed and turned her head to watch the sun sinking over the sea. With what high hopes she had bought the apartment that day, she thought miserably. It could have been such a good venture if only things had turned out differently.

"Something is troubling you," Antonio said gently. "I can tell by the sadness of your expression." All at once Jane became acutely conscious of his dark eyes intently regarding her and, as he reached out and took her hand, she felt almost shy in his presence.

"Can you share your trouble with me?" he asked.

Antonio had heard Terry's frantic footsteps clattering down the stairs and stepped aside, but Terry had not been aware of the Spaniard's greeting as he ran past, his eyes wild and unseeing. What his mother had told him had been the very last thing he'd expected to hear. And the very worst!

Terry strode across the parking lot, undecided where he would go. He had made a date with one of the English girls but he didn't want to keep it. She was pretty and trite, and he felt a terrible boredom at the thought of spending another evening with her.

He glanced up at the sky in frustration. He longed with all his heart to be up there now, soaring through the clouds. In the darkness of his soul Claire was the only bright light and she was no longer shining for him.

He was about to step down on to the street and then, almost by their own volition, his footsteps turned again and he began climbing the hill to a spot high above the apartment block. As he climbed he remembered a night in April when, his head whirling with Jane's disturbing story about his father and Claire, he had taken the same leafy overgrown path. He would be quite alone up there and, in his pain and rejection, solitude was what he craved.

Terry shivered with shock and a desperate kind of sadness. Claire had belonged to him since before time began, or so it seemed. In his youthful arrogance he had considered she could not have been more completely his if she had been given to him in bondage. Now she was being taken from him and he knew he had only himself to blame.

Terry cursed his failure to see that what occurred between his father and Claire had not been sick and perverted not on Claire's part. She had been merely the victim of his father's unbridled lust, and her own loneliness and childish innocence the snare which had led to her downfall. He remembered her anguished cry, 'I was lonely'. Why hadn't he been more understanding? He'd known loneliness himself, all those teen years missing his father. He should have understood yet he'd deliberately blinded himself to her needs. Why? he agonised.

Terry had always held on to what he had. Even as a child no-one had ever taken anything from him without a battle. Now he thought about flying back to his squadron next day and leaving Claire behind with Fernando Gonzalez. Claire, his Claire – he saw her grey eyes and gleaming fair hair, and felt as deprived as a soul cast into exterior darkness at the moment it hovers on the very threshold of heaven. Despair washed over him in an icy black wave.

Listlessly he turned and looked back down at the sea. Far below it was a leaden shimmer, capped with silver. A cry of anguish rose from the depths of his being and broke in his throat. Didn't she know they were destined for each other? He was visited by an image of her lying in his arms and softly speaking of a love which nothing, not even earthquakes or floods, could destroy. Dammit! Terry swore. He couldn't, wouldn't give her up. He didn't care if she was expecting triplets by that bloody Spaniard. He had known and loved her long before Gonzalez ever set eyes on her.

Terry knuckled his eyes and turned back to the path. He would fight for her, he resolved. He would seek out the man and they would engage in primitive battle for possession. And he would win! Terry clenched his fists and imagined the sweet satisfaction of slamming them hard in that aristocratic face.

As Terry reached the crest of the hill, sweat glossed his forehead and he was breathing hard. His dark waving hair flopped on his forehead and he forked an impatient hand through it, irritated by the unaccustomed length. Almost a month away from the Air Corps and it was curling on his neck.

It was minutes before he realised that he was not alone on the grassy knoll.

A woman was sitting on a rock, her legs gracefully curled under her, her chin propped pensively on her hand, her face side-lit by the dying sun. He saw that it was Claire.

At the sight of her, Terry's heart swelled in his chest and his breathing grew shallow. She was so beautiful, he thought, the light from the sky lending radiance to her skin and bathing her in a rosy glow. He moved forward and the sandy gravel softly crunched under his shoes. She turned her head and froze at the sight of him.

"Terry," she whispered, her face lighting with strong emotion. With a slight awkwardness of movement she got to her feet and came slowly towards him.

When Terry thought what might have been his heart yearned hopelessly within him. But time could not be reversed.

"Claire." His voice sounded hoarse in his own ears, and she came closer and stood before him, unconsciously adopting the classic stance of the expectant woman, hip slightly thrust forward, weight resting on one foot. Her grey eyes were soft and luminous in her heart-shaped face.

His gaze swept down her body and she saw that he knew. A pulse beat in his cheek and his eyes were very bright. Claire returned his gaze steadily and a little apprehensively.

Terry tried to speak but the words died in his throat in

the face of her new blossoming maturity. He no longer felt the fires of jealousy raging in his blood. Let her marry Fernando if that's what is required, he thought wearily. Somehow in the space of a few minutes Claire's needs and happiness had become of paramount importance to him and his own desires as nothing.

After a long moment he spoke as though with great difficulty. "My mother told me. I don't know why you felt you couldn't tell me yourself. He'll stick by you, I suppose?" There was a white line about his mouth and his eyes had again that wounded look in their golden depths. She drew back and stared at him, her own eyes very bright.

"Is that what you think?" she asked. "That it's Fernando's baby?"

"Who else's?" Terry looked at her aghast. "Surely there weren't others?"

"None at all," Claire said, almost cheerfully. "Not even Fernando."

The sky seemed to drop on him. He stared at her for a long moment. "Are you saying it's mine?" he asked quietly.

When she nodded he grabbed her to him so hard she gasped. "Oh my love," Terry cried and his voice cracked with emotion. "If you only knew what I've suffered thinking it was his and that you . . . He could hardly take in this wonderful change of circumstances. She was still his and had never been anyone else's. Words of love and gratitude tripped on his tongue and he could not hold her closely enough.

Claire stood close-pressed in his arms, feeling his heart beating rapidly against her. Nothing has changed, she tried to tell herself, but as her bewilderment turned to joy, her determination wavered.

"It's the best news . . . the greatest, Claire."

The blackness receded and light and hope flooded her soul.

"Claire . . . you'll never know how much I've missed and wanted you." Terry's voice was fierce with longing. "But this – this makes up for everything."

She was almost afraid to trust her ears. He didn't feel trapped. He was glad! And, Oh God! He loved and wanted her. She covered his mouth with hers, overwhelmed by the weight of her love for him.

The last glow was flaming the sky and still Jane and Antonio sat on the balcony, gazing at the distant coastline. For some time no words had been spoken. Both were still savouring the moment when Jane had finished tremulously confiding all that was troubling her and Antonio had been moved to take her in his arms and begin the tender task of reassuring and comforting her.

And what a good job he made of it, Jane thought contentedly. Perhaps he's right and everything would come right again. "Do not try and force a solution," he had told her softly. "Time is all that is needed for Sheena to forget the horrors she has endured and for the young lovers to find a way out of their dilemma."

And then Antonio delicately broached the subject closest to them both.

"Out of respect to the memory of my beloved wife," he told her, "I must wait out the period of mourning but then I hope with all my heart I may speak to you with the intimacy of a lover."

Jane couldn't help smiling to herself when she recalled the many warm conversations they had shared. Certainly none of them had lacked emotion. She composed herself, however, and continued to listen to what he had to say with fond attention, as always impressed by his sensitivity. When he fell silent at last she warmly gave him the assurance he sought.

"How I look forward to that time," she told him, "It will make me as happy, if not happier, as you have already professed yourself to be." In answer Antonio had placed a kiss in the palm of her hand and gently closed her fingers over it.

"Until that time comes," he told her seriously. With this, Jane knew, she would be content.

Now, having shared her worries, Jane felt more hopeful and was able, at last, to enjoy the rosy heavens.

"Red sky at night," she said softly, hardly aware that she said it, "shepherd's delight."

Antonio stretched out his hand and took hold of hers again.

"Jane, my delight," he said softly. "Look at me."

She did so.

"At the time of your car accident," Antonio said in heart-felt accents, "I thought providence had brought you back into my life only to take you from me a second time."

"And now?"

"I believe we have been given a second chance at happiness."

Jane looked into Antonio's eyes. When he gazed at her with the same tender look she had surprised in his eyes the day he came to meet her at the airport, she felt as though she had come into a safe haven at last and would never again know the rough and perilous seas she had sailed on for so long and alone.

All light was quite gone from the sky and the stars overhead were so many glittering diamanté chips. Terry and Claire lay close together on the stalky grass, their heads pillowed on Terry's shirt as he held her to his heart. His lips brushed the curve of her throat and he murmured over and over, "Clairey, my Clairey," and she trembled against him.

In the months since they had made love her body felt the same, and yet there were subtle differences. Her breasts were heavier and fuller and more satiny than before, her hips and belly softly rounded. He registered these changes as he loved her and heard the sighing moans that escaped her parted lips with a satisfaction that was all the more deeply felt for having waited so long and come so close to losing her.

"You are even more beautiful than before," he whispered, tracing the swollen curve of her belly with gentle, possessive fingers. And Claire kissed the healing scar on his neck with equal gentleness and marvelled at how tender and accepting he had become.

And when they had desperately meshed together, straining as close as they were physically capable, seeking total fusion of their bodies, he wanted her all over again and felt he could never get enough of her. The feeling they experienced transcended anything that had gone before, because they had each learned, in the lonely separateness of spirit, the true meaning of love.

They talked lying close to each other, she looking steadfastly into his face and he gazing down into her grey eyes. "You were so harsh and angry about Spain and the Spaniards that I thought you meant it," Claire said softly.

"I was angry," he told her, his voice trembling in his throat, "but only because I loved and wanted you and was desperately afraid you would marry him."

"Oh Terry, hold me!"

A little later, they made their plans and rejoiced in a future that they would share together. Claire spoke shyly of Jane's suggestion that she should live with them and continue to go to college until the child was born.

The earth was growing cool. "Let's go and tell Mum," Terry said, and when Claire thought how she would soon be living with the two people she loved most in the world she felt, as Elena had once said, that truly her cup was overflowing.

Terry raised her solicitously to her feet, and sealed the pact with a long kiss.

Was this at last happiness? Claire believed that it was. And when the earth steadied, she lovingly joined hands with him and together they walked down the blossom-scented hillside to the apartment.

Acknowledgments

I am grateful to my brother Dr Donal O'Holohan for sharing his medical knowledge on the rare disease porphyria. My loving thanks both to him and to my brother Terry for their constant support. With affectionate appreciation also to my other brothers and to my sisters. Warm thanks to my good friends Mary Dowling and Colette McDonnell who have been very helpful, the former with her Spanish expertise and the latter for giving me the idea of the *abecedario*. And to two other good friends Kathleen Sheehan O'Connor and Kay Maloney for their affectionate support. My gratitude to Betty and Sean Ryan for their kindly and practical support and to Comdt Kevin Byrne for his patience and good humour when answering my questions about the Irish Air Corps. And last but by no means least sincere thanks to Ailish Collins, Niall Meehan and Pat Balfe for generously sharing with me their computer know-how.

J. M. O'NEILL

Rellighan, Undertaker

A dark, intriguing modern gothic tale. The final novel by a writer who was a master of his craft.

In a small rural town in Ireland, nothing is as it appears. Ester Machen brings with her a mystery, and death is stalking the young people of the town. Though 'the town is talking', the only person determined to get to the bottom of the mystery is the detective Coleman. He has few allies, but Rellighan the undertaker gradually assists him in attempting to reveal and rid the town of the terror that has grown within it. They both risk death but unfalteringly continue to unveil the mystery, becoming deeply embroiled in the dark world of the occult as they strive to eradicate evil.

ISBN 0 86322 260 9

Original Paperback £8.99

J. M. O'NEILL

Bennett & Company

Winner of the 1999 Kerry Ingredients Book of the Year award

"O'Neill's world owes something to the sagas of Forsyte and Onedin, and his plotting has, at times, some of the pace and complexity of John Buchan, but the novel is, nonetheless, uniquely Irish with its sanctuary lamps, street-children, moving statues and bitter memories, and it is a contribution to an overdue examination of Irish conscience. The poor and the middle classes are indeed those of Frank McCourt and Kate O'Brien, but O'Neill's is a strictly modern and undeluded vision of the past. The writing is shockingly credible." *Times Literary Supplement*

"He is an exceptional writer, and one we must take very seriously." *Sunday Independent*

ISBN 1 90201 106 6

Original paperback £7.99

JOHN TROLAN

Slow Punctures

"Compelling. . . his writing, with its mix of brutal social realism, irony and humour, reads like a cross between Roddy Doyle and Irvine Welsh." *Sunday Independent*

"Three hundred manic, readable pages. . . *Slow Punctures* is grim, funny and bawdy in equal measure." *The Irish Times*

"Fast-moving and hilarious in the tradition of Roddy Doyle." *Sunday Business Post*

"Trolan writes in a crisp and consistent style. He handles the delicate subject of young suicide with a sensitive practicality and complete lack of sentiment. His novel is a brittle working-class rites of passage that tells a story about Dublin that probably should have been told a long time ago." *Irish Post*

ISBN 0 86322 252 8

Original Paperback £8.99

STEVE MACDONOGH (ED)

The Brandon Book of Irish Short Stories

"This impressive collection." *Times Literary Supplement*

"Ranges hugely in setting, style and tone. The confident internationalism of these mostly young writers reflects something of the spirit of the new Ireland but it is grounded in an undeceived realism . . . On the evidence here, the future of Irish fiction is in good hands." *Observer*

"This exciting collection of short fiction." *The Irish Times*

"A host of the best contemporary Irish writers." *Ireland on Sunday*

ISBN 0 86322 237 4

Paperback £6.99

KITTY FITZGERALD

Snapdragons

Sometimes shocking, frequently humorous, often surreal, *Snapdragons* is a unique and extremely engaging rites of passage novel about a young woman who grows up unhappily in rural Ireland after World War II. She is disliked – for reasons she cannot understand – by her parents, and has a running feud with her sister. Yet the mood of this story is strangely light-hearted, frequently comic and absolutely memorable.

She makes her escape to the English midlands, and works and lives in a pub in Digbeth, Birmingham, where her sister has settled with her husband. Her already difficult relationship with her sister is further strained when she discovers how she is living. She also learns the sad reason for her parents' hostility towards her.

A captivating story of a young girl in Birmingham and the North of England in the 1950s, its main protagonist, Bernadette, who carries on a constant angry dialogue with God, is one of the most delightfully drawn characters in recent Irish fiction.

ISBN 0 86322 258 7

Original Paperback £8.99